D0007918

THE
FIRST FAMILY

ALSO BY **MICHAEL PALMER** AND **DANIEL PALMER**

Mercy

Trauma

ALSO BY **MICHAEL PALMER**

Resistant

Political Suicide

Oath of Office

A Heartbeat Away

The Last Surgeon

The Second Opinion

The First Patient

The Fifth Vial

The Sisterhood

Side Effects

Flashback

Extreme Measures

Natural Causes

Silent Treatment

Critical Judgment

Miracle Cure

The Patient

Fatal

The Society

MICHAEL PALMER
AND DANIEL PALMER

THE
FIRST
FAMILY

ST. MARTIN'S PRESS ≈ NEW YORK

This is a work of fiction. All of the characters, organizations, and events portrayed in this novel are either products of the author's imagination or are used fictitiously.

THE FIRST FAMILY. Copyright © 2018 by Daniel Palmer. All rights reserved. Printed in the United States of America. For information, address St. Martin's Press, 175 Fifth Avenue, New York, N.Y. 10010.

www.stmartins.com

The Library of Congress Cataloging-in-Publication Data is available upon request.

ISBN 978-1-250-10742-8 (hardcover)
ISBN 978-1-250-10744-2 (ebook)

Our books may be purchased in bulk for promotional, educational, or business use. Please contact your local bookseller or the Macmillan Corporate and Premium Sales Department at 1-800-221-7945, extension 5442, or by email at MacmillanSpecialMarkets@macmillan.com.

First Edition: April 2018

10 9 8 7 6 5 4 3 2 1

To Dr. Richard P. Dugas, a loyal and steadfast friend to the Palmer family.
We thank you.

THE
FIRST FAMILY

CHAPTER 1

The terror never went away. It should have by now. After all this time, she should not have been so afraid. Her long legs shook beneath the silky fabric of an elegant red gown. She inhaled deeply to calm herself, but perspiration coated her fingers anyway. *That could be a problem.* Her ears picked up each twitch, rustle, and breath in the cavernous room. They were watching her every move. Her delicate face stared back at them with a blank expression that hid her mounting anxiety.

The concert hall was sold out. Thunderous applause for her had just died down, and this was the brief interlude before the music began. Her heart beat so loudly she feared the microphone would pick up the sound. She stood alone in the center of a large stage, a spotlight targeting her as if this were a prison break. In her right hand she clutched a violin with a bright amber finish and stunning marbled flame, expertly antiqued.

Scanning the hall, she searched for the rangy man with square shoulders and the slender woman who was an older version of herself. There they were in their usual location, third row: Doug and Allison Banks, her parents. Her name was Susie Banks, and she was their only daughter, their pride and joy. Without their support Susie would not be standing on the stage of the Kennedy Center, chosen from hundreds of hopefuls to open the National Symphony Orchestra's evening performance with a solo piece.

This moment had seemed inevitable from Susie's earliest days. She was two years old when she played her first song on the piano—a ringtone from her mother's cell phone she had replicated by ear. Soon she began

1

plinking out melodies she heard on the radio. By the age of five, Susie could play Bach's Minuet in G Major, never having taken a lesson. Words like "prodigy" and "special" got bandied about, but Susie did not understand what it all meant, nor did she care. She had found this amazing thing called music, and the music made her happy.

The day her mother put a violin in her hand, Susie's whole world came into even sharper focus. She felt a kinship with the instrument, understood it in a profound way. One year into her study she flawlessly performed Mozart's Violin Concerto No. 5 during a student recital. For Susie, the notes were more than dots on the sheet music. As she played, she could see them dance before her eyes, swirling and twirling like a flock of starlings in flight. She would practice daily, hours passing like minutes, her joy unfettered and boundless. She did not have many close friends growing up, always needing to practice, or rehearse, or perform. Yet she never felt lonely, or alone. Music was her constant companion, her first true love.

Now nineteen, Susie was poised for a professional career. She had taken a gap year between high school and college to work on her craft. With hundreds of concerts on her résumé, she had hoped her stage fright would be a thing of the past. But it was present as always and would remain with her until she played the first note.

This was a hugely important showcase. The conductor of the Chicago Symphony Orchestra was in the audience specifically to hear her play. If all went well, it was possible she would be moving to Chicago.

Susie set her chin on the smooth ebony chin rest and pushed the conductor from her thoughts. All sound evaporated from the room. She had no sheet music to follow. She had long ago committed the Chaconne from Bach's Partita No. 2 for solo violin to memory.

She took one last readying breath, drew the bow across the strings, and conquered the powerful opening double stop like a pro. The audience, the hall itself, seemed to vanish as she drifted into the other place where the music came from. Her body swayed to the rhythm and flow as Bach's notes poured from her instrument.

The bow and her fingers became a blur of movement. Susie kept her eyes open as she played, but she saw nothing while she felt *everything*. A brilliant shrill wafted from the violin, a melody sparkling and pure in triple time, followed by an austere passage of darker, more muted tones. Years of dedication, all the things she had sacrificed, were worth it for this feeling alone, such indescribable freedom.

She had reached measure eighty-nine, near the halfway point. Drawing the bow toward her, Susie geared up for the next variation, where the bass became melodic and the diatonic form resumed. Up to that point her playing had been perfect, but suddenly and inexplicably came a terrible screech. Susie's arms jerked violently out in front of her, the bow dragging erratically across the strings. Her chin slid free of the chin rest as her violin shot outward.

A collective gasp rose from the audience. Shocked, unable to process what had happened to her, Susie repositioned the violin. Her professionalism took over. Her reset was more a reflex than anything. She drew the bow across the strings once more, but only a warbling sound came out. The next instant, her arms flailed spastically in front of her again in yet another violent paroxysm, as if her limbs had separated from her body, developed a mind of their own. She tried to regain control of her arms, willing it to happen, but it was no use. The wild movements occurred without her thought, like those body starts she'd been having before she fell asleep: first the sensation of falling, followed by a jarring startle back into consciousness. Only this time she was wide awake. No matter how hard Susie strained, she could not stop her arms from convulsing. It was the most terrifying, out-of-control sensation she had ever experienced.

When the next spasm struck, Susie's fingers opened. The violin slipped from her grasp and hit the stage floor with a sickening crack. Another gasp rose from the audience, this one louder than the first. Susie was helpless to do anything but stand facing everyone with her arms twitching like two live wires. As suddenly as those seizures came on, her limbs went still, as if a switch had been turned off. She raised her arms slowly, studying them with bewilderment. Then, she directed her gaze to the violin at her feet. For a moment she could not breathe. Murmurs from the audience reverberated in her ears.

Bending down, she gingerly retrieved the broken instrument, fearing another attack was imminent. She stood up tall. The violin dangled at her side with a gap in the wood like a missing tooth. She searched the audience for her parents, but could not see them through the haze of lights and the blur of tears.

Frozen in the spotlight, her cheeks red and burning, blinking rapidly, Susie gave one sob as she backed away. A voice in her head howled: *What happened to me?* She stumbled into the back curtain, fumbling for an escape, pawing at the fabric, desperate to get away. Realizing her mistake, she reoriented to the right and dashed offstage.

The quiet concert hall carried only the echo of Susie's heels, tapping out a fast, unsteady beat.

ROW EIGHT, center seat.

His name was Mark Mueller, but those who knew him well called him Mauser—a reference to his favorite weapon, the German-made Mauser C96 semiautomatic pistol, last manufactured in 1937. Mauser kept his thick blond hair combed back to expose a wide and flat forehead. The green shirt he had picked out for this concert covered his tattoos and fit snugly against a body that bulged with muscles from years of pumping iron in the yard.

Calmly, Mauser watched Susie come unglued. His gray eyes sparked and his top lip curled, putting an arch in his bushy blond mustache. When people in the audience got up from their seats, Mauser did the same. He strode into the foyer with his cell phone out.

"It happened," Mauser said. He described what he'd seen.

It was all the information Rainmaker needed to mark Susie Banks for death.

CHAPTER 2

Distilled to a few words, Karen Ray's job description was: *protect the president's family with your life*. The family consisted of Ellen Hilliard, aka FLO-TUS, the first lady of the United States, and Cameron Hilliard, the first family's sixteen-year-old son and only child. She had done this particular job for six and a half years now. When she started, Karen had towered over Cam, but these days, standing only five foot four in heels, she was considerably shorter than everyone she protected.

Ellen thought Karen looked like Sandra Bullock with shoulder-length auburn hair. Karen could not see the resemblance herself, but as a woman approaching fifty, she took the comparison as a compliment.

Karen was a special agent, not a "suit guard," a term popular with members of the Uniformed Division. The differences in the divisions of the Secret Service were not subtle. Uniformed guards interacted with the public, wore mostly white shirts and black slacks, and intentionally did not blend. Karen wore tailored Ralph Lauren suits to work, and her domain consisted of anywhere members of the first family happened to be.

At the moment, Cam Hilliard was still in his bedroom on the second floor of the White House. If he stayed there much longer, he would be late for school. Again. The first lady had instructed Karen to make sure that did not happen.

Ellen was busy with a television interview, and her order had sent Karen off in a hurry. She took the same elevator President Geoffrey Hilliard used when his bum hip made it difficult to take the stairs. The elevator could make eight stops, from the subbasement up to the third floor. Karen exited on the second floor.

She marched down the Center Hall, an airy seventeen-foot-wide corridor adorned with landscape paintings and comfortable sitting areas arranged by the first lady. Compared with the ornate décor of the previous administration, Ellen Hilliard's style was more understated, in keeping with her middle-class upbringing.

The president embraced Ellen's choices wholeheartedly. He had a measured approach to just about everything, and cared more about public perception than aesthetics. Anything that did not create controversy (think: expensive remodeling) he supported fully. There was good reason that Ellen Hilliard's favorability rating seldom dipped under 80 percent.

The two floors the president and his family occupied comprised thirty-six rooms and fifteen bathrooms, but these days Cam confined himself mostly to his bedroom. It seemed just yesterday he'd been bouncing around the third-floor game room, or building with Legos in the spectacular solarium that the Clintons had constructed. But Cam had been a nine-year-old boy back then, sweet-faced and innocent, unsure of his family's newfound prestige and privilege. Now Cam was entering a new phase, carried forth on a raging river of teenage hormones. Perhaps when his father's second term in office ended, Cam would emerge from this period of seclusion like a bear waking from hibernation.

Bigger kids, bigger problems. That was how Ellen summarized her recent challenges with Cam—a saying that applied to most parents, regardless of stature. Karen could relate. Her twenty-five-year-old son, Josh, knew perfectly well how to use a phone but rarely bothered to call.

From a distance, Karen could hear the steady beat of electronic music coming from Cam's bedroom, directly across from the Yellow Oval Room where Ellen frequently entertained. Aside from pulsating music, the floor was library quiet. Secret Service agents seldom patrolled the upper levels, and the White House staff were busy elsewhere. Karen and Cam were alone.

She knocked on his door—softly at first, then again with a bit more force—but Cam did not answer. Karen thought she knew why.

Chess.

She peeked inside and saw Cam, his back to her, intently staring at a digital chessboard on his computer. She figured Cam was winning, because he always won.

Cam was serious about chess, supremely talented, and committed to playing tournaments, each functioning as a rigorous exam, so he could become one of a handful of young players to earn the title Grandmaster, the highest level of chess mastery. Karen did not know how close Cam was to obtaining his lofty goal, but if she had money to bet, hers would go on Cam.

She spoke from the doorway.

"Cam, it's Karen."

She did not have to identify herself. Karen was Cam's shadow; he knew her voice perfectly well.

"Your mom sent me to get you."

Cam held up a finger—a give-me-a-minute gesture.

Karen checked her watch. A minute was all they had.

"You're going to be late for school if we don't leave now."

At first glance, it would be hard to tell a teenager lived in this tidy room. The only giveaway was a mini-mountain of PlayStation games scattered on the carpeted floor in front of the television Cam had fought so hard to have in his bedroom. When it came to winning arguments, Cam's persistence and tenacity could rival some of the president's toughest adversaries. But that was the Cam from before—the kid with spunk and spirit, not the boy who had become withdrawn. For a kid accustomed to the limelight, always quick with a smile, lately Cam had trouble making eye contact.

"Knight c3," Cam mumbled to himself. "Why didn't I see that?"

To Karen's ears, Cam sounded distraught. He was out of his pajamas and dressed in his school uniform—a good sign she could still get him there on time.

"Cam, let's go. You're going to be late."

"Please, Karen, can you give me another second," Cam said. "It's super important."

His pleading tone won out.

"My queen's got the high ground," Cam said under his breath. "Try to castle, Taylor, go ahead and try it."

Taylor.

Now Karen understood Cam's intensity. Taylor Gleason, a high
school classmate of Cam's, was the son of the chief White House physician, Dr. Frederick Gleason, and the second-best junior chess player in
D.C. To Karen's knowledge, Cam had never lost a match to Taylor, and
he did not intend to start losing now.

Cam adjusted the volume on his computer speakers and a mechanized
voice rose above the din of electronic music.

"Rook takes e5."

Cam smacked his hand hard on his desk, and Karen could not help but
think *gunshot*. Her whole body tensed.

The computer voice spoke rapidly as the next sequence of moves
occurred in quick succession. "Queen takes e5. Queen takes d7. Rook a8
to d8. Queen takes b7. Queen e3, check."

"Got you now, Taylor."

Karen was pleased. Cam sounded animated, when lately talk of chess
seemed to bring him down.

The match went on a bit, until the computer announced Taylor's last
move: "Bishop b6, checkmate."

Cam clutched the sides of his head as if experiencing an intense
migraine. He lowered his hands and took a drink of water from a glass on
his desk. After a swallow, he swiveled in his chair, cocked back his arm,
and hurled the glass with force at the wall near his bed. The glass shattered on impact.

Karen rushed to him. "Cam! What's going on? Are you all right?"

Cam rose from his chair and began to pace. He was a tall boy, slim like
his mother, with short, sandy-colored hair. Beneath his wire-rimmed
glasses, Cam's eyes were cornflower blue, also like his mom's, and a jawline
was starting to emerge as the cute boy transformed into a handsome man.

"Cam, talk to me. What's wrong?"

Instead of answering, Cam muttered incoherently while he continued
to pace.

"I'm going to call Dr. Gleason," Karen said.

"No!"

Cam barked the word with force. Karen had not expected such a pro-
test, but then again it did mean seeing the father of his rival so soon after
a painful defeat.

"Not him. Don't call him."

Cam's shoulders were slumped as he got into bed. He pulled the covers over his head. Karen sat on the edge of his bed. She was his protector, and over the years a bond had formed that went well beyond anything written on an employment contract.

"Talk to me, Cam. Tell me what's going on."

Cam poked his head out from beneath the covers, his eyes reddened as he fought back tears. "I don't know what's wrong," he said. "I don't get it. He beat me. He never beats me, and I'm losing to him now."

Karen was glad to hear him acknowledge that *something* was wrong.

"Is it the pressure, Cam?" she asked. "It's got to get pretty intense at times. There's no stigma in needing help for—well, your mental health."

Cam bristled. "You sound like Dr. Gleason. He thinks it's all in my head. He's run all sorts of tests and whatnot, but he doesn't get it and now he has my parents convinced I need a shrink."

Karen and Ellen were close, confidants even, but for whatever reason Ellen had kept these developments a secret.

"They're wrong. There's nothing wrong with my head. I'm just—off."

"Have you tried talking to your parents about it?"

"Yeah. A bunch of times, but you know how much influence Dr. Gleason has over my dad."

The answer there was "plenty." Dr. Gleason, a navy doc, had come to the president's attention through the True Potential Institute, a unique educational center dedicated to helping D.C.'s most gifted children develop mastery in a variety of disciplines. It was where Cam and Taylor both studied chess. A friendship blossomed between Dr. Gleason and the president when they discovered a shared passion for sports, golf and tennis especially, though Gleason was by far the more competitive of the two. Their camaraderie led to Gleason getting the plum appointment to head up the White House Medical Unit. Cam had made a valid point. The president had complete confidence in Dr. Gleason.

"They won't listen to me," Cam said. "They only listen to *him*. Maybe if those stupid tests showed something, they might change their minds."

Karen mulled this over. She believed Cam. The way he had been acting could support Gleason's theory, but perhaps something else was amiss, something undetected. The president might not be open to outside consults when it came to his family's health, but the first lady was a different story.

Karen said, "Let's get you to school and I'll work on this from my end. It's possible I can convince your parents to consider the opinion of somebody other than Dr. Gleason. Do you trust me?"

Cam might have caught the mischievous glint in Karen's eyes. He returned a small smile as he climbed out of bed, the blue sport coat of his school uniform now a bit wrinkled.

"With my life," he said with a wink.

CHAPTER 3

The half-dozen medical residents, all part of a family practice residency program, were dressed similarly in hip-length white lab coats. These were junior doctors who had graduated from medical school but had not yet completed on-the-job training. All of the residents were required to wear shorter lab coats until they completed training, at which point they'd receive a longer coat to wear. Patients at the hospital had no idea that coat length equated to doctor prestige, but the residents were well aware of the status symbol.

Like a gaggle of geese, they followed close on the heels of their attending for the day, Dr. Lee Blackwood, a family practitioner with admitting privileges at MediHealth of D.C.—MDC for short—a renowned nine-hundred-bed hospital complex in downtown Washington. As their leader, Lee wore a white coat that went down past his knees.

By law, all residents needed a supervisory attending for questions as they conducted hospital rounds. Thanks to Lee's long relationship with the hospital, he and his partner, Paul Tresell, were the only family practitioners with a medical practice independent of the MDC who were allowed to serve as attendings. During contract renewal discussions, Lee would make it a point to tell the hospital administrators how he enjoyed mentoring young doctors, when the truth was more pragmatic: he needed the extra cash to help offset losses incurred in his family practice.

Most attendings were only a few years older than the residents they supervised, but at fifty-six Lee could have been the father of these newly minted docs. He felt like the old man of the group, too, his right knee aching as they walked. He vowed not to let this lingering discomfort impact his nightly run. An undesirable HDL result from his last physical had inspired him to take up jogging late in life, and he'd learn how to run through the pain.

Getting old was not for the faint of heart.

Neither was family medicine.

I should have been a dermatologist, Lee thought as he marched down a long corridor on his way to do a consult for a fellow family practitioner. Ten different family practices regularly sent patients requiring hospitalization to the MDC. Five years ago that number had been closer to twenty, before practice after practice ceased operations. Lee knew all of the local family docs, and all were hurting, but each remained committed to the tradition of caring for people soup to nuts. Which was why Lee was happy to cover for a fellow family doc on a patient who had a bad ankle break requiring surgery. If the family docs did not stick together, then the big business ethos of cutting costs wherever possible would eventually turn their profession into an anachronism.

Lee wondered how many of the docs enjoying their morning coffee were thinking about meeting daily patient quotas, or which specialists they could direct their patients to see. Headaches to the neurologist. Asthma to the pulmonologist. It was all about the Benjamins, and these days Lee was seeing far fewer of them in his bank account.

The residents Lee was supervising faced a seriously steep uphill climb. People wanted a relationship with their doctor—someone in whom they could confide, someone who could sense when they were truly sick. Even so, specialists would forever look down on them, while less expensive hospitalists, doctors assigned to administering general care to hospitalized patients, would continue to replace family docs in settings like the MDC. If these residents could endear themselves to their patients, prove their worth, they might be able to make a living in a dying profession.

Lee glanced at his Timex watch that barely kept on ticking, saw he was running a bit behind schedule, and lamented the fact that most dermatologists could afford a Rolex.

THE FORTY-SEVEN-YEAR-OLD man, rock-jawed and preternaturally tan, was propped up in his hospital bed while an orthopedic surgeon hovered over a discolored, badly swollen ankle. The surgeon lifted his head, his eyes closing to slits as he surveyed the processional of doctors who followed Lee into the cramped hospital room.

"Can I help you?"

Lee had met this surgeon before, but was not surprised by the man's lack of recall. Staff at the MDC changed with the tides, and learning names was often wasted effort.

"Dr. Lee Blackwood," said Lee. "I'm here to do a consult for Dr. Anthony Gavin."

The patient, Wendell Prichard according to the medical chart, brightened at the mention of the name.

"Hey! How is Doc Anthony doing? I thought *he* was coming to see me."

Doc A, like all of us, is drowning in a sea of paperwork, trying to keep his business afloat, thought Lee glumly.

"He got caught up with something and couldn't get to the hospital today. He knew I was escorting these fine residents on morning rounds, and asked if I'd stop by to check on you pre-op as a favor. Hope that's okay."

Lee thought he saw the surgeon's eyes roll, if only slightly, as he reapplied the patient's air splint. He could guess what the surgeon was thinking: a family doc consult would be as useful to Wendell Pritchard as a treadmill.

"Exam away," said Wendell. "But be sure to tell Doc A that the only thing really hurting is my ego."

Lee checked the medical chart on his clipboard and saw that poor Wendell had hurt his ankle falling down a flight of stairs, hence the bruised ego.

"You can always say it was a skydiving accident," said Lee.

Wendell returned a hearty laugh, while his surgeon did not so much as crack a smile.

"We're doing him tomorrow morning," the orthopod said flatly. "Just make sure he's stable for surgery, take an admitting history, whatever you need to do. You can have me paged if you need."

But you won't need me, the man's eyes said. *Because you take throat cultures and placate worried moms all day.*

"Thanks," said Lee, addressing the surgeon's back as he departed. The residents moved aside to let him through and reformed as a group at the foot of Wendell's bed.

"Do you mind if there's an audience while I do my exam?" asked Lee. "This is the future of family medicine right here, and I'm sure they'd appreciate the learning opportunity."

"Also fine," said Wendell, his smile surprisingly congenial for someone who had to be in a good deal of pain.

Lee passed around Wendell's medical chart, which showed a low dose of Ancef to fight infection and included results from various labs and blood work. No alarming finds in those pages. He doubted the residents would learn much from this exam, but they were his charges for the day and every moment could be a teachable one.

Wendell gave Lee his general medical history, including the few prescriptions he took for various aliments, none of which would cause problems for tomorrow's surgery. Overall, Wendell appeared to be the picture of good health, minus his badly injured ankle.

"Anything else troubling you?" Lee asked, using an ophthalmoscope to peer into Wendell's eyes. "Even something from before the accident?"

"No, not especially. Except maybe a little shortness of breath."

Lee stood back and appraised Wendell thoughtfully.

"Tell me more," he said, feeling the residents closing in, perhaps sensing something might be afoot.

"I dunno," said Wendell with a shrug. "I'm super tired all of the time. Before the injury I would get winded just walking my dog."

Lee placed his fingers on Wendell's wrist and measured the radial pulse. It was dramatic, brisk—a water hammer pulse. Next, he checked Wendell's blood pressure. The result, 150 over 50, indicated a wide pulse pressure of one hundred.

"Wendell, do you mind if I share my findings with the residents so they could benefit?"

Wendell gave his permission.

"The patient's blood pressure is one fifty over fifty," Lee announced, "and his radial pulse is a bit dramatic and brisk. What should we think about?"

Dr. Cindy Lerner, a stylish young woman in her second year of residency, lowered her horn-rimmed glasses to the tip of her nose.

"That's a wide pulse pressure," she said. Lee acknowledged her acumen with a nod. "The difference between a systolic and diastolic blood pressure should be around forty, more like one twenty over eighty. A wide pulse pressure suggests he has hyperdynamic circulation."

"Which makes you think of what?" Lee asked, arching an eyebrow.

"Well, aortic valve insufficiency would be my guess," she offered, ignoring or not seeing the mildly alarmed expression that appeared on Wendell's face.

Again, Lee nodded.

"Heart pumping blood, but leaking back into the body because of a damaged valve," he said. "So if he has an aortic valve insufficiency, we should hear a diastolic heart murmur. Let's have a listen to his chest."

Using his stethoscope, Lee gave a brief listen to all five precordial landmarks.

"To save time," he said, "I'll tell you there's no heart murmur, nothing to suggest a leaky valve. What else?"

"How about anemia?" Cindy Lerner was not going to give up so easily.

Lee appreciated her doggedness. "But the blood count is normal," he advised.

"How about hyperthyroidism?" The new voice belonged to a Korean fellow with a head of moppish dark hair.

"Observation is key," Lee reminded him. "There is nothing physical about the patient's appearance that should make you think of that. But it's something to consider, and we should double-check the blood work. There is something else observable about Wendell, something we should all be paying attention to. Anybody?"

No one spoke.

"Watch his head," said Lee, pointing. "He's nodding it slightly. It's his wide pulse pressure being reflected in his head. Wendell, were you aware your head is bobbing?"

Wendell looked perplexed. He had no idea.

At that moment, Lee was feeling mildly stumped himself. Wendell was right. Someone in his physical shape should not be so easily fatigued, constantly winded. Lee conducted a differential diagnosis in his head, running through the symptoms and various possibilities with the speed of a supercomputer, arriving at an unusual idea.

"May I ask something about your past history?" he asked Wendell. "It might seem a little out of the blue, but indulge me."

"Shoot," answered Wendell.

"Actually, that's my question," said Lee. "Have you ever been shot?"

Wendell's face flushed with sudden embarrassment.

"My wife says I'm accident prone for good reason," he answered sheepishly. "I got shot in the leg last year. Hunting accident. At least that's what my brother called it. He's the one who shot me. All kidding aside, it was an accident. No charges filed."

"Mind if I take a look at the scar?"

Wendell winced with discomfort as Lee lifted his leg, the same leg with the injured ankle. Pushing aside the hospital gown, Lee revealed a quarter-shaped scar behind Wendell's thigh. Placing his stethoscope directly over the scar, he gave a listen and heard a distinctive *whoosh whoosh* sound indicative of the exact issue concerning him. One by one, each resident used their stethoscope to listen as well.

"Any thoughts?" asked Lee after the last resident took their turn.

Cindy Lerner appeared ready to speak up, but retreated into herself. Lee was mildly disappointed. He viewed her as the sharpest of the lot and would have preferred she take a guess, show her thinking rather than hold back.

"It's all here," Lee said after a moment of silence. "Brisk radial pulse, head bobbing, wide pulse pressure, shortness of breath, fatigue, gunshot wound, *and* a prominent murmur of blood rushing between a major artery and vein. I've put it all on the table. All you have to do is put a name to it."

The room remained silent, so Lee settled his gaze on Cindy, trying to encourage her.

"Could it be . . . be an arteriovenous fistula in his leg?" she said, uncertainty leaking into her voice.

Smart as these docs were, they hated to be wrong in front of their peers. It was Lee's job to push them out of their comfort zone.

"No, it couldn't be that," Lee said, holding a grim expression, watching

Cindy's face fall. "Because it *is* that, no question. Blood is flowing directly from an artery into Wendell's vein because he got shot and that's how it healed. Well done, Dr. Lerner."

Cindy's crestfallen expression brightened.

"But here's the thing," Lee continued, holding up a finger for emphasis. "If the surgeon were to fix Wendell's ankle tomorrow, this fistula would cause some serious complications. Not only would the wound not heal properly, but they'd have a dickens of a time controlling the bleeding."

Wendell's eyes widened with alarm. "For real?"

"I'm afraid so, Wendell," said Lee. "We'll have to fix the fistula before tackling the ankle."

Lee turned his attention to the residents, his eyes beaming with delight. "*This* is what I love about medicine." He pumped the air with his fist for emphasis. "In a way, we saved this man's life by taking a good history and doing a good physical examination. I hope today gives you as great a feeling as it gives me."

Before anyone could respond, a man appeared in the doorway. He was tall and clean-shaven with short, dark hair only a hint longer than what the marines might allow, dressed in a charcoal gray suit, white collared shirt, and bold red tie.

"I'm looking for Dr. Lee Blackwood," the man said in a steely voice.

Lee stepped forward. "I'm Dr. Blackwood."

The man removed a badge from the inner pocket of his coat and flashed it at Lee. He was intimately familiar with the brass engraving of an image of the White House below a blue circle surrounding the presidential seal.

"I'm Special Agent Stephen Duffy with the United States Secret Service. I'm going to need you to come with me, Doctor. Right now. It's urgent."

The words "imposing" and "hard" came to Lee's mind and he made a quick determination about this special agent. Stephen Duffy was not someone who would take no for an answer.

CHAPTER 4

Lee and Duffy had a private chat in the hallway. He was worried about the residents he had to oversee. Duffy stood ramrod straight, and Lee wondered if the agent's rigid shoulders ever slumped.

"The hospital CEO arranged for another doc to take your place," he said. "You're ours for the day."

"She put you up to this, didn't she?" asked Lee.

"Who?"

"Karen, my ex. Is this about her?"

"All I know is that I'm to bring you to the White House. It's not an invitation many people pass up."

Before he agreed to leave, Lee had the orthopedic surgeon paged. Over the phone, he divulged the discovery of Wendell's fistula. It would have been more satisfying to see the man's disbelieving expression, watch him squirm with embarrassment at having a family doc save the day, but there was no time for ego boosting. Next, Lee checked with the hospital CEO, Dr. Chip Kaplan, and confirmed that another attending would supervise his residents for the day.

"So why does the Secret Service want you, anyway?" Kaplan asked. "Have you been making threats against our president in your off hours, Lee?"

"Funny, Chip," said Lee. "To be honest, I have no idea why they want me. But I'll let you know if I can."

Lee followed Duffy out the front entrance, leaving his car parked in the employee lot out back. The sun shone brightly off to the east and wispy clouds looked brushed upon a sparkling blue sky. A massive Suburban the color of midnight idled curbside, with windows tinted so dark it was impossible to see inside.

Duffy opened the rear door and Lee climbed in. He sank into the plush leather interior, inhaled the new car smell, and caught a whiff of perfume in the spotless gray carpeting. The car was stocked with plenty of snacks and bottled water, and lots of napkins and glasses, all adorned with the presidential seal.

E Pluribus Unum. Out of many, one.

Duffy introduced the driver, a tall, lean gentleman, handsome as a movie cowboy, as Woody Lapham. Judging by the suit and dark glasses, Lee guessed Lapham was also Secret Service. Both men reminded Lee of the boys he used to play basketball and football with—athletic, strong. Though he knew it was petty, Lee felt a pang of jealousy over their youth and vigor.

Lee had managed to keep his body in relatively decent shape, though now in the middle of middle age he could feel it starting to slip. Every slice of pizza these days seemed like the metabolic equivalent of half the damn pie. But Lee was still strapping at six foot two and a healthy 215 pounds. His firm jaw jutted out slightly and complemented a natural smile bracketed by a pair of dimples. A broad, flat nose fit his face just fine. Arresting hazel eyes might have been his most notable physical trait were it not for his wavy, reddish hair, which he kept well trimmed and always cut above the ears.

As the car pulled away from the curb, Lee took out his cell phone and tried Karen's number again. "Are you sure Karen is all right?" Lee asked from the backseat. "She's not answering."

Lapham drove the speed limit, telling Lee this issue of national importance was not an actual medical emergency.

"K-Ray? She's fine," Duffy said. Lee knew "K-Ray" was the nickname Karen's team sometimes used for her. Karen's last name was Ray before it was Blackwood, and Lee would be lying to himself if he said it did not hurt when she became Ray again. "You'll see her soon enough," Duffy added.

Duffy's fingers drummed a restless beat against the car's dashboard. He was looking back at Lee, but not seeming to fix his gaze on anything.

Duffy slipped off his sunglasses to get a better look at something outside, maybe the cherry blossoms in Dumbarton Oaks Park that were still in full bloom thanks to an unusually cold and wet April. Lee noted how Duffy's eyes darted about like Jason Bourne seeking all exits, and how they bulged slightly from the sockets.

Interesting . . .

Duffy looked forward again, but didn't bother putting his sunglasses back on. Lee was curious to get a look at his eyes again.

"What exactly will I be doing at the White House?"

Lee hoped that would get Duffy to look at him and indeed he glanced back, his expression oddly cryptic, fingers drumming restlessly against the front dash.

"Afraid that sort of intel is above our pay grade," he said.

Lee noted how Duffy's eyelids seemed to hesitate, leaving the white of the sclera visibly exposed rather than staying with the top of the iris as it normally does during downward eye movement.

Lee decided to distract himself with his favorite pastime: diagnosis.

"Agent Duffy, could I ask you to hold up your arms and close your eyes?"

Duffy screwed up his face. "What? Why?"

"Hey, indulge him," said Lapham, elbowing Duffy in the arm.

"Fine. Fine."

With a bit of reluctance, Duffy lifted his arms as if a kicker had made a field goal, and Lee observed a fine rapid tremor in both outstretched hands. Lee keyed in again on Duffy's prominent stare.

"Do you mind if I ask you something personal?"

Lapham and Duffy exchanged knowing glances, something Lee found a bit peculiar.

"Sure thing," Duffy said.

"Has your doctor ever mentioned hyperthyroidism to you, Graves' disease specifically? It's an autoimmune problem involving the thyroid gland."

From the driver's seat, Lapham pumped his fist in the air. Duffy, shaking his head in dismay, took out his wallet, removed a crisp hundred-dollar bill, and handed it to Lapham.

"I was diagnosed last month," Duffy said. "Started with the hand tremor, but wasn't long before other symptoms came up." Lee felt certain he could find all his other symptoms were he to give Duffy a proper exam. "It's not bad enough to put me on medical leave, but it is a pain in the ass."

"Why did you give Agent Lapham a hundred dollars just now?" asked Lee, nonplussed.

Lapham's grin broadened. "Because Duffy's always betting on something," he said. "K-Ray said you'd diagnosis his Graves' disease just by looking at him. Said you were that good. Duffy bet you wouldn't, and, well, I won." Lapham waved the bill in his outstretched hand.

"Now I feel badly," Lee said to Duffy.

"You should," Duffy replied. "This job pays crap and I got serious bills to cover. No joke."

Duffy's intense stare made it hard for Lee to pick up any levity, but he assumed it was there.

Fifteen minutes after leaving the clinic, they reached the well-marked and highly restricted checkpoint at Fifteenth and E Streets Northwest. A duty guard checked Lapham and Duffy's credentials. The rear window came down, and the same guard peered into the backseat at Lee.

"So this is Shaman?"

"Yeah," Duffy said.

The guard checked Lee's ID before retreating to a concrete guardhouse where he accessed controls to lower a barricade emblazoned with the word STOP.

Lapham drove forward a few feet before stopping at an area marked with white paint. An imposing K-9, handled by an equally imposing guard, canvassed the Suburban with its nose in search of explosive material. Other guards checked under the car with angled mirrors on a stick. It seemed everybody was subjected to rigorous security, even the people assigned to protect the first family.

"Why did the guard back there call me Shaman?" asked Lee.

"It's your code name," Duffy said. "The White House Communications Agency assigns names to people of prominence, but Lapham and I came up with your name all on our own."

"A shaman is a Native American medicine man," Lapham said, "and given how Karen talked you up we thought it was fitting."

Lee nodded. "Can you tell me the president's name?"

"Believe it or not, you can look it up on Wikipedia," Lapham said. "POTUS, that's the president of the United States, is Brave Heart, and FLOTUS, she's the first lady, is Black Bear."

"Why that name?"

"You know how a mother cub defends her young."

Lee got a picture of a fiercely devoted parent.

"What about Cam Hilliard?" Lee asked.

"There's a tradition of alliteration with these names, so he's Bishop," Duffy said.

Lee returned another nod. Cam's exceptional talent at chess was well documented. Bishop was a fitting nickname, and Lee thought Shaman was a pretty fine one as well.

After passing the K-9 checkpoint, the Suburban continued up a snaking driveway toward the White House. Lee had been here before, on a tour Karen had arranged. The same feelings of history and majesty swept over him.

Eventually they reached the distinct oval design of the South Portico entrance. Everyone got out of the Suburban, while a lone guard held open a door into the main building. Lee soon found himself standing in the middle of the resplendent Diplomatic Reception Room. He took a moment to marvel at the pastoral mural painted on the room's round walls, the federal-era furniture upholstered in gold fabric, and the massive, plush turquoise-and-gold rug with the image of an eagle dominating its center. A portrait of George Washington hung over an ornate marble fireplace. If Lee had not left his cell phone in the car, per Lapham's instructions, he might have been tempted to snap a selfie.

Duffy and Lapham led Lee down a long corridor paved with black-and-white marble tiles, arranged in a chessboard pattern. Lee followed them through a doorway and into a warmly lit room with muted brown carpeting and straw-colored walls decorated with original oil paintings. It was a waiting room of sorts, though nothing like the one at Lee's family practice. The furniture was upholstered in the highest-quality fabric, the lamps resting on burnished wood end tables were all antiques, and the magazine rack, adorned with the seal of the president, held a selection of military-themed journals.

Karen was inside the waiting room, along with someone Lee did not expect to see: Ellen Hilliard, the first lady of the United States, who came right over to Lee and extended her hand. Karen stayed back, giving the first lady the first greeting.

"Hello, Dr. Blackwood. Karen has told me so much about you. It's a pleasure to meet you in person."

The first lady's handshake was practiced and confident.

"It's an honor to meet you," Lee managed. In a blink, his throat had gone completely dry.

"Thank you for being here under these—well, unusual circumstances."

Ellen's voice was warm and intimate, lacking any pretense. She could have been a friend, a patient, anybody really. Her kind eyes, an electric shade of blue, were inviting, and her bright smile made it easy to forget she was one of the most powerful women in the country.

The first lady's stature was an oft-discussed topic for the fashionistas on TV, but in person Lee realized she was nearly his height, without heels. She wore her dark blond hair shoulder length, and her sleeveless pink dress, the color of the cherry blossoms, showed a body fit and trim from rigorous exercising. Her workout routine and diet were also well documented and frequently discussed in the media. She had an understated strand of white pearls around her slender neck. Glowing, near-flawless skin gave Ellen the appearance of a woman much younger than her fifty years.

Lee found her so warm and engaging, he forgot to be intimidated. Living in the fishbowl of the White House could not have been easy, yet Ellen Hilliard had managed it with grace and aplomb. Karen had always spoken highly of FLOTUS, and meeting Ellen for the first time, Lee understood.

More than a few political pundits speculated that without Ellen's sharp mind, campaign know-how, and financial acumen (she had been the chief financial officer with Boys and Girls Clubs of America), Geoffrey Hilliard, then a U.S. senator from Maryland, would never have won the election.

Lee believed Hilliard had won a second term because of a favorable economy and nothing more. The world was still going to hell in a handbasket, and he hadn't voted for the guy. He hoped Karen had never shared his political leanings with the first lady.

"I'm happy to be here," Lee said. "Though I'm not really sure what this is all about."

Karen, dressed in a stylish dark blue pantsuit, stepped forward. She and Lee embraced briefly, but warmly.

"You look well, Karen."

Lee's annoyance at Karen for ignoring his many calls passed through him like a breeze. Divorce had taught him not to sweat the small stuff. These days, most of their correspondence about Josh happened through e-mail and text messages. Lee had not seen Karen in—what, months? It was hard to keep track of time. When Josh was little, the days were long and the years were short. Now it was all just a blur.

"You do, too," Karen replied. "Sorry to put you through all this."

"You didn't have to send a surprise escort," Lee said. "I would have come in a heartbeat."

"That wasn't actually Karen's decision. I'm afraid my husband doesn't like to leave things to chance," Ellen said.

"You mean the—" Lee cleared his throat. "The president?"

Ellen's slight laugh came across as endearing. "Well, he is my husband."

Lee shook his head, only mildly mortified. He hoped he had not gone red in the face.

"Yes, of course. I knew that. Have you asked me here to see a patient?"

Ellen gave a nod. "Yes. The patient is my son, Cam."

"Got it." Lee took a moment to collect his thoughts. "I'm afraid I'm still trying to sort this all out. I assume the first family has a physician, and I'm guessing a pretty good one at that."

"That they do," Karen said. "Several, in fact. You're actually in the White House Medical Unit. Three private exam rooms and a full-time staff of twenty-five to look after everyone from dignitaries to White House visitors."

"Sounds like a mini urgent-care center. Why do you need me?"

"My son means the world to me, Dr. Blackwood."

"Please, call me Lee." He thought of her code name: Black Bear.

"Lee it is. I have full confidence in our medical staff. Dr. Frederick

Gleason has given Cam a very thorough examination, but Karen, who spends a lot of time with my son, has me convinced we'd benefit from a second opinion, an *outside* opinion. I told Karen if we did bring in a consult, it would have to be someone with exceptional talent, which is why you're here."

Lee sent Karen an appreciative glance. They might not have been perfect spouses, but they still held each other in extremely high regard.

"I trust Karen's judgment implicitly," Ellen continued. "However, not everyone agrees these extra measures are necessary. Which is why I wanted to meet you first, to give you fair warning."

Uh-oh, thought Lee. Nothing was worse than butting heads with another doctor over a patient's diagnosis, and it was especially concerning when this patient happened to be the son of the most powerful couple in the world.

"I'm flattered by your confidence, and I hope I live up to the praise," Lee said. "But who is Dr. Gleason?" The name was familiar, and Lee thought Karen might have mentioned him before.

"He's a navy captain and physician to the president," Ellen said. "He's our family doctor as well."

That's not all, Lee thought. The twenty-fifth amendment gave Dr. Gleason the power to decide whether Geoffrey Hilliard was fit to lead the country. Lee's authority did not go much beyond writing a prescription.

"Has Dr. Gleason made an official diagnosis yet? What are Cam's symptoms?"

"You can ask him yourself," Karen said, motioning to a closed door on the east side of the room, decorated by yet another embossed White House seal, this time partnered with a caduceus. "Everyone is waiting for you inside the exam room, the president as well."

CHAPTER 5

The exam room, bright and airy, was as typical as any Lee had seen, with the notable exception of the president of the United States standing in a corner, talking on his specially encrypted cell phone. Karen, along with Lapham and Duffy, hung back in the waiting room. This was a private family matter.

Lee inventoried the array of ultramodern medical equipment: all the essentials, including integrated diagnostic systems, instruments for checking vital signs, an ECG machine, and defibrillators were on hand. Various medications and medical supplies were neatly arranged inside tall, glass-fronted cabinets.

Cam Hilliard, perched on the vinyl cushion of a durable exam table, sported a glum expression. He used the sleeve of his blue dress shirt to clean grime off his wire-rimmed glasses. He reminded Lee a little of Harry Potter. He did not look anything like his father, but Lee could certainly see his mother in him.

A man in his late forties sat on a rolling exam stool not far from Cam. He was athletically built, with brown hair cut to military standards. He had a prominent nose, and for someone with a five o'clock shadow, quite a youthful face.

Lee guessed this was Dr. Gleason and got confirmation when he saw the stitched monogram on the right pocket of his lab coat. Affixed to the left pocket was the seal of the president. No doubt about it, the White House was big on branding.

The president ended his call and came over to Lee with the practiced smile of someone expert at glad-handing. Lee could not help being a bit starstruck. It was the president, after all.

President Hilliard, who was shorter than his wife by two inches or so, had a presence Lee found magnetic and energizing. Nevertheless, the aging effect of the White House was impossible to ignore. Hilliard's dark hair, balding from the front, featured brush strokes of gray not present when he first took office. The lines on his face were more deeply set, and his brown eyes no longer sparkled when he smiled. Hilliard had been a bit of a jock at Yale—baseball and crew—and his powerful jaw and well-muscled physique kept him from looking beaten down by the rigors of his job.

"Dr. Blackwood, thank you for being here," the president said, his voice a bit plummy, all trace of his Baltimore accent well disguised. Born and raised in a blue-collar neighborhood in Baltimore, Hilliard often referred to his hardscrabble upbringing in his speeches, but critics noted he had done little to lift former friends and neighbors out of the economic doldrums. Speeches were easy—governing was hard.

"It's my honor, Mr. President," Lee said, giving Hilliard's hand a firm shake.

"I'm sorry to bring you here without notice," the president said. "But Ellen convinced me we needed to take immediate action. Karen tells me you have a son together, former military, I understand."

"That's right," Lee said. "Josh was an Army Ranger. Did three tours in Afghanistan. Now he's a ski instructor in Colorado. Quite the shift."

"Please tell him the president thanks him for his service."

"I'll be sure to give him that message," Lee said. "I know he'll appreciate your gratitude."

"Speaking as fathers, then," Hilliard said. "I assume we can count on your discretion here. This is a rather—well, delicate situation." The president glanced briefly at Cam.

Dr. Gleason took that as his cue to come over and shake Lee's hand. It was a fishy handshake, weak and limp, the first unmilitary thing about him.

"Dr. Blackwood, we appreciate you being here." Gleason did not sound like he meant it. "I'm glad to have your counsel. I want to do everything I can to help ease the concerns of the president and Mrs. Hilliard."

Lee had a pretty good BS meter, honed from years of dealing with patients lying to him about their health habits. His was pinging loudly. Gleason wanted Lee here as much as he wanted the flu.

"I'm happy to be another set of eyes," said Lee, addressing Cam directly. The boy kept his head down.

Lee moved away from the president and Dr. Gleason so he could focus on Cam. He was not here for some meet-and-greet, after all; he had a job to do.

"Hey there, Cam, my name is Dr. Lee Blackwood. I'm Karen's former husband. Your parents thought it might be a good idea if I talked to you about what's going on."

Lee spoke to Cam the way he would any new patient. Cam flashed his father a withering look.

"What Dr. Gleason isn't saying is that you're wasting your time," Cam said in a low voice. "Everyone's mind is already made up."

"Made up their minds about what?" Lee asked. "I don't even know your symptoms."

Ellen approached from behind and placed her hands on her son's shoulders, but Cam remained sullen and silent.

"Sweetheart, please talk to Dr. Blackwood. Tell him what you told us."

"Why bother?" he said, his voice still low. "I'm not depressed, but you all think I am."

"It seems we're at a bit of an impasse," Ellen said, exasperation evident, her face betraying the strain.

Dr. Gleason stepped forward. "If it's all right with the president and Mrs. Hilliard, I'd like Cam to step into the waiting room for a moment so we could speak privately."

"That's fine," the president said. "Cam, give us a second, will you please? We have to talk about you."

The president's attempt at levity seemed utterly lost on Cam, who slipped off the table and slunk to the waiting room.

Dr. Gleason waited for the door to close before he spoke. "I'll start us off, if I may."

The president nodded.

"This past year Cam has become increasingly withdrawn. He's apathetic, moody, irritable, and it wouldn't be a stretch to say he shows signs of clinical depression. Recently there was an incident with a water glass, which Karen witnessed."

Gleason gave a brief explanation of the incident, though Lee sensed details were missing. He was curious to learn more from Karen or Cam.

"There's nothing physically wrong with Cam," Dr. Gleason continued. "And I'm happy to show you the charts. But as you can well imagine, the White House is not an easy environment for a child. No offense, Dr. Blackwood, but it's my belief—and before Karen inserted herself into the situation, the belief of Cam's parents as well—that he would benefit from seeing a psychiatrist, not a—family doctor." Gleason said "family doctor" as if the words were "country bumpkin."

Lee said, "Thank you for the information, and no offense taken." He noted the icy stare Ellen gave Gleason.

"What Dr. Gleason has left out," Ellen said, "what Karen has convinced me of, is that we want a second opinion from someone who is not affiliated with the White House, someone with no prior relationship to Cam. I don't want to drag him to a psychiatrist. The process has to be collaborative. We just want another point of view. If Cam was to hear the opinion of someone from outside the White House it might make him more receptive to receiving the help we believe he needs. Isn't that right, Geoffrey?"

"Yes, that's right."

The president moved next to his wife. The president's edginess made it obvious he wanted Lee's involvement over with quickly, and for Cam to move on with treatment for depression. Lee felt even better about voting for the other guy.

"What do you think, Dr. Blackwood?" Ellen asked.

"I think I'm happy to do an exam, but my conclusions might not support your hypothesis," Lee warned. "I'm obligated to form my own opinions. If you're in agreement with that, I think we should bring Cam back in here."

A moment later, Cam strolled into the exam room, his gaze on the floor.

Lee rolled over a metal stool, lowered it a bit, and sat down. Up on the exam table, Cam had the height advantage—the power position.

"Why don't you tell me in your own words what's going on?"

Lee tried to sound encouraging, but Cam remained tight-lipped.

"I wouldn't talk to me either, if I were you," said Lee eventually, speaking in an almost conspiratorial tone. In a whispered voice, loud enough for all to hear, he added, "Usually when I do a physical exam, there isn't an audience present."

Cam almost cracked a smile.

Lee glanced at the president, next over to Gleason, and lastly to Ellen Hilliard. "What if Cam and I spoke alone for a bit?" Lee was addressing Ellen, his advocate. "I'll do my usual exam, and we can talk after that. Does that sound good to you, Cam?"

Cam returned a half shrug to go along with his half smile. Ellen sent Lee a look of quiet gratitude.

"Yeah, I guess," Cam said.

"Mr. President, Mrs. Hilliard, are you all right with this as well?" Lee asked.

President Hilliard spoke for them both. "Yes, that would fine. Thank you, Dr. Blackwood."

Dr. Gleason said nothing at all.

CHAPTER 6

Except for the dark circles around his eyes, and an ashen complexion, Cam appeared to be in relatively good health. Still, it was clear from his demeanor that something was amiss. Lee cleared his mind and got centered. He needed Cam's cooperation, and judging by body language—eyes downcast, arms folded across his chest—it would be hard to get.

"Cam, I know this is difficult, but I'm here to help. If you're honest with me, I'll be honest with you."

"Are you going to tell my parents I don't need to see a shrink?" Cam looked at Lee pleadingly.

"I can't make that promise," Lee said. "I have to examine you first."

"Then you can't help me," Cam replied glumly. "I've already been examined. Everyone says the same thing."

"That you need a shrink."

"You got it."

"Why are you so against therapy?" Lee asked. "I know it sounds scary, but it's helped millions of people suffering from all sorts of issues."

"I'm not against therapy. I'm just not depressed."

Lee nodded, as if to say, *Touché*.

"Look, I'm here now, so why not make the most of it. Perhaps I can help."

"Please, can you tell them I'm not depressed? It's something else. I can *feel* it."

But Cam's whole demeanor seemed morose. He barely made eye contact, and he spoke in a flat voice with hardly any facial expression.

At first blush, Dr. Gleason's concern did not seem without merit. But Lee could not reach any conclusion until he completed a thorough exam, and for that he'd need Cam's cooperation. Clearly, he needed another strategy to win this patient over.

Thinking of strategy gave Lee an idea. He took out his cell phone and launched a chess application he had downloaded a while back on a whim. He had played a few games, without winning one, and maybe that was why he had forgotten about the app until now.

Lee moved the pawn in front of his bishop forward one space and handed the phone to Cam, whose face screwed up, confused.

"What's this?" he asked.

"It's chess," said Lee.

"I know it's chess," Cam said. "Why are you handing this to me?"

"I'm playing you in a game."

Cam shrugged and moved the pawn in front of his king forward two spaces. He handed the phone back to Lee, who studied the board intently. Eventually, Lee settled on moving the king-side pawn in front of his knight forward two spaces. He handed the phone back to Cam and thought little of his sly smile.

Cam said, "Queen h4. Checkmate."

He gave Lee the phone. Sure enough, Cam's queen had a diagonal line to Lee's king.

"It's called the fool's mate," Cam said.

Lee grimaced. "I feel so much better knowing that's the name. Thank you."

Cam returned a quiet laugh. Even though Lee had lost the game to an embarrassing two-move fool's mate, he took it as a victory. The lines of communication were now open. It was a start.

"You're pretty good at this game," Lee said.

"Got an Elo rating over twenty-six hundred."

"Elo? What's that?"

"The FIDE uses it to rank players."

"FIDE?"

"Fédération Internationale des Échecs," Cam said, speaking in an exaggerated French accent. "It's the World Chess Federation. They're the governing body of international chess."

"You compete internationally?"

"I told you my Elo rating. I'm one of the top junior players in the world." Cam did not sound cocky, just reciting the facts.

"Impressive," said Lee, who took a moment to think about what he would say next. Every word with this patient mattered. He knew he had one and only one chance to be of help. "Look, Cam, I promise you I'm not here to put a rubber stamp on Dr. Gleason's diagnosis, if that's your worry. I'm here to do my own exam, and it's medical, not psychological. Will you let me help you?"

"I don't know what else to tell you," Cam said.

To Lee's ears, Cam sounded desperate. He wanted to have something useful to reveal.

"You've been irritable. Tell me about that."

"I take it you heard about the water glass," Cam said.

"You mean the projectile?"

Cam gave a shrug typical of any teenager.

"What was the glass all about?" Lee asked.

"I lost a chess match to Taylor Gleason, Dr. Gleason's son. Guess I was pissed."

"You don't lose to him?"

"I don't usually lose to anyone."

"What's Taylor's Elo rating?"

"He's high for the U.S., but not as high as me."

"Why do you think you lost?"

Cam gave another shrug.

"Any chance you're feeling extra anxious for some reason?" Lee asked. "You might be under a lot of stress. This isn't an easy place to grow up, I'd imagine."

"Now you sound like Dr. Gleason."

"I'm trying to understand how you're feeling."

"I don't know. I'm just—just angry a lot of the time."

"Angry about what?"

"I don't know."

"Have you felt angry before?"

Cam mulled this over. "I thought this exam was going to be medical."

"Your feelings are medical."

Cam seemed to accept Lee's explanation. "I mean, sure, everyone gets angry sometimes, but I don't typically throw things."

"Would you say the anger began around the same time you started losing to Taylor?"

Cam thought it over and gave a nod. "Yeah. Maybe around then. It's probably hard for you to understand because it's not sports or something normal like that, but chess is what I do. It's who I am. Chess means everything to me."

Lee could see the distress on Cam's face and his heart broke for him.

"It's not hard for me to understand at all," said Lee. "Any star quarterback would be equally devastated if they couldn't play because of an injury."

Cam nodded in vigorous agreement. "But this isn't like a normal injury," he said. "It's more like that quarterback one morning suddenly couldn't throw the ball and nobody knew why."

Interesting, thought Lee.

"How's school going for you?" he asked.

"It's okay, I guess. It's easy for me, but I don't like going as much anymore."

"Are you losing interest in things?"

Cam shrugged again. "A little. Maybe I'm bored or something."

More signs pointing to some sort of depression.

"What about girls?"

"What about them?"

"Do you date?"

"I'm the president's kid. It's not really easy to date." He put "date" in air quotes. "And besides, there's no one I'm that interested in anyway."

"What about your friends?"

"They're cool. We hang out."

"What do you like to do with them?"

"Um—I dunno, we just hang out. My friends think it's cool here."

Lee made a little noise to underscore the observation. "It *is* cool here."

Cam gave what Lee now thought of as his signature shrug. "Guess I'm used to it," he said.

To Lee's ears, Cam sounded more apathetic than adjusted.

"Do you play chess with your friends?"

Cam shook his head. "I go to the TPI for that, or to tournaments."

"What's the TPI?"

"The True Potential Institute. It's where I learned to play. I still go there because they have some of the best chess instructors in the world. Every few years the FIDE hosts the junior team championships, and this year the tournament is being held in New York."

"Big deal?"

"Very. Teams from all over the world compete. I'm captain of the U.S. squad."

"Lots of practice?"

"Online mostly, but there are some weekend retreats, and we're expected to work on our own. That's why I go to the TPI so much. The competition is really intense."

"Are you the best player at the TPI?"

"I was until Taylor started beating me. I'm team captain and Taylor is first alternate. I shouldn't be losing to him. Now, I'm thinking I might quit playing altogether."

Lee was looking again at those dark circles around Cam's eyes, thinking how important concentration was to winning at chess.

"Are you having any headaches? Confusion? Issues with your vision?"

"Dr. Gleason checked my vision and gave me a new prescription. You think my eyes are the reason I'm losing?"

"I'm not sure yet. Does your vision ever go blurry on you?"

Lee was thinking back to when he first came into the exam room and saw Cam cleaning his glasses with the sleeve of his shirt. Maybe he was trying to clear his vision and not clean away the grime.

"Sometimes when I'm reading, the words get blurry for a moment. Even with the new prescription."

"Are you sleeping well?"

Cam turned his head, a giveaway something was amiss. "I guess. Some mornings I wake up and I'm super tired. It feels weird, like I was beat up in my sleep or something. I dunno how else to describe it."

Lee was keenly interested, but for reasons Cam could not have suspected.

"Achy muscles? Foggy feeling?"

"Yeah, all of that."

"Do you ever feel confused?"

"That too. Like a 'where am I' kind of thing."

"Does it happen often?"

"Maybe a couple of times a month. Maybe more."

Lee thought again of the glass Cam had thrown. Irritability now coupled with unexplained and intense fatigue after a night's sleep. Cam might need to be evaluated by a discerning psychiatrist after all. There were enough arrows pointing toward depression, but they pointed somewhere else, too, and that was the direction Lee wanted to go.

"Tell me, Cam, have you ever bitten your tongue?"

Cam leaned back, perplexed. "My tongue?"

"Yeah, does it ever feel sore when you wake up feeling tired?" Lee asked.

Cam thought it over, but seemed unsure. "Maybe," he said. "Everything feels sore on those mornings, but not so bad I can't go to school or anything."

"Let me have a look."

Cam stuck out his tongue.

Nothing abnormal. Maybe it was somewhat generous in size, but the tissue and color appeared normal and there were no bite marks or indentations from Cam's teeth to suggest macroglossia, the medical term for a pathologically enlarged tongue.

"Are you having any other issues with your sleep?"

"No." Cam said this too quickly, too sharply.

Waking up tired and sore, possibly biting his tongue—these were telling clues. Diagnosis was 90 percent history and 10 percent physical exam. To get real answers Lee needed to probe deeper, but some questions were difficult to answer, like the one he was about to ask.

"Cam, I want you to be honest with me. Have you wet the bed?"

"No." Cam would not look Lee in the eyes.

"It's nothing to be embarrassed about, I promise. But I need to know. It could be important."

He hesitated, but Lee could tell Cam's walls were coming down.

"Once. A couple weeks ago," Cam eventually said, looking away.

"Was it one of those mornings you felt achy and fatigued?"

"Yeah," Cam said, making eye contact now.

"Did you tell anyone?"

"No."

Lee wondered if Cam hid the sheets out of embarrassment, or if it really did happen just one time.

"Cam, from what you're telling me, I think we may need to do some further testing." Lee's voice was reassuring, his expression earnest. "I'm thinking this might not be entirely a mental health issue."

Cam seemed overcome with relief—it was in his eyes, the way his facial muscles relaxed.

"I want to do a complete physical, and after that I'll speak with Dr. Gleason and your parents. Is that okay with you?"

"Are you going to tell my dad? About the bed, I mean." He appeared to be horrified by the thought.

Poor kid is more worried about disappointing his father than his health.

"Let's not even worry about that for now."

"What's wrong with me?" Cam asked. "I've never done that before."

"Well, I'm not sure, but let's see what the exam tells us. Deal?"

"Deal," Cam said.

And they shook.

CHAPTER 7

Lee got the first lady's permission to conduct a more thorough physical exam before he asked Cam to put on a hospital gown in a private changing area. Lee took Cam's vitals—blood pressure a healthy 114 over 65, heart rate sixty-five, temperature and respirations all normal. Cam said he took no prescription medications.

All visual field tests, eye movement, speed, and quality came out normal, and Cam's pupils were equal and briskly reactive to light. Using an ophthalmoscope, Lee examined the retinas of Cam's eyes so he could directly observe the arteries, nerves, and veins, looking for evidence of papilledema—swelling of the optic nerve head that might indicate increased pressure within the skull. The marginated optic nerve and the visible pulsations of retinal veins were normal and reassuring, but did not exclude an underlying tumor.

No sign of one-sided facial weakness. Touch felt equal on both sides of his face, no signs of any sensory loss.

"Can you hear this?" Lee asked as he ever so gently rubbed his fingers together beside each of Cam's ears. He got a thumbs-up. No problem there.

Next, Lee aimed his penlight inside Cam's mouth, checking the soft palate, the back of his throat, and seeing Cam's uvula rise symmetrically and stay midline when he said, "Ahhhh." The gag reflect was as expected. Cam hated that test. That was expected, too.

Lee asked Cam to stick out that slightly large tongue of his once more, and noted it did not deviate to one side or the other. His neck muscles were strong and equal. After finishing the cranial nerve examination, Lee directed his attention to the remainder of the neurologic exam. Motor function, fine. Strength, good. Coordination intact. No involuntary movements or tremors. With Cam's eyes closed, Lee tested for sensation, touching a light cotton swab gently over his limbs.

"You feel that?"

"You mean the cotton swab?"

Passed.

All other sensory tests were normal: vibration, joint position sensation, temperature, and the like.

"Now let me see you walk," Lee said.

Lee could glean plenty of information by observing a patient's gait. Was there a subtle drag of the leg? Were there signs of imbalance? Did he have equal and normal arm swings? Everything checked out fine.

Lee tested Cam's reflexes. Those were normal, too. He finished with a general examination, listening to the heart and lungs, palpating and listening to the belly, looking for any unusual skin rashes or lesions or birthmarks, finding none. Physically, everything appeared normal, except for his slightly enlarged tongue and complaint of occasional blurred vision. Lee could hardly be sure those were even signs of any significance.

But that did not mean Cam Hilliard was out of the woods.

When the exam was over, Cam dressed in his street clothes and went back in the waiting room with Lapham and Duffy. Lee felt almost sad to see him go, because he was unsure if their paths would cross again. He had come to like Cam in the short time they'd spent together. The boy was witty, sweet-natured, and obviously exceptionally intelligent.

Ellen Hilliard and Dr. Gleason returned to the exam room, but the president did not join them.

"The president has a meeting he cannot miss, but I'm to report your findings to him."

Lee wondered if Gleason had encouraged the president to brush off his debrief, and got the vibe he was prowling in the territory of the alpha male. His preference was to speak to both parents, but no matter. The mother was here and Lee had findings to share.

The three sat in a circle facing each other. Ellen's blinking was rapid and nervous, her jaw firmly set.

"Well, I didn't find anything physically wrong in my exam, but I'm concerned. Cam told me he's been waking up some mornings feeling confused and extremely tired, with sore muscles."

Ellen seemed baffled. "He never said anything to me. You, Dr. Gleason?"

Gleason shook his head. "Don't we all have those days?"

Lee had seen this coming.

"Yeah, but he's only sixteen, and these episodes seem to come out of the blue," Lee said.

"Have you ever been depressed, Dr. Blackwood?" Gleason asked.

Lee gave the question some thought. On the life happiness spectrum, he typically swung pendulum-like from full-on joy to a bit morose, but never manic, and never so low that he could not pull himself out of a tailspin dive. Sure, he would like to find love again, have some sort of companionship. His last girlfriend, a nurse from the MDC named Bethany, had recently ghosted him. At first Lee thought she might have lost her phone, until his son Josh explained "ghosting" as the process of suddenly ceasing all communication in an effort to end a relationship without hurt feelings. Soon after Bethany went radio silent, Lee spotted her out on the town with an orthopedic surgeon. Bethany had never struck him as the materialistic type, but not many family docs cruised around in an eighty-five-thousand-dollar Mercedes, either.

Despite Lee's dismal love life and the stresses of a diminishing medical practice, he had managed, miraculously even, to live a relatively happy existence.

"I have never had depression," Lee finally answered.

"But you do realize fatigue, morning aches, are symptomatic of the condition?"

"I'm well aware," said Lee. "But there is another, more sensitive matter Cam was reluctant to discuss."

Ellen folded her arms across her chest, bracing herself for the news. "What did he say?" she asked.

"He told me that he wet his bed at night. He said it happened only once, and I'm inclined to believe him."

Ellen seemed bewildered, but also relieved Lee's discovery was not worse.

"He's never been a bed wetter," she said, "but one time, an accident, a really deep sleep maybe, it's not so remarkable."

"I agree," Lee said. "But it's also unusual, and I'm here looking for anything unusual that might give us a different window into what's troubling your son."

"And has this window shown you something?" Ellen asked.

"I saw nothing in my exam to indicate the presence of a tumor, but I'm worried that Cam might be having seizures during sleep. I thought his tongue was a little generous in size, possibly from having bitten it at night, and waking up tired and achy, the bedwetting, those are all possible indications of nocturnal seizure activity."

"Are you diagnosing Cam with epilepsy?" Dr. Gleason's voice had a harsh edge.

"I can't tell you that, but I do think he needs to see a neurologist, and he needs more tests."

Ellen pressed her palms together, fingertips to her mouth as though in prayer.

"What does it mean?" she asked. "There's no history of epilepsy in either of our families."

"At this point, having a seizure doesn't mean having epilepsy. If the findings are indicative of seizures, those could be affecting his mood as well."

"What could cause that?" Ellen asked.

"Scarring in the brain, perhaps, or a genetic predisposition of some sort."

Ellen shook her head in disbelief, unsure how to process this information. She eyed Dr. Gleason as if to say, *How come you didn't know all this?*

"No offense, Dr. Blackwood," Gleason said, "but I believe you're in over your head here, and I'm afraid you're alarming the first lady for no particularly good reason. Now, hats off to you for getting Cam to open up, but nothing you've described makes me think anything different.

"If you take into account all the evidence—Cam's moodiness, the behavioral changes, and now add bedwetting to the mix—I think you've helped to bolster my case that the real culprit is anxiety and stress. I think we should rule that out before we make Cam any more anxious with what may be unnecessary tests," Gleason said. "Then, I guess, we could let someone who knows the brain take a look at him."

With all the evidence he had presented, just about any doc Lee knew would be willing to suspect seizures, but not Gleason. Again, Lee caught the strong scent of Gleason's alpha male aura. If Cam was going to receive a neurological consult, it would be at Gleason's direction, not Lee's.

"Cam's not had any previous problems, and he says he's not under any undue stress," Lee said. "Something else may be going on here."

"Your exam was normal," Gleason said.

"That doesn't rule out anything. You have his visual complaints to consider as well," said Lee. "I think you should rule out all medical issues before declaring him in need of psychological help."

"Dr. Gleason, what are we going to do here?" Ellen asked. "All I hear is you two arguing, and that's not helping my son."

Her eyes bored into Gleason. She was task-driven, Lee could tell. She wanted clearly articulated next steps and a resolution.

Dr. Gleason returned a wan smile. "We will certainly take Dr. Blackwood's assessment under careful advisement. I want to thank you for your time today. You've been of great service."

There were more thank-yous after that, and a lengthy handshake with the first lady, and a promise to let Lee know he would be called upon again if they felt he could be of further help.

Lee was not expecting his phone to ring anytime soon.

CHAPTER 8

Mark Muller, the man his friends called Mauser, parked the cable company van across the street from the home belonging to the parents of Susie Banks. Mauser knew nothing about the cable business, but his friend who worked for the company servicing this home (as well as most in the area) did. His friend also happened to have a serious love affair with drugs, and had lent his van along with some technical know-how in exchange for the kind of help Mauser could provide.

The street where Susie Banks lived was nothing special. Nice brick houses nestled closely together on postage-stamp lots. There was one car in the narrow driveway. It would be the father's. He was the one who'd called the company when his Internet went down after Mauser's friend disconnected the service using his work laptop.

Now his friend was in the back of the van, high and happy, so it was Mauser who ambled up the stone-lined walkway to the front door. These were older homes—modest dwellings with a price tag nipping at the obscene level, but such was life in Arlington, Virginia.

Mauser's digs were not so cheap either. He lived in Fort Dupont, just east of the mostly forgotten Anacostia River area. It was centrally located to two steady sources of drug-dealing income: the sketchier parts of southeast D.C. and the far more upscale neighborhood of Capitol Hill. Cam Hilliard lived only a few miles from his apartment. Mauser had no idea how he'd deal with that problem when the time came, but he knew it would not be nearly as easy as pretending to be a cable repairman.

Mauser rang the doorbell, summoning Douglas Banks, tall with square shoulders, to the door. He was a family therapist who had an office on the first floor of this home. His wife was a high school history teacher. His daughter was a violin prodigy. The only other thing Mauser knew about this family was they had little time left to live.

Doug Banks checked over Mauser's uniform and saw the van parked outside. His face showed relief.

"Thank you for getting here so fast. Can't believe how dependent I am on the damn Internet. A few hours without it and I'm utterly lost." The man chuckled.

Mauser returned the pleasant smile of someone who heard that a lot in the course of a day. Tucked under his arm was an official clipboard, a prop his friend had provided. In his pants pocket Mauser carried a number of nine-volt batteries he had drained using a nine-volt connector and several LED lights purchased from an electronics store. He hoped those dead batteries would come in handy soon.

Mr. Banks invited Mauser inside, but first Mauser covered his work boots with plastic bags as a professional courtesy. Never track dirt into a customer's home. That would be poor form.

The home was decorated modestly and kept clean and neat. Music posters hung on the walls, along with framed photographs depicting a happy family proud of their talented daughter.

Mauser should have felt something akin to remorse, but the money he was making thanks to the arrangement with Rainmaker occluded his conscience.

"May I see your router?" Mauser asked.

Doug Banks led Mauser to a tidy little office directly off the kitchen. On a bookshelf the router's lights blinked a distress signal of sorts. Mauser examined the router and the cables, looking like a man who knew what he was doing.

"This might take some time," Mauser said, his voice implying the problem was a serious one. "The issue could be anywhere. I'm assuming you have a cable box upstairs?"

"Yeah, we do."

"Okay, I'm going to have to check throughout the house. Is that all right with you?"

"You have free range," Doug Banks said. "I'll be hiding out in my office if you need me for anything."

Mauser thanked the man and headed upstairs, where he found the first carbon monoxide detector stuck to the ceiling in the hallway. There were no prongs for an outlet, but a little green light indicated the unit was operational on battery power only.

Good.

He had a backup plan if the system was connected to a central alarm, but this setup made things considerably easier. Stealthily, Mauser snapped open the cover and replaced the working battery with the dead one, using a hand to dampen the sound of a chirp. Mauser checked the light and confirmed his dead battery had rendered the unit useless. He surveyed the rest of the floor. A single detector was all it took to safeguard the upper level from the odorless, tasteless, and deadly gas.

Down in the kitchen, Mauser found a second unit. He replaced that good battery with his dead one while Doug Banks toiled away in his office on the other side of the kitchen wall. The house was not alarmed, and the only other home safety products were two smoke detectors that would not go off for a gas leak.

Mauser found Doug in his office.

"Mind if I check the basement?" he asked. "I think the issue might be with the splitter. If so, it should be easy for me to get you back up and running in no time."

Mauser did not know what a splitter looked like, or what it even did. But his friend had given him a couple buzzwords to toss around before he got buzzed on oxy.

Douglas Banks brought Mauser to the basement door. "Do you need anything else?" he asked.

"No, nothing at all," Mauser said.

Mr. Banks returned to his office without Internet, while Mauser descended a varnished wooden staircase to the basement. He entered a spacious unfinished room, dimly lit, with a clean cement floor and boxes of various sizes all neatly arranged on shelving units. A pegboard displayed a nice collection of tools, but the workbench functioned as storage for additional boxes.

Mauser rendered a third CO detector useless before answering one of his last remaining questions: the home was heated with a gas furnace. This was a good thing. An oil furnace might not do the trick, but a big, nasty crack in the heat exchanger of a gas furnace would flood the house with carbon monoxide.

Some naysayers would argue that a cracked heat exchanger in a gas furnace was no cause for alarm. They'd say it was a sales job from an eager repairman looking for a good payday. They were wrong.

Mauser might not be an expert at cable, but he knew heating and cooling systems. It was his cover job—gave a plausible explanation for all his money. His father had taught him the trade, and Mauser had spent years working alongside his dad, learning the nuances of maintaining and fixing complex machinery.

The real money, however, came from dealing drugs. Profits kept climbing, even though he had to share the take with his crew of seven, all part of the Blitzkrieg motorcycle gang. These days his crew was busy expanding their operation and territory, thanks largely to his arrangement with Rainmaker.

A lot of people saw the name Blitzkrieg, and the emblem on the back of his leather jacket—a fiery skeleton clad in leather, wearing an Imperial German Pickelhaube helmet, riding a sleek chopper—and thought Aryan Brotherhood, but he was no neo-Nazi. Mauser's affection for all things German, his prized Mauser C96 pistol included, was born out of respect for a small, economically depressed country that nearly took over the world.

It was hard to get more badass than that.

Mauser checked the furnace tag. The model was ten years old. In five or so years the unit would be a candidate for replacement. If something were to malfunction, not many eyebrows would rise. The incident would be logged as a terrible tragedy and a grim reminder to test carbon monoxide alarms monthly and replace the batteries at least once a year.

The basement had a single door to the outside, with a steep set of concrete stairs up to ground level. The lock on the door was nothing special, easy to breach.

Everything was in place except for one final detail. Mauser called his friend in the van. Five minutes later he called upstairs.

"Mr. Banks, could you try the Internet for me?"

"Sure, hold a second," Mr. Banks called back. A moment later he exclaimed, "Hey, you're a miracle worker!"

No, Mauser thought. *I'm Death riding a chopper with a German Pickelhaube on my head.*

CHAPTER 9

Karen watched Cam's touch football game from the shade of a massive magnolia tree that President Andrew Jackson had planted sometime around 1835. Off to her right, White House gardeners were out in force, taking advantage of a dry day to prune the shrubs that lined the west colonnade bridging the Rose Garden and the South Lawn, where Cam's game took place.

In the days since Lee conducted his physical examination, Cam's chess game had continued to decline and with it his confidence had sunk to new lows. He hid out in his room and didn't even want to go to the TPI for chess practice anymore. Ellen, desperate for a breakthrough, arranged the football game as a way of possibly achieving one.

At first, Cam had resisted, calling it a scheduled play date. School was closed because of a teachers' professional day. Somehow, the first lady had convinced Cam to extend himself, see if a little fun might lift his spirits. She made the plans before he had a chance to change his mind.

Normally, Karen did not have to watch over Cam so diligently inside the compound. The kids could not have been safer. But Karen had promised Ellen she would keep a close eye on him, and her perch by the tree offered a view of the action without making her a presence on the field.

Cam was not the best athlete in the game, but he had a decent enough arm and probably would have been QB even if he were not the president's kid. To Karen's surprise, Taylor Gleason was playing. She was glad to see that Cam's string of losses had not soured their long-standing friendship. It showed great maturity, strength of character, and could mark a turning point in Cam's steady decline. One could always hope.

Cam dropped back to pass and connected with a boy named Rodger Winchester for a solid gain followed by a series of spirited high-fives. The smile on Cam's face was a major relief.

Maybe the first lady's play date would work after all.

Karen had had high hopes that Lee's exam would reveal some hidden cause for Cam's issues. Instead, his findings gave Gleason reason to dig his heels in even harder. The president was now thoroughly convinced the best course of action was for Cam to see a psychiatrist right away. That plan would have made perfect sense, except for one small detail: Cam kept insisting his issues were with his body, not his mind. He vehemently opposed any psychiatric help, but Cam had a hard time making his case.

For years, he had essentially lived his life above the busiest store in all of D.C., on display for the public's endless scrutiny. While the children of presidents were off-limits from muckraking (one of a few unwritten rules in Washington), living in the public eye had to be tremendously difficult. Cam had never asked for this role, and until recently, he had managed it well.

If Lee had done anything, it was to reinforce Cam's belief that his diminishing chess skills were rooted in something physical. While Ellen supported Gleason because he, not Lee, was the trusted doctor, the first lady's request that Karen oversee the football game told a different story. Football was a physical game, so perhaps Ellen worried Cam was physically fragile, which would support Lee's thinking. If Karen was right about that, then Lee had made an impression after all—just not enough of one to trump Gleason.

Karen had learned details of Cam's exam results from Ellen, not Lee. There were several reasons Ellen placed her trust and confidence in Karen. For one, Karen was older than most of her Secret Service colleagues, only a few years younger than Ellen, in fact. Culturally they shared many of the same reference points. Personally, they had bonded over fertility issues. The first lady had used IVF to get pregnant with Cam, while Karen had given up trying for a second child after a string of devastating miscarriages. Those difficult times might have been long past, but they had left scars, and their shared experiences helped to forge an unusual bond.

At times Karen felt less like Ellen Hilliard's protector and more like a personal friend. Some in the Secret Service wondered openly if Karen's rapid career trajectory was based entirely on merit. In addition to her close relationship with FLOTUS, Karen's father was former Secret Service, and whispers of nepotism followed her.

They could think what they wanted. Karen knew the truth.

From a young age, she had dreamt of following in her father's footsteps. But woman plans and God laughs. At nineteen, Karen met a dashing young doctor, Lee Blackwood, eight years her senior (scandalous) from her hometown of Beckley, West Virginia. Her job at the bank, followed two years later with the birth of her son Josh, brought her great joy. It was a fulfilling existence until her dad, a vocal proponent for Secret Service reform, had rumpled the wrong suit.

Her father believed the numerous shortcomings of the Secret Service, which he openly discussed with Karen, dated back decades. In his opinion, almost every embarrassing security lapse was the result of poor employee screening, crazy schedules, not enough quality agents, and no time to plan.

"When a president gets shot, maybe then they'll take me seriously," he often said.

Her father wrote lengthy e-mails and memos to his superiors, in essence telling them the emperor had no clothes. While management expressed appreciation for the thoughtful feedback, Karen always worried such candor could cost him his job.

Around this time, Karen's mother had moved from Beckley to Virginia to be closer to her husband, who traveled constantly for work and was seldom home. Aside from his family, the job was her father's greatest love, which was why Karen's heart sank when her dad phoned with news that he'd been fired. The defeat in his voice, the absolute sorrow, foreshadowed his rapid decline.

Josh was eight back then, Lee was working in his father's practice, and Karen had a new mission in life. Without telling her family, she had applied for the Secret Service. A long-simmering passion for the job and a desire to fulfill her father's reform wishes drove her. She had worried her dad's controversial legacy would work against her, but to Karen's surprise she was accepted. Fifteen years later, Karen had a brutal work schedule that had contributed significantly to her failed marriage, and not a single reform idea of her father's put into practice.

From her hideout by the tree, Karen watched Cam take a snap from Edgar Feldman. Feldman, who inhabited a heavy body with legs and arms like tree stumps, maintained an A average at school, had been in detention only once for tardiness, and had yet to decide if he wanted to be a lawyer like his father or a doctor like his mother. All of Cam's close friends had full background checks on file.

Cam's friends were accustomed to the metal detectors, the facial recognition software, the nondisclosure agreements, and other procedural hurdles necessary to get inside the wall. Kids by nature were adaptable, and for the most part, the mystique and magic of the White House had yielded to the more pressing demands of having a good time.

And these kids were certainly doing that.

Cam's pass was incomplete, though Feldman had put a good block on the rusher, a school chum named Arnold Chang, who happened to study advanced math at the TPI. On the next play, Rodger Winchester ran a buttonhook pattern several yards downfield and was wide open because the defense decided to rush two players instead of one. Feldman moved in front of Chang, leaving Taylor Gleason unblocked. Taylor, who looked like a mini version of his father, slim and athletic, with sandy blond hair and a handsome, albeit boyish face, was hardly an imposing figure, but he was quick on his feet and deceptive with his movements. Dr. Gleason's competitive drive had pushed Taylor to excel at sports in addition to chess. As far as Karen could tell, Taylor was the only real athlete on the chess circuit.

He charged the quarterback with quick strides and managed to smash into Cam's left side—the blind side—with a great deal of force. Taylor got the flag, all right, but the impact threw Cam's legs out from under him. Karen held her breath as Cam went airborne. He seemed to float above the ground for a moment before he came crashing back to the turf with an audible thud.

By the time Karen got there, winded from her sprint, Cam's buddies were already helping him sit up.

"Are you okay?" Karen tried not to sound like an overprotective parent, but she knew the hit had to have hurt.

"I didn't mean to hit him that hard," Taylor said, his voice shaky. "I was going for the flag."

Maybe Taylor was upset after injuring his friend, or maybe Karen's hard stare terrified him. Either way, the kid was rattled.

Cam winced in pain as Karen and Taylor helped him to his feet. He kept his hand to the left side of his chest, his breathing shallow. Scouring the ground, Karen checked for any sticks or a stone Cam might have landed on, but the White House landscapers kept the lawn clear as a putting green. Stone or no stone, though, that hit was pretty solid. Karen worried Cam might have fractured a rib.

"Let's get you to the medical clinic," Karen said.

"I'm okay," Cam said, still clutching his left side. He shot Taylor an aggrieved look. "What the hell, Taylor!" he said.

"I was just going for the flag . . . I'm sorry, Cam. I didn't mean to hurt you."

To Karen's ears, Taylor sounded genuinely distraught, and she did not believe there was any malice behind the collision.

"Let's have Dr. Gleason decide if you're all right," Karen said. "You boys wait right here."

Soon enough, Cam was back inside the White House clinic. Karen called Gleason's cell phone and explained what had happened.

"Taylor did it, huh?" Gleason sounded oddly proud of his son's prowess. "I doubt it's a broken rib," he added, assuaging Karen's concern only somewhat, "but I'll be there in a moment to check him out."

CHAPTER 10

The nurse, who had been a White House fixture for several administrations, took Cam's vitals while awaiting Dr. Gleason's arrival. They checked out fine. Dr. Gleason showed up five minutes later and asked Cam to lie down on the exam table.

"Sounds like you took quite a shot to the side," Gleason said as he pushed on the lower part of Cam's left chest. Cam winced again. "I'll speak with Taylor when I get home. Can't have my son injuring my patients."

He said this facetiously, but again Karen picked up a trace of pride in his voice. Winning was everything with Gleason. It was possible he viewed Taylor's prowess at chess or football as an extension of his own abilities, his worthiness. Karen had encountered similarly misguided parents years ago at Josh's sporting events.

"No abrasions or lacerations," Gleason said, continuing with his exam. "No obvious fracture. Now take a deep breath."

Dr. Gleason listened with his stethoscope.

"Full and equal breath sounds on both sides," he announced. "Abdomen is soft and not particularly tender. Cam, I think you'll be fine, but no more football today."

Cam did not seem disappointed.

"What about my friends?" he asked.

"We'll get them all home," Karen said, ruffling Cam's hair. "Not to worry."

"Tell them I'm sorry," Cam said.

"Of course," said Karen.

"And tell Taylor we're cool."

Karen knew this was teen-speak for "I'm not angry" and returned a warm smile. "Sure thing," she said.

"Now, I want you to go up to your bedroom to rest," Dr. Gleason said. "I'll get you an ice pack and some Tylenol, but no aspirin or ibuprofen. Nothing else unless you ask first."

Cam nodded.

"Dr. Gleason," said Karen. "May I speak with you a moment—in private?"

In addition to the examination rooms, the White House physician's clinic had an elegant three-room office suite situated directly across the corridor from the elevator to the first family's residence. Karen followed Dr. Gleason into his office. He took a seat at his expansive cherrywood desk, clearly perturbed, as though he sensed Karen was about to waste his time. Karen shut the door and stood in front of his desk, arms akimbo.

"How do you know he didn't fracture a rib?" she asked. Her voice had an edge. "You saw he had pain when he was breathing."

"I listened to his chest, and he took nice, full breaths without a problem. He's fine. A bit bruised is all."

"But how do you *know*?"

"Your concern here is appreciated, but it's also misplaced. Trust me on this, okay? I know. I'm his doctor."

If Karen had learned one lesson about Gleason from Cam, it was that there was no changing his mind once it was made up.

"You're the expert, of course. But if anything changes with him, will you please keep me apprised?"

"No problem, Karen."

From a storage compartment in his top desk drawer, Gleason removed a brass key hooked to a tennis racket keychain. Karen recalled the time Gleason broke his racket by slamming it on the ground after a poorly played point during a tennis match against Ellen. Needless to say, Dr. Gleason and Ellen had not played a match against each other since.

"I'll give Cam a pain reliever. Then he should go to his room and rest. You can keep a close eye on him if you want, but he'll be fine. Trust me."

Karen followed Gleason back into the clinic. Using the key he had taken from his desk drawer, Gleason unlocked a large glass-fronted medicine cabinet where all the clinic's medicines, from aspirin to prescriptions, were kept. He put two pills into a Dixie cup, got a glass of water, and handed both to Cam.

"Keep ice on that bruise and take these, buddy," Gleason said, locking the cabinet. "You'll feel better in no time."

Cam downed the pills in a quick swallow before departing for his bedroom. Karen wanted to go with him, but he insisted on going on his own. He trundled off to the elevator bay, holding the ice pack to his side, and Karen watched him go. Ellen Hilliard was giving a speech over at the Renwick Gallery, but had she been around, she would have insisted on tucking Cam into bed. She was Black Bear, after all.

Once Cam was gone, Karen called Donna Whitmore, the first lady's chief of staff, and got a message to Ellen about what had happened. Her next call was to the White House kitchen, where she ordered some chicken soup for Cam, thinking that's what his mother would have done. She had Duffy dismiss Cam's pals early, relaying Cam's message to Taylor, before returning to her small office in the basement of the West Wing, which was just roomy enough for a metal desk to hold her computer, business phone, and coffee mug.

Karen gave it twenty minutes before lingering concern got the better of her. She telephoned Lee, who was seeing patients at his practice, and related what had happened for his benefit.

"I'm sure Dr. Gleason is thrilled that you're calling me for a consult."

"He doesn't know," Karen said.

"I was kidding. I figured you hadn't told him."

"I forgot how subtle your sarcasm could be," Karen said.

"You realize Cam could have fractured a rib."

"That's what I said, but Gleason thinks he's fine."

"Maybe he is, but I'd err on the side of caution. Better safe than sorry with these types of injuries. You're going to have to use your judgment here. But if he has fractured a rib, he'll need to be watched closely for complications. Pneumonia, for instance. If he's not breathing fully because of splinting, the underlying lung tissue may not clear secretions sufficiently and infection can set in."

"What should I do?"

"Keep an eye on him, and call me again if he's acting abnormally in any way."

"Will do," said Karen. "Thank you, Lee." And she meant it, too.

"You do remember that Josh and I are leaving for our camping trip tomorrow morning?"

"I do," she said. "He called yesterday to make plans to see me. Said he was coming alone. What do you make of that?"

"I wouldn't read anything into it," Lee said. "Hannah isn't the outdoorsy type."

"I have no idea what type she is, to be honest," Karen said caustically.

"I wish he'd see in her what I see."

Karen shared Lee's concern. She had met the love of Josh's life, as he put it, this past September, when after some prodding Hannah had flown with him from Colorado to Washington to meet the parents. Karen had been excited to get to know the woman who had captured her son's heart. Hannah was stunningly beautiful, tall and willowy, with brown hair and alluring green eyes. She might have been an incredible skier, but she was as chilly as the slopes where they had met.

Karen wanted Josh's new girlfriend to adore him, to look at him the way he looked at her. But Hannah was more "selfie" than "selfless." She talked fondly of old boyfriends in front of Josh, boasting about their accomplishments, and in almost the same breath would discuss future plans that did not include Karen's son. And because Karen was trained to be observant, she noticed that it was always Josh who showed affection—a hug, a squeeze of the hand. Karen hoped that Josh coming to D.C. alone also coincided with a change to his relationship status on Facebook.

After saying good-bye to Lee, Karen went to check in on Cam, who seemed well enough for her to leave him alone. She attended an hour-long meeting with Lapham and Duffy to go over preparations for the first lady's visit to a public school in a not-so-lovely part of town, and afterward, returned to Cam's room to check on him again, guided more by intuition than anything else.

She knocked on the half-open doorway and peeked in, finding Cam lying in bed. The ice pack was on the floor beside an empty bowl of soup. Cam seemed restless.

"Just checking on you, pal. You doing okay?"

"I guess," Cam said in a quiet voice. "But it still hurts when I take a deep breath, and I feel a little sick to my stomach. I don't feel like throwing up or anything, just a little queasy."

Karen entered the room, went over to his bed, and immediately noticed Cam was sweating a bit. She thought he looked pale, too, and wondered why he spoke so softly. Something was not right with him, not right at all, but when she took out her phone to call Gleason, Karen ended up calling Lee. It went against protocol, but Gleason had brushed off her earlier concern and she feared he'd do so again.

She stepped out into the hall and told Lee what she thought of Cam's condition.

"Where is Gleason?"

Karen saw the president's schedule in her head—an ability she'd gained from years of reviewing schedules. She checked the time on her Marc Jacobs watch, a gift from Josh she wore every day. Gleason had left the White House to accompany President Hilliard to Walter Reed, where he was to deliver a speech on improving health care for veterans—an important agenda item of the president's second term. As part of his responsibilities, Gleason had to go wherever the president went, or he had to appoint another White House doctor as his stand-in.

"He's at Walter Reed," Karen answered.

"What's your take on Cam?" Lee said. "You lived with a doctor long enough, you have good instincts even if you don't have the training."

"I think something is wrong with him."

"I agree. Bring him to the hospital. You can take him anywhere, but I'd go to the MDC. I'm affiliated there, so I can help."

Karen's stomach dropped. "Is it that serious?"

"I don't know, but like I said before, better safe than sorry. The White House Medical Unit is a fine place to suture a cut, but I wouldn't want to have abdominal surgery there."

"No, of course not. Cam needs to go to the hospital for that."

"My point exactly. A broken rib could have caused some internal damage. Let the hospital do a CT scan."

"We don't have a CT scanner in the White House Medical Unit,"

Karen said, convincing herself there was good reason to go elsewhere for his treatment.

"I sure hope not. Otherwise my tax dollars really are being wasted. I'll call Brian Seneca at the MDC and have him arrange for Cam to be brought to the fancy suites. You can't just bring the president's kid to the ER waiting room. Seneca is a superstar surgeon, but hopefully he won't mind coordinating Cam's care."

"What about Gleason?"

"What about him?"

"He's the doctor. I should at least consult him or the other doctors here."

"The other docs will defer to Gleason. And how many times has Gleason backed you, me, or Cam, for that matter?"

"None."

"By my count, he's had three chances to do the right thing. You really want to give him a fourth? You tell Gleason you want to bring Cam to the hospital and he'll do the exact opposite because his ego won't let you be right."

"He'll go ballistic. He'll probably get me fired."

"I thought your job was to protect the president's son at all cost."

Karen thanked Lee for his advice and kind of wished she had not called him.

CHAPTER 11

Karen did not go over Gleason's head, at least not entirely. She got the first lady to back her decision before bringing Cam to the MDC in an armored black SUV. It was a little after one o'clock in the afternoon when they arrived. What Karen had told Ellen mirrored what Lee had told her: he should have a CT scan, and it would be best if Cam were already at the hospital should he require emergency surgery. She did not cite Gleason's attitude as a factor in all of this, but the first lady was exceedingly bright. She must have figured it out on her own, because she asked Karen only to notify Gleason, not consult him on the decision. Karen waited until they were almost at the hospital to make that call.

Two armored SUVs, one ferrying Cam, arrived at the rear entrance of the MDC at the suggestion of Brian Seneca, Lee's colleague there. Duffy and Lapham had gone on ahead and conducted a thorough security assessment that included a sweep for explosives to make sure Cam's private suite on the northwest wing met all standards.

Duffy was happy to be summoned back into work, because he qualified for Law Enforcement Availability Pay, essentially a type of overtime. "Don't get me wrong, K-Ray, I'm psyched for the OT, but I'd prefer you get me a promotion," he said.

There was always some money complaint with him, but lately Duffy's gripes about pay were becoming an obsession. Karen understood his frustration. Agents were stretched too thin, working too many hours for too little pay. The solution to every staff shortage was not better organizational planning, but rather more overtime, one of her dad's major complaints. Karen frequently shared her staffing concerns with Ellen. Having the first lady in her corner gave her a shield behind which she could toss barbs in the hopes of bringing about meaningful changes.

Lapham and Duffy locked Cam's hospital room down. Only approved people would be granted access to the floor, including the doctors and nurses who tended to this VIP patient. All of Cam's caregivers would receive expedited background checks. Visitors would have to leave their names and be subjected to a search before they could enter the floor.

Cam seemed better to Karen on the drive to the MDC. Though still a bit peaked, he was not nearly as sweaty as before, and his breathing had returned to normal.

That's when the doubt set in. If this trip to the MDC proved unwarranted, Gleason would use it as ammo to attack her. Angering the president's doctor was not a wise career move under any condition.

Karen was helping Cam out of the back of the SUV when Gleason finally returned her call.

"What in hell's name do you think you are doing? How dare you make this decision without consulting me!"

Karen felt the heat of Gleason's rage radiate through the phone.

"I checked on Cam. He didn't seem right to me, so I called Lee."

"No, Karen. You call me, the doctor assigned to the president and his family. I'm going to be there as soon as I can. The president is coming, too, so do your job and make sure security is in place. And from this point forward, *nobody* is to call Lee Blackwood for *any* reason, and that goes for the doctors and nurses at the MDC. Is that understood?"

"Fine. As you wish."

Karen had no problem tossing him a bone. If the first lady or the president wanted Lee's consult, they would override Gleason in a heartbeat.

"What you've done here is beyond all authority," Gleason said, his tone still irate. "*I'm* the one who makes decisions on Cam's health, not you. Last time I checked, you were hired as his supernanny. I swear I'll have you fired for this."

"You didn't see what I saw, Fred," Karen said assertively. "If you had, I'm pretty sure you'd be thanking, not threatening me."

CHAPTER 12

The three-bedroom bungalow in Cleveland Park, a neighborhood of approximately fifteen hundred residents tucked away in the northwest section of D.C., had been Lee's home for the past twelve years. It was a spacious place for a single occupant, which could explain why it had all the personal touch of an IKEA showroom.

Lee had bought the property not long after his divorce from Karen, but before the cost of modest homes in the area skyrocketed. Usually the place did not feel too big, but on weekends, or the occasional quiet evening, especially now that he and Bethany were on the outs, Lee would think about selling, taking the profit to do something else with his life. He wanted to spend more time hiking and camping, two of his greatest pleasures.

Growing up in West Virginia had kindled a boundless love for the forest. Many of his fondest childhood memories involved forays into nature, and to this day Lee found the fresh mountain air rejuvenating in profound ways. While he romanticized the possibility of a second career as a park ranger, Lee's pragmatic side told him it was nothing but a pipe dream. More likely, he would work at his family practice until his partner, Paul Tresell, got his way and they sold out to a hospital or some medical conglomerate. Then he'd retire and take up golf like the rest of his aging pals.

Lee noticed the time on the stove clock in his modest kitchen and thought about Karen. It had been more than two hours since she had agreed to bring Cam to the hospital. He had tried her cell, but his calls kept going straight to voice mail. His contact at the MDC, Brian Seneca, was not returning his calls either. Lee figured one of them would be in touch eventually.

At four o'clock the doorbell finally rang and there was Josh, standing on the front porch with a big smile on his face. A car parked curbside honked as it drove away. Josh gave a slight wave. Lee suspected the driver was one of Josh's D.C. friends who he'd be seeing later in the weekend.

Josh wore a backpack from REI and had nothing in his hands. Lee opened the screen door and embraced his son. It was hard to believe he had not seen his boy since September, but at least he looked much the same. He was still tall and broad-shouldered, with short dark hair and a face dotted with scruff. A flannel shirt and dark jeans made Josh look even more ruggedly handsome. His big brown eyes still held a hint of mischievousness when he smiled. The earnestness of his face warmed Lee's heart.

"Hiya, Pop. Good to see you."

Having spent his career caring for the sick and dying, Lee should have had more appreciation for the ephemeral nature of time, should have been insistent on getting together more frequently. But Josh was here now, and that was all that mattered. His son asked for a beer, and Lee got himself the same. No run for him tonight, but Lee would get plenty of exercise on the hike. Tomorrow they would set off at first light. Tonight, they could chat, maybe catch the Wizards game on TV.

They spent some time looking over the camping gear laid out on the living room floor, discussing what they should bring. Afterwards, they settled on the comfy living room armchairs and sipped beer from chilled glass bottles.

"When are you seeing your mom?"

"Sunday, I think," Josh said.

"When do you go back?"

"I don't know." A dark look crossed Josh's face, his eyes suddenly brimming with sorrow. "I'm missing some pretty sick spring skiing."

Lee squinted, appraising his son carefully. Something seemed off.

"Everything all right?"

"Yeah . . . it's all right."

But talk of Colorado had zapped the sparkle from Josh's eyes and given him a saturnine face.

"You'll be back on the slopes in no time," Lee said encouragingly.

"Actually, I might not go back at all."

Lee's insides clenched. "What? Why?"

Josh went silent.

"Hannah dumped me," he eventually said in a flat, monotone voice, folding his arms like a hermit crab retreating into its shell.

Lee groaned as though the wound Josh had suffered physically hurt him as well. "Oh, buddy, I'm so sorry." *But not at all surprised,* he thought. "What happened? When? Do you want to talk about it?"

"Not much to say," Josh said glumly. "She, um—just stopped all contact with me. A friend of hers said she was back with her old boyfriend, but that's an unconfirmed rumor."

At Josh's description, Lee could not help but think of his last girl-friend.

"She ghosted you," said Lee.

Josh returned a little laugh. "Oh yeah, I forgot you know all about ghosting. What was her name?"

"Bethany." A hint of animosity seeped into Lee's voice.

"Well, it sucks," said Josh. "Hannah was—she was so great, Dad. I really thought she was the one."

"There'll be another," Lee said. "You're a terrific guy. Any woman would be lucky to have you." He knew not to say anything disparaging, such as "You're better off" or "She wasn't good for you anyway." Now was the time to be supportive, to be a friend more than a parent.

"I'm here for you," said Lee. "That's the best I can offer right now."

"Thanks." Josh sounded genuinely appreciative. "I'll figure it out."

That was Josh's life motto. He'll figure it out. He went where the wind blew him. After high school that wind blew him into the military instead of college. Josh did four years active service and after that two more years of individual ready reserve (IRR, in military parlance) before his career came to an end. While he was going overseas on deployments, knee-deep in the shit as he would say, Josh's friends were back home posting to social media all sorts of fun and carefree pictures from their college and spring break antics. Josh would be the first to admit he simply got the itch to try something new.

By that point the military had already turned his son from a boy into a man. Josh had picked up leadership and technical skills to go along with self-discipline and tenacity. He could fire a weapon accurately under the most stressful conditions one day, and the next day dress up in his military uniform for formal dining under the microscope of the strictest social standards.

After he left the military that proverbial wind blew again, this time sending Josh out west, to Colorado, where he'd been working as a ski instructor, while avoiding conversations about what he was going to do with the rest of his life. Maybe this Hannah jolt would help get him unstuck. Maybe over the course of a few days camping, Lee could find a way to speed that process along.

The doorbell rang.

"Are you expecting someone?" Lee asked.

"Nope. No one."

When Lee opened the door his jaw fell open. Standing on his front porch were Woody Lapham and Stephen Duffy from the Secret Service, dressed in their trademark dark suits and sunglasses.

"Dr. Blackwood, we need you to come with us right away."

"Is it Cam? I've been trying to reach Karen for hours."

Josh rose from his seat and joined Lee at the front door.

"It's Bishop," Duffy said, using the code name. "Brave Heart has requested we bring you to the MDC right away." Brave Heart: the president. "He wants your opinion. I guess you made an impression."

Lee's mind clicked into gear. "What's going on?" he asked.

"We don't know," said Lapham. "That's why we need you to come with us, right now."

Lee glanced at Josh. "I'll only be gone for a little while," he said. "Keep getting our gear together. I'll explain everything when I come back."

Josh gave a nod, but Lee could see where this was headed. Their big camping trip was over before it had even started.

CHAPTER 13

Lee had never been to the ninth floor of the MDC's northwest wing before. He knew the deluxe rooms were up there. They had been modified to attract the rich and powerful, and D.C. had plenty of foreign dignitaries who did not have to contend with insurance-imposed spending caps. The floors on the private wing were carpeted, the walls decorated with fine art, and many rooms had a glorious view of the National Cathedral.

Lapham and Duffy escorted Lee to the concierge desk, where two agents from the Secret Service stood guard. The agents perked up like Dobermans as Lee reached for his wallet to show them his ID. After authenticating Lee's ID, an agent used a wand to check for hidden weapons. Satisfied, they opened the frosted-glass doors and Duffy and Lapham led Lee into the reception area. An aroma of some splendid cuisine wafted down the hall, which Lee found incongruous with a hospital setting.

A perky receptionist seated behind a mahogany desk offered a genuine smile at Lee, who smiled back. Duffy and Lapham gave her no notice. A cadre of Secret Service agents stood guard outside a set of solid oak doors leading to the waiting room.

"Karen is in there," Duffy said, pointing, "probably getting an ass-chewing from Gleason and the president."

"The president is here?"

"He and the first lady. You know, historically speaking, a shaman had the most influence over the chief."

Duffy's glib manner and a trace of foreboding Lee picked up in the agent's voice set him on edge. It was Lee who had ultimately set this chain of events into motion. If this all proved unwarranted, Karen would not be the only one taking heat.

At that moment, Brian Seneca popped out of a hospital room and waved Lee over. The two shook hands. Seneca, who had an athletic build, wore a long white lab coat over his blue scrubs. His well-trimmed beard and thick head of dark hair enhanced his olive complexion. He was a talented and committed golfer, which was why Lee saw Seneca at the hospital and nowhere else.

The name "Lincoln Jefferson" was written on a small whiteboard mounted to the wall outside the room from which Seneca had emerged. This was the alias the hospital had picked for Cam, aka Bishop. Lee peeked inside the room, which more resembled a suite at a fancy hotel than a hospital, and found the bed was empty.

A nurse in floral-pattern scrubs was busying herself with the telemetry monitors that transmitted Cam's vitals to the nurses' desk down the hall.

"Where's Cam?"

"Coming back from CT."

Lee turned to Duffy. "Do you think you can give me a little time before I speak with the president and first lady? Let them know I'm here and getting a debrief from Dr. Seneca, and I'll come see them in a moment."

Lee could not believe he was asking the president of the United States to wait for *him,* but he needed to get abreast of the situation privately before confronting parental royalty.

"The shaman speaks, the chief listens," said Duffy with a tilted smile, before he slipped into the waiting room to inform the president.

"I think he's going to be okay, Lee," said Seneca after Duffy departed. "He was a bit tender when I compressed his left lower ribs, but he's not splinting to avoid pain. I went over the scans with the radiologist, Dr. Patel."

"Do you mind if I take a peek?" Lee asked.

"No problem."

Lee followed Seneca over to the nurses' station, which was expensively constructed from dark wood. He was mindful of the plush carpeting under his feet and fragrant air piped through the vents. Comfortable as he was roughing it in the woods, Lee liked how the 1 percent lived.

With a few clicks of the mouse, Cam's scans magically appeared on the high-definition monitor. If Lee's father were alive, he would have marveled at the advancements in medical technology. Then again, his dad was an amazing diagnostician without all the gizmos, and had taught Lee to rely more on his observations than on machines.

Come home, son. Come back to Beckley and run the practice for me.

Lee heard his father's voice in his head all the time, even at the most unlikely moments. The practice his father opened back in 1961 was the only one around for miles, nestled within the mountains of Appalachia, where coal mining was still thriving, guaranteeing its share of black lung disease, poverty, and alcoholism, but also a binding sense of family and pride.

Lee had revered his dad. He did it all. Delivered babies, treated the mumps and measles, doled out pills, and stitched up the wounded. Lee spent most of his free time in high school helping his father out in the clinic. He'd say that's where he caught the bug to be a family doc, and taking over his father's practice had always been Lee's plan. But Karen had given him no choice, or so he told himself. She was committed to her new career, and Lee was committed to her.

He knew his father would grow too old to run things on his own. Sure enough, when the hospitals came courting, Lee's dad sold his practice for a fraction of its worth and tried settling into retirement. He grew morose, then got sick, and was dead five years later—a death Lee believed he had hastened. A year after his father's death, Lee's mother was gone. Now his sister, a pastor at the church where he and Karen had married, was the only Blackwood living in Beckley.

Lee's dad might not have been an early adopter of new medical technology, but there was a place for advanced machinery, and high-resolution CT imaging was extremely useful for uncovering rib fractures that x-rays might miss. The CT scan also made injuries to soft tissues and blood vessels easier to spot, which was why Lee had encouraged Karen to have Cam brought to the MDC in the first place. The variety of angles and cross-sectional slices of the body's internal structures gave Lee a crystal-clear view into the underlying architecture.

What he saw was not particularly alarming. The lungs were healthy, the bones intact, the tissue unbroken, the vessels functioning fully. But

Lee's eyes narrowed when Seneca brought up a scan showing Cam's spleen.

"That doesn't look enlarged to you?" asked Lee.

Seneca gave it a closer inspection. "No. Dr. Patel would have said something if he thought so. I'd say normal."

Lee did not feel like getting into a heated debate about spleen sizes. He could perform other tests to rule out his concern. Out of his peripheral vision, Lee caught sight of an attendant and nurse pushing Cam in a wheelchair down the carpeted corridor on his way back to his room. Three Secret Service agents, disguised in casual business attire, accompanied them. If Lee did not know to check, he never would have noticed the earpieces all three wore.

Lee waved to Cam as he rolled by him.

"I'll be in to see you in a minute," said Lee.

Cam returned a slight hand wave and away he went.

A few moments later, Lee entered Cam's room and found the patient already tucked into his hospital bed. Dr. Seneca had gone off to check in on another patient. A different nurse, this one with the body build of a greyhound, busied herself hooking up Cam's telemetry leads and adjusting his IV.

"Bet you haven't had one of those in before," Lee said to Cam, as he checked out the IV for himself. It was a saline drip, standard hydration for any hospital patient.

"The nurse said I had good veins."

"Just one of the many privileges of being young," Lee said.

"Hopefully another privilege is getting out of here soon. I hate hospitals."

"You kidding me? This place is like the Ritz!"

"I live in the White House, remember?"

"Point taken," Lee said with a smile. "Sorry you're here, but Karen told me your symptoms, and well, they didn't sound great. I like to err on the side of caution."

"All I know is you're not going to make Dr. Gleason's Christmas card list," Cam replied.

Instead of answering with a smile, Lee burst out laughing. "Good to see you haven't lost your sense of humor. Dr. Seneca told me you're doing fine. Maybe this will be just a quick overnight stay."

"Hmmm," Cam said, sounding contemplative. "Now I'm wondering if Taylor might have hit me on purpose."

"Why is that?"

"Because he's first alternate for the U.S. team at the world juniors tournament. If I'm out of commission, he takes my place."

It was obvious Cam said this only in jest.

"I have all the confidence you'll be able to play, but I'd still like to examine you again, if you don't mind?"

"No problem," said Cam.

Lee wondered if he needed to get the president's permission to proceed. He decided to follow the same advice he had given Karen, and ask for forgiveness instead.

CHAPTER 14

Cam's plush hospital room quickly cleared out. Lee thought he looked a bit pale, and a bit bloated from the IV fluids he had been receiving, but in good general health.

"First, tell me how you're feeling. Any pain?" Lee asked.

"Not too bad," Cam answered quietly, "except when I cough or take in a full breath. Then, I feel a little twinge in my left shoulder."

"Anything else?"

"I'm a little sick to my stomach. Can I have a Coke, maybe?"

"No can do, pal," Lee answered without hesitation, thinking about Cam's spleen and the CT scan. "Let's see what we find, shall we?"

Compressing Cam's lower ribs, Lee confirmed the slight wince that Dr. Seneca had observed. He took out his stethoscope and listened to Cam's chest. Good equal breath sounds on both sides. No signs that he was splinting, favoring movement on one side that could be a clue to a tiny rib fracture missed on the CT. He listened over the belly. No bowel sounds. That could mean a sign of irritation in the abdomen. *Leaking blood, perhaps?* Next, Lee pressed down gently over the abdomen and let go quickly. Cam winced ever so slightly.

"Sorry. That hurt?"

"Yeah, a little."

Lee finished his examination and put away his stethoscope. He glanced at Cam's vital signs on the monitor. *BP 96/60, P 104, R 18.* Oxygen saturation 99 percent. No fever. All normal.

But then again . . .

"Cam, I'm going to do what all doctors on TV do about this time."

"You're going to talk with my parents and tell them you're still worried."

"How come you're such a smart kid?"

Lee and Cam both said, "Chess," at the exact same moment. "And I can see it on your face," Cam added. "I could really use that Coke. I'm feeling queasy."

"Sorry, Cam. You can't take anything orally until we decide on whether you need surgery. I'll talk with the nurse and get you something for your nausea."

A SECRET Service agent guarding access to the president and first lady frisked Lee at the doors to the family waiting room before letting him inside. The first person Lee saw when he entered was President Hilliard. He sat on a cracked leather armchair, poring over documents in a folder embossed with the presidential seal. Mounted on the wall behind him, a CNN broadcast showed stock footage of President Hilliard walking the grounds of the White House. The volume was turned off, but according to the graphics they were running a story about a recent flare-up with Iran.

The first lady sat on a different leather sofa, her attention fixed firmly on her cell phone. Her shoes sank into the plush gold carpeting. Two Secret Service agents, each as animated as houseplants, stood in the corners opposite the door. Karen was seated on an upholstered armchair looking extremely uncomfortable, while not far away sat Dr. Gleason, wearing a suit instead of his white lab coat, his focus also on his phone.

Off in a far corner, Lee spied a military aide wearing the bold blue uniform of the U.S. Navy, white hat under his arm, gold aiguillette draped from the shoulder, holding a large black briefcase. The nuclear football, Lee mused. The gravity of this moment, of the patient he was treating, came into sharper focus.

The first lady sprang up from her seat the moment Lee entered. She might have been one of the world's most recognized figures, but in that instant, she looked like any mother worried for her son.

"Lee, thank you for being here," Ellen said quickly. "Is Cam all right?"

"He's doing fine," Lee said. "But I'm glad he's here for now."

"Me too," added Karen, joining Lee and Ellen in the center of the room.

Dr. Gleason came over, conspicuously avoiding eye contact with Lee. The president approached and Lee shook his proffered hand. He had to remind himself that the president and first lady put their pants on one leg at a time, just like he did.

Dressed in a charcoal suit, his eyes strained and tired, the president could not hide his utter exhaustion.

Congratulations, Lee thought. *You spent millions of dollars and fought countless battles to win the worst job in America.*

It was hard for Lee to fathom the constant pressure Hilliard was under, now compounded with worry over the health of his only child.

"I had you brought here because I wanted Cam to have consistency with his medical care," President Hilliard said to Lee. "You're a part of this process now, and I want you to know, I fully support Karen's decision to bring Cam to the hospital."

Hilliard shot Gleason a stern glance, putting an end to any possibility of fisticuffs with Lee.

"Please," Ellen said, taking a disparaging tone. "Don't pretend you wanted Lee here. It was my idea to bring him back. Let's not make *this* political too."

"Regardless of who instigated the call, we are both glad you're here," said the president, tightening his lips some. "So what's your opinion? How is Cam?"

"Mr. President, I think Cam will need to have surgery today. I think we need to remove his spleen."

"You just said he was fine," retorted Gleason with a smirk of pique.

"He is fine—right now, that is."

"Is this connected to his . . . other issues?" Ellen asked.

"I can't say for certain, but possibly, yes. His examination—"

Lee could not complete the thought because Dr. Seneca entered the room, interrupting the conversation. He seemed relaxed, but then again Seneca had grown accustomed to dealing with high-powered clients, the way a mountaineer could adjust to thin air. He immediately assumed command, the dark shade of his beard and blue surgical scrubs adding to an oracular aura.

"Sorry, I'm late," Seneca said. "I got caught up with a patient. What have we discussed?"

"Lee thinks Cam will need surgery to remove his spleen," Ellen said.

"I strongly doubt that," Seneca said. "His scans looked good. It's most likely nothing more than a bruised rib. He'll need rest and observation, of course."

Relief registered on the faces of the president and first lady. Lee should have seen that coming when he and Seneca had not agreed on the interpretation of those scans. Good chance this was going to get contentious.

Gleason shot Karen a look that might as well have been a slap in the face. "Mr. President, I'm deeply sorry for all the trouble Karen has caused. We need to reevaluate roles and responsibilities so this won't happen again."

The president offered Gleason only a fleeting glance. "Later, Fred," he said dismissively. "Can we take Cam home now?"

"Actually, I don't agree with Dr. Seneca, and I don't think you should take Cam anywhere."

Brian Seneca stared piercingly at Lee, clearly taken aback by his candor. This was surgical turf. What right did a family practitioner have interfering with more experienced judgment? But Lee felt he had no choice. He would have preferred a private conference, out of earshot, a consensus opinion with a family briefing to follow. But now Seneca had put the battle out in the open with everyone taking notes, and friendship would have to take a backseat, at least for the moment.

"I agree that the CT scan looks fine for the most part," Lee said. "But there could still be a tiny rib fracture. More important, I thought the spleen looked a little enlarged."

Lee demonstrated the spleen's anatomic location by pushing up against his stomach just beneath the rib cage.

"Lee, I reviewed the scan with Tushar Patel, the radiologist. He did not comment on any splenetic enlargement. He's good. I've relied on his judgment for years."

Gleason said nothing, though his gloating expression spoke volumes. The president and first lady listened attentively, neither showing any hint of emotion.

Lee cleared his throat, sensing a need to convince and take command while minimizing any threat to civility or ego. "You know me, Brian. I still put a lot of weight on old-school history and physical examination in making a diagnosis. First, Cam certainly suffered the type of injury that could fracture a rib, or lacerate his spleen. So, history alone should make us suspicious."

"Agreed."

"I've just examined him. He tells me that he feels pain in his left shoulder when he coughs, which could represent referred pain from the diaphragm, most likely irritation from blood. And he has rebound tenderness when I release from pressing down on his abdomen. Another sign suggestive of blood from a leaking spleen. And—"

"We can treat him expectantly," Dr. Seneca interrupted. Clearly, he too wanted to minimize any suggestion of public disagreement between doctors who were treating the president's son. "We'll watch closely and wait. If his blood pressure falls, we'll go in."

Seneca would have preferred the conversation to have ended at that point, and to debate with Lee in private. Lee refused to pick up on his cue.

"I stand by what I said. Cam is going to need surgery, and if we wait for major bleeding to occur, we will be putting him at greater risk. I say we go in now, laparoscopically. Just a tiny incision. It's much easier on Cam and clearly safer than putting him through a full laparotomy should the whole spleen rupture."

"You're rushing this, Lee," Seneca said.

At that moment, everyone's attention went to the waiting room door, which burst open with Cam's nurse in the threshold. "Dr. Seneca, the patient's blood pressure is down to eighty and he's diaphoretic!"

Seneca exhaled loudly.

"Call the OR and tell them we're on our way," he announced, eyeing Lee as though he were a soothsayer. "Cam's already been typed and crossed. Change the IV to Lactated Ringer's at two hundred cc an hour. We'll put in a central line in the OR. Lee, I'm going to try this laparoscopically. I hope we'll have time. Mr. President, Mrs. Hilliard—I will speak with you as soon as I can."

Seneca raced from the room.

Lee stayed behind and put his hands on the arms of the president and first lady.

"Dr. Seneca is a supremely talented surgeon. Please take comfort in knowing that Cam is in the best possible hands and in the right place. And for that, we all have Karen to thank."

CHAPTER 15

Lee was in the operating room, sent there to observe at the president's request. The game had changed. President Hilliard had come off the sidelines and was now draped in the colors of Team Lee, much to Dr. Gleason's chagrin.

It was six thirty in the evening according to Karen's watch. Normally at this hour, the first family would be sitting down for dinner prepared by the White House chef. Family time was sacred for the president and his wife. They had vacated their Maryland home for the White House with a pledge to live as normal a life as possible. Any chance he got, President Hilliard would trumpet the importance of the family meal, but Karen thought it was just his way of relating to voters.

When it came to politics, Geoffrey Hilliard was an unabashed centrist who shamelessly cut deals both ways, which was why people both loved and despised him. His centrist position made it difficult to know what was truly important to him.

There was no question what was most important to the first lady. The anxiousness on Ellen's face was pronounced. She sat on the leather couch next to Geoffrey, holding his hand. Hospital staff had switched off the television, which had been broadcasting CNN. The president followed the example of his predecessor and rarely watched the talking heads or politicos on the twenty-four-hour news cycle. The media was seldom centrist, and skewered him based on their leanings.

Ellen did her best to stay dignified under the relentless scrutiny, but the spotlight of the White House was a harsh glare to live in. The public could be profoundly cruel. The pitfalls of public life that she had experienced early in her marriage to Geoffrey, then a young state senator from Maryland, grew exponentially when he decided to run for the U.S. Senate, and it got even worse after he announced his candidacy for the presidency. Ellen played the good wife, ever supportive, careful to curate an image she felt was digestible to the American people, while behind closed doors she was dealing with personal losses from multiple miscarriages.

Right now, however, public scrutiny and political appearances were the least of her concerns. In this regard, hospitals were the great equalizer.

Eventually, a nurse entered the waiting room—a bit starstruck at first, but she pulled it together enough to deliver a message from Lee. The operation was going well. They could do laparoscopic surgery as opposed to an open splenectomy, which would greatly reduce recovery time. Cam would need a day or two in the hospital before returning to the White House to rest at home.

The media, unlike Cam, would not rest, not even for a moment. Presidents were unable to move about without media teams, pools of reporters following their every step. The media and the White House press office had an understanding: play by the rules, follow at a distance, and your question may be the one the president answers during a briefing. But in this situation, the press could not be allowed to tail the president to the MDC, so a diversion was hastily arranged. A fake motorcade had departed from Walter Reed for the White House with a body double playing the role of President Hilliard, while a separate motorcade, this one smaller, had ferried the president to the MDC without arousing suspicion.

It would not be long, however, before reporters figured out they had been duped, and that a patient at the MDC named "Lincoln Jefferson" was in fact Cam Hilliard. Like hyenas to carrion, the media were expert scavengers who picked away at privacy until no meat remained on the bone.

Ellen found the lack of privacy one of the most difficult aspects of her life in the White House. There were innumerable restrictions on her movements, many of which Karen had to enforce. She would gripe almost daily about not being able to stand in front of an open window in her own home or breathe fresh air while out for a drive. Those were big no-nos for the Secret Service. Good guys with guns had to take extraordinary measures to protect her from bad guys with guns.

For a career-minded, brilliant businesswoman, a woman with ambi-
tion and drive, the White House was a challenging bubble. Ellen had
well-formed opinions about important matters, but instead of her
thoughts, people were more interested in the brand of her pumps. Right or
wrong, any policy matter she discussed ended up reflecting negatively on
Geoffrey.

The White House had sandwiches couriered over, saving the Secret
Service from having to test the hospital cuisine. Good as those sandwiches were, Gleason hadn't taken a bite. He was too busy trying to find
ways to contradict Lee.

"In addition to my own research, I've had several calls with colleagues, and I can assure you, Mr. President, Mrs. Hilliard, nothing
about an enlarged spleen correlates with Cam's psychological issues."

Karen leapt to her feet. "Why do you keep insisting Cam's troubles are
psychological?" she said. "With all due respect, Dr. Gleason, Lee had
reached a very different conclusion."

The president sensed the tension and opted to play referee. "Easy,
Karen. Let's not make a bad situation worse."

Gleason was not about to let it go. Backing away from a challenge ran
counter to his makeup.

"Where do you get off, Karen?" Gleason said. "You're not a doctor.
You have no footing to stand on here."

"Now, Fred, you take it easy."

Gleason held his angry stare for a beat before redirecting his attention
to the president.

"What I'm trying to say, Mr. President, is that Cam's symptoms developed when Taylor started to beat him at chess. That's when all his moodiness began."

Ellen joined the circle. "What are you getting at, Fred?" she asked.

"I'm simply saying that we both admire our kids' abilities to play the
game, but we also know that Cam was the better player up until recently.
Now I'm not trying to say that Taylor has outworked Cam, but he's been
going to the TPI every day after school to practice. Every day. The results
speak for themselves. Taylor's game has improved remarkably."

"You're talking about chess, while I'm starting to wonder if you should be the one to look after Cam," Ellen said, ice in her voice. "First you missed diagnosing a possible epileptic event, and then you completely dismissed Karen's concerns over Cam's injury."

President Hilliard's jaw clenched. "Ellen, please," he said. "Let's be reasonable."

Karen could hardly believe her ears. Not what Geoffrey had said—that was entirely expected. He would cling to the middle ground like it was the last life jacket on the *Titanic*.

What had surprised Karen was how forthcoming Ellen had been, so openly critical of one of her husband's confidants—a personal hire, in fact. This was more like Ellen from Geoffrey's first campaign—brash, unabashed, and unafraid to speak her mind. It was refreshing to hear, and Karen enjoyed watching Gleason squirm.

"I understand that you could perceive the events in that way," Gleason said. "But I stand by my earlier assessment that Cam's initial symptoms were indicators of depression and nothing more. I respectfully disagree with Lee Blackwood's assessment, but let's get Cam neuro-tested if that's what's needed to bring us some closure. Of course I'm all for that. What I'm trying to point out is that suddenly Cam isn't at the top of his chess game, and well, I hate to say it, but I think it's gotten to him. It's completely understandable, but it's also completely unrelated to this current injury.

"Had Karen done her job and watched Cam closely, called me instead of Lee when she grew concerned, I would have ordered her to bring him to the hospital right away."

Karen managed to stay quiet, but inside she was seething. Not only did Gleason find a way to bash her while refusing to acknowledge she had made the right call, he was gloating about his damn kid to the president and first lady at the most inappropriate time.

"You're saying that a few months of extra work at the TPI brought Taylor up to the level of Cam? That's utterly outrageous," Karen said, taking a step toward Gleason, hands on her hips.

"So now you're a chess expert as well as a medical professional," Dr. Gleason said.

"No," Karen replied. "But if it were that easy to get as good as Cam, everyone who loved the game would do it."

"Maybe Taylor is that good. Maybe the TPI needed to help him unlock his true potential. It is the True Potential Institute, after all."

"In a way Dr. Gleason is right, Karen," Ellen said, her anger settling. "The TPI has done wonders for many of the children who go there through my Aim Higher initiative."

Karen knew this to be true. Aim Higher was the program Ellen had developed as part of her signature cause to enhance arts and science curriculum for disadvantaged students across the country. She modeled her efforts in part on the TPI's unique approach to learning, believing that without the support and structure Cam received there, he would never have excelled at chess.

Karen felt a tickle of doubt. Maybe Gleason was right, and Taylor had discovered his own potential for excellence. Maybe Cam's issues *were* all psychological. Chess meant everything to him, and Cam's identity was entwined with his game like a Gordian knot. His personality change, the moodiness and irritability, it all coincided with a sudden and inexplicable losing streak to Taylor, a far lesser player.

The founder and director of the TPI was an enigmatic Japanese man named Yoshi Matsumoto. Yoshi's methods were thought to be part science and part magic. Perhaps Yoshi had taken a sudden interest in Taylor and worked hard to foster the boy's latent gifts. Or maybe Taylor had eclipsed Cam in a less conventional way.

Cheating.

Karen knew the unsavory practice was commonplace in most every arena these days. Just this morning, she had read a news story about a competitive bicyclist who'd managed to sneak a miniaturized motor into the frame of her bicycle.

If Taylor had somehow gained an unfair advantage—conceivably with the help of his ultracompetitive father—it stood to reason that knowing this might help pull Cam out of his funk.

Karen decided she could no longer wait and do nothing. The president and first lady had plenty of agents to watch over them. She could take an hour to go to the TPI and see what exactly went on at the famed institute.

CHAPTER 16

The name of the place—the TPI, the True Potential Institute—was a bit hippy-dippy for Karen's taste. She did not believe in a secret key to unlocking greatness, other than lucky genetics and lots of hard work.

From the outside, the TPI was about as remarkable as any inner-city middle school. It was a two-story gray brick building with an arched entranceway and a mauve-colored metal door. Mauve. About as kumbaya a color as there was.

Karen drove there in the same SUV she had used to shuttle Cam to the MDC, and probably could have made the trip blindfolded. The TPI was a little over two miles north of the White House, and she'd been to this residential street lined with quaint two-story brick townhomes near the Mount Pleasant Library countless times. She knew every inch of the building where Cam studied chess, every sightline where a determined sniper might be able to take a shot, every entrance and exit where his would-be kidnapper could make off with the prize.

Normally, Karen would have arrived with an entourage. This evening, she had come alone.

This was how she lived her life: with colleagues, or alone. She squeezed seeing friends into slivers of free time, but as far as dates and lovers went, those were few and far between. The job was all-consuming. When she did have downtime, it was hard to spend it on potential soul mates. Karen was not around enough to properly nurture a new relationship. Though she had never taken a physical bullet for any member of the first family, she had already sacrificed much of her life for them.

Her father had said it best: "You live this job, you don't work it."

Tonight's work involved her getting information from the head honcho himself—Yoshi Matsumoto. Karen did not have a card key, so she pressed a buzzer, then waved at the security cameras mounted above the front door. Irene, the TPI's lone administrator, buzzed Karen inside from her glass-fronted office in the main foyer.

Karen stepped into a clean and brightly lit entranceway. The linoleum floor was shiny and newly buffed, the brick walls freshly painted in a muted tan tone. Hanging on those walls were attractive artworks students themselves had created. Many were good, well above average for sure. Glass cases displayed pottery and sculptures, also of high quality.

One of the walls held framed posters, stylishly designed, showcasing TPI's current students as well as distinguished alumni engaged in their respective disciplines. Most of the posters featured young people, few over thirty, but the accompanying text described an array of impressive accomplishments. Two were MacArthur Fellows and several others had started successful consumer technology companies. There were posters of musicians working for some of the world's most prestigious orchestras, and of artists who had created attention-worthy pieces or had installations in reputable locations.

Sandwiched between a poster of a glamorous Indian woman who had become a successful magazine publisher, and that of an African American male who had founded a clothing Web site, was one of Cam playing chess. Karen saw no poster of Taylor Gleason on any wall.

The hallway in front of Karen branched off in an east-west direction. Just beyond, a wide staircase led to the basement and second level with more studios, practice rooms, and lecture halls. Even though it was nearing eight o'clock in the evening, the halls still bustled with activity. The TPI stayed open until 10:00 P.M. to give already overscheduled kids the chance to be even busier. Yoshi was often here late at night, which had worked in Karen's favor when she called to make this impromptu appointment.

Karen exchanged waves with Irene, a sturdy woman with a tangle of brown hair, who'd been working for the TPI from the beginning.

Moments later, she heard footsteps descending the stairs in front of her. She saw a slight Japanese man approaching. He was short in stature, about Karen's height, and dressed all in black. He had a rakish look to him. His hair was cut like a rock star's, longish in the back, shorter and choppy up front, white as fresh snow, and framed a face far younger-looking than his fifty-three years. He approached Karen with hurried steps. An aura seemed to follow him, as if a chorus of trumpets should have announced his arrival.

"Karen Ray?" His accent was slight, but detectable—English was not his first language.

Rattled from the day's event, Karen extended her hand, forgetting that Yoshi would not extend his. Instead he placed his hands to the sides of his legs above the knees, feet together, and delivered a short, clipped bow of twenty degrees. Karen reciprocated awkwardly.

"I don't shake hands," Yoshi said. "Germs and culture."

"I'm sorry, I knew that," said Karen, still thinking about her bow, wondering if she had done it properly.

"Irene told me you had an urgent matter to discuss. Is there a security issue?"

"No, nothing like that," said Karen. "But I am here about Cam. He isn't in any physical danger, so to speak, but he's suffering because his chess game has suddenly gone flat. I'm hoping to figure out why."

Yoshi leaned back on his heels, arms folded, his expression troubled. "As a policy we never discuss our students with anyone other than family."

Karen had anticipated his response. It was why she'd come here in person instead of trying to garner information over the phone. She felt she'd be more convincing face-to-face.

"Yes, I understand," she said. "Cam's parents would be here to address the issue personally, but as you can imagine they're quite busy, so I thought I'd take the initiative. It would mean a great deal to them, and to Cam, if we could get to the bottom of things."

"My apologies," Yoshi said, his mouth dipping into a frown. "Perhaps we could get them on the phone now."

Yoshi was not at all awestruck by Cam's parents, as others might be. The TPI catered to many of D.C.'s elite and Cam was not the first child of a president to have attended the institute. But Karen could not get the first family on the phone to talk about chess, not when they had all they could handle with Cam's surgery.

Besides, she had come here to try and figure out if Taylor was cheating at the game. She was already on shaky ground with Gleason and did not need to further escalate the situation with him.

"I'm afraid they're occupied," Karen said.

"Well then, I'm sorry to have wasted your time," said Yoshi.

"Please, Mr. Matsumoto—"

"Dr. Matsumoto," Yoshi corrected abruptly.

"Doctor," Karen said, cringing inwardly at her second flub of this meeting. "Cam is very special to me. I want to help him. Could you please consider an exception to your policy? It makes no sense that Taylor Gleason is suddenly beating Cam when he couldn't win a game against him before."

Yoshi's headshake was barely perceptible. "It would be inappropriate for me to discuss Cam, Taylor, or any of my students with you."

"Then maybe we could speak in generalities," Karen suggested. "You could tell me what it is you do here, your teaching philosophies, methods, and such."

Yoshi made a low sound from somewhere deep in his throat, a thinking noise.

"Forgive me if I sound rude," he said, his brown eyes darkening a shade. "I truly mean no disrespect, but I don't see how our methodology is relevant to the work of the Secret Service."

"It's not," Karen admitted. "But I care about Cam and I know he's hurting. Maybe if I learn more about what goes on here, I could, I don't know, somehow help him."

Yoshi glanced at his watch, a Patek Philippe, which told Karen the TPI must have been on more-than-sound financial footing.

"When Irene put you on the calendar she made it sound like this would be a relatively quick discussion. I'm afraid I don't have time to give you a proper explanation of what it is we do here and how our methodology works. We have plenty of literature you can have."

"I prefer primary source material," said Karen.

"You'd have to make an appointment for that," said Yoshi. "Another day perhaps, when I have more time to give."

Karen could read body language, mannerisms, a variety of nonverbal cues the Secret Service had trained her to detect and interpret. Yoshi's feet were pointed away from her, in the direction where he wished to go, telling Karen he could not have been less interested in the idea of a second meeting. His eyes cooled and his expression became as revealing as stone.

Just then, the front door to the TPI opened and a stocky man in his late sixties entered with a smile on his face. Karen recognized him right away. He was Dr. Hal Hewitt, who had sat on the board of the TPI for the past ten years.

"Our students are getting older," Hal said, eyeing Karen with a friendly smile.

"Ah, Dr. Hewitt. This is Kelly Ray, she's with the Secret Service."

"Karen," Karen said, annoyed. She wondered if this was Yoshi's subtle revenge for her having failed to acknowledge him as a doctor of some sort.

"Yes, of course," said Hal.

Karen offered her hand and, unlike Yoshi, Hal Hewitt had no qualms about shaking hello.

"Hal, Karen is interested in learning more about what it is we do here, why we're unique. I'm afraid I don't have time to give her the explanation she deserves, but maybe you could stand in for me—if you have the time, of course."

"Absolutely," answered Hal, sounding delighted.

"Hal's been affiliated with the TPI for a long time. He knows as much about our processes and methodology as I do. Rest assured he'll be more than an adequate substitute."

"I have a half hour before the board meeting," said Hal. "I'd be happy to share what I know."

"Very good," said Yoshi. "I'll leave you be. Ms. Ray."

Yoshi bowed as he had before, short and clipped, twenty degrees precisely. Karen reciprocated with a bow of her own, no less awkward than her first attempt. With that, Yoshi turned and off he went like a wisp of smoke rising, back up those stairs to where he kept a small office.

Hal appeared bemused. "I'm guessing you haven't had many interactions with Yoshi," he said. "He's a brilliant man, but he does take some getting used to."

"Well, I didn't make it easy for him," said Karen. "I'm trying to help a friend."

"Would that friend be Cam Hilliard?"

"Good guess."

Hal looked around, curious. "Are you here alone? Usually you travel with a posse."

"No, this had to be a solo mission—a failed mission at that. I'm trying to figure out what's gone wrong with Cam's chess game. Dr. Matsumoto wouldn't discuss it with me, so I was hoping a better understanding of what goes on here will give me some insight that might help."

"Would you like a tour? And I don't mean of the entrances and exits. I'm sure you're already well aware of those."

"I'd love for you to show me around."

"In that case," Hal said, taking Karen by the arm, "it would be my pleasure. I've been here a long time, and I can tell you *exactly* how Yoshi works his magic."

CHAPTER 17

Almost immediately Karen felt far more relaxed in Hewitt's company than she had with Yoshi. There was something about the director of the TPI she found off-putting that had nothing to do with his unwillingness to discuss Cam's issues. His personality was searingly intense, and the way he eyed her with that penetrating stare made her secrets feel vulnerable.

"Why don't we go to the cafeteria, we can get a cup of coffee and chat," Hal suggested.

Karen liked the idea. She put her hands on her hips as they ambled down a long hallway, feeling the butt of her weapon through the fabric of her blazer, a reminder that this visit was about the job, about protecting Cam from danger, even if the threat was not so obvious.

They passed classrooms with lectures in progress, active art studios, and music rehearsal rooms where future maestros honed their craft. Karen might not have embraced Yoshi, but she did embrace his mission to help the best and brightest reach their personal zenith. Even if that zenith—hello, Taylor Gleason—seemed out of a person's reach.

Karen paused to respond to a text from Lee: Cam had come out of surgery, was in the surgical ICU, and was doing just fine. Fortunately for Cam, Seneca had been able to remove the spleen laparascopically. Lee had said this would speed up Cam's recovery time dramatically. The president and first lady had been notified. All was well. Lee had no idea she had gone to the TPI on a reconnaissance mission. So far she had nothing to tell him, but hoped Hal Hewitt would be able to shed some light on Taylor's newfound abilities.

Karen sent a text to Lee, thanking him for the update, and letting him know she was out and would return to the hospital soon.

Lee was a brilliant doctor and Karen was grateful for involving him in Cam's care. While she did not dwell in the past, the past echoed more loudly in his proximity. It made her think and reflect, neither of which was her favorite pastime.

There was no big aha moment, no last straw that snapped their marriage apart. It had been limping along for a while, a simmering series of issues that eventually broke into a roiling boil.

At the heart of it was Karen's obsession with the Secret Service. She had wanted to salvage her father's legacy while forging a legacy of her own. If she had stayed in Beckley, if Lee had taken over his father's medical practice as he had wanted, maybe they would still be married. She never doubted Lee would forge a quality life here, but she had underestimated how much he'd come to resent her for having to do it. When Lee's father died, his resentment grew exponentially. He blamed himself for abandoning his father and the practice. When he needed a place to put all that anger, Lee put it onto Karen. It was not all his fault. It was near impossible to create intimacy with Lee when Karen gave all she had— her heart and soul—to protecting another family.

Karen and Hal walked and chatted pleasantly, eventually arriving at a modest cafeteria tucked away in the basement of the building. Students and faculty milled about, and the scene reminded Karen of an ultracool liberal arts college. She had gone to West Virginia State, studied accounting, and thought people who majored in the arts were destined to starve. These kids all seemed well nourished—for now.

Hal pulled out a chair and motioned for Karen to take a seat.

He was gentlemanly and came from an era where courtesy spoke of character. His suit was rumpled like his skin. His face was kind, with a broad and flat nose and big ears. She graciously accepted his offer to get her a coffee.

"I take mine black," she said.

"Ah, a kindred spirit," Hal replied with a wink.

He returned moments later with two black coffees. She noticed a slight tremor in his hands as he set the coffees on the table. Karen was not lucky enough to have seen her father grow old. For whatever reason, Hal's shaking hands made her miss her dad.

"How is it you came to join the TPI board?" asked Karen.

"I guess you could say my day job led me here."

"You're a fertility doctor," Karen said. "Head of the Greater Washington Fertility Center. You've been practicing there since 1987."

Hal was impressed. "I feel naked and exposed in your remarkable presence, my dear," he said. "How did you know all this about me?"

Karen's expression turned contrite, her shoulder shrug intended as an apology of sorts.

"We have backgrounds on everyone who works here," she said. "It's standard protocol for folks of my ilk. But I would have remembered your job even if I didn't have such excellent recall. My ex-husband and I looked into IVF after a number of miscarriages, but ultimately we decided one son was enough for us."

Karen was not sure why she felt comfortable to share such a personal detail about her life. Maybe it was Hal's profession or the way he reminded her of her father that had inspired such candor.

"How old is your son now?"

Hal's brown eyes seemed to glow. It was obvious he took delight in hearing about children, regardless of how they came into existence.

"Josh is twenty-five, but he won't see twenty-six if he doesn't call his mother soon. It's amazing how you can create life in a lab, but there's no miracle formula for raising the perfect person."

"Yoshi might disagree with you there."

"How does he do it?" asked Karen. "How does he get results like these? The list of alumni is a who's who of the amazing."

"It's all in the mind," Hal said, sounding darkly mysterious as he tapped a finger to his head.

Karen gave a slight roll of the eyes. "The Secret Service doesn't do new-agey well," she said.

"It's hardly new-agey," answered Hal. "His approach is grounded in real science. Yoshi's methods enhance the direct connection between the mind and body. He believes our thoughts drive our actions."

"Well, that's common sense, not science."

"No, it's much deeper than the idea of thinking of walking before you move your legs," Hal corrected. "Our minds and emotions play a critical role in our health. Hippocrates, the father of Western medicine, taught that good health depends on a balance of mind, body, and environment."

"Is that how you became involved? Because of a medical interest?"

"In a way, yes. Through my work, I was extremely aware of the psychological difficulty couples experience in struggling with fertility. My curiosity led to an interest in the mind-body connection, and I studied techniques to improve conception rates without medical intervention."

"Wouldn't that put you out of business?"

"I wasn't thinking like a businessperson. I was thinking like a healer."

This made sense to Karen on a profound level. She knew from many discussions how Ellen's fertility doctor had healed the giant hole in her heart by helping to bring Cam into this world.

"But my interest in mind-body techniques evolved beyond just fertility and into child development when my son, Liam, became a drug addict."

Karen grimaced slightly in a show of sympathy. "Oh, I'm sorry to hear that," she said.

"Liam was—is, I guess—an incredibly gifted artist. His drawings honestly look like photographs to me. But he also got it into his head that he needed drugs to enhance his creativity, foster his gifts. You know, the suffering artist trope."

"Where is Liam now?"

Hal ran a wrinkled hand through the wisps of gray hair receding from his sun-spotted forehead. His sweet smile flattened.

"I don't know. He's lost to me. I tried to get him help, but drugs don't care how much a father loves his son. When I heard about the TPI, I was immediately intrigued. Not only did it align with my interest in the mind-body connection, but it also made me keenly aware of the need for support systems beyond the family. I couldn't help but wonder: if Liam had a support network like the TPI, would he have ever turned to drugs?

"I started volunteering my time as a medical consultant and eventually was offered a seat on the board of directors. Over the years I've become more passionate about Yoshi's work, not less so. He's a special man."

"What makes him so special?" Karen asked.

"How much do you know about his teaching philosophy?" Hal responded.

"I know about would-be kidnappers and snipers. I don't pay attention to the curriculum."

Hal quickly dispensed with Yoshi's résumé. Ph.D. in clinical psychology from Taisho University in Tokyo. Research and teaching positions at Harvard and Stanford Universities.

"There's a lengthy tradition in Eastern cultures of exercises that are specifically mental in nature," Hal said. "Yoga involving meditative techniques, for instance. If Yoshi taught me anything, it's that the power of mental training to influence neurological and physiological functions should not be underestimated. In more Western terms, think about the job of a sports psychologist. They use mental rehearsal, or imagery re-creation, to re-create an event or image in the mind, so when the player goes to the field they can execute at a higher level because they've already visualized their success. They've enhanced the mind-body synchronicity."

"So students here meditate?"

"Meditation, breathing exercises, visualization techniques, all of that and more."

"So you're like sports psychologists for the arts and sciences."

Hal gave a laugh. "In a way, yes. Students are taught how to relax, how to breathe right, how to calm the mind to open it more fully. Every mental state has some physiology associated with it—some effect, positive or negative, felt in the physical body. Outside of the TPI students are required to practice meditation for twenty minutes a day, five days a week. They work on breathing exercises. While training here, instructors help students use positive mental imagery to learn complex new skills, to better understand the material, and manage anxiety and negative thinking."

"And it works?"

"You've seen the posters. I'd say it's miraculous. There's a reason we have a five-year wait list. Yoshi's methodology far surpasses what could be achieved through diligent practice alone. In some cases he's taken the ten-thousand-hour rule to mastery and flipped it on its head, getting amazing results in a fraction of the time."

"So what happens if you don't have a gift, some special talent? Does this technique work for everyone?"

"Yoshi believes, and I've come to concur, that everyone has some type of creativity locked inside. It's his job to find the key to let it out."

"Not me," Karen said. "Give me a pen and I'll give you a stick figure. Hand me a musical instrument and I'll give you a headache."

"That's because nobody gave you a chance to explore your inner self."

"My new-agey alarm is going off again."

"Young students come here without a focus in mind. They are encouraged to explore a variety of disciplines, the goal being to unearth an individual's innate creativity, regardless of his or her area of interest."

"Right," Karen said, sounding as if she'd just remembered something. "Cam started off in the music program before he demonstrated an aptitude for chess. Then he switched his focus of study."

"That sounds typical. Once the students discover their True Calling, as we've named it, they learn from the best instructors. Some of our teachers are world-renowned. They come here because they believe in Yoshi, and he's given them plenty to believe in. What we offer here is a holistic approach to learning."

"You know how good Cam is at chess," Karen said.

"He's remarkable," said Hal.

"In your opinion, could a student like Taylor Gleason suddenly eclipse Cam with extra holistic training?"

"Anything is possible, that's what we teach our students."

"What about cheating?"

"Here?"

"Yes."

"Well, I guess anything is possible," said Hal, repeating himself. "But I doubt it."

"So it's all in the mind," Karen said, still trying to grasp it. "I think it and it will come. I wish to be better than Cam and therefore I am."

"No, it's not all about thought here," answered Hal.

"What do you mean by that?"

"Yoshi is a trained herbalist. He has a second doctorate in naturopathic medicine."

"Which is?"

"Alternative medicine using natural modalities, especially herbalism."

"So he gives these kids brain-boosting herbs?"

"He did for a time, yes, only to those who expressed interest. But over the years his thinking has taken a decidedly more Western turn, and he's brought nootropics to the school."

"Nootropics?"

"Colloquially they're known as smart drugs."

Karen's face scrunched up in confusion. "He's peddling pills?"

"No, he's providing access to a new type of cognitive enhancer that's part of a billion-dollar industry and growing rapidly."

"Are these FDA-regulated?"

"I don't believe so. For the most part nootropics are not considered controlled substances, which means it's legal to use and own these compounds without any restrictions."

"I can't believe parents would give their kids something like that."

Hal chuckled. "At first very few did," he said. "But the company that markets the nootropic we sell—"

"What's the name?"

"ProNeural, they started showing up here regularly and doing neuro-feedback testing, quantifiably measuring brainwave activity, memory, and concentration. They found that the kids taking the nootropic performed significantly better than those who did not in a number of key areas. Well, you can imagine what happened next."

"Parents wanted to give their kids the pill," answered Karen.

"Almost all of them. Nobody wants his or her child to be at a disadvantage."

"Including Cam?"

"Yes, including Cam."

Karen had no idea Cam was taking anything, but it was not her place to track his prescriptions. That was Dr. Gleason's arena, and despite what he thought of her, Karen did not go traipsing willy-nilly onto his turf.

"Is it safe?" asked Karen.

"I'm a fertility doctor and a board member. I'm not a nootropics expert, but what I can tell you is that many of the students take the nootropics, and they all seem to do fine on them."

"Not just fine," said Karen. "Better."

CHAPTER 18

Maybe it was the chicken.

It was the only thing Susie Banks's father ate that nobody else did. They had gone out to their favorite Italian restaurant for dinner and upon returning home all seemed normal, until her dad complained of feeling queasy. He went upstairs to lie down. Moments later, Susie heard the sound of him retching in the bathroom.

Nothing about the meal had upset Susie's stomach, but it was knotted just the same. Tomorrow she would get the results of her blood work and MRI. Nobody could yet explain what had brought on the episode of what her doctor had called myoclonus.

The word itself sounded scary to her. It had the ring of a rare disease—*oh, I'm so sorry you've come down with myoclonus*—but it was not, according to her doctor, a disease at all. It was a symptom of something else gone awry.

Susie had experienced more twitches and jerks since the first incident. Though none were as severe as the initial attack, each episode induced intense spikes of anxiety and fear. They occurred as a sequence of muscle contractions and relaxations, but sometimes had no discernable pattern at all. Susie's doctor told her most people experienced some form of myoclonus—a hiccup, or a sleep start when the body jerks as it falls asleep—but this gave her little comfort. Most people did not experience such a violent attack while onstage, performing for a sold-out audience. She felt like a bomb was ticking away inside her, only she couldn't see the timer and had no way of knowing the intensity of the forthcoming explosion.

Her doctor had rattled off a litany of possible causes, including brain tumors, infections, and even issues with Susie's kidneys, describing the condition as a short circuit in the electrical activity in her brain, which made it sound treatable. But when Susie got home she did what most people would do: she Googled the term.

An onslaught of information greeted her, most of it distressing. Whatever disease caused the symptom, Susie sensed it was progressive to the point where she might not be able to walk, or talk, or heaven help her, play.

Since the horror show at the Kennedy Center, Susie had yet to play her backup violin (the cracked one was still in repair). Twice she had gotten as far as holding the instrument in her hand, but before she could draw the bow across the strings, a flash of that terrible night made her stop. The scenario played out in her mind in excruciating slow motion. She would see her arms flailing out in front of her; feel the violin slip from her grasp; hear the gasps of the startled audience ring loudly in her ears.

She wondered if she would ever find the strength to play again. These occasional moments of self-pity made her think of athletes determined to walk after being paralyzed playing a sport they loved, or a young child with cancer committed to beating the odds. That was when the guilt would set in. She'd feel ashamed for allowing one incident to define her. But the memory would return like a speeding train, and fear would take hold, and the violin went back into its case.

Susie sat on the living room couch, absently flipping through a *Home & Garden* magazine, wondering what her life would be like without her music. Upstairs she heard her father get sick again.

"Mom, is Dad okay? He sounds awful."

"He'll be fine, dear," her mother called back. "I'm afraid he may have food poisoning. Are you feeling all right?"

"I'm okay."

Actually, she was feeling a bit light-headed, but did not say so. Her dad needed her mom's attention right now.

"Have you taken your pills?"

Her mother was like a clock when it came to the TPI supplements. *Why bother?* Susie asked herself. Unless she could take a pill to rein in her myoclonus, her playing days were all but done.

She went to the kitchen anyway, and took the supplements mostly out of habit. Her nightly ritual felt weighty and pointless. Three pills down the hatch: one white, one yellow, and one brown. She did not know what exactly these supplements contained, but her parents approved of her taking them, and that was good enough for her.

Susie's mother called down to her from upstairs. "Sweetheart, could you please bring Dad a glass of ice water from the kitchen?"

Susie traipsed upstairs with the water glass in hand and recoiled slightly at her father's green and sickly pallor.

"Daddy, are you all right?"

Douglas Banks clutched at his stomach. "Just be grateful you didn't eat what I ate," he said.

Addressing her husband, Allison said, "I'm going to tuck you into bed, and I think I'm going to go to bed myself. I'm not feeling all that great, either."

Her mother had the fish, and Susie ate pasta, but at some point they must have eaten the same thing, Susie thought, because she was starting to feel worse. *Could it have been the olive oil?*

Doug Banks staggered over to the bed and collapsed onto the mattress with a thud.

"I'm a little queasy myself," Susie said. "We are *never* going back to that restaurant."

"Three cases of food poisoning from three different meals," Allison said. "Maybe I should call the restaurant."

But her mother did not look well enough to call anybody, and Susie doubted she would pick up the phone.

Susie's stomach clenched and released. For a moment she feared another myoclonus episode, and was strangely relieved to realize it was just plain old nausea.

"I'm going to bed, too," Susie announced. "Feel better, Daddy." She kissed her mother on the cheek and gave her father a little hug. Doug mustered enough strength to pat his daughter on the arm tenderly.

"I love you both so much," Susie said, feeling tears come to her eyes. She could cry at soap commercials these days. She was so moody and out of sorts, lost without her music. "Thank you both for being there for me."

"We love you too, sweetheart," Allison said. She gave Susie's forehead a gentle kiss. "Get some rest. If you don't feel well, come wake me. We have some Imodium or Pepto that might help. Damn restaurant!"

Susie let out a little laugh and off she went. Her bedroom had become her sanctuary in the days since the incident. The incident—what other name could she give it? Decals of the Eiffel Tower, a symbol of Paris, a city where she dreamed she would play one day, decorated her closet door. She kept her room intentionally uncluttered. It flowed like a good piece of music that way. She liked things to be simple and understated. She had sleek furniture, and mini blinds on the windows, and pretty framed photos hanging on the walls. She wondered what would happen next year—if she'd go to college or somehow resume her music career.

She slipped on her pajamas and slid into bed, feeling the light-headedness a bit more intensely. She hated throwing up, and the idea of having food poisoning on top of her other issue felt like an unfair string of bad luck. She contemplated getting that Pepto, but decided to wait it out. If it got really bad she'd wake her parents, but it wasn't that awful. Just a little queasiness was all. Her heart felt like it was beating funny, but that had to be a trick of the mind. The fear of getting sick must have made her heart race. A good night's sleep was all she needed.

As she drifted off, Susie's last thought was of her arms shooting forward as her violin tumbled from her hands.

SHE AWOKE later with a shattering pain ripping through her head. The room seemed to be spinning and the dizzy sensation would not let up, even after she managed to get both her feet on the floor.

Food poisoning, she thought, standing on wobbly legs. She took a tentative and unsteady step toward the door, then winced. The headache was like a vise compressing her temples with brutal force. She felt incredibly light-headed as she stumbled down the carpeted hallway, careening off the walls. Her balance was so off it seemed as though the house were riding atop ocean waves.

"Mom, Dad—I don't feel well—"

Susie's weak voice sounded far away and very faint in her ears. Her head was buzzing like static on the radio and the pain kept intensifying, making it hard for her to see. Her stomach was doing spins.

"Mom—"

She staggered into her parents' bedroom, breathing in sputters, and saw them on the bed. Their bodies lay perfectly still.

"Mom! Dad!"

Fear wormed into Susie's gut as she pulled on her mother's arm. Her mother's skin felt cool to the touch. The arm fell limply back onto the mattress. Terror replaced worry. The room teetered and twirled. Intense nausea and a blinding headache eclipsed her dizziness. With great effort, Susie managed to come around to her father's side of the bed, where she tried to rouse him. She shook his body, but he did not wake up. Instead, his head lolled awkwardly from side to side as though he had no muscles in his neck.

Not food poisoning, Susie thought. *Too sick . . . feel . . . too strange . . .*

"Help—" Susie's voice sounded like it was underwater. "Help me— please—"

Her parents' eyes remained closed. They seemed so at peace.

Peace . . .

Susie saw a strange blackness coming toward her, a shapeless thing, like a rolling cloud of pure emptiness. It was an entity swallowing everything in its path, leaving nothing in its wake. It felt so difficult to breathe, as though air were being systematically pumped from her lungs. A thought came to her. If she closed her eyes—if she slept—if she let the blackness overcome her, then all these feelings would go away.

Susie resisted the urge and tried to push the blackness back, but it was coming on stronger, moving faster. Through the haze of her vision she spied a lamp on the bedside table. Wielding it like a spear, she hurled the lamp through the bedroom window, shattering the glass on impact.

Air—I want to breathe . . .

A gust of wind seeped into the room and filled her lungs with a rejuvenating effect, but only for a precious few moments. The blackness was once again sliding into her mouth, burrowing up her nostrils. She grabbed the cordless phone from the table and lurched out of her parents' bedroom on legs made of rubber, gulping for air as she went. She peered down from the top of the stairs. They seemed to descend into infinity. She took an awkward step, lost her balance, and tumbled the rest of the way down. She fell end over end, feeling the hard wooden stairs as they slammed into her legs, back, head, and arms. Something might have broken, but the sharp pain of the fall was nothing compared to the burning sensation inside her head.

After landing in a heap at the bottom of the stairs, battered and badly bruised, Susie managed a slow crawl to the front door. From there, she reached up, and, using the doorknob for leverage, got onto her knees. She pulled the door open and fell outside onto the concrete front stoop. The phone was still clutched in her hand. Fresh air filled her lungs, but the blackness was a relentless predator and would not let her go. At last the pain and nausea were lessening. She had the wherewithal to dial three numbers on the phone: 9-1-1.

She managed two words before the blackness finally took over.

"Help me."

CHAPTER 19

Susie awoke in a new place. She was in a room with a curtain and bright lights overhead. From somewhere far away she heard a low voice speaking slowly.

"Nineteen-year-old white female. Banks. Susie Banks."

There was a woman talking to a bearded man wearing a white coat.

"Carbon monoxide poisoning," the woman said in her distorted speech. "We brought her to the MDC because you have the hyperbaric oxygen unit."

"Smart thinking," said the bearded man.

Carbon monoxide. Not food poisoning.

"BP was sixty when we got to her. Couldn't get a pulse, but got leads on her quick and she was in sinus tach, one forty per minute. Respirations very shallow, only six to eight. We strapped on an O2 mask, started an IV, and got a finger stick sugar of eighty."

While the doctors spoke, people dressed in scrubs placed things on Susie's body, and connected her to monitors with wires. A dollop of cool gel made Susie's skin tingle. Her eyes were closed, but Susie could hear people talking all around her. She could hear the bearded doctor clearly, even though she did not understand what all his words meant.

"I want a carboxyhemoglobin, stat! Let's get a carbon monoxide oximeter reading as well. Add a urine myoglobin and blood for lactate and cardiac enzymes. Also a toxicology screen and cyanide level. Increase her oxygen to one hundred percent."

At that moment, Susie wished the blackness would come back to take her away. She could smell the soaps and astringent cleaners; she could feel the prodding, pricking, and poking against her limbs; she could hear whispers, low voices amped up with anxiety.

"Blood pressure is stable. Ninety over sixty."

Moments passed. For Susie, time had lost all meaning.

"Carboxyhemoglobin is twenty-five percent, and most of the other labs are back."

Susie's breathing echoed in her ears, making it hard to pinpoint the location of the woman who spoke.

I want to go to sleep now, Susie thought.

"CBC is normal except for a slightly high white count of eleven point five. But I'd expect that with carbon monoxide. Tox screen is negative. Arterial blood gases seem pretty good, considering. Lactate is high at one point seven. Again, fits the situation. Her liver function tests are mildly high, too. Not sure what that means."

"She's nineteen. Where are the parents? Are they coming, too?"

I want them . . . where are they . . . I want my mom . . .

"Her parents are dead." Susie startled briefly. "They were found in the second-floor bedroom. Nothing we could do. We think Susie broke a window with a lamp, but it was too late for them."

In the next instant, Susie's heartbeat accelerated. She could hear it racing in the monitors, too, the beeps getting louder and faster.

Mom . . . Dad . . . no . . . they can't be . . .

Everything felt suddenly strange, as if Susie had gone hot and cold simultaneously. The odd warning seemed to signal a coming explosion from inside her body. Something horrible was about to happen to her, she could just tell. An intense chill came over her. For a moment she felt simultaneously weightless and unbelievably heavy. A strange whiteness filled her eyes and she could feel her whole body shake.

"She's seizing!"

She heard the voice cry out, but could see only white.

"BP fifty-six over thirty-six, pulse one fifty. Sinus rhythm, but with frequent ectopy. A very unstable heart. Not much time before she codes. Respirations too shallow to even register. Temp one oh one. Call anesthesia and let's get her intubated. Now!"

Time slipped away and then returned. Faceless voices spoke from the void where Susie had gone.

"Amp of D-fifty now. Diazepam eight milligrams IV. Where's anesthesia? Open the IV to two hundred an hour. Let's get fosphenytoin ready. I doubt the diazepam alone is going to hold her seizures."

"Ready to intubate. Let's stop these convulsions. How much does she weigh?"

"Fifty kilograms by the bed scale."

"Let's get a portable chest film, and get her on a ventilator. Where's anesthesia? We need to tube her!"

CHAPTER 20

THURSDAY, APRIL 20

Being the president stinks.

On the morning after Cam's surgery, this was the only thing about the case Lee knew for certain. Last night, Mom and Dad, aka the president and first lady, had to say their good-byes to Cam in the surgical ICU while he was still heavily sedated. There was no easy way for them to hang around until their son woke up fully, because some damn fool had alerted the media.

Maybe it was a patient on the deluxe floor, or perhaps someone on the MDC staff had put out the word. However the leak got out, news vans were soon parked outside the hospital in convoy numbers, and a crush of photographers blocked the hospital entrance. Police had to be called in to clear the scene. Requests for privacy were ignored. Anything involving the president was news, including his kid's spleen—or lack thereof.

Dr. Chip Kaplan, CEO of the MDC, gave a news conference that failed to placate the hungry mob. It was deemed no longer safe for the president to be on the premises. Hordes of Secret Service agents descended like locusts on the MDC and quickly whisked the first family, minus Cam, back to the White House.

Karen was there for the fracas. She had something to tell Lee, but the conversation had to wait, as she got swept up in the commotion and did not even have time for a two-second chat.

Being a Secret Service agent also stinks, thought Lee.

As for Ellen Hilliard, she planned to return today to visit with Cam, but told Karen to check first with Lee so she knew the best time to come.

Lee was her conduit now, and it seemed she trusted him more than Dr. Gleason to relay important information about Cam's care. She gave Lee her private cell phone number, which he stored in his phone's contacts under her code name: Black Bear.

Cam had come out of surgery like a champ. They still had to watch for signs of infection, but Lee was not overly concerned. Considering Cam's age he should be able to bounce back in no time. Another bounce-back was Lee's relationship with Dr. Seneca. All seemed forgiven there.

"I'll admit you embarrassed me a bit in front of the president," he had said to Lee post-surgery. "But I'm also big enough to admit you were right. Feel free to inject yourself into my job anytime."

Lee hoped Dr. Seneca would not forget those words, because he had no intention of standing on the sidelines. As far as he was concerned, Cam was as much his patient as he was Dr. Gleason's.

Even though Lee had admitting privileges at the MDC, he still had to be searched for weapons and show ID to the Secret Service agents guarding the entrance to the hospital suites. They checked his name against the approved list.

At the nurses' desk, Lee ran over Cam's chart, reviewing the lab results from 5:00 A.M., and the portable chest x-ray from 6:00 A.M. He listened in as the overnight nurse gave the day nurse an update on Cam's condition.

"Any problems, Wendy?"

Lee did not work on the fancy floor, but he had made it a point to learn the names of all the nurses who did. Wendy, who was short with a chipper smile, was one of the better ones.

"Not a one," said Wendy. "His vitals are enviable. Afebrile. His crit's stable. Hemoglobin nine point eight. White count ten point seven. Didn't even ask for Tylenol, even though he's obviously having some discomfort. A genuine stoic. Very minimal drainage. I'm sure Dr. Seneca will be able to remove the drain tube this morning. Getting a call from the president and first lady in the middle of the night was sure something! I'm glad I could tell them Cam was doing so well. I was so darn nervous."

"I understand, but at times like this they're just worried parents. I'm sure you handled it well."

Lee glanced at Cam's labs and again noted the asterisks next to his liver enzyme values. AST 47, ALT 68, both minimally elevated. *Most likely nothing,* Lee thought. Could have bruised his liver a bit in that hard tackle. Coagulation profile was normal, so nothing to worry about in terms of any major liver injury or bleeding risk.

Still . . .

Lee signed off the computer and glanced up, only to notice Dr. Fred Gleason standing behind him.

"Kind of early for a family doc to be making rounds."

He was headed straight for Cam's room.

"He's doing great," Lee said, falling into step behind him. "Glad you asked. We'll get that drain out soon, and gradually advance his diet. Hopefully, we'll have him home tomorrow."

Lee intentionally left out the neurological consult he had ordered last night. Normally, he would have waited longer to do the testing he wanted, but there was no telling when Gleason might try to pull Cam out of the MDC. If that happened, those tests might never get done.

Dr. Marilyn Piekarski was one of the best neurologists Lee knew. He wanted her to advise him on Cam's behavioral issues. He was especially keen to get her take on seizures and whether she thought, as he did, that Cam might be having them at night. The president and first lady were aware, and had approved the consultation and testing beforehand. Lee was a bit disappointed not to see the results logged in Cam's medical records. He had hoped for a rush job. Either way, Dr. Piekarski was due back here this morning and could update him then.

Cam was sitting upright and alert when Lee entered his hospital room. Dr. Gleason was busying himself with a check of Cam's IV and vitals, work the nurses had already done.

"How's it going, Cam?"

Dr. Gleason asked the question, but Cam directed his answer to Lee.

"I'm feeling pretty good. Just a bit hungry."

"An appetite. Now that's good news," Lee said, coming to Cam's bedside. He placed his hand over Cam's belly and examined the surgical dressing.

"Dr. Blackwood, I think you can go back to your office now," Gleason said. "I've got it from here." The look he shot Lee could have chilled ice.

"May I please speak with you at the nurses' station a moment," Lee said through gritted teeth.

He left the room, not waiting for an answer, and sure enough Gleason followed. Lee checked to make sure they were out of earshot.

"Look, Fred, I don't know how to say this, so I'm just going to come right out and say it. I know you don't want me involved with Cam's care, and I don't blame you. But I am involved. The first lady and the president are looking to me for guidance right now. I admit that's a lot for a *family doc* to handle, but I feel pretty confident I'm up to the task."

Dr. Gleason stared Lee down like a heavyweight at the prefight ceremony. At that moment, Dr. Seneca came bounding down the hall, cheerful as could be.

"How's our patient this morning?" Seneca asked. "I was coming to take the drain out."

"Cam's doing fine," Gleason answered quickly. "We want to get him back to the White House as soon as possible. It'll be better for him there."

"Understood," Seneca said.

Lee thought it was too soon to move Cam, but knew it was a battle he'd lose if he tried to fight it. His bigger concern was for Dr. Piekarski's neurosurgical consult, which he hoped had been done last night as he had requested. Now with Cam leaving the MDC it might not get done at all.

"What about the pathology on the spleen?" Lee asked.

"Should get it back in four to five days," Seneca said. "By the way, the spleen weighed two hundred twenty grams. They're usually less than two hundred. Funny how you picked that up looking at the CT. You've got quite the eye, Lee. And the liver, too, was maybe a little large."

Lee's thoughts went spinning. The moodiness, possible epilepsy, and now he had a mildly enlarged spleen and liver to add to the mix. Cam's elevated liver enzymes suddenly took on a whole new significance. *But what does it all mean?* Lee had tremendous confidence in his ability as diagnostician, but these symptoms did not fit any medical condition he could name. He knew better than to try and brainstorm all this with Dr. Gleason.

"You get that drain removed right away, Dr. Seneca," Gleason said with authority. "I want Cam out of here by noon sharp. The president and first lady are in agreement. Cam can be monitored at the White House clinic, and it'll be safer for him there."

Gleason was not going to wait around for a response. He spun on his heels and bounded down the hall.

Some minutes later, Dr. Marilyn Piekarski arrived on the floor. She was trim and prepossessing, with dark-rimmed glasses, long black hair, and pretty brown eyes. Much to Lee's disappointment, she was also happily married.

"Hey Lee, Brian. How are we this morning?"

"We're good," Lee said, trying not to sound anxious. "How about those tests?"

"Showed what I suspected," Dr. Piekarski said. Lee was glad to hear the tests had actually been done. "The spinal fluid is clear and colorless," Dr. Piekarski continued. "No cells. Normal protein and sugar. The EEG shows normal background rhythms. Normal sleep architecture for the most part, but we did capture two isolated generalized spikes and wave discharges during sleep that would be consistent with primary generalized epilepsy."

"And the MRI?"

"The MRI does show some subtle signal abnormalities in the basal ganglia, but I think the radiologist may be overreaching. I see findings like this all the time, and it usually means nothing."

"Would you say definitively that he's been experiencing nocturnal seizures?"

"Definitively? No. But I can't rule it out either. The tests were inconclusive."

While seizure activity was not always related to epilepsy, as Lee had previously explained to Ellen, the symptom could have resulted from some disruption of normal brain function. Lee and Dr. Piekarski spent some time discussing Cam's other abnormalities, including his elevated liver enzyme values and slight organ enlargement, but those seemed to have no correlation to brain function.

"I have no idea what to make of that, Lee," Dr. Piekarski said. "Really puzzling there. What I think we should do is treat the symptoms and put Cam on a course of levetiracetam and see how he does. If he's not waking up unusually exhausted, or wetting the bed, well, then, we can assume he has been experiencing nocturnal seizures of some sort and take it from there."

"Sounds like a good plan. Thanks for getting this done so quickly," Lee said.

"Hey, he's the president's kid. I'm supposed to wait for preauthorization from his insurance company before ordering an MRI?"

"Just to be clear, you wouldn't say he was a depressive?" Lee asked.

"Not at all," Dr. Piekarski said. "If you ask me, I think he'd resent being seen by a psychiatrist at this point, but I already told that to Dr. Gleason."

Lee's mouth fell open. "Dr. Gleason? When did you—how? I didn't even tell him you were involved."

"Well, somehow he found out," Dr. Piekarski said. "He asked me not to enter any of the test results into the computer. He wanted all the records handwritten and sent to him. I guess it was a security concern. But he did say he would pass on all this information to you right away. I'm surprised he didn't call you last night when the results came in."

CHAPTER 21

Lee sat in his Honda Civic, letting it idle in the MDC parking lot, while he got his temper under control. In his irascible state, an errant honk from a fellow driver could lead to road rage. The only person deserving of his ire was Gleason, who would do anything, it seemed, to keep Lee in the dark about Cam.

His conflict with Gleason had overtones of the political arena into which he had been thrust. Lee hated politics, and hated subtlety. For those reasons alone, he would tell the president exactly what he thought: he could not in good conscience continue as Cam's medical advisor without clear ground rules in place.

He tried to convince himself he'd be fine if the president fired him, but he was doing a poor job of it. He was too invested now, and Cam's symptoms troubled him too greatly to let it go. Hopefully, Gleason would raise no objections to Cam going on the antiseizure medication, levetiracetam, as he and Dr. Piekarski both wanted. Even without an official diagnosis, they should still treat his symptoms.

Then again, anything Lee advocated was reason enough for Gleason to object. He'd probably say the EEG was inconclusive. Lee thought again of the asterisks next to Cam's elevated liver enzyme values recorded in his medical chart. It was almost certain Gleason would come up with some equally outrageous explanation for those abnormal function tests.

What Lee needed was a clear and irrefutable narrative. For that, he decided to turn to Paul Tresell for help. When it came to stitching together seemingly unrelated symptoms, few were better diagnosticians than Lee's longtime business partner. There was no doctor he respected more.

On the drive to his medical practice, Lee used hands-free calling to get Josh on the phone. He had thought that maybe they could still salvage an abbreviated excursion into the Blue Ridge Mountains. But the more he pondered, the more he knew such thinking was pure fantasy. He could not be without cell phone service, or even an hour's drive away, in case the first family needed him. Dr. Gleason might not have wanted Lee around, but it would take an executive action to get him off the case now.

"Calling to cancel, Dad?"

Josh always had good intuition, except when it came to picking girlfriends.

"I can't be far away right now. He's the president's son."

"Don't take this the wrong way, but I kind of figured we were off and made other plans."

"What plans?"

"Bringing some army pals to camp for a few days. They want to throw me a good-bye Hannah party."

Lee's mouth ticked up into a smile Josh could not see.

There was some back-and-forth chitchat before Josh ended the call with a good-bye, but no "I love you." Lee said it, though, and that was good enough for him.

The camp Josh was planning to visit belonged to Karen. After her father died, Karen's mother bought the property where they had vacationed for years. There were four well-maintained cabins spread out on twelve secluded acres of woodland in Caroline County, Virginia. The cabins were close to the shore of a pristine lake, and each had running water and electricity. Karen's father was something of a sportsman and he liked his weapons, which he kept in a gun safe in the main cabin.

For years Karen's mom had rented the place, but it was never a moneymaker. Karen inherited the camp after her mother died. The mortgage was paid off and the camp was meant for them to use as a family. After their divorce, Karen could have used the money from the sale, but her mother had loved the camp and selling it felt like uttering a final good-bye she was not quite ready to say.

These days, the cabins got little use, and Josh and his friends would probably have to do some cobweb removal before settling down with their cans of Budweiser.

A few minutes later, Lee arrived at his medical practice, located on the first floor of a four-story modern glass building in Tenleytown, a historic neighborhood in the northwest quadrant of Washington, D.C. There was a Starbucks in the building and he went there first to get a little pick-me-up for Paul. The Starbucks was busy as usual, though not many cars were parked in the spaces reserved for his practice. Even though they had convenient access to Nebraska Avenue and Yuma Street, the new location, as of a year ago, had not brought in a flood of new patients as Lee had hoped. What it did do was add new costs to a business already struggling to stay in the black.

Lee saw expenses everywhere he looked. He had to pay the salaries of the office staff, two women who handled the scheduling and billing. He had to do the same with the three nurses he employed. The four exam rooms had supplies to refill. The waiting area had to be stocked with new magazines. Someone had to foot the bill for the electricity.

Bottom line: it was up to Lee and Paul to keep the lights on, and nobody else.

Lee greeted his staff warmly, as was his norm. They had no idea of the financial pressures he and Paul faced; how dangerously close they were to selling the practice to one of the hospitals looking to establish a satellite operation.

After a quick check of the mail, and a review of his messages and patient follow-ups, Lee found Paul seated at his desk in his wood-paneled office, talking on the phone. No surprise there. It was what they did the most these days: fought to do what was right for their patients, not what was most cost-effective for Medicare or some other insurer. Every hour they could not bill, Lee knew, was an hour closer to selling the practice. And fittingly, Lee's involvement with Cam Hilliard had so far not put a single dime into their business coffers. If his involvement went on much longer he might have to find a way to invoice the White House.

"I don't care that I was already at the nursing home the day before," Paul said into the phone. "I didn't need to see that patient on that particular day. I needed to see another patient, and then the next day I had to go back there to see patient number two." Paul fell silent as something was said. "You mentioned that already, several times in fact, but I still don't see how that's any reason to pay me less for the second visit."

Over the years, stress had turned Paul from a fit and trim athlete to a man with a double chin, a bit of a paunch, and gray at the temples of his thinning black hair. In other words, this place had made him old.

"Well, please see what you can do about it," Paul said. "I'm actually a very nice person, but I'm afraid I didn't pass groveling in medical school, so forgive me if I'm not doing it correctly. Yes, you too. Have a pleasant day."

Paul hung up the phone and rubbed at his tired eyes. He was eight years younger than Lee, but it was hard to tell. A professor they both had at Duke had introduced them to each other not long after Lee moved to Washington, back when Josh was still excited to ride his bike. Paul had a three-year-old daughter and a baby on the way back then. He also had the hunger to be his own boss, while Lee had the means and the experience to help make it happen. Plans were hatched over whiskeys and burgers, a friendship blossomed, and it was not long before The Family Practice of Tenleytown opened its doors for business. The years sped by in a blur, and Lee wondered if he looked as beaten down as his good friend. He pulled a chair over to Paul's desk, sat down, and presented the coffee he'd bought at Starbucks.

"Triple, venti, soy, no-foam latte, just the way you like it," Lee said.

"Thanks for that," said Paul, taking a sip without an ounce of joy on his beleaguered countenance.

"Not that I have any idea what that concoction actually means," Lee added.

"I want to sell," Paul said. He sounded definitive.

Lee made a grimace. "I'm pretty sure no-foam latte doesn't mean that."

"I'm not kidding, Lee. The MDC has courted us for years. Let's get a message to Chip Kaplan. Tell him we're open to a deal."

"Our numbers aren't that bad."

Lee had no idea why he bothered with the lie when he and Paul shared a bank account.

"Abby is headed off to college next year, and Kyle is not far behind. I can't afford it. I've tried, Lee, I've really tried, but this is misery."

"Misery? I think that's a bit harsh, don't you agree?"

"No, it's not harsh enough. Really. I thought I'd be practicing until they carried me out in a body bag, but this is best for us both. Everyone owns the doc now—the government, insurance companies, not to mention the hospital that actually wants to buy us. We've got no choice but to sleep with the devil we know. We have to sell out."

Lee could not mask his disappointment. "When people talk about their doctor—*their doctor*—it's guys like you and me they're referring to, not some faceless hospitalist at the MDC," he said.

"I get that, I really do. But you heard me on the phone just now. They wanted to pay me less because I made *two* trips to the nursing home when I could have made one. It's out of control, and I can't afford to be the one to fix it."

"I hate the stupidity and paperwork as much as you do," said Lee. "But trust me, Paul, you're going to hate the alternative even more.

"The MDC will make us see patients every five minutes. It'll be all bottom line, and there will be no heart left in what we do. You're not an automaton doing just what the hospital demands. You're the guy who does the right thing, no matter how difficult it is."

Lee leaned back in his chair as Paul took another sip of his triple venti whatever.

"Are you through?" asked Paul.

"Yeah. How'd I do?"

"Pretty convincing that time," he said with a nod. "But next week I'm definitely going to demand we sell, and I'm not going to be so easily swayed."

"That must have been one heck of a pep talk," Lee said. "Usually I only buy myself a couple of days."

"Don't get cocky. I'm pretty sure that's your last one."

"Speaking of how amazing you are," Lee said, "Cam Hilliard's case is troubling me."

Lee spent the next several minutes on the details, getting Paul up to speed on everything, including his troubles with Dr. Gleason.

"I think I'm right about the seizures, but the enlarged spleen, possibly enlarged liver, and the minimally abnormal liver tests are really puzzling. Maybe I'm reaching, but I've never come across an enlarged spleen that's not indicative of something more serious."

"Are you thinking cancer?"

"Have to. He's a young guy, so lymphoma's a possibility. Mono spot and EB virus titers are both negative, so it's not mononucleosis."

"I take it his CBC showed nothing to suggest leukemia. Palpable lymph nodes?"

"Nope. And serologies were negative for hepatitis."

"What about sarcoid?"

Sarcoidosis was a disease involving abnormal collections of inflammatory cells. Though most often located in the nodules of the lungs, any organ could be affected.

"Unlikely," Lee said. "Cam's chest x-ray is normal. I guess we'll see what the liver biopsy shows."

"Infection?"

"He's not sick enough. No fever or elevated white count. His sedimentation rate is normal."

"But his chess game is off."

"Which is more mental and also plays into Gleason's theory this is all psychological."

Paul had to sense Lee's frustration. Both doctors enjoyed the detective aspect of medicine in the abstract, but flailing around in the dark was a different matter entirely when a patient's health was at stake.

"What about a metabolic disorder?" asked Paul.

"Something systemic?" answered Lee.

"Something along those lines."

Lee gave a nod. "Could be," he said.

Before they could discuss it any further, Karen called. She and Lee exchanged a few quick pleasantries. He was glad to hear Josh had taken the initiative to call his mother and clear his plans before actually inviting all his friends to the camp.

"We're all tied up moving Cam from the MDC back to the White House, so I don't have even a minute to come by and see you," she said. "But I wanted to tell you about what I learned at the TPI."

Karen recounted her time with Yoshi Matsumoto and what Dr. Hal Hewitt had told her. Lee ended the call with a promise to get together soon to discuss her findings in more detail. He was most struck by what she told him last, and for Paul's benefit conveyed what Karen had said.

"These kids are taking nootropics? Why on earth would their parents allow that?" Paul sounded incredulous.

"Obviously it's not mandatory, but according to Karen, most parents chose to opt in. The drug maker runs some sort of neurofeedback testing to measure brainwave activity. Apparently the results have been impressive. Improved memory. Improved concentration. Improved focus. No reported side effects."

"Makes sense," Paul said, sounding a bit dismayed. "Soon as one group of kids has access to something potentially beneficial, parents get competitive about that. They want their kids to have those benefits, too."

"Studies say these nootropics are safe," Lee said, recalling what little he knew of the industry. "But I don't like giving them to young people."

"No doubt, their brains are still developing," said Paul. "Then again kids as young as five are taking ADHD meds these days."

"And nootropics are marketed like vitamins and nutritional supplements more than the cognitive enhancers they are," added Lee.

"What's the company?"

"ProNeural," Lee said.

Paul did some Google searching.

"Good gracious," he said, skimming some Web page. "They have millions in VC backing from Silicon Valley. When did high tech get into the supplement business?"

"Probably when they realized there were big dollars to be had."

"So the TPI kids are taking nootropics. What does that mean for Cam and his symptoms?" asked Paul. "Obviously what's happening to him isn't a widespread problem, otherwise there'd have been an uproar."

"Cam told me he wasn't on any prescription medication, but I'm willing to bet Gleason is the one doling out his daily dosage of ProNeural."

"And he has been acting very protective of Cam," Paul said, hitching onto Lee's train of thought.

"Oddly so," said Lee. "It's hard to explain Cam's dip in mental acuity, and there're no widely reported problems with ProNeural, as you said. Karen thinks he's been taking the nootropics for years. So why would he suddenly start having issues now?"

"Are you thinking what I'm thinking?" asked Paul.

"That's right," answered Lee. "Poison."

CHAPTER 22

The signs posted at the E Street entrance to the White House read NO STOPPING and AUTHORIZED VEHICLES ONLY. Lee stopped anyway. He was authorized.

Karen stood near the guardhouse waiting for him. She waved to Lee as he drove up. Standing behind Karen, a stern-faced uniformed guard, white shirt, no tie, kept a close watch on Lee. With a glance Karen got the guard to relax.

"Don't you look dapper," she said, leaning into the open window of Lee's car.

For his meeting with the first lady, Lee had selected his best suit from Brooks Brothers, and did an extra-careful job with his morning shave.

"Thank you," he said. "I actually tried."

"How come you never dressed like that when we were married?" she asked playfully.

"I did. You were never home to notice." Lee said this with an equally playful wink.

Karen, who wore her usual attire—a navy blue pantsuit and durable shoes, good for chasing down wall jumpers—facilitated the ID check. She climbed into the passenger seat of Lee's Honda, directing him to the next checkpoint, where a bomb-sniffing dog, sleek and muscular, waited for work.

"Speaking of home, Josh is with me for a few days," Karen said.

Lee raised an eyebrow. "I thought he was going to the camp."

"He is, but I guess his plans got delayed for some reason, and he didn't offer to explain."

"The less you probe, the better."

"My thoughts exactly," said Karen.

Lee noticed the time on the car dash. "I have to be at the MDC for morning rounds at eight thirty. Do you think I'll be late?"

"Ellen is about the most directed and task-oriented person I know," said Karen. "I'd be surprised if your meeting lasts more than five minutes. Are you going to talk to her about the nootropics?"

Patrolling outside Lee's car, the dog, a glorious German shepherd, sniffed away busily.

"And say what? We want to have them tested to make sure Cam's doctor isn't poisoning him so his son Taylor can play in some chess tournament? Are you crazy? I'd be thrown out of here by the same people who work for you, and you'd be tossed out right after me."

"I don't disagree," Karen said, sounding a bit frustrated.

"Look, I don't trust Gleason to do right by Cam with or without Pro-Neural in the picture. That's why I can't be cut off right now. We have to tread carefully here."

The guard handling the canine waved them through. Following Karen's instructions, Lee drove slowly down East Executive Avenue with the White House looming nearby. He came to a stop at an open parking space near the covered East Wing entrance.

"So what's this meeting all about?" Karen asked as they exited the car. "I thought you had already convinced Ellen to have Cam take the antiseizure meds."

"No, I did not. She said she wanted to discuss it in person before speaking with Gleason."

After his meeting with Paul, Lee called Ellen to follow up on Cam's condition since his return home, and more important, offer his opinion about the meds. Never having used the private number before, Lee figured he would be patched through to Donna Whitmore, Ellen's chief of staff, but no: the first lady answered as if he had phoned a close friend.

In a preemptive strike, Lee voiced his concern that Gleason might not put Cam on levetiracetam as he and Dr. Piekarski recommended. Instead of coming to an understanding, Lee got an invitation to come to the White House to present his case. He hoped Dr. Gleason would not be there, waiting in ambush.

Karen escorted Lee into a long, richly paneled hallway and past a manned security desk. They took a right turn into another corridor lined with stiff-backed wing chairs and artwork in gilded frames.

"For your information, this area is *not* part of the official tour," Karen said in a conspiratorial tone.

The first lady's office was located on the second floor of the East Wing, just down the hall from the White House calligrapher, a job Lee did not know existed until Karen pointed him out.

"What does he do exactly?" Lee asked.

"The calligraphy for all the official White House invitations."

"Sounds torturous."

"Not if you enjoy calligraphy. Don't worry, Lee. I've seen your handwriting. You're in no danger of getting the job."

The last door in the long hallway was wood paneled and stood out from the others. Karen knocked on that door. A moment later, Ellen Hilliard appeared, invited them inside, and gave them both a warm greeting. She looked like she did on TV, completely put together, wearing a black skirt and white blouse topped with a black cardigan, a strand of pearls secured around her neck.

"It's wonderful to see you, Lee," Ellen said in a pleasant voice. To Karen she said, "If I may, I'd like to speak with Lee alone for a few minutes. Would you mind waiting outside? I'll have you escort him out when we're through."

"Of course."

Ellen had a spacious, nicely decorated office with a cream-colored carpet and upholstered couches and chairs. She worked at an eye-catching, two-tone executive desk, framed by two built-in bookcases painted the same color white as the house and stacked full of books. On the walls, in addition to some modest artwork, hung pictures of Cam (some taken during chess matches) and several of her and President Hilliard in various phases of life.

"Tea? Anything to drink?" Ellen asked.

"No, thank you, I'm fine."

She took a seat on a comfortable-looking couch and motioned for Lee to take a nearby chair and join her.

Ellen spent a few moments expressing her gratitude for Lee's involvement with Cam's medical care. As was the case during their brief phone conversation, the pleasantries did not last long.

"How's he feeling?" Lee asked.

"Sore. Tired. Out of sorts."

"That's not at all unexpected. He'll feel much more like himself in no time. What did you decide about the medicine?"

"Dr. Gleason went over the side effects with me in detail. Moodiness, fatigue—the same as Cam's earlier symptoms, but now add to that the possibility of *hallucinations*! Goodness, Lee, are you sure this is absolutely necessary? Dr. Gleason doesn't seem to think so."

"Well, like I said on the phone, I'm not surprised there," Lee replied. "But Mrs. Hilliard—"

"Please, call me Ellen."

"Ellen, then. This is not just my opinion, but the opinion of the neurologist, Dr. Marilyn Piekarski, as well. We can start Cam on a very low dose and build it up slowly to a more therapeutic level. We'll watch closely for side effects. If his symptoms resolve, if he stops waking up extremely fatigued, we will be that much more confident in our diagnosis that Cam is experiencing seizures. It could have a positive impact on his mood. We won't know until we try. This is Dr. Piekarski's plan, and she will repeat his EEG and MRI in six to eight weeks."

Ellen got up from the couch and went over to a window, which showed off a view of the South Portico and White House grounds.

"It's funny," she said. "Weekday or weekend, every day is a workday around here. My husband's at work in the Oval Office right now, getting his morning debrief, keeping the world from imploding, all the weight and responsibility of millions of lives on his shoulders—and here I am, responsible really for one life in addition to my own. Yet somehow it feels equally as weighty."

"He's your son," Lee said. "I understand your struggle, but I strongly advise he take the medicine."

Ellen returned to her seat. "My job, my—role, here at the White House, can be challenging at times."

"I can imagine."

"There's no clear objective, no defined path for a first lady, but it comes with tremendous scrutiny. One wrong move can get you branded in the harshest possible way. Motherhood feels a bit similar. You do your best without much guidance, and you hope you don't do damage to your kids."

"In this case, I don't believe you will."

"Perhaps that's true. But I'd like to make another observation, if I may. My job here, Lee, is mostly to stay on the sidelines and support my husband. Sure, I have my causes. My Aim Higher initiative. My work with military families. But my most important role, aside from motherhood, is to present a unified front to the American people. That's what they want from a first family, and it's what they'll remember most when we leave the White House. We're role models whether we like it or not. And people want a team. They like things to be together, not fractured."

"I can sort of relate to your struggle," Lee said. "I was married once. Didn't do a very good job presenting my own unified front."

"Well, I need you to do a good job of it now. I'll confess it's not always easy for me to play the good wife, not let the East Wing affairs mix with those in the West. I may not agree with everything Geoffrey has done as president, but my support of him has never wavered. Not for one instant. For Cam's sake, I need you to take a similar approach with Dr. Gleason. You might not agree with everything he says and does, but I do think he has Cam's best interests at heart."

If ever there was a time to bring up the nootropics it was then and there, but Lee worried it would add confusion to the levetiracetam issue.

"I'll make sure Cam takes this medication you're recommending," Ellen continued. "But you need to do something for me."

"What's that?" Lee asked.

"I don't want to be at odds with my husband over the direction of Cam's medical care. I need you to get on the same page as Dr. Gleason. Immediately."

"I'm trying, he just seems—opposed to the idea." Again, Lee resisted the urge to say more.

"None of us has an easy job, Lee. I know you have your work cut out for you. I'll cover all of your expenses for Cam's care, and not to worry, no scandal here. It's not the government paying, it's me. I'll have my chief of staff, Donna Whitmore, coordinate. Just make sure Dr. Gleason sees things your way from now on. I've come to trust you, so I believe your way is the right way."

Ellen stood again. This time Lee took it to mean, and correctly, that he should do the same. He shook Ellen's proffered hand.

"For now, I'm content standing on the sidelines, doing my part while my husband fights the bigger battles," Ellen said. "But when it involves my son, I'm the one in the game getting muddied and throwing punches. I'm counting on you, Lee, to make it all work out."

Ellen opened her office door. Karen was standing there.

"Thank you again for your time," Ellen said.

She closed the door, leaving Lee and Karen alone in the quiet hallway. Meeting adjourned.

"What did she say?" asked Karen.

Lee chuckled softly to himself as they ambled down the hall past the calligrapher's office.

"I think she and Geoffrey are perfectly suited," said Lee.

"How so?"

"She wants me and Gleason to get on the same page and then in the next breath tells me she trusts me completely."

"Bit of a double message, don't you think?" said Karen.

"More like a pitch right down the center of the plate."

CHAPTER 23

Lee was still processing his meeting with the first lady when noon rolled around. He had arranged with Paul to have the time off, but with his camping trip canceled, Lee decided to take a shift at the MDC supervising medical residents. It was good in a way to get back to business as usual, and the extra pay did not hurt. But it was hardly a return to normal.

He was supposed to form some sort of alliance with a man who might be intentionally harming the first family's son for personal gain. Either the man was so egotistical he would risk medical malpractice just to be right, or he was devious, trying everything possible to keep Lee from discovering what was making Cam Hilliard sick.

Lee headed straight to the coffee station in the MDC lounge to fuel up for his afternoon rounds. He poured himself a cup of coffee thick as mud and chuckled, thinking Paul would never suffer such a beverage. He had called to see if Josh wanted to meet up for lunch, but he was already out with friends. Dinner remained a possibility, though Josh had made plans to eat with his mother.

On his walk to a nearby empty chair, Lee noticed his knee acting up again. It was a nagging little pain, right where the patella connects to the ligament. His nightly run was suddenly in question. Someday those runs would turn into walks. After walks, maybe downshift into a stroll. The next phase after that got a little grim.

Lee took his seat, sipped at his coffee, and pondered ways to get Gleason on his side. His focus wandered when he overheard a snippet of conversation between two nearby doctors he did not know. Both were young, with full heads of hair (one blond and curly, the other straight and dark). They probably had good knees.

"We've weaned her off fosphenytoin," the curly-haired doc said. "But she's still on a pretty aggressive course of diazepam."

"No more seizures?" the darker-haired of the two asked.

"No, but I was hoping the diazepam might bring her myoclonus under control. It hasn't. She's had episodes even when we had her sedated. Her arms keep snapping like whips without warning."

"What did the CT scan show?"

"Slightly enlarged spleen and liver, but nothing else."

Lee's ears perked up like a dog hearing a whistle. He was standing in a flash, knee pain be damned. The two doctors watched him approach.

"I'm sorry to bother you, but I couldn't help but overhear," Lee said. "Your case sounds similar to a patient of mine. Have you figured out what's causing her symptoms?"

"No, she's a young girl who came in the other day with CO poisoning," the dark-haired doctor said. "She lost her parents. It's a real tragedy."

Lee had heard about the fatal gas leak on the news, but yesterday it seemed like a sad headline and nothing more.

"Say, if you come up with something on your patient that can help ours, let us know."

The curly-haired doc fished a business card out from a leather wallet and handed it to Lee. The doc was a hospitalist, a physician who cares for patients while they are hospitalized—the same profession helping to put Lee out of business.

"Will do," said Lee, shaking hands good-bye. He had no intention of involving them in his case, because they could not know his patient was Cam Hilliard. But still, seizures and an enlarged spleen and liver? Even though he was not her doctor, there were enough symptoms overlapping for Lee to investigate. Using his phone to check the news, he quickly found the girl's name, Susie Banks, and decided to pay her a visit.

Locating the patient was a matter of locating a hospital computer. He entered his log-in credentials into the terminal and was soon directed to the ICU on the sixth floor of the main building. While Lee was not re-sponsible for Susie's care, he was at least dressed for the part in a white lab coat, striped cotton shirt, blue tie, and the slacks from the Brooks Brothers suit he had worn to his meeting with Ellen.

He marched over to the nurses' desk, taking confident strides, acting like he was in a hurry, but pretending not to know exactly where he was headed.

"I'm looking for Susie Banks's room," Lee said to a dour-faced nurse with dyed black hair. She peered out from behind her expansive monitor and appraised Lee with some skepticism.

"And you are?"

"Dr. Lee Blackwood. I'm a member of the internal medicine practice. I'm consulting on the case for Dr. Sarah Anderson. I thought you were informed."

He used a name of a doctor who he knew worked on this floor. The tone Lee had taken implied any lack of cooperation might result in a ding on this nurse's next performance review.

"Of course, Dr. Blackwood," the nurse said, feigning awareness as convincingly as a Broadway actress. "She's in 601."

Lee thanked her and moved on. The scene inside Susie's ICU cubicle was a familiar one. Sick person, lying on a bed, hooked to an array of machinery. The sweet-faced girl with long brown hair was on high-flow oxygen therapy delivered via a nasal cannula. Her eyes were closed, but only because she was sleeping, not sedated. He was glad to see she was not on ventilation, which was far more invasive and would leave her prone to infection.

The telemetry monitor showed good vitals. Steady sinus rhythm, though her oxygen saturation was a low ninety-two percent: safe, but far from normal.

From a plastic pouch affixed to the end of the bed, Lee removed Susie's medical chart and began to give it a careful read while keeping an eye out for one of Susie's doctors or a nurse. They would be harder to fool than the duty nurse. It was all clear for the moment. The only person nearby was a maintenance worker, standing on a ladder, with his head and shoulders hidden inside the drop ceiling.

Lee resumed his evaluation. Susie's medical history was sparse. There was no primary care physician listed, and with her parents gone, nobody could fill in the blanks. The line for next of kin was also a blank. Lee felt heartbroken for this girl. Her parents were dead and either she did not have, or could not provide, the name of her closest living relative.

She was alone, and had to be terribly frightened.

A CAT scan confirmed what the doctors in the lounge had said—both the spleen and liver were enlarged. Lee could think of no reason why CO gas would have affected her organs in such a way. She'd been given urine myoglobin in the ER to combat rhabdomyolysis, but that would not cause organ enlargement, either.

Lee felt a jolt, a tingle telling him to read on. After suffering a grand-mal seizure in the ER, she had briefly slipped into a coma before regaining consciousness. Later, she began experiencing myoclonic jerks, another type of seizure, unrelated to her acute carbon monoxide poisoning. Neurological issues, liver and spleen enlargement—indeed, her case was sounding a lot like Cam's.

When Lee read Susie's labs, his eyes went wide. The liver enzymes were elevated, only slightly, again similar to Cam. Susie's doctor noted something else: a very unusual cherry-red spot in the retina of both eyes, a rounded red dot surrounded by a halo of pallor, like a target's bull's-eye right where the macula was, that part of the retina where rays of light are directly focused. There were multiple comments about it in the record, the consensus being it was most likely a rare manifestation of carbon monoxide poisoning. But Lee wondered: *If CO gas could produce a red spot in the eye, could a different toxin also do the same?*

Lee called Paul's cell, but after several rings got patched through to his voice mail.

"Paul, it's Lee. There's a patient at the MDC with a possible connection to Cam Hilliard. Could you do some research for me on cherry-red spots in the macula? Curious to know if you can find any connections to these red spots in the eyes and various toxins like we discussed. Thanks much, and I'll see you soon."

Lee put his phone away and went back to flipping through pages of Susie's medical chart when he noticed her eyes flutter open. He could see her struggle to focus her vision. When she spoke her voice was whispered, soft as a breeze.

"Are you my doctor?"

Lee returned a friendly smile, slipped the chart back into its pouch, and came around to the side of the bed. He poured water into a plastic cup and gave her a drink.

"I'm *a* doctor," Lee said. He set the water cup on the side table after Susie finished taking a sip. "How are you feeling?"

Tears flooded Susie's big round eyes. Answer enough.

"I'm okay," she said without any conviction.

Lee gave her hand a squeeze. "You stay strong, Susie Banks. I promise, I'm going to check up on you again very soon."

Lee did not tell her his checkup would happen after he dilated Cam's pupils and used an ophthalmoscope to look for a cherry-red spot on his macula.

WITH HIS tools and ladder, Mauser was dressed for the part. He had come to the ICU to decide how and when to take care of Susie Banks permanently. This was Rainmaker's order, and Mauser could lose his supply if the deed was not done. The miracle of Susie's survival confounded and infuriated them both, perhaps Mauser more than Rainmaker. He was not accustomed to failure. Susie should be dead like her parents, but no, she had to go and complicate things. No matter. Mauser had other ways to eliminate her. Other tools at his disposal.

Now was not the time to take care of business. Too many people were on the floor. He would come back later—perhaps after dinner, when things quieted down. He'd show up with some complicated piece of machinery he'd say was needed to complete a job he was pretending to do. Being an actual heating and cooling repairman made this a relatively easy ruse. Nobody at the front desk had asked questions when Mauser presented a bogus work order. Nobody wondered what he was doing moving ceiling tiles about. Nobody asked why he was peering into dark spaces with his flashlight.

At first Mauser thought nothing of the doctor who had come to see Susie. His perspective changed dramatically when he overheard him talking on the phone. If the acoustics up in the ceiling had not amplified the call, Mauser would have missed the conversation entirely. He knew from Rainmaker there was a connection between Susie Banks and the president's kid. Now he knew the doctor was connected as well.

He could inject Susie easily later tonight, but the doc was another story. Perhaps Mauser would inject him as well. Or maybe it would happen during a mugging gone wrong. Could be something else entirely. He would check with Rainmaker, and together they would decide this doctor's fate.

CHAPTER 24

Lee finished up at the MDC and then drove to his office. Stacie, the office manager, had business to discuss.

"I think the new scheduling software is extremely buggy," Stacie said.

Stacie's earnest face showed grave concern. In her world, scheduling issues were matters of extreme importance, as they should be. She proceeded to provide an in-depth explanation of the software's many perceived shortcomings. Lee listened as intently as he could until his patience ran out.

"Look, Stacie, I can't even get my e-mail to work on my phone. You're in charge of scheduling. Handle it. Whatever you have to do, whatever it costs, I trust you'll do the right thing here."

"Right isn't going to be cheap," Stacie said.

"Seldom is," answered Lee.

With Stacie satisfied—for the moment, at least—Lee headed off in search of Paul, whom he found in his office, back on the phone. Of course he was on the phone.

"Yes, I know. You're a doctor," Paul said snippily into the receiver. "Happy for you. But you work for an insurance company, and I am responsible for the care of my patient. And I'm telling you that Margery Theilman needs an MRI of the lumbar spine to confirm a herniated disc—yes, I have examined her. She has excruciating back pain radiating into her leg and foot and a partial foot drop from weakness. . . . No, she cannot wait to see a neurosurgeon. She needs the MRI today. Why are you making her suffer unnecessarily? . . . No, she doesn't first need to see a physical therapist. . . .

"Okay, I get it, I really do. You're reading from a playbook called Back Pain. I'm not trying to put you down, really, but stop being an obstructionist. You're practicing medicine on my patient from an office five hundred miles away—are you serious? You call this a peer-to-peer evaluation? Good gravy, you are so deep in the pocket of the insurance company there's not a rope long enough to help you climb out. I live by my reputation. You live by making insurance companies even richer. That right there is our problem and our conflict. Great job, Doc. Honestly, how do you sleep at night? I hope Mrs. Theilman sues you. I'll be sure to give her that advice."

Paul hung up the phone, cursing under his breath.

"I thought you handled that well," Lee said with a straight face.

"You are looking at a man who is on the verge, Lee."

"Of greatness?" Lee sounded hopeful.

"Insanity. I can't take it much longer. I really can't." Paul shook his head in disgust. The place was wearing him down. Paul's paunch seemed paunchier, his gray grayer, and the bags under his eyes bigger than usual.

"The first lady is going to pay us for Cam's care. She told me that today. Maybe we'll get a bonus if we figure out what's going on with him. Did you get my message?"

"I did. What was it about? All you said was a cherry-red spot in the macula and a possible connection to Cam."

Lee launched into a detailed review of how he'd come to know Susie Banks and her enlarged organs. He made a point to emphasize that Susie and Cam had similar results for their respective liver enzyme tests.

"You know a cherry-red spot could be a feature of a metabolic disorder, a storage disease like Tay-Sachs or Niemann-Pick."

Paul knew all this without having to look it up, which impressed Lee greatly. Much about Paul impressed Lee. A sense of profound gratitude for their years of friendship and partnership overcame him. It hurt Lee to see his partner in such distress over the state of their struggling business. Perhaps Lee was holding on to the practice for the same reason Karen held on to the camp: saying good-bye simply felt too final.

"Well, if I remember correctly, both of those metabolic disorders are diseases of infancy, and I can assure you Susie and Cam are well beyond that."

Lee and Paul spent a quiet moment pondering the possibilities.

"It would almost be easier if CO exposure caused myoclonus," Lee said. "I know it doesn't, but then it would be one less link between Susie and Cam."

Paul's face lit up as if a sudden thought had left him thunderstruck. Lee could not recall a time when he saw his partner this animated.

"Did you say myoclonus?"

"Yeah, I thought I had said it before. My brain's a bit rattled. Susie's been experiencing myoclonic jerks in addition to the grand mal seizure she had in the ER."

"Hang on a second. Hang on," Paul said. "A few years ago I took care of two sixteen-year-old twin boys, Richard and Scott Stewart. Now, I don't know if they had a red spot on their maculas or not, but I do recall their mother brought them here because each had presented with a case of myoclonus."

Given there were so few family docs around these days, Paul treating twins with a symptom Susie had was no great surprise. But it was *what* they had that left Lee breathless with excitement.

"In fifteen years, how many cases of myoclonus have we treated?" Lee asked.

"Treated? One or maybe two others, in addition to the twins. People get those jerks all the time, but sleep starts aren't a reason to go see a doctor. The severe cases are rare, and they all went straight to the neurologist," Paul said. "But here's the thing, Lee. Those boys never received follow-up care, because they died."

"Died how?" Lee swallowed hard.

"Car accident," Paul said. "The father lost control in Shenandoah National Park and went right off a cliff. No brake marks, just tire tracks. Both parents died with them."

It was a chilling image. How many nights had Lee woken with a chest-tightening panic when Josh went out with his friends for a good time? If his years in medicine had taught Lee anything, it was that nothing in life is guaranteed, and everything we hold dear could be taken away with a twitch of God's eyelash.

"Was it investigated? Murder-suicide, perhaps?"

"Not that I'm aware of," Paul said. "It was a tragedy, nothing more."

Lee had no memory of that particular car accident, but it was no surprise. The news pummeled him daily with stories of loss and grief. Another thing medicine had taught Lee was that good people suffered bad outcomes all of the time. But it was interesting that two of these tragedies happened to touch the lives of three people who had presented with myoclonus. He shared that thought with Paul.

"Cam doesn't have myoclonus, though," Paul commented.

"True, but he's potentially been having seizures at night while asleep. And his seizures could even present as myoclonic jerks. Seizures of any type point to something wrong with his brain. Something that makes neurons hyper-excitable and fire off without control."

"It's possible," Paul said.

"I wish we knew more about those poor twins."

"I'll see what I have on file. Like I said, I had referred them to a neurologist, but never got the chance to check up on them myself."

Paul's voice held an ache Lee could hear and feel.

From his computer, Paul accessed the medical records of the Stewart twins. A few years back, Stacie had put the full-court press on the practice migrating to an electronic recordkeeping system. The expense would be worth it for the convenience alone, she said. She was right, to a point. If she had asked them this year, after such dismal earnings, Paul would have nixed the notion without much consideration. Lee would have told Stacie to do what she thought was best. They were different in that regard.

Lee drummed his fingers restlessly on his armrest, while Paul perused the files.

"Nothing here that will help," he said. "Though I feel really awful now."

"Why is that?" asked Lee.

"Not only are the boys dead, I didn't buy their CD like I had promised.

I even put a note in their file here to remind me. Dammit. You don't think it was foul play, do you?"

"It *is* a little odd for three patients with such unusual conditions to all suffer these terrible accidents," Lee said. "These boys were musicians, you said?"

"Incredible musicians," Paul answered. "One played cello and the other piano. Their mother was distraught about the myoclonus because it was starting to interfere with their practice and performances."

"Hold a moment." Lee sounded excited. "Cam is an incredibly gifted chess player, world-ranked. Supremely talented. Are we talking that level?"

"They were concert-level performers, as I recall," Paul said. "It was their life. They were destined for Julliard and great things after, at least according to the mother."

"So we have myoclonus in three cases at least," said Lee. "The same condition perhaps presenting in Cam as well. Add to that some tragic incidences—CO exposure for one, a car accident for another, resulting in two fatalities, and we have at least two patients with enlarged organs and elevated liver function tests, one of whom we know has a cherry-red spot on the macula that could be a rare side effect from the gas exposure, or it could be related to these other symptoms, we just don't know. Sound about right?"

"Does to me. Is Susie Banks gifted in any way?" Paul asked.

"Google her," Lee said.

Paul put the name "Susie Banks" into a search box, and in a blink of Internet magic, the Web browser produced a series of links. Lee confirmed they referenced the same Susie Banks who was in the hospital. Among those links was a story about a recent performance of Susie's at the Kennedy Center that had ended horrifically when she appeared to lose control of her limbs.

"Myoclonus," Lee said.

Paul did some more clicking, and it was not long before another article related to Susie caught Lee's interest. He pointed it out to Paul.

"Have a read. Pretty interesting where Susie Banks honed her craft," Lee said.

"The True Potential Institute," Paul said, reading from a profile about Susie that had appeared in a local newspaper.

"I'll bet anything the Stewart twins had studied at this TPI place as well," said Lee.

"And I bet you're going to want me to stop what I was working on to find out if there are any toxins other than carbon monoxide known to cause a cherry-red spot on the macula," Paul said.

"Damn straight," answered Lee.

CHAPTER 25

Lee got Karen on the phone while she and Josh were out doing some shopping. She invited Lee to join them for a bite to eat. He could not remember the last time the three of them had dined together, settled on too long, and decided the idea was a good one. Rather than launch into a long explanation of all he had discovered on the phone, Lee thought they could brainstorm an action plan over dinner. They would meet at Olivio's, an Italian restaurant they had frequented when Josh was young.

A maître d' escorted Lee over to a table where Karen and Josh were seated with drinks already served.

"Thanks for including me," Lee said to Karen, taking a seat. The restaurant, dimly lit and well appointed, was not particularly crowded at 5:30 in the afternoon. The waiter approached and took their orders. Josh settled on the fish, but only after some internal debate. Lee ordered a glass of red wine and opted for the eggplant special, while Karen went for the chicken. If he had to guess each person's order beforehand, Lee would have been right on all three counts (including Josh's hemming and hawing). He knew their personalities, had their habits and tastes ingrained.

This was his family. Fractured and small as it was, it brought him great joy to be in their company. His parents were gone, his sister an infrequent visitor, but Karen and Josh were constants in Lee's life. They were signals that all was right in the world, everything was as it had been and as it should be.

"You got here just in time," Karen said to Lee, her tone a bit off. "Josh was just telling me that he's quit his job." She turned her head so only Lee could see her eyes grow wide as her expression shifted from pleasant to deeply upset.

Yessiree, all was right in Lee's world.

"I figured Josh should be the one to tell you," Lee said in his own defense.

"When are you going to tell him that he's throwing his future away? He has to commit to something, Lee. Anything, really."

"I committed to Hannah and look how that turned out," Josh said. The comment was meant in jest, but it was obvious to Lee he still hurt over the breakup.

"Let's give him some space, Karen," Lee said. "He's dealing with enough as it is."

"What he said," Josh tossed in.

"Well, I'm glad you waited until just before your father sat down to break the big news."

Karen shot Lee another hard-eyed stare over the rim of her wineglass as she took a long swallow to chase down the bread she'd been chewing. A waiter brought over Lee's wine.

"Look, I know it doesn't seem like I have my act together," Josh said, trying out a placating tone. "But I don't need rehab, or cash, or anything like that. I just need to have a nice dinner with two people I love more than anybody else in this world."

"To that, I propose a toast," said Lee, hefting his glass of wine. Karen and Josh raised their respective glasses as well. "To family. We might not be together like we once were, but we'll never be apart."

They clinked and drank, and the talk turned breezy and easy for a while.

"So, Karen," Lee said, the tenor of his voice changing to signal a shift in topic. "I think we need to take a careful look at those nootropics Cam is taking."

"Why's that?" Karen asked.

Lee gave a little speech, mostly for Josh's benefit, about this being privileged information not to be shared or discussed with anyone. The consequences could be dire for him, he explained.

Once all were in agreement, Lee launched into a detailed rehash of the conversation he had overheard in the doctor's lounge; the links he had made to Susie's symptoms and those of Cam; a connection between Susie and the twins who had also presented with myoclonus; how they had died while Susie miraculously survived; and lastly a connection, at least in two cases (perhaps all four, if the twins attended as well), to the True Potential Institute.

"No wonder you need help," Karen said at last.

"Typically a cherry-red spot is caused by a genetic defect. But carbon monoxide can produce a cherry-red spot on the macula as well. Given that, I'm thinking why couldn't some *other* compound produce a cherry-red spot, something Susie and Cam both had exposure to?"

Lee opened the question to the table. No one had an answer.

"Why can't it be genetic?" Josh asked.

"Well—if we assume Susie, Cam, and the twins all experienced some type of seizure activity, most likely myoclonic jerks, and if we assume the twins studied music at the TPI, it would be highly unusual, no—make that statistically impossible—for four kids connected to the same place to have the same incredibly unusual metabolic disorder. It has to be something environmental, a compound, something they've been exposed to. It's more like a cancer cluster from contaminated groundwater than a genetic disease."

"The cherry-red spot is a disease?" Josh asked.

"It's a sign of a disease," Lee clarified. "What I want to know is could the cause be something intentional, possibly even malicious?"

"Malicious?" Josh sounded surprised. "What's the motive for that?" He was always a practical thinker like his mother.

"There's a big chess tournament coming up," Karen said. "Cam's the captain of the U.S. junior squad and Taylor is the alternate. We've tossed around the idea that Gleason wanted Cam out so that Taylor can be in."

"How competitive is this Gleason guy?" Josh sounded incredulous.

"Pathologically so, I'd say," Karen answered. "I've seen him on the tennis court, and I hear he's just as bad playing contract bridge and golf."

"As a doctor, I'd say he protects his ego to the detriment of his patient," Lee added.

"Or, like we've discussed, he's keeping the patient from *you*," said Karen.

"Precisely," Lee answered. "He clearly wants me at more than an arm's length. The question is why."

Josh did not appear convinced. "That motive's pretty weak, if you ask me," he said. "All that effort just so his kid can play in some chess match?"

"If I told you a mother once hired a hit man to take out her daughter's rival on the cheer squad you'd have said that's preposterous too, but it happened. Google Wanda Holloway," said Lee. He was thinking of the Lifetime movie about the crazed Texas mother he'd seen not too long ago, on one of those dreary evenings when the wine bottle was half empty, his ex-girlfriend left a dull ache in his heart, and regrets about not becoming a surgeon took center stage.

"So explain the connection to Susie and those twins," Karen said. "Gleason would have no reason to hurt them. They're musicians, not chess players."

The only good idea Lee had was to take another drink of wine.

"I honestly don't know," he said. "You raise a good point."

"Maybe Yoshi's the one administering something experimental on behalf of the nootropics company, and getting paid for it while making his students' personal information part of that research."

"Could be," Lee said. "That's a stronger motive for sure, and it would explain similar symptoms in other students, but it doesn't explain why Gleason's been so cagey with Cam."

"What's the next step?" Josh asked.

"I'm sure as heck not going to Ellen without actual proof," Karen said. "Real, hard, irrefutable proof."

"Why don't you get some samples of what Cam's taking?" Lee suggested. "We could have them tested."

"It's a good idea," Josh said.

"I don't have access to those," Karen said, her voice flattening. "What are you proposing? That I break into Gleason's office and just take them?"

Josh and Lee studied each other before nodding simultaneously. Karen exhaled loudly.

"No," she said.

"Then we may never know," Lee said with a shrug.

"Fine, I'll do it," Karen snapped.

"You didn't really need a lot of convincing, did you, Mom?"

"No, I guess not," Karen said softly. "To be honest, I've been thinking along those lines myself."

"A bunch of my army buddies used to take something called modafinil," Josh said. "They called it the 'go pill' because it kept them super alert on patrol. Kind of sounds like these nootropics you're talking about. I can talk to some of them, see what they can tell me. Might help."

"It's a great idea," said Lee. "These smart drugs seem like your generation's kind of thing anyway. Whatever you can dig up, I'm sure it will be useful. So, when are you going to get the samples?" Lee directed his question to Karen.

"I might as well go now," she said. "The clinic should be quiet at this hour."

"And you?" Josh asked his dad the question, with his eyes focused on his cell phone.

"Soon as we're finished eating, I'm headed back to the hospital," Lee said. "I want to check in with Susie, see if she takes ProNeural or some other TPI-supplied nootropic."

Josh handed Lee his phone to show him an article he'd found—a promotional story about the TPI identifying the Stewart twins as star students at the institute. Lee's expression darkened as he read the relevant passage.

Josh said, "While you're at the hospital chatting up Susie, maybe find out if there were rumors swirling around the TPI about the twins' deaths not being an accident."

CHAPTER 26

Karen dropped Josh off at her place, a modest apartment in Shaw, a neighborhood close to Logan Circle, the place she slept and sometimes ate, but didn't really live. Her real home was in her small office in the lower level of the White House, or in hotels (always the cheap rooms), or in the cars, airplanes, and helicopters that ferried the first family from one place to the next. Home was wherever this other family went. She was the turtle shell, along for the ride, good for protection. Despite all the challenges, the brutal schedule, the lack of progress on her reform efforts over the span of two different administrations, Karen was proud of the work she did, proud to be a human shield.

She caught a cab to the White House, showed her ID to two different guards stationed at two different gates, and then strode up a lonely stretch of paved road on the western side of the compound. Twilight was nearing an end and city lights twinkled all around her.

Off to her right, Karen saw the White House. To her left stood the ornate Eisenhower Executive Office Building, a fine example of French Second Empire architecture. The EEOB, as it was better known, housed most of the offices for White House staff. Plenty of lights still glowed in the windows of the five-story building. The head honchos at the White House could not care less about work/life balance. The same could be said of the Secret Service. Love of country trumped all else.

Karen turned right and passed under a long white awning before she entered a door leading to the West Wing. Another guard station was just inside, and again she showed her badge. Returning to work to break into the office of the physician to the president would be, to say the least, severely frowned upon. She was not entirely sure this was a risk worth taking. Lee's theory about Gleason intentionally harming Cam felt like a stretch. Would he do that just so Taylor could be king of Chess Mountain for a while? Perhaps. The memory of that broken tennis racket flashed in Karen's mind.

The interior of the West Wing was a far cry from the rococo style and elaborate wood carvings of the East Wing, where the first lady worked. The aesthetic here was more like the lobby of a Ramada Inn. Tan carpeting. Hotel lobby furniture. The halls were lined with pictures of President Hilliard at work in his office, signing legislation, meeting dignitaries, or just looking presidential. Once Hilliard left office, pictures of the next president would occupy these walls.

Beyond the guard station was a stairwell leading to the upper and lower levels of the West Wing. Downstairs were the navy restaurant, offices for the Secret Service, and the Situation Room.

All was quiet, like a museum at night. There were no crises afoot. All of the people trying to make policy happen were stuck over at the EEOB, burning the midnight oil. At this hour, the first family was upstairs on the second floor of the residence.

Karen walked past the vice president's office, and next to that, the office of the president's chief of staff. As with real estate, with these offices there was only one rule: location, location, location. Proximity to power was itself a kind of power. Reflected glory. The deputy national security advisor was typically offered a palatial suite in the EEOB or a broom closet next to his boss and steps from the Oval Office. Every single person to hold the position had chosen the broom closet.

Karen continued down the hallway, passing between the Oval Office and the Roosevelt Room, the primary meeting spot for the West Wingers. Soon she was back outside, strolling along the West Colonnade, not having encountered anybody other than uniformed security. She passed through another door and entered the main residence where, up ahead, she spied Stephen Duffy, keeping watch. He was one of several agents placed on duty while the first family was at home.

Duffy did a double take when he saw Karen headed his way.

"K-Ray! What are you doing here?" he asked. His voice was louder and carried farther without bodies around to absorb the sound.

"Dr. Gleason left a prescription for me in his office. I came to pick it up."

Karen invented the lie on the spot. Duffy was stationed near the entrance to the diplomatic reception room. He might have noticed her going into the clinic, raising eyebrows she did not want raised.

"Hey, listen, Karen, I'm glad I caught you alone." Duffy touched his temple and winced, as if confronting a sudden pain. He did not blink. That penetrating stare of his made Karen a bit uneasy, but tonight it seemed a little more pronounced. His fingers tapped against his legs as if he were playing a piano. Duffy had said his Graves' symptoms got worse with stress. The Secret Service did not have a less stressful assignment than guard duty inside the White House residence at night.

What could be bothering him? Karen wondered.

"I wanted to know if you've given any more thought to my getting a raise," he said.

Karen tried but failed to keep from rolling her eyes. Duffy was a recording on repeat these days.

"Look, Stephen, I don't set your salary. We've discussed this before."

"But you can put in a good word with the folks upstairs." He sounded desperate.

"What's going on here? Why are you so hot on this?"

"Nothing—I'm just—"

"Are you in debt?"

"No."

But the way he said it made his "no" sound a lot like a "yes."

"Are you gambling?"

With all the strict and rigorous testing procedures in place, Karen doubted it could be drugs.

"No, I don't do that. You're making it seem like a big deal."

Karen closed the gap between them. It *was* a big deal.

"I hope there's nothing hanging over you that could compromise your integrity, Stephen," she said.

Duffy raised his hands in defense. "Easy. Easy, it's nothing like that," he said. "I just have some health expenses—you know, related to my condition—and a little extra scratch would ease the pressure, that's all. It's not dire. You're freaking out over nothing."

Karen took a cautious step in retreat.

"Good to hear," she said. "In that case, you can stop peppering me for a raise. There are procedures in place for promotions, and you'll have to get in line and follow them. Do your job well, Agent Duffy, to our standards, and I'm sure things will work out in your favor. Understood?"

"Understood," Duffy said, yielding to her with a conciliatory nod.

Karen did not often pull out the boss card, but when necessary she could castigate her subordinates like unruly children.

"I'm going to grab my meds and then I'm getting out of here," said Karen. "I'll see you tomorrow. And don't bug me anymore about your raise, Stephen. I mean it. If you need to borrow some money, ask me. I'll help you out as much as I can."

"It's cool," Duffy said. "Thanks for the offer. I'll let you know."

Karen made an about-face and backtracked to the clinic area. She had a master key on her person—the Secret Service could not be locked out of any rooms in case of an emergency.

The clinic was dark, and Karen flicked on the lights. She ventured into the exam room where not long ago Lee had conducted his physical exam on Cam, and made her way into Gleason's spacious office. She found the key attached to the tennis racket key chain where she had seen it before—in the top drawer of Gleason's cherrywood desk. In no time, she was back in the exam room, rifling through the medicine cabinets in search of those damn TPI neurological supplements.

Only now did her heart start pounding. Drops of sweat traveled the contours of her neck and slid all the way down her back to stain the blue shirt she'd worn to work that day.

This is wrong . . . this is dangerously wrong. . . .

Karen pushed those thoughts aside as she scanned the contents in the meticulously organized cabinets. The plastic bins were clearly labeled, so it was easy for Karen to distinguish Cam's medicines from those of his parents and other White House staff who came to the clinic for their prescriptions.

On the third shelf Karen spotted a bin marked CAM TPI. In it she saw three different clear plastic jars with the ProNeural branding. The jars were similar in width and size to the container of face cream she favored. The graphic design made the containers look more like vitamins than prescriptions. The labeling was bold and professionally done. Emblazed on one jar was the word "FOCUS," next to a line drawing of an open eye. The front of another jar read "SUPER O-3," with a lightning bolt for a corresponding image, while the third jar, this one called "SOAR," had wings sprouting from the letters.

Karen opened each jar and dispensed some of the contents into the plastic bag she'd put in her purse for this exact purpose. FOCUS was a yellow pill, SUPER 0-3 a white one, and SOAR came in a brown casing. The pill casings themselves revealed a powdery substance within.

Using her phone, Karen checked the ProNeural Web site and saw that the products in the medicine cabinet matched the inventory available for purchase over the Internet. No FDA regulation. No age restriction. All it took to FOCUS or SOAR was a home address and a valid credit card.

Karen took a pill from the plastic bag and examined the casing closely. It did not look like it had been tampered with, but that did not mean anything. It stood to reason that Dr. Gleason had the medical knowledge to replace the ProNeural formula with his own special concoction. All he would have to do is seal the casing to conceal his tampering.

For being such a practical woman, Karen was a bit surprised at the faith Ellen Hilliard had invested in Yoshi Matsumoto and his cognitive enhancers, but she recalled what Hal Hewitt had said about parents being ultracompetitive with their progeny. For these high-achieving kids it was easy to see how *not* taking ProNeural would seem like a major handicap, especially considering the dramatic results from the neurofeedback testing.

The professionalism of the design, testimonials, and reviews from well-regarded publications like *The New York Times* lent added credibility to the product. But ultimately, all that would be required for Ellen and the president to approve of Cam taking these pills was Dr. Gleason's endorsement.

Satisfied with a job well done, Karen closed and locked the cabinet, and returned to Gleason's office. She put the key back in the desk drawer exactly where she'd found it.

She was on her way out when a figure materialized in the doorway. Karen froze. She tried to take in a breath, but the air seemed to have left her lungs. A cold, terrifying chill swept through her.

"What the hell are you doing here, Karen?"

No thoughts came to her. No excuses like the one she gave Duffy popped into her head.

"Dr. Gleason, I'm sorry about this."

"Again, what are you doing in my office, Karen?"

Fred Gleason had on a suit and tie, but his workday was long over. *What is Fred doing here?* Probably checking up on Cam, Karen realized. She had been careless. Of course Dr. Gleason might have been on the premises. His charge was still recovering from surgery.

"I had some work to do, and I got a terrible, terrible headache. I was hoping there might have been some Advil in the clinic. I'm sorry, I should have called."

She sounded sincere, but she could read the skepticism in Gleason's eyes. She clutched her purse with the supplements inside close to her side.

"Did you touch my computer?"

Gleason's rage was palpable.

Confusion sparked on Karen's face. "No, no, I told you. I needed something for my headache."

Gleason closed the gap between him and Karen in a blink. He did not get right in her face, but got close enough for her to want him to take a step or two back.

"I'll ask you again." Gleason's eyes became slits, his shoulders going back as his chin jutted forward, the posture entirely threatening. "Did you look at my computer for any reason?"

Karen glanced behind her, where the computer was, and only now realized that the monitor resting atop his desk was aglow, a screensaver displayed. But no, she had never touched his computer, and said as much.

"I'm sorry for being here, Fred, honest I am, but my head was killing me."

Gleason held a menacing stare for several beats.

"Don't ever come in here again without my permission," he eventually said, "or by God, I swear I'll have you fired."

Karen slipped past him and Gleason let her go without so much as offering her an aspirin.

CHAPTER 27

Lee had no idea if Susie Banks would be awake or asleep when he arrived at the MDC at seven thirty on Friday night, though he did know she'd been transferred from the ICU on 6 to the medical floor on 5. His heart ached for all her suffering. *Has she had any visitors? Is someone making arrangements for her parents' funerals?* Hopefully someone was hard at work trying to locate the right people to care for her. The doctors and nurses could see to Susie's physical recovery, but the wounds she had suffered went far beyond anything medicine alone could cure.

Lee made his way along several quiet corridors en route to the elevator bay. After the sun went down, a certain hush settled over the hospital, and tonight was no exception. Plenty of foot traffic was about, but the pace had downshifted to a noticeably lower gear.

Lee liked it here at this hour. Hell, he liked it here at any hour. Medicine may have become a terrible business, but it was a calling he would do for free if he could afford it. His father would have done the same.

He rode the elevator alone, reminding himself to keep it brief for Susie's sake. Later, he would try to find the name of the social worker assigned to her case, assuming the assignment had been made.

Another thought came to him. If the eye exam he planned on giving Cam revealed a cherry-red spot on his macula, Lee would have to align himself quickly with Susie's primary care physician. A medical mystery connecting the president's kid to other gifted students attending the TPI would send shock waves through Washington and beyond. Lee had to brace himself for the coming tsunami, and that meant getting to Susie's doctor before Gleason had the opportunity.

Thoughts of Gleason made Lee think of Karen. He wondered how she had made out. By now, if everything had gone to plan, she should have secured samples of the nootropics Cam was taking. An itch of worry raced up his neck. *She's fine,* he assured himself. Karen was always fine. But he wondered. Was he telling himself this, or trying to convince himself of it?

The elevator came to a bouncing stop and Lee got out. He waved his badge in front of the card reader, unlocking the secured doors to the medical floor. Having admitting privileges granted Lee full access to the MDC's many units.

To Lee's left were the hospital rooms, and to his right were stretchers and wheelchairs. A set of portable oxygen tanks stood near the curved nurses' station.

Lee waved to the nurse in floral scrubs seated behind the desk. Other nurses popped in and out of rooms like whack-a-moles, appearing and disappearing at random intervals. Down the hall a tired-looking nurse with hunched shoulders, dressed in blue scrubs, a stethoscope clasped tightly around his neck, came toward Lee with his face buried in a medical chart. Lee had his eyes peeled for Susie's room and the two almost collided in front of the nurses' station. Were it not for Lee's fast and fancy footwork, they would have.

"Sorry, sorry!" Lee called out, leaping to one side.

The nurse made a startled noise and apologized as well. The brief commotion caught the attention of a repairman farther down the hall, a small ladder slung over his shoulder. He was walking toward the stairwell exit at the opposite end of the long hallway. A flicker of recognition came to Lee and he tried to place the man with blond hair and a thick mustache. He thought he'd seen him before, when Susie was up on the ICU. A repairman on both floors where Susie was a patient nagged at Lee, but he pushed that thought from his mind to make room for other considerations.

Lee glanced at the repairman as he walked away. Nothing about his behavior was suspicious, and yet . . .

He noticed the man wore blue sterile hospital gloves, not the heavy-duty kind he would have expected a workman to need.

"Is the heat turned down in 5-H?" the nurse in blue scrubs asked. "It was a terrarium in there last I checked."

"Maintenance fixed it a few minutes ago," the other nurse answered.

"Excuse me, I'm looking for Susie Banks's room," Lee said, interrupting.

"And you are?"

The nurse in floral screwed up her face. The medical floor did not receive many house calls after hours.

"I'm Dr. Lee Blackwood, a hospitalist assigned to Susie's case."

He said this with the same authority as before, and again, got no pushback. Hospitalists were a common practice these days, so his coming to see Susie, even at this hour, had a logical explanation.

Lee took another glance at the repairman, who was walking slowly toward the exit. Again it was probably nothing, but the encounter irritated him for some reason, like the steady ping of radar going off, a sound letting him know something was there. But what?

At that moment, alarms started to sound. The nurse in floral scrubs studied the telemetry monitors before her.

"She's in 5-H. Speaking of Susie, her vitals just took a little dip." The duty nurse spoke in the flat voice of someone accustomed to vitals dipping all the time. Lee's internal radar pinged louder when he glanced again at the repairman, walking a bit faster than before.

First maintenance fixed a heat problem in Susie's room and now there's a sudden dip in her vitals?

The gas exposure was already suspect in Lee's mind, and this repairman, his presence here and before, congealed to form a worrying picture.

Did he do something to her?

The repairman moved along, stepladder slung over his right shoulder.

"Hey!" Lee called out to him. "Wait a second, please." Lee wanted him to stop before he disappeared down those stairs.

Instead of stopping, the repairman quickened his strides. Lee started after him in a trot that soon became a run. He paused to glance into

Susie's room and saw clusters of nurses gathered around her bed, doing what needed to be done.

Lee hurried his steps. Susie was in capable hands and he had questions needing answers, but the repairman was at the exit now.

"Hold a moment!"

Lee's voice boomed down the hall.

The repairman glanced back, and the man's icy blue eyes flared before they cooled. He tossed the full weight of his body (considerable weight, too; all muscle, Lee speculated) against the exit door's metal push bar, letting the stepladder fall off his shoulder and clatter noisily to the ground. The door swung shut and Lee lost sight of the man.

Worried he'd lose him entirely in the stairwell, Lee raced ahead, feeling tightness in his knees and chest. "Stop!" he yelled, sounding a bit winded.

Without slowing, Lee leapt over the discarded stepladder to hit the push bar with both hands. The door sprung open with force and Lee stumbled off-kilter into an echoing concrete stairwell. From below, he heard the sound of fast-moving footsteps, already two or three floors below.

Lee descended the first set of stairs like a slalom skier bounding down a slope. As he approached the landing, he leapt several stairs to gain ground on his fast-moving quarry. Airborne, he misjudged the distance and had only a second to brace for impact before slamming into an unforgiving cement wall. His shoulder took the brunt of the blow before he ricocheted off. A rush of adrenaline swallowed the sharp pain.

Reorienting himself, Lee repeated the same speedy descent to the next landing, and to the one after that, trying not to focus on the repairman's footsteps beating an even faster retreat. The urge to get upstairs and check on Susie was hard to resist. He pushed ahead, paying no mind to the gap between him and the repairman.

Two floors from the bottom, Lee heard the exit door bang shut. Dismayed, he knew there was no way to catch the repairman now, but he went to the bottom anyway. There he paused, hands on his knees, panting to catch his breath. Soon, he was moving toward the exit, thinking he'd make a quick check of the first-floor hallway, when a gruff voice spoke to him from behind.

"Hey, guy."

Lee turned and came face-to-face with the repairman. He must have opened and closed the exit door to make Lee think he had gone. Without another word, the repairman uncorked a punch to Lee's chest, just below the midline. The blow turned his vision white as he fell to his knees.

A gauzy film descended over Lee's eyes, but he could still see the repairman lift one of his big black work boots. His body tensed, fearing a devastating strike to his side. A tattoo on the repairman's muscled forearm came into sudden and sharp focus. A skull head wearing a spiked helmet appeared to be grinning right at Lee.

Instead of giving him a steel toe to the ribs, the repairman placed his boot on Lee's back, applied pressure, and pushed him to the floor. Lee turned his head to the side. Air, blessed air, had finally begun to work its way down his throat.

"I don't like doctors and I don't like being chased," the man said in a raspy voice. He kept his boot on Lee's back. "You try following me, and I'll kill you."

The repairman stepped over Lee. The stairwell door opened and closed. Just like that, he was gone.

Eventually, Lee managed to get to his hands and knees, his breathing still severely compromised. Gripping the banister for support, Lee pulled himself to a standing position. He checked the hall. The repairman was gone. He took out his phone to call security as he started up the stairs to check on Susie. There was still time to hunt the repairman down. As he climbed higher he heard a strange, muffled sound from above— screaming, he thought. He climbed higher. The voice sounded familiar, and if he was right, Susie Banks was in terrible agony.

Lee put his phone away. There was no time for phone calls. He had to get back upstairs, had to help, do anything and everything he could. Whatever the repairman had done to Susie, it was not going to hurt her.

It was going to kill her.

CHAPTER 28

Lee felt as if a sledgehammer had bludgeoned his chest. He struggled up each step, moving as quickly as his rubbery legs would allow. Eventually, he returned to the bright lights and harsh glare of the medical floor. The antiseptic odors acted like smelling salts, bringing him more fully back to his senses. He rushed toward Susie's room, battling for balance. Orderlies, visitors—basically, anyone not confined to a bed—lurked in the hallway, listening to Susie's primal screams.

The scene inside Susie's room was utter chaos. On her bed, the girl thrashed about wildly. Not only had she pulled out the leads to her monitors, she had managed to rip out her IV as well. Blood spurted from the open vein, splattering the floor and spraying the white hospital sheets crimson. Nurses moved quickly to get the bleeding under control.

A nurse heroically managed to reattach Susie's IV, but the floor was now slick with blood. The room warmed with the heat of many bodies. Nurses gathered around Susie's bedside, fighting what appeared to be a losing effort to keep her limbs contained. She wanted out of her bed, out of this hospital, and was willing to do anything to break away from those attempting to hold her down.

"Let me go!" she screamed. "They're crawling all over my legs!"

She unleashed a bloodcurdling yell.

Surveying the room, he noticed no white lab coats present. Everyone here was a nurse. As if to put an exclamation mark on his observation, the nurse in blue scrubs, the one Lee had almost knocked over, cried out, "Dammit, page Dr. Rajit again. We need him here, STAT!"

Lee stepped forward.

"I'm a doctor at the MDC," he announced. "I'll take over until Dr. Rajit arrives."

One of the nurses recognized Lee and nodded vigorously, encouraging him to take charge. Susie's agitation was intensifying—a funnel cloud forming into a tornado.

"Get them off me! Get them off! I hate spiders!"

Susie shrieked while violently brushing her arms and legs, as if arachnids actually were crawling on her limbs.

"Susie, sweetheart, you need to calm down. There's nothing on you."

The nurse, a dark-haired, stout woman, had managed to pin Susie's arms to her sides using significant force. Susie fought hard to free herself, and when that failed, tried to get one leg over the bed rail so she could climb out.

"They're biting!" She yelled as if in extreme pain, staring at her legs with horror in her eyes. She was seeing something though nothing was there.

What are these hallucinations all about? Lee wondered. He knew it was not a symptom of CO poisoning. Could it be a bizarre reaction to a medication? Or did the repairman do something to cause her delusions?

"They're all over me," Susie whimpered, her body convulsing as she bucked and writhed in an effort to rid herself of these imaginary creatures.

"What's been her status?" Lee asked. Basically, he wanted to know what had happened during his footrace with the repairman.

"This! This has been her status!" The nurse holding Susie's arms sounded exasperated. "We've tried reasoning with her, but she's completely delirious."

Crazed is more like it, thought Lee. He had seen *The Exorcist* plenty of times, and the way Susie flailed and contorted was terrifyingly reminiscent of the film.

"They're in my ears! I feel them crawling in my ears! Biting me!"

Susie's bloodcurdling scream caused several nurses to jump.

"No, nothing is biting you, sweetheart." The stout nurse did her best to sound reassuring.

No good. If anything, Susie's paroxysms intensified. Sweat glistened against her pale skin. She was warm to the touch, probably febrile, but no one could get a temp on her just yet.

"We need to restrain her, right now," Lee said.

He spoke in a commanding voice, but tried not to sound overly aggressive. He had to keep everyone calm. Or maybe he was trying to keep himself calm. A flutter of nervousness came and went. He'd been a resident the last time he triaged a patient in crisis. On a daily basis Lee dealt with sore throats, fussy kids, odd ailments; not what appeared to be delirium tremors on steroids.

Lee joined three other nurses in holding down each of Susie's limbs, while another nurse lashed restraints onto the metal bed frame. Susie resisted with the strength of a wrestler escaping a pin. She arched her back, bucked her hips, and swiveled violently from side to side, all while groaning and shrieking incoherently. With Lee's help, the team won the battle and got her secured. Thick fabric straps, impossible to rip, bound her wrists and ankles.

"Is she on any new medications?" Lee asked.

"No," a nurse replied, as she worked to reapply the leads for the telemetry monitors.

"Has her blood sugar been stable?"

"Stable," another nurse said. "But she's anuric."

Indeed, the bag used for collecting and measuring urine output through the Foley catheter that had been inserted into Susie's bladder was empty.

"Forty milligrams furosemide. Increase the IV to one fifty cc's per hour. D-five normal. How about renal function?"

"BUN thirty-six, creatinine two point eight," a nurse said.

"K?" Lee said, meaning potassium.

"Five point one."

Borderline, but likely on its way up too, thought Lee. Any higher could mean a potential fatal cardiac arrhythmia. Trouble. But what was doing all this?

Susie grunted and groaned, then violently rolled her head from side to side.

"Please, please, they're in my hair, they're crawling toward my eyes—please—" Her voice had softened to a whimper.

"Haloperidol five milligrams," Lee ordered, hoping that would stop the hallucinations. "Got those leads back on?"

"Almost there," a nurse replied, her voice a bit breathless.

The monitor showed Susie's heart racing at 160 beats per minute. There were frequent premature beats, PVCs. Her BP was 176 over 112, way too high, but not high enough to worry about an imminent brain hemorrhage.

"Labetalol twenty milligrams," Lee called out. "Then start a drip at two per minute. Get a twelve-lead ECG."

They had to get her BP down.

"Temp's one oh two point four," shouted one of the nurses.

"Get me a tox screen, and blood cultures. And a stat thyroid panel. Repeat her chemistries and CBC. Let's check blood gases."

Lee paused to review the cardiogram. Brief runs of ventricular tachycardia. The T-waves were inverted in the inferior leads, worrisome for myocardial ischemia, a heart attack. In a nineteen-year-old? He felt baffled.

Why was this girl acutely delirious? He needed answers, but those would have to wait.

Susie's bucking and thrashing had finally begun to subside. She gazed unblinking at the overhead fluorescent lighting. The haloperidol and restraints were doing the job.

At that moment, a team of doctors burst into her cubicle. The one of Indian descent, who a nurse identified as Dr. Rajit, glared at Lee.

"Who are you?"

He did not sound pleased.

"Dr. Lee Blackwood, I'm with the MDC. I was here to speak with Susie when she crashed."

Dr. Rajit's eyes widened, his body tensing as he readied for a confrontation. "Speak with her? What on earth for?"

The answer would have to wait. Susie's back arched as her limbs stiffened. She moaned loudly, a strange wounded noise that escaped her pale lips just before her face turned crimson. She started to tremble, imperceptibly at first, and then with larger synchronous jerks. The restraints kept her from hitting herself.

"She's seizing!"

"Get anesthesia in here! We've got to intubate!" Dr. Rajit yelled the order, sending the nurse closest to the door scrambling for the phone.

Turning Susie's head to one side, Lee prevented her from aspirating the foaming saliva into her lungs. *Could anything more go wrong?*

"Two milligrams lorazepam IV and load her with fosphenytoin IV. What's her weight?" Lee asked.

"Forty-nine kilos," a nurse replied.

"Okay. Eight hundred milligrams phenytoin equivalents at one hundred per minute. Now!"

Dr. Rajit nodded at Lee. He would have ordered the same.

Susie's seizure subsided quickly, but in a matter of minutes she was yelling out again, pulling at her restraints, talking about spiders.

"Let's get her sedated," Lee said. "Start her on a ketamine drip. Labs back yet?"

Suddenly, Dr. Rajit seemed blindsided by Lee's orders. "Dammit, this is my patient!" he growled at Lee. "And who ordered labs?"

"Dr. Blackwood did," a nurse said.

Lee returned a slight shrug before ordering an increased dosage of haloperidol, which seemed to quiet Susie down.

Before anesthesia arrived, the labs came back. A nurse read the results.

"BUN forty-eight, creatinine four point six."

Lee did a double take. Her creatinine was rising too rapidly, crazily so, from two point eight to four point six. He had never seen anything like this. It made no sense.

"Her blood gases show a metabolic acidosis," one of the residents intoned. "PH seven point ten."

"It's got to be lactic acidosis," Lee said. "Give her two amps of bicarb in the IV."

"I'm still confused. Is this your patient, Dr. Blackwood?" Dr. Rajit's eyes bored into Lee.

"Listen, Dr. Rajit, you're a resident, right?" Lee made the guess solely based on Rajit's young-looking face.

"Yes, so?"

"Where's the intensivist on call?"

"Dr. Sears is in the surgical ICU," Dr. Rajit said. "I've got this."

"I'm sure you do," Lee said. "But I'm an attending here at MDC. I've got the experience to help you. Let me help. Please. This patient—she's—she's very important to me."

For a moment, Lee was not sure which way Dr. Rajit would go. Was he another Gleason? To his relief, Lee got the consent he wanted.

The anesthesiologist, a silver-haired man with wire-rimmed glasses, stormed into Susie's room. A female resident pushing the anesthesia cart, along with a nurse anesthetist, came in soon after.

"I'm Dr. Cochran," said the anesthesiologist. "And what's happening here?"

Lee summarized the essentials. Dr. Cochran listened while giving Susie 100 percent oxygen through an Ambu breathing mask.

"I've given her ketamine, one hundred milligrams," Lee said.

Dr. Cochran nodded his approval while he extended Susie's neck to advance the laryngoscope over the back of the tongue and epiglottis. He worked the tube beyond her vocal cords, inflated the cuff to ensure a seal, and listened for breath sounds through his stethoscope.

"Sounds good," he said. "Let's get a portable chest to confirm the tube's placed right."

And with that, Susie finally appeared to be resting comfortably. All it took was giving her ketamine, getting her anesthetized, and then putting on a ventilator.

Lee noted Susie's temp was still high, at 101.6. Her blood pressure was also elevated at 160 over 110, and her heart rate still too fast, at 140 beats per minute, with frequent ectopic premature beats.

"Let's increase the labetalol," Lee said. "Start her on a drip, fifty milligrams per min. Dr. Rajit, you concur?"

The young resident looked as though he had just leapt from a moving train.

"Yes, yes, of course," he said.

Blood still had to be cleaned off the floor. The nurses would have to change their clothes, their sneakers, too.

The room was a total mess.

At least Susie's ECG showed normalization of those inverted T-waves.

"CK-MB and troponin levels normal, Dr. Blackwell."

"Let's get another serum creatinine test," Lee said. A normal jump might be one point per *day* for someone in kidney distress. Susie's had gone up more than that in under an hour. Lee had never heard of a patient whose levels had risen so rapidly.

A nurse administered the serum test while Lee kept close watch. A shocked expression came to her face as she read the results.

"Her creatinine level is nine point oh."

Lee's mouth fell open.

Impossible.

"We've got to get her to the ICU, get her on dialysis STAT! Now! Now!"

Orderlies, nurses, gathered around and rushed Susie out of the room, headed for the elevator to take them to the ICU one floor above. The critical care physicians, with the help of the radiologist, would get her started on dialysis before her creatinine levels shot up to the point of no return.

Lee watched Susie get wheeled away, wondering if her kidney failure could be related to her other symptoms—the ones she and Cam had in common. He desperately wanted those tox screen results. It was certainly a possibility the repairman had injected Susie with something to manifest her delusions; exactly what, he could not say. But he doubted the tox report would explain the sudden and alarming rise of Susie's creatinine levels.

Nothing in medicine Lee knew of could do that.

CHAPTER 29

Lee visited the ICU to instruct Susie's doctors and nurses not to allow her any visitors. While he doubted the repairman would return, Lee knew there was a chance he could. It was a risk trusting the staff to keep a vigilant watch, given how patients on this floor were in constant crisis. A discomforting image of the repairman slipping into Susie's ICU cubicle with the stealth of a serpent made him shiver. Maybe he'd return as an orderly, or a doctor, or even a hospital security guard. Lee believed anything was possible.

When he returned to the medical unit, Lee counted six members of the MDC security team roaming the floor. These were not rent-a-cops. They wore light blue shirts with shiny badges pinned to their breast pockets, dark neckties, and dark slacks. Most were armed like patrol officers.

Joining the investigation were two police officers from the MPD—D.C.'s Metropolitan Police Department. They were fit-looking young guys, early thirties, who were treating this as a straightforward case of assault and battery. Depending on what the tox screen revealed, the police might have to upgrade the alleged crime to attempted murder.

As it was, these two cops were taking statements and making every effort to gather evidence. Forensics was coming to get fingerprints, even though Lee told the police the man had been wearing gloves. In the description Lee gave, he made sure to call out the tattoo of a skull wearing a spiked helmet on the man's forearm. He offered to work with a sketch artist, and was told it might be arranged.

"What about security cameras?" Lee asked.

"We're looking into it," the shorter of the MPD cops said.

Lee understood. It was going to take time to scrutinize the security footage, speak to all potential witnesses, and do whatever was required to track down the repairman. All the while, Lee believed Susie's mystery illness would continue to confound her doctors.

The more Lee pondered, the more Susie's rapid spike in creatinine levels puzzled him. A jump like hers should have taken days, weeks, or even months, not hours. These MPD officers were not the ones to confide in regarding a possible connection to the Stewart twins' suspicious car accident, Susie's equally suspicious CO exposure, and potential links to the TPI and Cam Hilliard. They were too low-level and it was all too nebulous, too much conjecture.

What Lee needed was hard evidence. Looking in Cam's eyes using an ophthalmoscope was the new priority. Cam's body could be a ticking bomb as well.

Having found an empty chair behind the nurses' station, a respite from all the commotion, Lee sipped at a ginger ale on ice while awaiting Karen's arrival. With his adrenaline rush subsiding, he became acutely aware of how much his body ached. His chest where he took the punch, legs, lungs, everything hurt.

Lee called the ICU, forgetting his last check-in was fifteen minutes ago. With luck the IVs would flush out most of the toxin, allowing Susie to come off the ventilator. He was eager to find out what had made her see spiders, naturally, and footsteps down the hall told him the answer was on the way.

Dr. Rajit approached in lockstep with the intensivist, Dr. Sears, a woman Lee had met only recently. Her sallow skin tone and tangle of hair escaping a loosely held bun hinted at too many hours spent in the hospital. Lee rose from his seat and greeted them in the hallway.

"We got the results from the tox screen," Dr. Rajit said.

"And?"

"And Susie Banks suffered from massive methamphetamine toxicity. It certainly would explain her hallucinations. There was enough drug in her system to kill a horse. I have no idea how you managed to save that girl."

Lee had no idea either. All he did was follow established procedures, nothing special. He wondered if the unexplainable spike in Susie's creatinine levels had somehow acted as a buffer against the narcotic. Did it also help her to survive the CO exposure that killed her parents?

"Has security made any progress tracking down this mysterious repairman?" Dr. Sears asked.

"No, but I suspect detectives will be brought in now," Lee said. "Please, make sure you get this report to them ASAP. And Dr. Rajit—"

"Yes?"

"I want to thank you for letting me help with Susie Banks. Dr. Sears, you should know it was a most unusual situation and Dr. Rajit handled himself admirably and professionally. I'm sure the police will be eager to talk with you both. If you'll excuse me, I have to go."

Lee shook their hands, making a fast exit, because behind them he saw Karen, still in her wall jumper outfit, flashing a badge to the security team guarding the entrance to the medical floor. Tension seared her face.

Lee led Karen to the waiting room, where they could speak in private. He went into details about his confrontation with the repairman and Susie's crazed hallucinations.

"She was injected with what should have been a fatal dose of methamphetamine," Lee said. "This repairman tried to kill her. No doubt about it."

"How's she doing now?" Karen asked.

"Stable," said Lee. "They moved her to the ICU. I've told the staff no other visitors."

"Good call," Karen said.

"I'm just glad my emergency medicine training came back to me. Otherwise I might not have been able to save her."

Karen's expression became strained. "You're sure there's a connection between Susie and Cam?"

"I think a lot of evidence points that way."

"And these Stewart twins, their deaths no longer seem accidental to you, do they?"

"No, they don't," Lee said. "Where are you going with this?"

"If Cam's connected to Susie, and Susie to the twins, doesn't it stand to reason that Cam could be a target, as well?"

Lee returned a grim nod of agreement. "You have those brain pills?" he asked.

"Getting them wasn't the best moment of my day, but yes, I've got them."

"Good. Let's get to the White House. Now."

"Why?"

"Because I want to shine a light into Cam's eyes. If there's a red spot on his macula, like there is on Susie's, it might as well be a laser pointer from a sniper rifle."

CHAPTER 30

Lee and Karen shared an Uber to the White House, which they exited nine dollars poorer. Lee was actually two hundred and nine dollars poorer, because he had slipped a security guard all he had in his wallet in exchange for a promise to keep an extra-close eye on Susie.

"You realize someone could pay a lot more money than two hundred bucks to do something other than keep a close watch," Karen said.

"Don't remind me," Lee answered glumly.

At the Pennsylvania Avenue security checkpoint, Lee was asked for identification. Phone calls had already been made, chains of events set in motion, which allowed Lee to enter the White House compound with little hassle.

Karen led Lee through the West Wing entrance to the clinic where the Hilliards, Cam, and Gleason all were waiting. Agent Duffy stood nearby, along with other members of the Secret Service. With the president downstairs, they needed to be a presence.

Everyone was dressed casually, including the president, who had on a navy polo shirt, dark jeans, and loafers. This was a side of the White House few ever saw. These were normal people, Lee realized, leading a truly extraordinary life. They may have been the first family, but right now it was family first.

Karen took Cam into the waiting room, so Lee could get everyone up to speed without alarming him. He started off explaining the possible medical connections between Susie and Cam—seizure activity, enlarged organs, abnormal liver function tests—and concluded with the cherry-red spot in Susie's eye, the big mystery.

"That can be a symptom of CO exposure, or were you not aware?" Dr. Gleason's tone carried some bite.

"I am well aware, thank you," Lee said. "But it is also a rare symptom. Which is why this eye exam is so important. If Cam has a red spot, it may suggest that the origin of Susie's spot is something other than carbon monoxide."

"Such as?" Dr. Gleason's arms refused to uncross.

"Such as whatever enlarged Cam's spleen and made him susceptible to splenic rupture, or caused his nocturnal seizures, or gave him abnormal liver function." Lee's voice was steady. "It's everything I just talked about. I don't know what exactly is causing these symptoms, and until I do, I suggest Cam stop taking any medication, supplements—anything other than what we've prescribed for his seizures. We need to be extremely cautious."

Lee also needed to tread lightly, at least until he got those nootropics tested. If that red spot was there, as Lee believed it would be, talk could turn to protecting Susie and Cam from outside threats. *But how do you protect a patient from his doctor?*

For now, Gleason was untouchable. Outlandish accusations might lead to Karen's dismissal, and that could put Cam in grave danger. She needed to stay near him, continue to serve as his protector.

"Now there's something more you need to know," Lee said to the group.

He told them about the repairman, his fight in the stairwell, and Susie's close call with death.

"Somebody tried to kill this girl?" Ellen sounded horrified.

"I believe this repairman tried to kill Susie at her home, and when that didn't go as planned, he struck again at the hospital."

Ellen shook her head in shock and disbelief.

"That poor, poor girl," she said, her voice brimming with emotion. "And nobody knows who assaulted her, or why?"

"No," Lee said. "There are a lot of police at the hospital right now, but it's a short-term measure. They're watching over the entire facility, not just Susie."

"Why on earth are they doing that? The attack was on Susie."

Ellen sounded incredulous and more than a little angry. Lee explained what the police had told him: Susie had never taken out a restraining order against a violent boyfriend; no one in the Banks family had ever reported receiving threats of any kind. Susie was the victim of a crime, but the motive and suspect were both unknowns. Since there was nobody for the authorities to detain, the heightened police presence was meant to deter the attacker from making a brazen return for a second strike against another random target.

"It hardly seems random to me," said Ellen, who seemed to share Lee's frustration. "If there's anything I can do for her, please, please let me know."

"There's actually more to the story," Lee said. He told them about the Stewart twins.

"And these twin boys had seizures similar to the ones Susie Banks suffered?" President Hilliard's paternal instincts came through clearly.

"And they died in an accidental way, which might have happened to Susie if she hadn't escaped from her house," Lee added. "Honestly, I can't explain how she survived either attack. It could have something to do with what's happening inside her body. We just don't know."

"Is Cam in any danger?" The president's stare was harder than stone.

"Sir, I can't say for sure," Lee said. "I'm only telling you the facts as I know them."

Almost all of the facts, he thought, eyeing Gleason.

Ellen's concern and worry were palpable.

"I'll speak with Karen," the president said to his wife. "We'll increase the size of Cam's Secret Service detail. Nothing is going to happen to him. He's the most protected child in the country. But this theory of yours, Lee, if I understand correctly, is predicated on Cam having the same red spots in his eyes as this girl does? Otherwise, their issues might not be connected after all."

The president impressed Lee with his quick understanding.

"If the red spot is in Susie and not in Cam, I'll have to assume her spots are the result of carbon monoxide exposure."

Gleason uncrossed his arms and approached Lee. "And what if Cam doesn't have this spot, Dr. Blackwood? What then? Can we agree at this point to stop worrying the president and first lady? Because that's what you're doing here."

"No, we cannot," Lee said firmly. "Because regardless there's something wrong with Cam. His moodiness isn't what made his internal organs larger."

"Back to the girl," Gleason said. "Susie Banks. If there's no red spot, does that mean there's no connection between them?"

"I can't say that for certain. There are symptomatic similarities in the four children who have a shared connection to the TPI," Lee said.

"How similar, Lee?" Gleason said. "Cam doesn't have myoclonus jerks like these other three."

"We don't know if that's actually true," Lee said. "They could be happening while he's asleep."

"Right. Those seizures of his that we've yet to prove he has." Gleason's voice was sharp. "Keep stretching, Lee, and eventually you'll figure out a way to make it all fit. Isn't that what people say about statistics? You can make them say anything, including the truth. The bottom line is that Cam isn't on dialysis. His creatinine levels are perfectly normal. Slight enlargement of the organs could be something viral or bacterial, something we can treat. But when we reviewed the EEG, it's inconclusive, and you put him on a medication with a host of side effects to treat his excessive tiredness in the morning—which by the way, is symptomatic of depression.

"Now, I'll grant you that we need to get to the bottom of his liver function and slight organ enlargement, but nothing you've said has steered me away from my original diagnosis of some form of depression. Perhaps there's something viral we haven't found in the blood work taking a toll on his mood. Perhaps. But in no way will I embrace the notion of some sort of murder conspiracy involving Cam and his TPI associates. Your imagination is truly a wondrous thing, but just because someone wanted to do away with Susie Banks doesn't mean there's any connection to a tragic car accident or to Cam."

"The clustering around the TPI is more than a little unusual," said Lee.

"Why do you say that? Did the twins have this red spot in their eyes? Enlarged organs?"

"No, only the severe myoclonus as far as I know," Lee admitted. "They weren't tested for any of the other symptoms."

Gleason shook his head in disgust. "What you're doing, Lee, is making it difficult for me to properly treat the boy, and that—that is my greatest concern, and the reason I have been vocally opposed to your involvement from the very start."

President Hilliard cleared his throat, and that got everyone's attention.

"Lee, I appreciate what you're trying to do for us," the president said, taking Ellen's hand. "But Dr. Gleason is right. What you've stated is quite outlandish. I'm worried we're missing the bigger point here, which is what to do for Cam. If there's no red spot in his eye, some definitive way to tie him to this girl—well, I'm honestly more inclined to focus on what Dr. Gleason has told us from the get-go.

"Ellen wants Cam on the new medication you've prescribed, and I'm fine with that, for now, but as for the rest, well, murders and whatnot, until there is proof, I'll have a hard time seeing how any of it is related to my son."

"I believe wholeheartedly that Susie Banks's life is in grave danger," Lee said. "I was physically assaulted by the man who injected her with methamphetamine."

"I've no doubt that it happened, Lee," the president responded. "But I'm responsible for the country and for my family, not for one girl who is being stalked. I feel for her, I honestly do. But without some direct, irrefutable connection to Cam, her situation is a matter for the local authorities, not the federal government, and certainly not the president.

"For Cam's sake, I want to keep his life as normal as possible. The World Junior Chess Championships are three months away, and Cam needs to train diligently if he has any shot of winning."

Lee's eyebrows rose, but he held back, said nothing about Taylor being first alternate. He was on shaky enough ground and things would get more complicated if Lee voiced suspicions about the TPI nootropics and Gleason's possible involvement.

"Obviously, Cam's health issues come before chess," the president said. "But I know he wants to compete, and I don't want to give him unnecessary reasons to be concerned. So, please do check for that red spot,

Dr. Blackwood, but as for Cam's ongoing medical treatment, I'm going to defer now to Dr. Gleason, unless—unless I'm given a *very* compelling reason to do otherwise.

"And as for Miss Banks's unfortunate situation, she's a private citizen and needs to be cared for within the system—*unless,* again, I have a compelling reason to do otherwise. I don't mean this as a putdown, Dr. Blackwood, but I've learned, as president, there comes a time when decisions must be made. And I believe now is that time. Ellen, since this involves Cam, your opinion carries equal weight here."

Ellen hesitated. "Yes, of course. It all sounds logical to me."

Lee sensed the first lady was holding back, but he was not about to put her on the spot.

Lee nodded solemnly. "Very well then," he said. "I guess I better have a look in Cam's eyes."

CHAPTER 31

Moments later, Cam sat on the edge of the exam table with his parents nearby. He was understandably edgy.

"Do you know a girl named Susie Banks from the TPI, a violin player, a good one at that?" Lee asked.

Cam thought it over and gave a nod. "Yeah, I know her," he said. "Not well. She's older. But I've seen her around."

Lee explained what he'd seen in Susie's eyes and how her medical situation could be connected to his. To answer that question he'd need to take a look in Cam's eyes.

"Is it going to hurt?"

"No," Lee said, "but I do have to dilate your eyes to get a better look at the retina."

"What if there is a spot?" Cam's voice quavered a little.

"One step at a time," Lee said. *But what would happen?* He shuddered at the thought. Lee would be proven right, Gleason proven wrong, the president would have a compelling reason to act, and Susie Banks would be taken into the protective care of the same people who watched after the first family. *What will happen if there's a red spot?*

Everything.

In his peripheral vision, Lee saw Ellen bite her lower lip. She was holding her husband's hand, and Lee wondered if she might be holding her breath as well.

Lee had brought the eye drops he needed from the hospital, even though chances were Dr. Gleason kept a stock at the clinic, stored in the same glass-fronted medicine cabinets where he kept those suspect TPI nootropics.

Dr. Gleason, perhaps tired of his backseat role, stepped forward. He placed a hand on Cam's shoulder.

"It will be a few hours of blurry vision and sensitivity to light because your pupils will be dilated from the drops," Gleason said.

Cam signaled his consent with a slight nod, but then did something rather odd. He shot Dr. Gleason a strange look, as if he knew something sinister about the man. Dr. Gleason's demeanor instantly turned frosty. *What's going on between him and Cam?* Lee wondered. Was Gleason angry because he thought the dilation was unnecessary, or was he worried about what it might reveal?

Lee cleared his throat and Gleason backed away.

"Look up," Lee said to Cam. He tugged at the skin below the right eyelid with a gloved hand, and placed the drops, phenylephrine hydrochloride, into Cam's eye. Cam winced. There was always some stinging, but nothing that lingered. Lee did the same to Cam's left eye.

"No online chess for a bit," said Lee.

Cam looked around the room, blinking rapidly as if trying to clear his vision. Lee retrieved the ophthalmoscope, a metal tube with an attached Xenon lamp, from the wall holder, and brought the instrument up to Cam's eye. Using an ophthalmoscope was one of the basics of clinical examination, so Lee was more than comfortable doing the procedure. First, he examined the optic nerve and great vessels, which all appeared normal.

"Look into the light, Cam."

He did so, and this brought the macula into sharp focus. Lee searched for an amorphous cherry-red area. He repeated the procedure in the other eye, moving the light around, probing—searching—but it was clear. No questioning his findings.

Lee moved the light away. He locked eyes with the president and first lady, his manner almost penitent.

"Well?" President Hilliard studied Lee intently.

Lee pursed his lips. Time to break the news.

"His eyes are good," Lee said. "All clear. No red spots."

A faint smile came to Dr. Gleason's face. Ellen and President Hilliard were clearly relieved. Part of Lee was relieved as well, because no doctor wanted their patient to be even sicker.

Unfortunately, the news also meant that Lee had just lost his best chance for protecting Susie Banks.

KAREN READ the mixed emotion on Lee's face. She understood the exam had changed everything.

"So, I'm okay?" Cam sounded relieved.

Even though his vision was blurred, he turned to Lee expectantly; he'd placed trust there, formed a relationship. This was what Lee did best: connect with his patients, make them feel valued and heard, take the time to listen, to show he cared. It was for this reason Karen had reached out to Lee in the first place.

"Buddy, I don't know," Lee said. "It's going to be up to Dr. Gleason to guide your care from here on out. I'll be available as consult anytime."

Cam leaned forward and whispered something in Lee's ear as Karen called Lapham and Duffy into the exam room.

"You need to bring Cam upstairs," she said. "He's had drops put in his eyes and can't see well."

Duffy helped Cam off the exam table. "Shaman fix you all up?" he asked.

"Shaman's my code name," Lee said, clarifying.

"I'm Bishop," said Cam.

Lee chuckled and his smile showed off the dimples Karen had fallen for so many years ago.

"Yeah, I know," Lee said. "I'll miss you, Bishop. If you're ever looking for a game of chess, you know how to reach me."

Karen heard it in Lee's voice—a little ache from knowing that most likely this would be the last time he and Cam ever spoke. In such a short time, Lee had grown fond of Bishop, which was no surprise. Cam was such a sweet, kindhearted boy. And yet, something was off between Cam and Dr. Gleason. Karen had noticed an odd exchange between them right before Lee's exam.

What did Cam whisper to Lee? Karen wondered.

Lee said his good-byes to the president and Dr. Gleason, with handshakes all around. Gleason gloated like a conquering gladiator, missing only a bloodstained sword clutched in his hand.

"Lee, you understand our need to put Cam under the care of a single person," the president said. "It's best for us all."

"Of course," said Lee. "It's been my pleasure to be of service, and as I said, I'm not going anywhere. I'm here for Dr. Gleason, if you're ever in need of a consult."

More handshaking, thanking, and that was it. It was done. Karen was asked to escort Lee out of the White House. Duffy and Lapham brought Cam back to his room. The president and first lady retreated to Gleason's office, where conversations about Cam's health would take place.

As for the TPI? There was one car accident and one girl being targeted by some mysterious assailant for unknown reasons, but there were no clear connections to Cam, nothing for anyone to latch onto. Unless, of course, the analysis of the compounds in those nootropics revealed something of consequence; something to tie all these disparate threads together.

Lee and Karen had just made it to the colonnade, walking together in silence, when the sound of footsteps from behind drew their attention. Ellen Hilliard came toward them, unaccompanied, in a hurry. Even though Cam had no red spot in his eyes, a worried look remained in hers.

"I'm glad I caught you," Ellen said to Lee, her breathing a bit labored. "You've done a lot for us, and I wanted to ask you something before you left."

"Anything, Mrs. Hilliard," Lee said. He caught himself. "Ellen."

"You don't think Cam not having those red spots in his eyes is conclusive proof of anything, do you?"

Karen could have guessed Lee's answer.

"No, I don't," Lee said. "But unless you can change your husband's mind, I don't think I'm someone he and Dr. Gleason wish to consult anymore."

"I can't change my husband's mind about much of anything. He plays it safe, Lee. You should know this about him. Dr. Gleason is safe. He's the known commodity, and well, your wild stories of murdered TPI students didn't help your case. I'm not saying I believe in your murder conspiracy theory, but I'm not willing to disbelieve it either. No matter how it seems, I've come to trust you as much as I've come to like you. There are too many strange coincidences for this to be nothing."

"What would you like me to do, Ellen? Your son is a fabulous kid, but he's not like my other patients. I can't just have my office manager call and make an appointment."

"What I want is for you to keep that girl safe," Ellen said. "If something happens to her, it could mean we lose a vital link to what's happening to Cam. I know that sounds cold, and judge me as you will, but if you think she's connected to what's wrong with my son, we can't let anything happen to her."

"If the president would help—"

"You heard Geoffrey just now. In his mind this is a local issue. But the girl needs an advocate, and unfortunately her parents can't do that job."

"What are you asking of me, Ellen?"

"I'm asking you to protect her the way a father would."

CHAPTER 32

Lee and Karen took an Uber back to the MDC. On the ride they discussed the nootropics.

"It's our last best shot of getting Hilliard back on our side," Lee said.

Karen fished the samples out of her purse. "Take them," she said, handing him the plastic bag with a collection of yellow, white, and brown pills. "Getting them wasn't exactly the best part of my day."

"I'll find a place to get these analyzed," Lee said, slipping the contents into the inside pockets of his blazer.

"What did Cam whisper to you back in the office?" Karen asked, suddenly remembering the odd exchange in Gleason's office.

"He said, 'Don't leave me. Gleason's a liar.'"

BACK AT the MDC, Karen and Lee headed to the sixth-floor ICU to check in on Susie. When they reached her cubicle, there was no sign of the security guard Lee had paid handsomely to keep watch.

Can't trust anybody but family to do the right thing, Karen thought.

"I'll call Josh," Karen said to Lee. "We'll get him to guard Susie for the night."

Susie could not voice her opinion either way. She was still ventilated and connected to a dialysis machine with two tubes, one taking blood from her body and the other putting it back in.

Lee reviewed her charts.

"Her vitals are stable. Heart rate and blood pressure both normal. Flow rates on her catheter are excellent, too, but her BUN and creatinine levels haven't come down substantially. Maybe her doctors could wean her off ventilation in a few hours, but she's not coming off dialysis anytime soon."

THIRTY MINUTES later, Lee and Karen were seated in a waiting room on the ICU floor with faded fabric armchairs and a coffee table papered with dog-eared magazines. Josh would be arriving soon. Lee had spoken with several nurses, and according to them there had been no luck locating Susie's next of kin. Ellen was right. The poor girl *was* truly alone.

"I'd sure like to get my hands on any TPI nootropics Susie may have been taking," Lee said.

"Maybe she can help us once she comes off the ventilator, but Lee, we've got to think about how we're going to keep her safe."

"You're the law enforcement expert. What do you think?"

"I think we should start by telling the police about the furnace, get them to investigate it for signs of tampering, but my guess is it's going to be hard to prove."

"A repairman who can fix things can also break them," Lee concurred. "Any chance of catching this guy?"

"While you were trying to find Susie's next of kin, I spoke with hospital security. Whoever attacked her knew how to avoid the cameras. I don't think they're going to be able to ID him."

"What about social services?" asked Lee. "Can they help with Susie?"

"Even though she's only nineteen, in the eyes of the law, Susie is an adult, so no. And the police can't take her into protective custody either. That's for federal trials."

"So the only thing we can do is deal with the next threat or incident when it occurs?" Lee sounded incredulous.

"That's about it," Karen said with a sigh. "The police presence here is going to drop off substantially by morning. We have to assume responsibility for Susie's safety starting now."

"And how should we do that?" Lee asked. "Should we look into hiring security?"

Karen leaned forward in her chair. "If we believe the same person who attacked Susie also sabotaged the furnace at her home, then we are dealing with an individual who is smart and extremely crafty. We could have

Susie moved to another hospital, but what if the killer returns? And what if he pays off one of our guards?"

"Or what if he's good enough to take those guards out?" Lee added.

"As long as Susie remains in a hospital, ensuring her safety will be tough. There are too many gaps for the repairman or some other hired gun to get through."

"What if we can track down a relative?"

"If *we* can track them down, so can the repairman," Karen said. "Which means anybody housing Susie—"

"Becomes a target," Lee said, finishing the grim thought for her. "I still can't believe Hilliard wouldn't put Susie and Cam into some kind of super protective custody." Anger rose in Lee's throat. "No offense to the Secret Service, but why not fly them somewhere safe until the police catch whoever is behind this?"

"What, like Camp David?" Karen said. "It's not going to happen, Lee. We've got to move on from there."

"Camp David." Lee's voice trailed off. Karen looked at him curiously.

"What are you thinking?" she asked.

"I'm thinking what if Susie wasn't in a hospital? If she's not in the system, nobody can find her. I don't care how good they are."

"But she's sick, Lee," Karen said. "Didn't you tell me she's going to need dialysis for a long time?"

"Right. She's sick. But her vitals are strong. Once her system is flushed, the only issue is her kidneys."

"I'm sorry, I'm not following," said Karen.

"There's no doubt in my mind that Susie is in danger," Lee said. "But bringing her to a relative, assuming we can even find one, puts them in danger. And keeping Susie in the city hospital leaves her vulnerable. But nobody can hurt her if they can't find her."

"And how do we make a patient disappear?" Karen asked. "She still needs treatment."

"She needs a nurse and a dialysis machine," Lee said.

"And a remote place to set up that equipment," Karen added, getting it now.

"You said it yourself, the president has a camp," Lee said. "And we do, too. It's very private. Very remote. We'll move Susie to one of the cabins.

I'll get a portable dialysis machine and all the supplies we'll need to keep her healthy, easy enough. All I need to do is hire a nurse to care for her."

"I have some vacation time saved up."

Lee raised a quizzical eyebrow. "Meaning?"

"Meaning, I'm sure the first lady wouldn't mind my using those vacation days to spend a little quality time at the camp."

"Well, now," he said, smiling, "if it's a bodyguard we need, who better than the Secret Service?"

LEE SPENT most of the next morning on the phone getting everything organized. Josh had kept a vigilant watch over Susie, given up a night's sleep to do so, and canceled the camp plans with his pals, all without complaint. He said he was happy just to be needed, which led to an epiphany of sorts for Lee. As long as he was not telling Josh what to do or how to live his life, it seemed he and his boy got along splendidly.

Almost fifty-six years old, and he was still learning.

To her credit, Ellen had put her pledge to help Susie into action by funding this entire operation. The funds allowed Lee to hire a nurse from his practice, Valerie Cowart, who had twenty years' experience and was certified in hemodialysis.

Valerie agreed to temporarily move to the camp in Virginia despite Lee's warnings that this assignment was not without danger.

"I have no children, no husband, only my work," Valerie had said when accepting the offer. "If other medical professionals can travel to war zones to administer care, the least I can do is help out this poor young woman. Besides, it's hard to say no to the first lady."

Everything they needed to prep the camp for Susie, including a portable blood analyzer that provided real-time, lab-quality results, Lee had procured either from his practice, or from ZASK, the largest medical supply outfit in the area. He had hired drivers from ZASK to transport the equipment to camp and assist Paul, who had gone on ahead, with the setup.

Lee was at Susie's bedside when doctors finally removed the ventilation tube, holding her hand as she came awake.

Protect her the way a father would. . . .

Naturally, she had plenty of questions, but Lee kept everything intentionally vague. It was a drug reaction that had sent her to the ICU, nothing more. Without revealing anything of the repairman, or the growing suspicion that her parents' deaths were not accidental, Lee managed to confirm what he had suspected: there was no angry ex-boyfriend or crazed stalker terrorizing Susie's life. Unless the police could identify her attacker, they were helpless to help, and Lee and Karen remained Susie's best and only hope.

There was, however, no skirting around the kidney issue. A new machine was connected to her, and Susie wanted to know its purpose. Wisely, nobody told her that dialysis was a forever thing until she got a kidney transplant. One step at a time. The poor girl had suffered enough.

"What about family?" Lee asked. "Is there anybody we should notify?"

Susie gave a nearly imperceptible headshake while biting at her lower lip, presumably to stave off tears.

"I don't have any extended family," she said, speaking in the raspy, quiet voice of someone who moments ago had a tube down her throat. "My grandparents are gone and my parents didn't have any siblings or cousins. It's always been just the three of us."

This time, there was no stopping the tears, which Lee helped wipe away with some tissues. After Susie calmed, she told Lee where they kept a key that would let him into the house. She also told him where they stored the nootropics she got from the TPI.

Lee spent an hour at the hospital, then drove to Susie's house in Arlington. The home looked normal from the outside, except for a broken window on the second floor that somebody had boarded up with plywood. There were no police on the premises. No caution tape strewn across the front door. This was not a crime scene. It was the scene of a terrible tragedy. The inside of the home was as normal looking as the outside. The furniture was in place, not a single picture hung askew. While everything looked in order, it was still deeply unsettling to be there.

Death was ultimately painless; this Lee knew. For the living, however, it left a profound wound, one that would never heal completely. Being a doctor had not inured Lee to people's suffering. If anything, it had made him more empathetic. Illness, accidents, those were facts of life, mostly cruel, often unjust, but an undeniable part of existence, something he could wrap his brain around. But murder was something entirely different. It was man-made. It required cognition, a willful desire to act, to inflict harm.

After Lee got samples of Susie's nootropics from a kitchen cabinet, he headed upstairs to the girl's silent bedroom. He packed a suitcase of clothes he thought she would need, gathered some books of hers he thought she might like, and, following a moment's hesitation, decided to take her violin as well as some sheet music in a folder beside the case. Sick or not, he reasoned Susie would need something to occupy her time at camp.

Lee locked up the house, stood on the lawn, bowed his head, and had a moment of silence for Susie's parents. He got back in his car and drove to XLR Labs, a privately run forensic testing facility in Falls Church, Virginia. XLR handled everything from DUI toxicology tests to forensic consulting and designer drug analysis. Because it was privately run, he had brought the samples he wanted tested directly to the facility. For an additional five hundred dollars, Lee got a rush put on his job.

There was nothing left to do except get Susie the hell out of there.

CHAPTER 33

Susie sat in the back of a roomy SUV, still in her hospital gown, wrapped in a warm blanket. A nurse named Valerie sat in the backseat next to her with a medical bag tucked at her feet. Positioned between them was a machine encased in white plastic, about the size of a printer, with a lighted digital panel on the front and clear tubes sticking out the sides. Some of those tubes were connected to Susie's IV. The machine—a portable dialysis unit, she'd been told—buzzed and hummed and made various noises.

Everything had happened so quickly, Susie had not had time to process it all. She had met Dr. Blackwood's son, Josh, only because he had been vigilantly keeping watch over her, though she did not know why exactly. But Karen and Valerie were new people to her. They'd come to her room with Dr. Blackwood, and it was a quite a scene with Dr. Rajit as they escorted Susie out of the hospital against his wishes. Now she was in a car with them, driving to who knows where.

"I don't understand what's happening," Susie said shortly into the drive.

Her voice, cracking slightly, rang distant in her ears. She'd never been carsick, but now her stomach was roiling with nausea.

"We need to take things one step at a time," Karen said from the driver's seat. "Let's get you to the camp."

"Camp? What camp? Why are we going to a camp?"

Susie felt so incredibly tired, as though she had woken from the deepest sleep ever, but no matter how she tried, her head would not clear. Perhaps worst of all was how badly her skin itched. It was that all-over sensation of spiders again.

At that moment, Susie's arms began to tingle. Without warning, both limbs flailed out in front of her. Her knuckles smacked the back of the front seat so hard Karen hit the brakes, confused. The next instant, Susie's arms shot upward, slamming into the ceiling of the car. They went spastically in different directions: up, down, left, right, no order, and she had no control over her body.

As fast as the body jerks turned on, they ended. Susie's arms fell limply to her lap and she could move them normally once again. Despite the violence of the episode, the tubes hooked to her had remained attached.

"Do we need to pull over?" Karen asked, alarm in her voice.

"No," Valerie replied. "Her kidney issues have probably exacerbated her myoclonus. Lee has medication. I'll text him. See if he wants us to stop."

Susie's heart sank. This latest episode was a reminder that she was still horribly broken, and in more ways than one.

Her thoughts turned to her mom and dad. She could not believe they were gone. She felt paralyzed with grief. It was impossible to bend her mind around it.

Gone.

They were just—gone.

The shock was overpowering, the loss incomprehensible. She knew bad things happened. People died every day. Accidents, illnesses, fires, anything could happen. An entire family she knew from the TPI had died in a car wreck a year ago. And now this horrible thing had happened to her.

Her parents were her best friends, her number-one fans, her only support in this world. A house was a house, but they were her home. And now, home was gone.

If she closed her eyes, Susie could still hear the sound of her mother's voice. She could feel the coarseness of her dad's stubbly cheek when he held her tight. For a moment, she allowed herself to believe that when she got to this camp—wherever camp was—her parents would be there, waiting.

In her heart, she knew her dad would never again go swimming every Tuesday and Thursday. Her mom would not take another Mandarin class, or try to teach her some words. They would never cook together again. They would never take drives to the country, like the one she was taking now. They would not be in the audience—third row just left of center, their usual seats—eagerly waiting to hear her play. Sadly, horribly, this was Susie's new reality. And it hurt to think of them, to remember.

It hurt to breathe.

HOURS PASSED and wide roads became narrow ones. Houses and buildings gave way to trees. Other motorists appeared less frequently. To the west, the sun was a pale disc hovering low in the sky, leaving a wake of delicate yellows and vibrant pinks as it settled. Susie's dialysis machine continued to churn and hum. Twice they had to stop for a bathroom break, but not Susie. She no longer had to go. The machine went for her. It put the liquids in and it took them out.

"Do you need anything to eat?" the nurse had asked.

Susie could not stomach the idea of food. Her nausea would not allow even a single bite. Valerie told her not to worry about eating. They could keep her nourished intravenously until her appetite returned.

More time passed. More miles were traveled. Susie had no idea where she was, or where they were headed, and that was fine with her. Everything was fine. *Fine.* The less she engaged, the better. The more she kept her feelings locked away, the better.

She sat quietly, watching trees zoom past her window, glancing up in time to catch an occasional glimpse of birds swirling against a darkening sky. Eventually they left the main road (which was hardly a main road) and turned onto a dirt road that was quite bumpy and made her poor stomach feel even worse.

In front of them, the Honda set the pace, with Dr. Blackwood driving and Josh riding shotgun. He kept his speed down because the road was narrow, full of potholes, and lined with trees on both sides. It was hard for Susie to believe that not long ago she'd been having dinner with her parents, eating a nice meal, having fun, enjoying pleasant conversation. Now she was an orphan with a Secret Service agent and a nurse she hardly knew. Life was strange. Life was sad.

She was fine.

Eventually the hilly, windy road flattened out and opened into a clearing. Ahead, Susie could see a single building: a two-story log cabin with a wide covered porch and slanted metal roof. A few plantings grew out front, but nothing like her mother's impressive gardens. The dirt road to the cabin branched left and right, but Dr. Blackwood drove onto the grass and parked his car parallel to the porch. Karen pulled in behind him. Valerie had finished dialyzing miles ago, freeing Susie to exit the car without any tubes attached.

She stepped onto the hard-packed dirt with slippers on her feet and the fuzzy blanket wrapped around her body. The air was clean and fresh. It overpowered the hospital smells she'd thought might never go away. She took a long inhale and gazed up at the stars just beginning to twinkle against a deep blue backdrop. She pulled the blanket around her shoulders and shook off a sudden chill.

"Go on inside," Karen said. "It's all set up for you."

What's all set up? Susie wondered.

Valerie raised the SUV's rear hatch. "Lee packed a suitcase of your clothes from home," she said. "I'll lay them out so you can change into something more comfortable whenever you're ready."

What is this place? Susie asked herself. *Why am I here? What's going to happen to me?*

Quick as those thoughts came, Susie pushed them aside.

I'm fine, she thought. *Everything is fine. . . .*

She walked gingerly up a rocky dirt path toward the cabin, clutching the blanket tightly in her hands. The forest was all around her; tall, dark trees encircled the cabin's modest plot of land. The sounds of the night were symphonic. No more beeps or hospital alarms. Susie took in these new noises: the steady chirp of crickets, something higher pitched like a soft whistle, the lonesome hoot of a faraway owl.

Lee and Josh disappeared through the cabin's creaky front door. Valerie collected bags from the trunk. Nearby, Karen was looking around cautiously, as if surveying the land.

What was she on the lookout for? Bears?

As Susie walked up the front steps, the cabin lights came on. Josh stepped onto the porch. She liked seeing him. Always a smile on his face, his eyes friendly and kind. He seemed indifferent to her sickness and fragility, as though he could look beyond all that at the person she remembered once being.

He took her hand to help her up the stairs. "Come on in," he said. His skin felt warm against hers. His touch was soothing. "Everything is ready for you."

Susie followed Josh into the cabin. A pair of portable lamps cast off plenty of light. Her mouth fell open as she took it all in.

Instead of rustic furniture, a gleaming hospital bed and stainless steel laboratory table took up a good portion of the room's center. Solutions already hung from the branches of an IV stand. Susie loved chemistry and recognized the pipettes, beakers, and flasks all neatly arranged on a wooden dresser. Stacked beside the dresser were boxes of syringes, gloves, and masks. On another table Susie saw a centrifuge machine (she had used one in science class) and nearby was a hard red case she guessed held a defibrillator. There was additional equipment including blood pressure cuffs, instruments to check ears and eyes, and other machines she could not identify.

Dr. Blackwood stood near the bed, a kind expression on his face, but there was sadness in his eyes, Susie thought. Valerie came huffing up the stairs, pulling Susie's luggage behind her. Josh and Karen leaned against a wall next to the door. Valerie walked the room, nodding her approval as she checked out all the equipment.

The rest of the cabin had an open floor plan that allowed Susie to see from the living room into a spacious galley kitchen containing older-looking appliances. Speckled pots and cast-iron pans dangled from a knotted support beam. The cabin walls were paneled with smooth logs shellacked to an amber finish. The floor was made of darker wood, with wide planks evenly spaced except where they had to accommodate a rear door and large stone fireplace just beyond a dining area.

The flickering fire warmed the room beyond what a wall-mounted heating unit would produce, but still a chill clutched at Susie and would not let go. The furniture had no real theme, no unifying design elements like her mother would have insisted on. It was a hodgepodge of fabrics and styles, a bit more to her father's taste. Susie took it all in while standing inside the doorway, still as could be.

"My partner, Paul, set everything up so it would be ready for you when we got here," Dr. Blackwood said. "You, Valerie, and Karen will sleep at the camp. There are two bedrooms upstairs, so plenty of room for all. Josh and I will be staying at another cabin down the road. There are four cabins total on the property, but none are occupied."

"Okay," Susie said in a quiet voice. "Thank you."

"We're going to take good care of you, I promise," said Josh, and because of his confidence she believed him.

Dr. Blackwood joined them in the center of the room. "I know it's not perfect, Susie," he said. "But it has everything we need to keep you healthy and get you better. Tomorrow we can talk more about why it's best you stay here for a while. There's a beautiful lake down the path. Karen will show you. And when you're feeling stronger, you can take the canoe out for a paddle. There are lots of walking trails, too; you don't have to be bedridden. It's not home, but hopefully you'll be comfortable here."

Home.

Home was gone and it was never coming back. Home was nowhere. She was here now. So be it.

"It's fine," Susie said.

CHAPTER 34

Lee awoke with the sunrise, feeling invigorated. His energy surprised him, given how frantic the previous day had been. Getting "The Cabin Clinic" operational had been a herculean effort, and he owed Paul more than a fancy Starbucks drink for his contributions.

Stepping quietly onto the front porch, Lee stretched his limbs and felt his back lengthen. Morning dew clung to leaves and tall grasses. He inhaled deeply, taking in the fresh pine smell scenting the air. All around him, birds were calling to each other in melodious tweets, chirps, and warbles. Lee sipped coffee from his mug, savoring the taste.

The peace he felt here was profound. His joints felt looser, including that troublesome knee. Even with everything happening to Cam and Susie, Lee could still take a moment to appreciate the beauty of this special place. No wonder Karen was so reluctant to sell.

The cabins had everything that was needed to live comfortably—working plumbing (well water and septic), and electricity. Come the winter months these cabins were closed down, but propane used for heating and cooking kept the pipes from freezing and insulation allowed for year-round use if anyone so desired. Eventually, Josh emerged from his bedroom to join Lee on the porch, clutching a mug of steaming coffee in his hands. His hair was a tangled mess.

"How'd you sleep, champ?"

Josh stretched, yawned lazily, and took a sip of coffee. "Not enough," he said. "The birds woke me."

Josh had loved coming to the camp as a boy. When Lee's work allowed, he and Josh would trek out here on weekends to dig for worms. Afterwards, they'd spend hours on the lake, fishing from the flat-bottom canoe, catching and releasing small bass along with the occasional trout. The time had gone in a blink, and while the idea of the days being long and the years being short was a cliché, that did not make it untrue.

Lee asked: "You sure you don't mind sticking around here a while to help your mother out?"

"Nope. Not at all."

Josh said this quickly—a little *too* quickly, actually—and Lee sent his son a knowing sideways glance.

"She's a pretty girl," Lee said.

"Who?"

Josh's attempt at ignorance would have fooled nobody. Lee just smiled.

"How you feeling about Hannah?"

"Who?"

This time Lee laughed.

"Anyway, Mom lent me her SIG, not to mention all of Grandpa's guns. Those are still in good working order. We'll keep Susie safe. You have my word."

Josh came with plenty of military training. Lee had no doubt about his ability.

"Once I figure out what's going on with her, make the connection to Cam, maybe we can get the president to take over protection duties. A lot depends on what the toxicologist reports back to us."

"Like I said, I'll be fine here for a while. No problems."

Lee put his arm around his boy, embraced the moment, and wished it could last longer.

When they finished their coffee, Lee headed to the kitchen, where he cooked up some scrambled eggs and wheat toast. They had brought enough groceries to last only a few days, but modern conveniences were reasonably close by. The supermarket was a twenty-minute drive and a major hospital was only thirty-five minutes from camp. If all went well, Susie would need dialysis and nothing more, but Lee was glad to have easy access to a hospital in case of emergency. He still did not understand what was causing Susie's symptoms, which meant the possibility of new symptoms occurring.

He and Josh ate their breakfast at the dining room table. The cabin walls were decorated with flea market paintings, the rug beneath the table had gone threadbare, but the view out the window into a verdant and vast forest made this a five-star dining experience in Lee's opinion.

When his cell phone rang, Lee figured it was Karen calling. The caller ID did show a D.C. area code, but it was not a number Lee recognized.

He answered the call. "Dr. Blackwood here."

"Hello, Dr. Blackwood, this is Vera Sacks from XLR Labs calling with results from your priority job."

Excitement rose as Lee thought about Gleason and finally getting some answers.

"Go on," he said.

"I have both sets of results for you. I'll start with the SB sample."

Susie Banks, Lee thought.

Lee had selected XLR Labs for their use of high-performance liquid chromatography and liquid chromatography-mass spectrometry, the two best techniques for identifying compounds by comparison. Like all doctors, Lee had suffered through organic chemistry, but the course was never in his wheelhouse, and he hated to admit the science XLR Labs used to analyze the ProNeural product line was a bit over his head. But the end result was easy enough to understand.

Lee found a pen and some paper on the bookshelf and wrote down the compounds and amounts present as Vera read through the findings in the three different pills analyzed: SOAR, FOCUS, and SUPER O-3.

In total, Lee's list contained twelve different naturally occurring substances, including bacopa monnieri, an herb native to the wetlands of Eastern India, and periwinkle, the seeds of which yielded vincamine, thought to be a natural memory enhancer. In addition to ginseng, rosemary, vitamin D and K, as well as omega-3, the ProNeural pill line contained huperzine-a, an alkaloid compound found in firmoss; theanine, found in green tea; and tryptophan, an amino acid and mood enhancer obtained only through diet and supplements, best known for its association with turkey. There was also spearmint, basil, marjoram, palm, wheat, daisy, and dracaena, which Vera identified as a houseplant. When Vera read off the make-up of Cam's supplements, they exactly matched the ingredients in the SB samples.

Lee asked Vera to repeat her findings on the off chance he had missed something important. He checked off each item as she read it back to him, and no, he had not missed anything.

"What is it, Dad?" Josh asked when Lee ended his call. "You seem a little freaked out."

But Lee did not answer. Instead he called his neurologist friend at the MDC, the person who had done Cam's MRI and EEG, Dr. Marilyn Piekarski. When she answered, Lee gave a quick overview of the issue before he read through the results from XLR Lab's analysis of the nootropics.

"There's virtually nothing in these," Dr. Piekarski told Lee, confirming his suspicion. "Just a bunch of herbs and plant compounds."

"What's your bottom line on this, Marilyn. Help me put some pieces together."

"I'm no expert, Lee, but I know some of these designer nootropics contain a class of drugs called racetams, which includes complex, synthetic compounds like piracetam. In the U.S., piracetam isn't FDA approved and can't be included in supplements like nootropics, but in the U.K. it's less regulated and used to treat myoclonus, of all things. So, if you told me that compound was present in the ProNeural samples, or something like it, I might give my answer more thought. But it isn't. Bottom line, these supplements aren't causing Susie or Cam's symptoms. Impossible."

FLANKED BY Josh and Lee on the front porch of Susie's cabin, Karen drank from her mug of coffee and dubiously studied Lee's handwritten list of ingredients from XLR Lab's report. She was dressed casually in jeans and a comfy sweatshirt; it was the way Lee remembered her when they'd come here in years past. Inside the cabin, Susie was still asleep. Valerie had gone out early to take a walk around the property and check out the lake.

"So this makes no sense to me," Karen said, focusing intently on the list. "I cook with a lot of these ingredients, and I don't feel any smarter for it."

"Dr. Piekarski said some nootropics contain synthesized compounds, complex drugs manufactured in a lab, as opposed to the natural extracts like what we found in the ProNeural line."

"So what does this mean? What about Gleason?"

"It means we're still at square one," Lee said. "It means that if this is what Gleason is giving Cam, it's not causing his moodiness, organ enlargement, seizures, none of it. Same goes for Susie."

"What about the red spot in Susie's eyes?" Karen asked.

"CO poisoning, most likely," Lee said. "We knew all along it was a possible cause."

"So this was all for nothing?" Karen's voice was distressed. "I don't buy it. Not for one second. Someone wants this girl dead, Lee. Someone wanted those twins dead, too. Something is wrong with Cam, and the link between all four of them is the TPI. There's a reason. We need to find it." She sounded sure of herself.

Josh snapped his fingers. "Go back to what you said at the restaurant, Mom. Maybe this stuff isn't the only thing Yoshi is giving his star students. Maybe he's feeding them something more complex."

Lee and Karen gave him their full attention.

"I mean—and I'm thinking out loud here," Josh continued, "what if Yoshi is giving these kids something other than his placebo supplements to achieve his impressive results, and when complications arise, he's burying the evidence? It would be easy enough to give Cam something without Dr. Gleason knowing—or maybe—" Josh paused, thinking it through. "Maybe Gleason's helping Yoshi out. I mean there's a reason Gleason's tried so hard to keep you away from Cam, right, Dad? If these guys come up with some brain-boosting breakthrough, they'll stand to make millions."

"Billions," Lee corrected.

"So call the president," Josh said. "Tell him what we found in those supplements."

Karen shook her head, dismissing the idea. "And tell him I think Yoshi Matsumoto may be experimenting on Cam and the others? Tell him we don't know if Gleason's involved or not? That some experiment, we don't know what, went wrong and now someone, we don't know who, is going to try to take out Cam to hide the evidence? Look at how our last conversation with the president went down, Lee. First he'll go apoplectic, and after that he'll push me right out of the White House. We are teetering on the edge here."

"Well, what do you suggest?" Lee asked.

"I'll go back to Washington, right now, and be extra eyes and ears around Cam."

"I'll go with you," Lee said. "Maybe the president would go crazy, but Ellen won't. I need to talk to Yoshi, see what else might be going on here. I'll tell Ellen we got samples of Susie's ProNeural nootropics tested and I have some questions, nothing alarming, but I'd like some clarification on a few things. She doesn't need to know what we found just yet. I'll ask for her help arranging a meeting for me with Yoshi and Dr. Gleason at the TPI. See where that leads us."

"What about me?" Josh asked.

"You stay on guard duty," Karen said. "We'll drive into town, rent two cars. That way you and Valerie will each have a vehicle here. I'll come back soon, but you can hold down the fort for a while, I trust."

"I spent years on patrol and post," Josh said, his eyes glazing with the memory. "I can handle it. Not a problem."

"Yeah, well, here's a problem, and I'm not sure how to fix it," Karen said. "Until we figure out what's going on, I've got to keep Cam away from the True Potential Institute, not to mention his doctor. He has the World Junior Chess Championships coming up. He's going to want to train."

"And Gleason's not going to suddenly drop Cam from his patient roster," Lee said. "What do you suggest?"

"I suggest you do more than just talk to Yoshi Matsumoto," Karen said. "You've got to hurry up and get us some real answers."

CHAPTER 35

When Karen arrived at the White House, it was early afternoon on a day when she was not scheduled to work. She went to the lower level, directly beneath the vice president's office, where the Secret Service had a break room and some offices, including Karen's small space.

Duffy was there, getting something to eat from one of the vending machines. When he saw Karen his expression shifted, as though he'd seen a ghost. After his odd reaction he slipped back to the normal Duffy—a fixed and pointed stare, jutting jaw, and rigid posture.

He had his suit jacket off, and Karen could see the butt of his SIG Sauer sticking out from the Cloak Tuck IWB holster he wore. She used the same inside-the-waistband hybrid holster, which hid her gun so well no one ever suspected she was carrying. She also wore an ankle holster for her backup weapon—a Ruger LCPII .380 that weighed only 10.6 ounces unloaded. She carried a backup in times that called for heightened security. This was one such situation, but only Karen was on high alert.

"What are you doing here?" Duffy asked in a clipped tone. "I thought you were on vacation."

"I came in to take care of some office work," Karen said. "What's Cam's schedule for the rest of the day?"

"Home from school, just hanging out in his room," Duffy said. "I'm bringing him to the TPI in a few hours for his afternoon practice. I'll tell you, I think that kid's coming around. This thing with Taylor Gleason has really gotten to him. All he wants to do is play, practice, and beat him."

"Yeah, well, I'll go talk to Cam. He's having a private lesson today, no

TPI. I already made the arrangements. His coach is going to come here this afternoon instead of Cam going there."

"Why?"

"Ellen thinks Cam needs as much time at home as possible while he recuperates."

Duffy seemed perplexed. "He's feeling fine. I mean, he's still Cam being Cam, moody and all that, but he's up and about, no problems there."

"Well, Ellen thinks it's best he limit himself to school and home for the next few days."

"All righty then. School and no TPI. Less for us to do. Fine by me."

This plan had been hatched hours ago, when Lee had made his call to Ellen. She had been glad to arrange the meeting with you, but regretfully could not join herself. To keep Cam away from the institute without revealing their suspicion of Yoshi and maybe even Gleason, Lee simply voiced concern about Cam overdoing it, and suggested he limit his activities for the time being. This was something Ellen was happy to present as her own idea so that Gleason and President Hilliard would not take exception. The only one who might be disappointed would be Cam. For that reason, Karen would go to his room to break the news herself.

But first, something about Duffy continued to nag at her.

"What's up with your financial situation?" she asked bluntly. "Are you fine about that for now? No major stress?"

Duffy took a big bite of the Snickers bar he had procured. "If the Nats don't win tonight, I'm going to be a lot lighter in the wallet, but no, no major stress. Why do you ask?"

Duffy might have been joking, but his constant betting had Karen worried. Even Lapham had said something to her about it.

"You seem anxious to me is all. Be honest. Are you in any kind of trouble?"

"Only if I don't get back to my post," Duffy said, his trademark smirk returning. "My boss can be a real hard-ass at times."

Duffy slipped his suit jacket on, giving Karen a chummy punch on her arm as he headed out the door.

KAREN TOOK the stairs to the second level. Once the White House had intimidated her, but that was ages ago. Now, it was just a home. Nannies to the rich and famous could probably relate.

While the tourists toured below, the second level was like a monastery and had a hush typical for this time of afternoon. Cam's parents were away, busy as always. Woody Lapham was leading the security team at West Point, where Ellen was to give a speech highlighting the contributions of women to national defense throughout history. Seniority should have made it Duffy's gig, but his medical condition made Karen rethink the assignments. These days, Duffy kept mostly to the White House and was part of the team shuttling Cam to school and back.

A separate team of agents had accompanied President Hilliard to Atlanta, where he was slated to speak at a major health-care summit. If Karen remembered his schedule correctly, he should arrive home in time for dinner, as was always his preference.

Walking down the hall, Karen could hear the steady pulse of Cam's electronic music bleating out at ear-damaging decibels. She knocked on his bedroom door, got no answer, so she knocked again, harder and with more authority.

"Come in," Cam yelled.

Inside, Cam's shades were drawn. The blue glow of his computer monitor lit the room like a nightclub. A pile of video games lay on the floor near some clothes that should have been in his hamper. No surprise, Cam had a chess game going. He had to be multitasking, because Karen saw other windows on his monitor displaying computer code that to her untrained eyes read like gibberish.

Cam turned down the music.

"Who are you playing?" Karen asked.

"Taylor," Cam said gloomily.

"Tell him I said hello."

Cam typed something. "He says 'hi' back."

Kids today, thought Karen, lamenting the inevitable demise of the phone call. Still, if Gleason were trying to give his son a competitive edge, Karen doubted Taylor was aware. He and Cam were friendly rivals, and that friendship seemed to be continuing despite the role reversal.

"Are you winning?" she asked.

Cam shook his head. "Nope. But he's helping me dox some of the players I'm supposed to go up against at the world championships."

"Dox?"

"Yeah, doxxing," said Cam. "It's computer stuff. Kind of a hacking thing. You know that group Anonymous?"

"Sure, vigilante hackers."

"Right. Well, they do doxxing all the time. It's basically hacking into systems, looking for public and private records to expose people, find secrets, that sort of thing. We try to get dirt on our competitors so we can trash talk during the match."

"Chess players trash talk?"

Cam shrugged. "Might not be a contact sport, but it can be a pretty brutal game."

"Where did you learn how to dox?" Karen said the word, still unsure what it meant.

"My computer club. It's all right."

"By 'all right,' I hope you mean legal."

Cam said nothing and Karen decided to let it go. He could dox all he wanted if it helped lift his spirits.

"Mind if I turn on some lights?" she asked.

Cam shrugged. She flicked a switch and blinked until her eyes adjusted to the glow.

"How are you feeling?"

"Fine," Cam said. "You know—the usual. I'm losing to a kid I normally beat. Again. What does that tell you?"

"That's something is still up."

"Yeah. Something."

Karen decided to switch topics. "I talked with your mom, and she wants you to stay home as much as possible. That means no trips to the TPI for a while. Just school and back, until you fully recover from surgery."

Cam spun around in his desk chair, looking frustrated. "If I don't practice, I'm going to get crushed at the tournament. Taylor might as well go ahead and take my spot."

"Your instructor is going to come here instead," Karen said. "It's all been arranged."

Cam shrugged his acquiescence, though a glum expression remained. "Okay. I just want my old self back, you know?"

"I do, buddy," Karen said, giving his shoulder a tender squeeze. Turning, she scanned his desk, trying to be discreet about it. He had schoolbooks open, a good sign. It meant he was still showing interest in his studies. She was curious about his work. Having dedicated so much of her life to protecting Cam, watching out for him, seeing him grow and change, it was hard not to feel like an overprotective parent at times. But the impulse was there and Karen did nothing to fight it.

"Everything good at school?" she asked. A little conversation might make it seem less like snooping, she reasoned.

"Yeah, it's all right." Cam had his one-syllable-word thing down pat.

She poked through a stack of his school papers. There was a history quiz. A+. A science lab. A+. Some notes from English class. All seemed normal, good even. Cam was dealing with a lot, but he appeared to be holding his own.

Then her eyes went to a piece of paper partially hidden underneath one of his notebooks. It was a printout from a word processing program. No name, no date, no heading at all, just the same two sentences repeated over and over again.

I know what you are. I know what you do.

I know what you are. I know what you do.

When she closed the notebook, Karen saw those sentences spanned the length of the page.

I know what you are. I know what you do. . . .

"Cam, what's this about?" Karen asked, holding up the sheet for Cam to see.

"It's nothing," he said, avoiding Karen's eyes.

She could tell right away his *nothing* was really *something*.

"I'm just curious, Cam," Karen said, using softer tactics.

Cam rose from his chair and reached for the paper. "It's nothing," he said, crumpling the page when Karen handed it to him. "I was just goofing off with some friends at school. That's all."

Cam did not act like it was nothing, and Karen was not quite ready to give up on her inquiry. She thought about what he had said to Lee after his eye exam.

Dr. Gleason's a liar.

"Is this about Dr. Gleason?" she asked.

"No," Cam said. He paused before answering, his head subtly nodding yes. Karen knew the brain was wired in such a way as to cause verbal and nonverbal behaviors to naturally match up. Cam might have picked up a lot of useful skills from the TPI, but lying was not one of them.

"You said something to Lee about Dr. Gleason being a liar. What did you mean by that?"

Instead of answering, Cam turned his back to Karen, a clear signal that this conversation had come to an end.

CHAPTER 36

Lee arrived at the TPI at precisely half past four in the afternoon. There was a lot riding on this meeting, and his anxiousness made the usual traffic and parking woes more bothersome than usual.

He pushed the front-door buzzer, heard a click, and was soon standing in a gleaming foyer with incredible works of art decorating the concrete walls. The institute was hardly quiet, and given the hour, Lee figured it was prime time for the after-school crew who came here to improve upon their respective disciplines. He wondered how many of those kids were consuming the ProNeural nootropics, believing they could not reach their personal zenith without them.

He was scanning the posters of TPI's famous alumni when a hardy-looking woman approached. A slightly officious air dimmed her friendly smile. She must have been the one who had buzzed him inside.

"Dr. Lee Blackwood?"

"Yes, that's me."

"I'm Irene Goodman, I handle the administration here. Yoshi asked me to show you to his office."

Lee followed Irene up a wide concrete staircase that brought them to a hallway lined with glass cases displaying TPI-related news clippings and announcements, and trumpeting various success stories.

Assuming the Web site was up to date (and Lee had no reason to believe otherwise), tuition here was on the steeper side. With a cost of $2,600 each trimester (scholarships available) and roughly 280 students enrolled at any given time, the TPI generated more than $2 million in revenue annually, an impressive sum by any measure.

He asked himself: if Josh were a student here, gifted in some way, competing against the best of the best, would he let him take the ProNeural supplements? Lee liked to believe he was above peer pressure, but if his kid wanted them, and if others were taking them with no issues, no reported side effects, why deny him the advantage? Cognitive enhancers were fast becoming normative. Lee speculated that the majority of people who ingested various weight loss shakes and powders probably had no idea what was in those products. Was ProNeural all that different? If the packaging looked professional, and the testimonials were believable, why the heck not take them?

Irene led Lee to a nondescript wooden door at the far end of the hallway. She knocked and a slightly accented voice invited them to enter.

Yoshi occupied a spacious but sparsely furnished room on the second floor. A few bamboo plants caught sunlight from a windowsill. Black bookcases contained neatly arranged volumes of what appeared to be textbooks. His pedestal desk was uncluttered. The walls were covered with framed photographs of Yoshi with well-known people. It was a Wall of Fame, similar to those in every elected official's office on Capitol Hill. Several of the pictures were of Yoshi and the first family (some with him and just the president). It was like a shrine to Yoshi, but Lee was not here to pay his respects.

When Lee arrived, three people were seated at the round conference table tucked in a corner of the room. He recognized only two of them. Irene excused herself as Lee reached across the table to shake hands with Yoshi and Gleason. Gleason gave Lee's hand a predictably fishy shake hello, but Yoshi left his hand dangling in midair. He stood instead, pushed back his chair, and bowed slightly. A bit unsure, Lee pulled his hand back and returned a slight bow of his own.

Yoshi wore a pair of John Lennon glasses, his rakishly styled white hair contrasting sharply against an all-black ensemble. Gleason wore a suit and tie and appeared a little less formidable without his white coat embroidered with the presidential seal.

Lee took the only available seat, next to the older gentleman with a stocky build, puffy eyes, and wisps of gray hair sprouting from a sunspotted forehead. He shook that man's hand last.

"Dr. Lee Blackwood," Lee said, introducing himself as he settled into his seat.

"Dr. Hal Hewitt," said the man, giving Lee's hand a vigorous shake. "I'm on the board of the TPI."

Hal's name was one Lee recognized from Karen.

"I asked Dr. Hewitt to join us," said Yoshi, "because from what Ellen told me this meeting is a medical one."

"That's great," said Lee. "And thank you all for arranging your schedules to be here on such short notice. I think what we have to discuss is rather important."

"Ellen said you wanted to know more about ProNeural, but wouldn't elaborate, said you were better equipped to explain." Gleason leaned forward, his leering look designed to inflict maximum discomfort. "I should be with the president right now, Lee, but as a favor to the first lady I'm here . . . with you."

"Fred, I appreciate it," said Lee, pouring himself a glass of water from a pitcher on the table. "We're here because I have some concerns about these cognitive enhancers, the nootropics the students are taking."

"ProNeural is perfectly safe, Lee," Gleason said smoothly. "All the products are manufactured in the U.S. and have been independently tested and verified by reputable labs. I've confirmed this myself. Do you think I'd let the president's son take anything if I wasn't a hundred percent confident it would do no harm?"

"Dr. Gleason is right," said Yoshi. "I have a doctorate in naturopathic medicine and mycology, and I can attest to the products' safety." Lee's face showed his confusion. He'd heard the word "mycology" before, but could not recall its meaning. Yoshi noticed Lee's puzzled look. "Mycology is the study of fungi for medicine, food, and other purposes," he explained.

"Other purposes like altered minds—and *poison*," Lee said, placing emphasis on the last word.

"Are you implying that ProNeural is poisonous?" Yoshi's eyes became fiery. "Because I can assure you that's not the case. Nootropics are as close to the natural supplements I've studied for years. They're made of herbs, things like caffeine, vitamins B6 and B12—all substances the FDA has approved as dietary supplements and regards as safe."

"That's not all they contain," said Lee. "A lot of these nootropics are comprised of complex synthetic compounds."

"But *not* ProNeural, Dr. Blackwood," Hal interjected, offering his first contribution to the discussion. "I know this because I've carefully reviewed the compounds at Yoshi's request. As a set, the ProNeural product line enhances neuroendocrine function naturally, improving memory and concentration by changing cognitive performance as it encourages the brain to naturally release things like dopamine and other cognitive enhancers. In a way it's comparable to a good night's sleep and some yummy dark chocolate. Both affect the brain in similar ways."

On his drive into the city, Lee had stopped at XLR Labs to pick up copies of the official report. He removed the folded pages from the inner pocket of his suit jacket and separated them into two batches. He gave one batch to Gleason and Yoshi to share; the other he slid over to Hal Hewitt.

"Confirming what you're saying, I had the supplements professionally analyzed," Lee said.

"Where'd you get the samples?" asked Gleason, shooting Lee a suspicious look.

"Susie Banks," Lee said.

Gleason gave a soft groan, clearly annoyed with Lee's unwillingness to let anything go. For Yoshi and Hal Hewitt's benefit Lee said: "Susie is your student. You may have read about, or seen her on the news. Almost died in a carbon monoxide gas leak that killed her parents, and later someone assaulted her in the hospital."

Both Yoshi and Dr. Hewitt expressed sympathy for the girl's plight, but Lee did not accept that as proof of anyone's innocence.

Yoshi scanned the pages quickly, while Dr. Hewitt studied them more carefully.

"And I agree with you, Yoshi," Lee said. "I'd say these products are perfectly harmless. Though I'm not sure they're all that effective."

Gleason's stare was cold. "Just hold it right there, Lee," he said. "This product is incredibly effective. Yoshi, do you have the binder from the last round of neurofeedback testing? I want to show Lee those results."

Yoshi got up from the table, went to a nearby bookshelf, and removed a black binder with the ProNeural branding running down the spine.

"Our partnership with ProNeural includes comprehensive neuro-feedback evaluations," Yoshi said, handing the binder to Lee, "and the results speak for themselves."

Lee flipped through dozens of laminated pages filled with colorful charts and graphs, all professionally rendered, each branded with the ProNeural logo—a trail of fast-moving electrons encircling a drawing of a blue-colored brain. These days, most everything was measured and tracked—sleep, steps, heart rate, and such. If it could be quantified, some sort of wearable device was out there quantifying it, so Lee was not at all surprised by the depth and breadth of data aggregated from the student population. The results clearly demonstrated improved cognition in a number of key areas for all three supplements: SOAR, FOCUS, and SUPER O-3.

"Better memory, better concentration, reduced time on task when mastering new skills," Yoshi said.

"How exactly did you collect all this data?" Lee asked as he leafed through the thick binder.

"Neurofeedback is essentially brain mapping," Gleason said. "I've observed these sessions myself, so I've seen firsthand exactly what the ProNeural team does when they come here on testing days. It's called quantitative EEG, qEEG for short."

Lee did not need Dr. Marilyn Piekarski's neurology training to know EEG was a way of measuring electrical activity in the brain. Every thought, every emotion is the result of electronic discharges from neurons firing.

"By studying the EEG in nineteen areas of the brain," Yoshi said, "we're able to help our students see opportunities for improvement, and we can also measure how the ProNeural nootropics can assist them in that process. That's essentially what all those reports you're looking at show."

Lee could not deny the results were impressive.

Hal said, "Students wear electrodes while they perform their respective skills and the qEEG process puts to use complicated mathematical and statistical analyses that literally allow us to see into their brains.'"

Lee turned a page in the binder, revealing a photograph of Cam and

Taylor engaged in a game of chess. Both boys had electrodes fixed to their scalps like space-age hairnets with wires.

"The first lady supported this?" Lee asked, showing Gleason the picture of Cam.

"At first she was a little hesitant, but I assured her the procedure was perfectly safe and completely harmless."

The accompanying graphs visually documented the qEEG results with and without the ProNeural nootropics. The conclusions were as evident as the concentration on the boys' faces. The ProNeural nootropics dramatically improved their cognitive function. In essence, the smart drugs did indeed make these kids smarter. It was all there in the data. Some measurements showed calmer brain waves for better focus, while others highlighted how their minds were optimized for skill mastery.

"ProNeural helps our students achieve a state of flow," Yoshi explained. "Instead of more brain activity, we train our students to have less. Have you ever been so absorbed in a task that hours can go by without your notice? You feel incredibly alert, your concentration unyielding, emotions positively charged, everything but the task forgotten. Achieving this flow is the purpose of our work here.

"We don't train people to win races, to reach some end. Instead, we train our students with meditation, relaxation, visualization techniques, and yes, cognitive enhancers, to help them maximize their true potential. The TPI is a blend of many Eastern philosophies with Western techniques to create a truly unique learning environment."

Any doubts Lee had about giving Josh the pills would have been tossed out the window had he been given these charts. ProNeural, in conjunction with Yoshi's Eastern methods, appeared to work wonders.

Yoshi continued: "With training, and these supplements, students here learn to quiet the mind, lowering theta, delta, and beta waves to heighten the alpha state, which is scientifically proven to be a state of relaxed alertness. With mastery, these neural connections become more ingrained, making it easier to achieve this state quicker, more efficiently. Our system simply speeds up this process."

"What percent of students take these nootropics?" asked Lee.

"Seventy-five, thereabouts," answered Hal.

"Clearly it benefits the kids," said Lee. "I'm curious to know how it benefits ProNeural."

"They're a private company," answered Yoshi. "We're not privy to their financials, but the CEO told us since we agreed to make the TPI results public, sales and interest in the products have risen substantially. It's helped them get PR and new adopters and there's been a snowball effect. Wouldn't you say, Hal?"

"Yes, for certain."

"What's your point in all this, Lee?" asked Gleason, his blue eyes turning frosty.

"My point," said Lee, fixing Gleason with an unblinking stare, "is that I'm aware of four children afflicted with mysterious ailments, all of them with connections to the TPI. Two of those four are dead, and somebody tried to kill the third. The fourth—well, he's safe for now."

Gleason eyed Lee contemptuously. "This is about Cam, isn't it? My God, Lee, you are tenacious."

"I gather we're talking about Susie Banks and Cam Hilliard, but who are the other children?" Hal asked.

"The Stewart twins," Lee said. "Both were students here. I use the past tense because both of the boys are dead."

Yoshi's dark eyes bored into Lee. "They died in a car accident," he said.

"Yes, I know," said Lee. "I want to know what made the twins sick enough to come see my partner at our clinic."

"How would I know such a thing? I am not their doctor," Yoshi said angrily.

"Are you suggesting ProNeural made them sick?" asked Gleason.

"No," said Lee. "I checked with a neurologist—you know her, Fred, Dr. Marilyn Piekarski. She shared some information with you about Cam that you didn't bother sharing with me, if you recall. Anyway, she told me the compounds in ProNeural couldn't cause these symptoms."

"What symptoms are we talking about?" asked Hal.

"I'll put the question back on you, Dr. Hewitt. Are you aware of other students here who have severe cases of myoclonus, cherry-red spots on the retina, enlarged organs, moodiness, and irritability?"

Hal shook his head that he was not.

"So if your friend at the MDC ruled out ProNeural as a cause, why are you here, Lee?"

Lee wanted to wipe the smug look off Gleason's face with his knuckles.

"Because it makes no sense that four of your students would present with the same, incredibly unusual affliction. Want I want to know is what else you're giving these kids."

Yoshi leaned back as an angry look came to his face. "Dr. Blackwood, I take offense at your insinuation. Are you suggesting that we're experimenting on our students?"

"I'm asking you to explain how there's a cluster of some unknown disease centered around your school, Mr. Matsumoto."

"Dr. Matsumoto," answered Yoshi. "And I cannot explain that, nor will I even attempt to try. This is not my area of expertise." Quick as his anger appeared, Yoshi's expression turned suddenly neutral. Lee recalled what Karen had said about him being sphinxlike when it came to body language. If Yoshi held his cards any closer to his chest, they'd slip right under his skin.

"I respect your position, Dr. Matsumoto," said Lee. "And I admit that I'm no statistician, but I'd wager several years' salary that the probability of four kids who attend your school all coming down with the same strange symptoms, independently of this place, then coming together here by random chance, is about the same as me winning Powerball—twice. It's not possible. This has all the characteristics of a cluster disease, and those are caused either by something environmental, the way contaminated groundwater can produce cancer clusters, or it's something these students are taking. I'm betting on the latter."

"I assure you, Dr. Blackwood, we do not, nor would we ever experiment on our students."

"In that case," said Lee, "I take it you wouldn't object to having some testing done. If you're not subjecting these kids to some experimental nootropic, perhaps there *is* something in the air or water here. I'm sure with the first lady's help we can expedite a thorough environmental analysis."

Yoshi rose from his chair, his brown eyes burning like two embers. "As you see fit, Dr. Blackwood," he said. "But what we do at the TPI not only works in demonstrable ways, it is absolutely, positively safe. You may be willing to bet your salary, but on this, I'd bet my life."

Yoshi strutted over to his desk, on which sat three jars of ProNeural. He unscrewed the lids, removed a pill from within each jar, opened his mouth, and swallowed them without so much as a sip of water to chase them down.

CHAPTER 37

Susie Banks pushed a button to raise her hospital bed so she could peer out the cabin window. She liked the woods, the birdsong, everything about this place. It was so quiet here, so peaceful.

But nice as it was, what she wanted more than anything was to be back home with her parents. In the kitchen, Josh was brewing a pot of coffee and cooking something for dinner. The delicious smells made Susie think about all the times she had cooked with her mother. A lump formed in her throat, so large that for a moment it was difficult to swallow or breathe. Funny how a simple smell could cause a flood of painful memories.

Tears flowed.

Gone. They're gone.

A few minutes later, Josh brought over a tray holding a plate of pasta in red sauce, a leafy salad in a ceramic bowl, and some meatballs steaming in a clear glass dish.

"I didn't know if you were a vegetarian, so I put the meatballs on the side," he said, carefully setting the tray on Susie's bed.

"Thanks," said Susie, feeling famished for the first time. "It all looks great."

Josh scrutinized his handiwork. "Hold on a second," he said.

Josh scampered back to the kitchen, returning moments later with a small glass vase containing a single yellow flower.

"I picked this for you," he said. "Thought it might brighten your meal."

Susie's smile was wide and deeply appreciative. She knew she looked awful, pasty, with no makeup, her hair a mess, but Josh did not seem to notice, or care, and this made her feel relaxed around him.

Valerie Cowart returned from outside and lifted Susie's arm, the one that had vascular access for dialysis. "How are we feeling?"

Susie liked Nurse Valerie immensely. In a way, she reminded Susie of her mother, only twenty years older. Valerie managed to keep in great shape thanks to a dedicated regimen of walking. She was tall and long-limbed, with a glowing, round face, deep brown eyes, and short dark hair streaked throughout with gray. She always dressed for outdoors, not in some nurse's uniform or scrubs, which made Susie feel a little less like a patient.

"What's wrong with me?" Susie's voice had become quiet.

Valerie pulled her lips together. "I don't know the answer to that one, I'm afraid. But I do know you're a fighter. You're going to pull through this. I can feel it."

Valerie checked Susie's vitals, which were holding steady. She retreated to the kitchen, where she washed the dinner dishes before sitting down to the meal Josh had left for her on the dining room table.

Josh stayed on the front porch while Susie ate, keeping lookout, eyes fixed to the vast forest before him, alert as an eagle guarding its nest. When he came back inside, Susie called him over to her bed.

"Why are you here?" she asked. "And why is the Secret Service involved?"

Josh lifted Susie's tray off the bed and set it on the floor. Susie sensed his reluctance to answer.

"We think somebody is trying to hurt you," he finally said.

"Who?"

"We don't know."

"Was the gas leak an accident?"

"We don't know."

A word flashed in Susie's mind.

Murder.

"Tell me the truth," Susie said. "Does Cam Hilliard have what I have? Does this have something to do with the TPI?"

"Guess my answer."

Josh's broad smile was the best part of Susie's day. A spark flared in her eyes. "You don't know," she said.

To Susie's surprise, Josh brushed a strand of hair that had fallen in front of her face, and his touch sent shivers through her body. He was older and extremely handsome and if she ever had a serious boyfriend she'd want him to be like Josh—strong and confident, not like the cellist she had once dated whose hand got sweaty whenever she held it.

"Just know I'll be here, watching over you. I might not be Secret Service like my mom, but the army trained me pretty good."

"Pretty well."

"Yeah, that too," Josh said, not skipping a beat. "Well or good, believe it when I say you're safe with me."

She believed him.

Josh pulled up a stool, sat down beside Susie's bed, and the two of them spent time talking as though they were out on a dinner date. She was curious about him. If he was going to guard her life, she wanted to know him better. Susie shared stories of her family that brought tears to her eyes, while Josh told her of his time in the military, his love of skiing, and mentioned a recent breakup with a woman named Hannah. Susie was not at all displeased by this breakup news. Their banter was effortless, and twice he made her laugh hard, something she had not done in ages.

Susie surveyed the room, taking inventory of all the belongings Dr. Blackwood had brought from home. The books and clothes were comfortingly familiar, but her eyes went to another object on the floor next to a stack of books—her violin case.

"Could you please hand that to me?" She pointed.

"Sure thing," said Josh.

Josh retrieved the violin and handed it to Susie. She sat more upright in bed. After undoing the metal clasps, Susie opened the case, brushing her hand against the soft, velvety interior, feeling the plush texture tickle her fingertips. She took the instrument, her backup violin, in her hands. The burnished wood gleamed brightly when it caught the glow of the powerful portable lamps near her bedside.

"Do you play any instruments?" she asked.

"Does Spotify count?" Josh's half smile was endearing.

"Not really," she said, crinkling her nose at him. "What do you like to listen to?"

"Um . . . Metallica?"

Her expression turned playfully curious. "Are you saying you listen to Metallica, or are you unsure of what it is you listen to?"

"I'm sure I listen to it, but I'm unsure if you've heard of them."

"Just because I play Bach doesn't mean I don't know who Metallica is," said Susie playfully. She paused, pondering something. "You do know who Bach is, don't you?"

"You mean my man, Johann?"

Susie's eyes went wide with surprise. "I'm impressed," she said.

She removed the bow from the case and ran her fingers along the thin ribbons of fine horsehair before placing her chin on the chin rest. Touching her instrument reset Susie's mood.

"My parents loved it when I played," she said.

Gone. They're gone.

But she could still play for them.

Susie pulled the bow across the strings and felt her spirits soar as the notes spilled out. Out of the corner of her eye, Susie saw Josh smiling at her as she played, and it sent her spirits soaring even higher.

MAUSER WAS sleeping on his couch when a phone call woke him. He checked the number and became fully alert in a blink. Rainmaker did not call often, or without good reason.

"I told you, I have no idea where the girl's gone to," Mauser said in response to Rainmaker's question. "I've checked all over. One of my best customers is a hacker working for the damn NSA. . . . Hey, easy, easy, he's not some outsider, I'm not an idiot. . . . You know him, hell, you hired him, remember? Anyway, I gave him a few freebies and he got into the electronic records systems of the largest hospitals. They all share patient information these days. He went looking for new patients with those symptoms you told me about, or close to it, and I've checked them all out, but none of them match our girl."

More grumblings from Rainmaker. Mauser was getting edgy. Meth was a steady trade, and access to the drug had certainly come in handy when he had tried to do away with the girl. But the real cash cow these days was in opioids. Synthetic crap, a lot of it coming from China, was flooding the market, driving up the price for the real deal. If he lost his oxy supply, which Rainmaker threatened would happen, it would crush his profits. Rainmaker warned him again of the coming drought.

"Well, what do you want me to do?" Mauser asked. "I can't find her."

Rainmaker expressed his displeasure at Mauser's failure to do away with the girl—again.

"Look, you agreed to the plan, it's not all on me," Mauser said.

Rainmaker thought it *was* all on him.

"Whatever," Mauser said. "The dose of meth she got should have killed her, but then again the gas should have killed her, too. What can I tell you, there's something weird with her. The doctor—Blackwood—I bet you anything he's the one who saved her."

Apparently that doc had been a source of surprise all around. Rainmaker went off on him for a while. Even gave Mauser a detailed dossier on Blackwood, including revelations that his ex-wife was Secret Service and his kid ex-military, all of which could complicate matters.

"So is that what this call is about?" Mauser asked. "The doc? He's got you that spooked?"

More chatter. Yeah, Rainmaker was spooked all right. If Rainmaker had given orders to do away with Doc Blackwood, he'd have died in that hospital stairwell, but no such mandate had been issued, and Mauser did not kill for sport.

"I've got bigger fish to catch and fry," Mauser said, thinking now was not the time to add a new target to his hit list. "I can't be stretched that thin."

Wrong answer.

Mauser sat up, rubbing at his face to wipe the sleep from his eyes. Light streamed into his apartment overlooking the D.C. cityscape from a bank of west-facing windows. By D.C. standards, Mauser's home was a pretty nice place to live. It had two generous-sized bedrooms, and the airy layout with high ceilings and wood floors was nicely furnished with a modern, industrial flair. The couch where Mauser had fallen asleep (low to the ground with durable red cushions) cost over two thousand dollars. The idea of trading these digs for a concrete cell made Mauser shudder.

"Why don't you listen before you get all crazy on me," Mauser said in an angry tone. "I can still do it. I can still handle Doc Blackwood *and* the other job, but I don't have to be the one to do it. I got a guy, name's Willie Caine. He rides with me. Kid's got a crazy long rap sheet, but he's also got skills. We'll take Doc Blackwood out at his practice. Bait him there if we have to. If something goes wrong—and I'm not saying it will, but if it does—the police will think Caine's a junkie looking for a fix."

At last, Mauser had said something Rainmaker agreed with.

"Now, what about the boy?" Mauser asked. Obviously, Rainmaker knew he was referring to Cam Hilliard. Rainmaker told him what was going to happen.

Mauser smiled to himself. It was cool to know the biggest news story in the world hours before it happened.

CHAPTER 38

Karen used the few minutes she had before Cam had to leave for school to check in with Josh. It had been two days since she had left, and guilt and worry were starting to take hold.

"It's all good, Mom," Josh said. "Valerie has been great, and Susie's doing well. No physical problems. Dialysis seems to be doing its job. She has these occasional body jerks. They're pretty freaky."

"Your dad calls it myoclonus. It's kind of like a mini seizure," Karen said.

"Yeah, Valerie told me. Not sure why, but her arms are itchy all the time and bruised for no reason. Other than that and the fevers that come and go there's no big change in her health, if that's your concern."

"I'm concerned about you needing to use that SIG Sauer," Karen retorted.

"If I do, I do," Josh said, sounding confident. "But nobody's come around. Susie's been playing her violin, which has been really nice and it seems to take her mind off things. I love listening to her play. I just hope she's going to be all right, you know—with her health."

"I hope so, too."

Karen did not know what else to say. She was glad not to hear the ache for Hannah in her son's voice. It was obvious that in Josh's short time guarding Susie he had developed feelings for the girl. They were only six years apart. Considering how Lee is eight years her senior, Karen fully understood the appeal of an older man. She would not be at all surprised if Josh's feelings were reciprocated.

"How's Dad making out?"

"Nothing so far. He's got some environmental company testing the air and water at the TPI. We'll see what that brings, but he's not expecting much. He's convinced Yoshi is giving these kids something other than ProNeural. No other explanation works for him."

"Makes sense," Josh said.

"He's been catching up with patients and researching nootropics in his spare time, trying to cross-reference different synthetic compounds with Susie and Cam's symptoms. So far no luck, but he's pushing ahead."

"Well, don't worry about us," Josh said. "We're fine here. I oiled all the guns, made sure everything is in good working order. I even drove into town and picked up a battery-powered infrared motion detector at Walmart. It's Bluetooth enabled, so if anybody drives down the road, I'll know they're coming before they get here."

"You sound like a Secret Service agent. You know, if this whole Colorado thing doesn't work out—"

"Love you, Mom," Josh said, interrupting. "But let's not worry about my career. Deal?"

"Deal," Karen said, and after a few more pleasant exchanges, ended the call.

She checked her watch. It was time for school, or more aptly, time to bring Cam to school. Until she fully understood the threat facing him, she would be a part of his escort team.

Duffy drove the SUV, a black Ford Explorer with tinted windows, up from the garage. Karen motioned for him to get out so she could drive. They had multiple routes to Cam's school, and she wanted to mix things up in case somebody had an ambush in mind. Duffy climbed into the passenger seat, muttering something under his breath, not happy about his boss taking charge.

Graves' disease, thought Karen once again.

She had noticed other odd behaviors in Duffy that morning. How he avoided making eye contact with her, how his fingers appeared extra animated, how sweat glistened on his skin even though the temps that morning were unseasonably cool. Something was indeed wrong with him, and Karen decided it was time to move him off Cam's detail permanently. Hard conversation to have, for sure, but Duffy's medical condition seemed to be worsening. She would call HR and make the move that afternoon.

Cam shuffled over to the idling SUV with Beats by Dre headphones clamped around his wiry neck. While he looked dashing in his school uniform, Karen thought he seemed extra melancholic.

"Hanging in there, buddy?" she asked, opening the car's back door.

"Yeah, just—a bad night's sleep, is all," he said in a quiet voice.

He looked and sounded tired. She wondered if he had suffered a seizure during the night, if Gleason had held back the medication Lee prescribed, if some toxin he'd been exposed to was wreaking havoc on his body.

The convoy—if two SUVs ferrying five Secret Service agents and one child of the president could be considered a convoy—was off with all the fanfare of a departing school bus. Karen drove in the lead, headed in a northerly direction on Sixteenth Street. Normally, she would have taken K Street to Rock Creek Parkway, but instead kept driving north on Sixteenth.

Duffy's face revealed his surprise. "What are you doing?" he asked, his expression almost a scowl.

"Changing things up," Karen said. "We're taking Beach Drive instead."

"That's—that's going—going to—to add ten minutes to the drive," Duffy said, stuttering.

Karen shot him a sideways glance. "Which is why I told you that we're leaving ten minutes early for school."

Checking the rearview mirror, Karen watched Cam stare absentmindedly out the window, his headphones in place, head bobbing slightly to the music.

"I don't even know what you're doing here," Duffy said in an angry voice. "This is my detail."

"Last I checked," Karen said in a neutral tone, "you worked for me."

As she weaved her way through the morning traffic, Karen kept a vigilant eye on everything: her surroundings, the distance between her car and the follow vehicle, and Cam. She took it all in with practiced efficiency. It was only because she was being so cautious that she happened to catch a quick glimpse of Duffy using his cell phone. The rules around cell phone use were ingrained in every officer. Few employee misconduct violations were more egregious than being distracted while on protective duty.

"Hey!" Karen said, pointing to the cell phone Duffy unsuccessfully tried to shield with his leg. "You put that damn thing away this instant. What the hell is wrong, Stephen? Keep your eyes open. BOLO—be on the lookout. That's the job!"

Karen exhaled a few calming breaths. If anything, Duffy was giving her more reason to do what had to be done. It was medical with him, she reminded herself. Maybe he couldn't control his impulses. Maybe those same impulse problems were contributing to the money woes he insisted he did not have.

She was driving along a leafy stretch of Seventeenth Street, almost to the turnoff, when Karen caught sight of Duffy texting once again.

"What the hell, Duffy!" she yelled. "Put it away!"

The force of her voice overpowered the music in Cam's headphones, causing him to jump in his seat. Duffy startled as well. He glared angrily at Karen, his breathing erratic and shallow. Sweat coated his face.

"What the hell is going on with you?" she said, furious. "Are you okay?"

"It's nothing," Duffy said, avoiding Karen's stare by looking out the window. "I'm fine. It's just an urgent thing. A personal matter. I'm sorry. I shouldn't have done it."

"Damn right, you shouldn't."

Some time later they were driving through Rock Creek Park, traveling along a narrow two-lane road lined on both sides with leafy trees. Running parallel to the road was a dirt pathway used by runners or bikers who could handle the ruts and stones. Karen was still trying to tamp down her anger, checking her rearview mirror once again, when she noticed what appeared to be a dirt bike with narrow tires, cruising down the jogging path at a high rate of speed. The bike's frame was small and light with a hydraulic and spring shock suspension.

Right away Karen's body tensed. Because the bike was on the path and not the road, it could easily pass traffic on the left. It was certainly a convenient mode of transportation for the rider and a fast-growing trend, but it was also illegal on D.C. streets, given how dirt bikes lacked such basic safety features as headlights or turn signals. D.C. police policy, however, did not allow officers to give chase. They could snap pictures of the offenders, but that did little to deter those urban riders, who were deemed a public menace. This rider could have been a harmless thrill seeker, but something in Karen's gut urged caution.

Her focus kept shifting between the rearview and the road with regular frequency. The dirt bike seemed to be gaining on them. Soon it would pass the escort vehicle. The rider was dressed all in black. The visor of his helmet was tinted dark, like the windows of the SUV.

A cold feeling of dread overcame her. She focused more on the rearview than the road. Cam, with his headphones on, was oblivious. Karen's fingers tightened against the steering wheel. Hairs on her neck began to rise as her muscles turned taut. The patter of her heartbeat became erratic.

When she heard the distinct whine of an engine revving for speed, Karen glanced back in time to see the dirt bike rocket forward with velocity. At the same instant, she observed the driver reaching behind him, and only then did she realize he had a backpack. The whine of the bike's engine intensified. The black-clad rider zoomed past the escort vehicle, driving one-handed.

Karen's world became a single point of focus. All her energy, her every intention, was not on the road, but on the threat behind her.

The rider's hand slipped inside the pack's open top. Quickly, his arm came forward. While she could not be sure what it was in his hand exactly, it looked long and made of steel. A thought flashed through Karen's mind: *This is what I trained for, the day I hoped would never come.* She had endured a variety of simulated attacks, navigated serpentine courses through tightly spaced objects, and learned evasive driving maneuvers all with one goal in mind: safeguard the lives of those in her protection.

With one hand gripping the wheel Karen reached behind her, stretching as far as her arm would allow. Seizing the lapel of Cam's school jacket, she gave a hard pull, yanking him forward. He let out a cry of surprise.

"Get down!" she yelled. "Down!"

Cam fell to the floor of the SUV just as the dirt bike pulled alongside. Now she saw it, the long black gun barrel rising up as the rider took aim at Cam's window. It was a massive weapon. More like a rifle than a handgun.

Instinctively, Karen jerked the wheel left, but she could not execute a 180-degree turn without causing a head-on collision. A sudden stop, slamming on the brakes, would cause a rear-end collision with the SUV traveling behind them.

From outside she heard a quick series of pops. The window held for two shots, but on the third it shattered, spraying shards of thick bullet-resistant glass inward like sea spray from a crashing wave.

Bright flashes ignited in her mirrors. Agents in the rear car were returning gunfire. Beside her, Duffy was reaching for his weapon, but his movements seemed languid. He got his window down as a car traveling in the opposite direction passed Karen's vehicle on the left. The road ahead was clear.

Now! she thought. *Do it now!*

Karen pumped the brakes while spinning the wheel hard and counter-clockwise. Duffy fired off a shot from his SIG Sauer that sank into the trees because the SUV had slipped into a skid. A loud screech of tires, rubber burning, came before acrid smoke stained the air. The dirt bike quickly abandoned the path, changing course sharply, now headed for the woods lining the parkway, where oversized SUVs could not pursue. Not that they would try, even if they could. The mission of the Secret Service was to protect and evade, not apprehend.

Glancing in the rearview, Karen saw the escort vehicle initiate the same evasive bootleg maneuver, sending a fresh batch of smoke skyward as tires screeched against the road. The escort vehicle sped up, getting right behind Karen's car, almost kissing the bumper while traveling at a high rate of speed. Cam lay curled in a ball on the floor, his body covered in shards of glass, arms shielding his head.

CHAPTER 39

Karen got on the two-way radio. She had to alert the Secret Service command post (aka "Horsepower") located in the West Wing directly below the Oval Office.

In addition to the team riding in the escort vehicle, agents from the UD, Uniformed Division, as well as the Secret Service, monitored the frequency Karen was using 24-7.

"Horsepower, Ray."

Everyone at work knew Karen by her maiden name.

"Horsepower here. Go ahead, K-Ray."

"Advise, we've had shots fired," Karen said, managing to speak in an even, steady voice despite the rapid canter of her heart. "Shots fired at Blitz. No injuries."

Blitz, a chess term, was code for Cam's convoy.

"Bishop is okay," Karen said with authority. "Follow-up. Bishop is okay."

Horsepower said, "Confirm, you wanna go to the hospital or back to the White House?"

"We're all right . . . back to the White House. Back to the White House. Bishop is okay," Karen said.

"Okay, okay," said Horsepower.

"Tell everyone to stay off the air for now. Bishop's all right. Request MPD escort at intersection Seventeenth and Piney Branch Parkway. ETA three minutes."

"That's a roger," Horsepower said.

Karen took another glance in her rearview and detected no threats behind them, none up ahead either. Speeding down the parkway, strobes flashing, horn honking, Karen forced cars onto the grassy patch lining the side of the road. Moments later, she could hear sirens off in the distance headed their way. MPD must have been close by.

When the intersection with Seventeenth Street came into view, Karen counted four police cars already on the scene, lights flashing and blocking traffic. She brought her vehicle to a hard stop with a slight squeal of tires. The escort vehicle behind her came to a stop as well. Exiting the car, gun drawn, Karen yanked open the passenger door and urged Cam forward with a wave of her hand. He needed to be transported to the White House in a more secure vehicle, one that had all its bullet-resistant windows still intact.

"It's okay, it's okay," she said. "You're safe. Come on, Cam. Take my hand."

As Cam lifted his head, shards of glass stuck in his hair cascaded to the floor mat with plinking sounds. He reached for Karen's outstretched hand, terror burned into his eyes.

Every second it seemed more police were arriving on the scene, sirens blaring, lights flashing. Joining them was an armored SWAT vehicle, several fire engines, and even an ambulance. It was an incredible show of force, and one that had assembled with startling efficiency.

Pulling Cam gently from the car, Karen shielded his body with her own as she scanned the tree line for movement, any signs of a possible sniper.

Sensing the all clear, Karen led Cam to the escort vehicle with her arm draped around him. Police officers rushed toward her. Above, an MPD helicopter hovered. Dirt kicked up from the fierce winds of the whirling blades got behind Karen's sunglasses to sting her eyes. Cam kept his shoulders hunched forward, shielding his face with his arms to guard against the winds.

"Get him home!" Karen yelled while easing Cam into the backseat of the idling SUV. She positioned him in the middle seat, in between two agents who had their guns drawn. "I want a rolling escort back to the White House," she instructed an MPD officer standing nearby. "No stops. Block traffic ahead. Go now! Get it organized. Now!"

MPD held joint training exercises with the Secret Service on a regular basis—they knew what to do and how to do it.

On the way back to her SUV, Karen noticed something she had missed. The other car was a Chevy Suburban, which had a bullet-resistant-glass rating of level seven, able to withstand five shots from a 5.56mm rifle. The Ford Explorer she was driving, while armored as well, only had a level-two rating on the glass, which could handle a couple shots from a .357 Magnum with soft-point bullets, considerably less firepower. It was hard for Karen to be certain because of all the commotion, the speed at which everything had unfolded, but she believed the gun the biker had used might have been a SIG MCX Pistol. If memory served correctly, and usually it did, the SIG pistol fired a 5.56mm round, enough to shatter the weaker bullet-resistant glass.

It was a disturbing observation.

Soon they were off. She took lead again, racing through red lights, traveling at a high rate of speed, the road ahead cleared for her passage. Through her peripheral vision, she watched Duffy closely, curious to see if he attempted to use his phone again. He did not. His expression was a blank. It was like he had switched off, gone into shock or something. His sweating had stopped. His fingers had gone still.

By now Horsepower would have altered POTUS and FLOTUS. Teams would be assembling. Gleason would want to examine Cam, while his mother and father would want to console him.

"How are you holding up?" Duffy asked, as Karen sped through yet another red light.

"Fine," she said in an icy voice. Her tone made it clear there would be no idle chitchat.

Eventually, the convoy arrived back at the White House. Pedestrians on the street and drivers trapped in their vehicles, waiting for the go-ahead from the police, rubbernecked with intense curiosity.

When Cam was out of danger, after the Uniformed Division had escorted the SUVs through the White House gates, Karen did not relax. Because she was the agent in charge of the first family detail, it was Karen's duty to lead the debriefing in the Situation Room. She would do this, but only after her colleague—her employee, really—answered her questions.

The SUV carrying Bishop headed to the West Wing entrance, where Cam could be brought inside the White House undercover. Karen got on the radio.

"Horsepower, Ray."

"Ray, go."

"Bishop is home safe. Parking my car. Will meet in the Situation Room."

"Roger, out."

The underground garage was dimly lit and deserted when Karen pulled into an available space. Duffy got out of the car at the same time as Karen. He started for the elevator, but stopped when Karen called his name. He turned to face her.

"Who were you texting?" she asked.

Duffy took a step toward her. Karen tensed.

"I told you, personal business." His voice was a low rumble.

"Give me your phone," Karen said.

Duffy's face registered surprise. "What? No."

"Hand it over." Karen took a step toward him, her hand already at her hip.

Duffy tensed and took a step back, fixing her with a scathing stare.

"Why did you bring up the Explorer from the garage?"

Duffy tried to act offended, confused, when in Karen's eyes he just appeared guilty. "What are you talking about?" he asked.

"The bullet-resistant-glass level on the Explorer is a two. I should have noticed, but I didn't. You didn't think I was coming on the drive in the first place. I saw you sweating, and don't try to tell me it was your medical condition."

"You're sounding crazy, you know that?"

Maybe, but Duffy's hand had moved closer toward his hip.

"How did the biker know where we were?" Karen asked. "I took a route we've never taken before. How did he know?"

"Maybe he was tailing us?"

"How did he know?" She said it more forcibly this time.

"K-Ray, think about what you're doing here." It sounded like a warning. Duffy's fingers were moving, nervously twitching, as his hand inched closer toward his gun.

"Who paid you?"

"This is wrong, Karen. You're accusing me of something I didn't do."

"Then hand over your phone."

Duffy got a distant look in his eyes, one Karen found deeply troubling. "You froze. I pulled Cam down to the floor—"

"What? You did—"

That was when Karen realized Duffy was concocting his explanation for what he was planning to do.

"You were petrified, crying even. I had to take over. You're not fit for duty—and when I told you I was going to have to report you—"

"Duffy, don't do this."

Karen pushed back her suit jacket so she could reach her weapon more easily.

"—went crazy—you pulled your gun on me—"

It was a crazy story, one that would never stand up to scrutiny, but Duffy was not thinking clearly. His fingertips brushed against his SIG Sauer, tapping a fast beat against the butt of his weapon.

We're alone down here, she thought, panicked now. *No witnesses.*

"There's another way," Karen said. "Hand over your phone and your gun. That's what you have to do. Are you working with Yoshi? Is Gleason involved? Is this about Cam's sickness? Talk to me, Duffy. Please—talk to me."

"You just—went—crazy—"

Karen kept a close watch on Duffy's hand, waiting for the slightest twitch.

When it happened, it was so stunning, so unbelievable, she almost failed to react. His left hand, his weak side, pulled his suit jacket back, clearly exposing his weapon. Karen did the same, only a fraction of a second behind him. But when he went for his gun, his right hand failed to make solid contact with the handle of his SIG. Karen did not have this problem. She cleared the gun from the holster first and slapped her left hand to her right as she took a firing stance. Her finger found the trigger only when she was ready to engage.

Her eyes were dry. Hands steady.

Duffy's gun was out of the holster, rising up from his waist when she pulled the trigger. The bang echoed off the concrete walls. The flashes were blinding. Her hearing was gone. Three bullets struck Duffy in the chest. He dropped to the ground, grunting, but there was no blood. Karen had fired knowing the body armor agents on protective detail were mandated to wear would keep him alive.

Duffy lay on his back, his breathing labored, chest heaving. Somehow, though, he had managed to keep hold of his gun. He was still a threat, but in too much pain, too immobilized to sit up and fire. He could still move his arm, though, and as he did, brought the gun barrel level with his temple.

Karen's eyes widened. "No!"

Her scream rang louder than the gunshot when Duffy pulled the trigger.

And then there was blood.

CHAPTER 40

Seven hours after the shooting, Lee found himself seated in the White House Situation Room. It was a state-of-the-art facility with high-tech video conferencing capability and a closed-circuit television system. The monitors mounted to the walls broadcasted breaking news from around the globe. No surprise, the attempted assassination of Cam Hilliard was the only story the media cared to cover.

The president had already given a statement, one that Lee had been watching on TV at home, when Woody Lapham showed up with orders to bring him to the White House. The information given to the American people was brief and, thought Lee, intentionally vague. A Secret Service agent was dead, Hilliard had said. No further details were given. A gunman was still at large. Again, no further details given. Several terrorist organizations took credit for the attack, but those claims had yet to be verified.

Homeland Security and the FBI were leading the investigation task force. In conclusion, the president reiterated the most important fact: Cam was unharmed, thanks largely to the actions of Karen Ray.

Now, he was with her, seated at the same massive conference table. The president sat at the head of the table, looking haggard, emotionally and physically drained.

"Dr. Blackwood, thank you for being here."

"Of course," Lee said. "I'm at your service, Mr. President."

Lee had expected a full room, maybe with decorated generals, the vice president, a bunch of cabinet secretaries. Instead there were lots of empty seats, probably because everyone else was busy tracking down the shooter. Ellen Hilliard was there, seated next to Karen, who sat beside the barrel-chested Director of the United States Secret Service, Russell Ferguson. The director is appointed, serving at the pleasure of the President of the United States, but unlike the Secretary of Homeland Security, to whom the director reports, the position does not require Senate confirmation.

The older gentleman seated across from them was the president's chief of staff, John O'Donnell. O'Donnell, slimmer, with salt-and-pepper hair, a pronounced Adam's apple, and a prominent nose, was widely respected for his candor with the media.

"I requested a scaled-down meeting," the president said, "because I would like to discuss some rather sensitive issues with you personally, Dr. Blackwood."

Lee strained to get his mind around the enormity of what had transpired and what role in all of this he could possibly play.

"Please, call me Lee, and yes, anything you need. How is Cam?"

"He's fine. Resting upstairs," Ellen said with an appreciative glance toward Karen. "Badly scared, of course."

"We're looking for a motive here," the president said. "Naturally, we're thinking terrorism and we're actively pursuing intelligence there, but Karen said you have a different theory."

"The TPI?" Lee was surprised Karen had been so candid.

"She's spoken with us extensively, and has convinced me that it's an avenue worth exploring. I have to confess, Lee, what she told me is hard to believe."

"I'm assuming you're referring to Yoshi Matsumoto."

"You really want me to believe that the director of an after-school program is the mastermind behind Cam's attempted murder?" The president shook his head dismissively. "I've known this man for years," said President Hilliard. "He's been a mentor to my son."

"I believe he may have been using Cam and other TPI students as test subjects, guinea pigs if you will, for nootropic drugs that enhance cognition."

"What makes you think that?" the president asked.

"Mr. President, I have no other explanation," Lee said. "I strongly believe some illness is affecting your son, as it is Susie Banks, and I believe the Stewart twins before they died. All of them attended the TPI, and from what I gather all were the best of the best. Diseases like they have don't cluster like this without some sort of an external catalyst—poisoned water, poisoned air, something ingested into the body."

"Well, what *about* contaminated groundwater or something like that?" Chief of staff John O'Donnell's voice was raspy from hours of issuing commands.

"We're testing for that now," said Lee. "But I believe those results will be negative. There'd be a lot more sick kids otherwise. I think the affected population is far more limited . . . and controlled."

"But Cam didn't have the red spot in his eyes," the president said.

"True," Lee said. "He did not. It could be that the red spot presents only after a certain length of time, or perhaps after a certain degree of exposure to this unknown toxin."

"I'm still not convinced there's a connection to Cam. He's different, that's what I think, it's what I believe," the president said. "But in light of the extraordinary and horrific events of today, I'm willing to keep a door open—explore this further."

Ferguson's brow furrowed, conveying his deep skepticism. "You honestly think this Yoshi fellow got to one of our special agents and turned him?" he asked.

"I don't know how Stephen Duffy is involved," Lee admitted with regret.

"The FBI has already done some serious digging into Mr. Duffy," O'Donnell said. "Forensic teams are still working on decrypting his phone, computers, and such, but a search of his apartment netted us some interesting finds."

Judging by the impassive looks around the table, Lee guessed he was the only one present not yet informed of these findings.

"Mr. Duffy evidently had a serious gambling problem. Some documents we've recovered indicate he went on a catastrophic weeklong bender and lost more than a quarter of a million dollars. Money he didn't have to lose. On a special agent's salary, that's an insurmountable hole. He signed over the deed to his mother's house as collateral, and the bookies he owed were ready to close the deal. His sixty-five-year-old mom was going to be out on the street."

Lee recalled the bet Duffy had made with Lapham about the Graves' disease test. What had, at the time, seemed a harmless and amusing wager in reality masked a deep and deadly compulsion.

"What we didn't find," O'Donnell added in a somber tone, "is any link between Yoshi Matsumoto and Agent Duffy, which, to Russell's point, gives us pause."

"I don't know what to say there," Lee offered. "I'm honestly as in the dark as you are. I just have my suspicions."

"And those are?" Ferguson asked.

"The nootropics."

"Cam's been taking the ProNeural supplements for years without a problem," Ellen said. "Dr. Gleason said they're as safe as vitamins, and Cam says it helps him."

"I'm not doubting that," Lee said. "But I don't think *those* ProNeural pills are the issue."

The president leaned forward in his seat, hands resting on the table, his fingers clasped tightly together.

"This is why I wanted you here," the president said. "Help us better understand your thinking, Lee."

"I've consulted with a neurologist, Dr. Marilyn Piekarski, who treated Cam at the MDC, and she believes, as do I, that the ProNeural products could not have produced the impressive results I saw on the neurofeedback testing. Something else these kids are taking is enhancing the brain's natural neuroplasticity."

"Neuro what?" Ellen's eyes were open wide.

"Neuroplasticity," Lee repeated for her benefit. "It's essentially the brain's ability to reorganize itself by forming new neural connections among nerve cells to learn faster and much more efficiently. It's how a person can become a master at a new skill. We all have this to some extent. But what if I could give you a drug, something that changes your brain's chemistry, speeds up your ability to learn? Take the ten-thousand-hours rule to reach mastery down to a few hundred."

"A pill to do that is only in the movies," Ellen said. "What you're saying seems like quite a stretch."

"I'm suggesting the folks at ProNeural may have found the chemicals to do what you see in the movies, and they're using the TPI to put their product to the ultimate test."

"So Yoshi's trying to put himself out of business with a brain pill, is that it?" Ferguson sounded doubtful, while Karen grimaced slightly at the harsh tone her boss had taken.

"I think he's trying to make a business," said Lee. "If a pill like that was shown to be safe and effective, millions of people would take it. No question there."

"And Duffy?"

"Somehow Yoshi knew about his financial troubles," Lee said. "Duffy's interacted with Yoshi before, when Cam was at the TPI. Maybe Duffy confessed to having serious money troubles, and maybe Yoshi saw an opportunity to—and I apologize for my phrasing here—deal with a problem of his."

"The problem being Cam," Ellen said coolly.

"Yes, Cam and Susie. The twins, too. Really, anybody who ingested this product and got sick because of it."

Lee contemplated accusing Gleason of being cagey with Cam to conceal his possible involvement with Yoshi, but without hard evidence feared it would further muddy these already murky waters.

"So every student at the TPI is taking experimental nootropics?" O'Donnell, who asked the question, drummed his fingers on the table in a way that reminded Lee of Duffy.

"I highly doubt it. Just like with air or groundwater contamination, there'd be a lot more sick kids if that were the case. I think—and again, this is conjecture on my part—he has some students taking the experimental drug, and the others are a control group of sorts, ingesting a harmless nootropic. Then he compares, measures if the test subjects can master skills with greater efficiency using neurofeedback testing, not realizing he's turning them into walking time bombs."

"So is Cam all right?" Ellen asked with alarm. "Physically, I mean. Is he a—a time bomb?"

"I don't know," Lee said, regretting his word choice. "We'll just have to see. I have no idea what course this may take with Cam. If these children are being poisoned, our goal is to find out, eliminate it, and work on a treatment."

He had to give her some hope.

Ellen exchanged nervous glances with her husband.

The president said, "Out of extreme caution, I'm willing to give Lee another chance to prove his case."

"Have other students besides those we know about experienced symptoms similar to Cam's?" Karen asked.

"That's a good question," Lee said. "There was another doctor at the meeting, Hal Hewitt, who is on the board of the TPI, and he couldn't say for sure."

"I know Hal," Ellen said. "He's a very good man, but he has nothing to do with the kids' medical health. He's just an advisor."

"Which is why I think we'd have to pull medical records for all the students who have ever attended the institute," Lee said.

"We can get subpoenas to do that," O'Donnell said.

"Then do it," the president said. "But for now, I want a low profile on this. We have a shooter out there, and our focus needs to be on tracking him down. This Susie girl, is she safe?"

"She is, for now," Karen said. "We have her out at the camp I own in Virginia. Our son Josh is looking after her, and there's a nurse, Valerie Cowart, monitoring her health."

"We think whoever tried to kill Cam also tried to kill Susie," Lee added, speaking for Karen.

"That might be," the president said. "I'm thinking if we find a link, some irrefutable connection, we'll take over protective duties from Josh."

"Why not move her now?" Lee never thought he would openly question the president's judgment.

"Because, believe it or not, Washington is not great at keeping secrets," the president said. "The public would think I've lost my mind if they found out I'm going after some schoolteacher and sheltering a musician when somebody just tried to kill my son. Our collective focus has to be on tracking down the shooter. That's the plan moving forward, unless I'm given reason to do otherwise."

Typical Hilliard, thought Lee. *Always thinking about perceptions, trying to keep equilibrium. Not doing too much, or too little. Never being bold.*

"As you wish," Lee said.

The president directed his attention to his chief of staff.

"John, I want you to take point on this," he said. "Let's get Yoshi in for questioning. Have Dr. Blackwood involved. He can handle the medical aspects of the interview."

Lee grimaced. *How does the FBI interview people?* he wondered. Were they going to waterboard him? Bring him to a black site? Lee had no idea how the government operated in this regard, and the thought that he had instigated all of this chilled him to the core.

"See what we can do about this ProNeural company, too," the president continued. "Coordinate everything with the FBI. Maybe we can conduct a records search or something, but whatever we do, I want it all aboveboard. Also, have Dr. Blackwood involved in reviewing the medical records of the TPI students. Cycle Dr. Gleason in as well. They'll both know what to look for."

Lee wondered how Gleason would feel if he knew a *family doc* had had such a large role to play in this operation.

"What about the shooter?" Ferguson asked.

"Hopefully, if Lee's theory proves out, Yoshi will lead us to him."

Ferguson's face flushed. "Mr. President, shouldn't we take the lead here? I can certainly coordinate with the FBI."

"Russell," Ellen said, interrupting before her husband could answer. "Your team was responsible for protecting my son. How did that turn out?"

"Mrs. Hilliard, I—"

"No. No," Ellen said, shaking her head dismissively. "As far as I'm concerned, the entire Secret Service may be compromised. Now, I've spent years hearing Karen's complaints about your agency, lack of resources, gaps in security, all that—well, shame on me for not doing more to fix it when I had the chance. But I'll tell you this, Russell. You'd better spend your time questioning every agent, every damn one of them, because I don't believe for one second that Stephen Duffy was the only employee of yours with dirty hands."

CHAPTER 41

It was almost ten o'clock at night when Lee got word that a car was coming to bring him to FBI headquarters. Since the 1970s the J. Edgar Hoover Building had occupied two blocks between Ninth and Tenth Streets in Northwest D.C. The building, Lee had read somewhere, was Brutalist architecture, a name derived from the French term *béton brut,* which, translated, meant "raw concrete." It was a fitting name. The concrete behemoth had hundreds of sunken squares for windows, covering an exterior more austere than a prison. Tours of the headquarters had to be arranged through Congressional offices, but John O'Donnell, along with a cadre of humorless G-men all dressed in dark suits, got Lee inside with no problem.

Lee followed O'Donnell and his FBI cohorts through security, and then down a mostly deserted hallway, eventually coming to a stop at an elevator marked RESTRICTED.

"We brought Yoshi in a couple of hours ago. We can hold him for a while without charges. Our agents have already spoken with him extensively."

"And?"

"And the president wants you to speak with him. I'm afraid that's all I can say on the matter."

The elevator arrived. All got inside.

"Okay . . . guess I'll wing it," Lee said, rubbing his tired eyes. He let his annoyance go. He had a job to do: take a medical approach and try and learn something from Yoshi that the professionals could not.

Down they went until the elevator doors opened to reveal a dimly lit corridor in the building's subbasement.

"Welcome to Disneyland," O'Donnell said in a humorless voice. He led Lee into a small room with a low drop ceiling, and some chairs placed around a table with a computer on it. Next to a second door across from the entrance was a rectangular glass window cut into the gray brick wall, through which Lee could see Yoshi, dressed in his trademark black, seated at a metal table.

"We'll be watching and listening from here," O'Donnell said, pointing to that computer.

Lee had to stoop to enter the room holding Yoshi. Inside he found a table, two chairs, a few plastic bottles of water, and nothing else. He noticed a wall-mounted camera in one corner of the room.

Yoshi glanced up as Lee entered, his face brooding, eyes weary. Lee exhaled loudly, trying to clear the uneasy feeling that washed over him.

I'm responsible for this.

The empty chair was made of metal with no cushioning. Nothing here was comforting or comfortable.

Lee sat down across from Yoshi. "I'm sorry it's come to this."

Yoshi glared at Lee, his expression furious. "*You*—you are involved? I should have known."

"Let's cut to the chase," Lee said. "I've already gone over with you what I think is happening here. There are people, lots of them, looking through the medical records of all the TPI students. It's going to come out in the open, so you might as well tell me. Are you testing nootropics, or some kind of smart drug, on your students?"

"I'll tell you again what I told the FBI: I am doing no such thing."

Lee was not trying to detect Yoshi's lies, nor interpret his body language. The FBI had that expertise. Lee would take a different approach. With Cam, he used chess to break the ice. With Yoshi, he would have to play to the man's ego.

"Look, Yoshi, I believe what you do at the TPI is pretty darn remarkable. The results of the neurofeedback testing are astounding. ProNeural seems to be a wonder drug. And yet, based on the compounds in those pills, I'm convinced there's no way *those* nootropics could achieve *those* results. So tell me how you *really* do it."

"My methods, Dr. Blackwood, blend ancient Eastern practices with more modern science. I've said this to you before. Meditation, guided imagery—"

"—breathing exercises, mindfulness, yoga, yeah, yeah, I've memorized your brochure, and I still don't buy it. The results are too impressive. The data in those reports suggests you've unlocked the secret to supercharging the brain's natural neuroplasticity."

"And what if I have?"

"Hey, I believe you're smart, but you're not *that* smart."

So much for kowtowing to his ego, thought Lee.

Pausing to regroup, Lee exhaled loudly. His eyes were dry with fatigue.

"This isn't about your school," Lee said through gritted teeth, getting angry now. "Someone tried to kill Cam Hilliard. I'm sure it's connected to his illness, and his illness, I'm sure, is connected to you and your damn TPI. The people reviewing those medical records are going to find more cases." Lee believed this was true, but he did not know how long it might take to find one. They had thousands of records to review, going back over a decade.

"Help us cure these kids before it's too late," he said, his voice softening. "Tell me what you've given them and maybe, with lots of smart people working the problem, we can reverse the effects."

Yoshi contemplated this, and eventually his demeanor shifted from angry to resigned. When he spoke, his voice held no trace of hostility.

"If you think you will do well at a job interview, you are more likely to do well. Think you'll win a race, you are more likely to win it. Science has shown this to be true, even Western science." Yoshi gave his first smile of this strange interview.

"And your point is?"

"The supplements I supplied were a part of what I do. I tell you to take these pills, because they will help you with focus, with concentration—you're more likely to believe it is true."

"How do you explain your results? So much improvement in so little time."

"I can't, Dr. Blackwood."

"Excuse me?"

"I've spent my life studying herbs and fungi, looking to them for healing powers, looking to nature for the key to human betterment. It's been my lifelong obsession."

"Until you found ProNeural, until you discovered nootropics," said Lee, trying to encourage Yoshi along. "And you thought that was the answer."

"Yes. I came to believe a blend of science and nature was the missing link."

"And?"

"And I was wrong. These nootropics might help in some small way, it's possible, but like you said, they do not help *that* much."

Lee did a double take, confusion etched on his face. "Wait, what are you saying?"

"I'm saying that if I tell you something is true, over and over again, eventually you'll believe me. But if I show you the data, the scientific evidence, your belief will come about much quicker and take far deeper roots."

Lee suddenly got it.

"My God, the data you showed me—what you show the kids, their parents, it's all bogus, it's forged. You made it all up."

Yoshi's guilty expression was answer enough.

"ProNeural doesn't make the students better, but those phony results made the company a lot of money." Yoshi held up his wrist to show Lee his expensive timepiece. "The company and me," he added, regret heavy in his voice. "I suspect I'll need a lawyer now."

"Wait . . . wait a second. Cam, Susie, the Stewart twins, they were all best of the best and they're the sick ones, but you're telling me you didn't give them anything special to do that?"

"No. Nothing. Never. I told you what I did. I helped falsify the results of the neurofeedback testing to sell more ProNeural pills and get more students for the TPI. That's my only crime, that's what I'll live with."

But what Yoshi had said still did not add up in Lee's mind. A cluster of some strange, never-before-seen disease, centered at a single location, and there's not a single external factor involved? It was inconceivable.

"Yoshi, I don't believe you're telling me everything. Please! Lives are at stake."

Yoshi leaned forward and lowered his head. His snow-white hair shielded his eyes.

"What I have given my students is a belief in themselves and their true potential." Yoshi became reserved, retreating into himself. "And that's the only thing I've ever given them."

CHAPTER 42

Two days later, Ellen and Karen were having coffee together in the Navy Mess, a restaurant in the basement of the White House run by the U.S. Navy. In light of the incident, the president had reneged on his plans to attend the upcoming White House Correspondents' Dinner. But to Karen's dismay, not everything was being put on hold.

"Honestly, part of me thinks he'll be safer there," Ellen said sharply.

They had been discussing when it would be the right time for Cam to return to school, and the gibe Ellen made had stung. Every gripe Karen presented over the years, Ellen threw right back at her.

"This is an agency in crisis," Ellen said. "Russell Ferguson is incompetent, and management isn't going to change. You're understaffed, overworked, and the screening standards have gone downhill. You've told me this a thousand times. Don't get me wrong. I'm beyond grateful for what you did. But if I'm being honest, you're the only one on the job right now I trust."

Karen's efforts to transform the culture of her workplace had served only to make her current job more difficult. There was no getting around it—the Secret Service was irreparably tainted in Ellen's eyes.

It would help if they had some answers. Who had gotten to Duffy? Who else had been compromised? Was it connected to Yoshi and the TPI? Why was Cam targeted? Who was the shooter? It had taken days for the FBI to produce useful surveillance footage of the Tsarnaev brothers in the wake of the Boston Marathon bombings. There was no telling when a meaningful lead on the Dirt Bike Shooter might come through.

With so much uncertainly swirling, Ellen was pushing to have the entire first family detail replaced (with Karen as the only exception), but the logistics were complex, not to mention her husband's opposition.

"He says it would show a lack of faith. That it sends the wrong message to the American people." Ellen set her coffee cup down. "Well, it should, shouldn't it," she said. "It's all about perception with him."

"I can work on it with Russell," Karen assured her. "I'm sure we can change the president's mind here. But it's not easy to reassign an entire team. It will take weeks."

"Well, it doesn't take weeks to pull a trigger, now does it?" Ellen retorted. "Anyway, don't bother. You'll just waste your time. I've already talked to Geoffrey and his mind is made up. Someone tried to kill Cam, and my husband thinks I'm overreacting. Enough terrorist organizations are raising their hands to claim responsibility that he thinks it was one of them. That they somehow got to Duffy, and Duffy is the only one. He also thinks Lee is off his rocker and he's pissed at himself for giving so much credence to his theory."

"Lee is seldom wrong."

"Which is the only reason Geoffrey was willing to investigate Yoshi. Now, it's in the hands of the FBI and DOJ. But as far as a link between Susie and Cam, or Lee's suspicions that Yoshi had been giving these kids something other than ProNeural, Geoffrey's done giving that any consideration."

"He said that?"

"No," Ellen said. "He was actually quite a bit harsher."

Karen was not surprised. Lee's narrative, while intriguing, had not fit neatly together. Yoshi was questioned and released, and while everyone believed his arrest on mail and wire fraud charges was imminent, there'd been nothing to validate Lee's thinking.

The media had picked up on the story and angry parents had begun unenrolling their kids from the TPI. Karen had no doubt some anxious executives at ProNeural's Silicon Valley headquarters were busy lawyering up. Lee had managed to uncover a juicy scandal, but nothing more. Even the environmental tests he ordered had come back negative. The medical records search, while not complete, had also been a bust.

Those records were Lee's latest obsession and his final hope. He spent every minute he could spare obtaining and reviewing medical records of hundreds of TPI students from over the years. The process was painfully slow and O'Donnell's task force had no extra resources to help, leaving it up to Paul and Lee to do much of the work.

If Cam were sicker, if he had the red spot in his eyes, something— but, no, he was simply tired, moody, and morose. Was it because he was depressed, traumatized, or having nocturnal seizures? The attack on him notwithstanding, something was not right with him. But it was not, as yet, enough of a something to keep him home from school.

Karen sighed. Ellen and Cam had formed a united front. "Has the president cleared this?"

Ellen's eyes turned fiery. "He's my son, too, you know."

"I'm sorry—I just—I really think it's too soon," Karen said.

"Well, Cam wants to go to school on Monday and I'm supporting his decision. I've spoken to several experts in traumatic experiences, and they've urged him to return to his normal routine as quickly as possible. If he just sits in his bedroom all day, he'll think obsessively about what happened. He needs to be distracted. He has to move around, engage with his peers, be with people he *trusts*."

Karen noted how Ellen emphasized that last word.

"And for your information, yes, the president thinks it shows strength of character, not only for Cam, but for America. Like it or not, we're sym- bols. We will not be deterred or terrified into submission. There are many reasons to resume our lives, but few to cower. If Cam needed the time to recover, of course we'd give it to him. But *he* wants to go."

In the end, what choice did Karen have? The parents wanted it, Cam wanted it, and she was not the decision maker. Still, Karen did hold a modicum of control. She doubled the detail, with four cars instead of two, and got the Uniformed Division to coordinate a rolling escort—no stopping at red lights this time. If Cam was going to return to school so soon, *too soon,* Karen was going to do everything in her power to ensure he got there and back safely.

MONDAY MORNING, Cam was in an armored SUV, headphones on, backpack at his feet. He seemed relaxed, eyes glued to his phone instead of scanning his surroundings for would-be killers. Karen did the driving. Woody Lapham rode shotgun.

Something is off with Cam, thought Karen. It was not just the odd bruising she had noticed on his arms that morning, or how he scratched his skin even though there appeared to be no bug bites, or how tired he still looked.

He's acting too relaxed for a kid with so much wrong with him, she thought.

When they got to the school, Karen and Lapham walked Cam into the building. At first, Cam's peers hung back, gawking at him, unsure what to do. It was not until Taylor Gleason came forward and put his arm around Cam that something shifted. More students surrounded Cam, spoke to him, and soon he was just another kid going to school. Karen wondered if she'd underestimated his resilience.

Cam took a few steps in lockstep with the masses before breaking away from the crowd. He spun around, calling Karen's name. Karen whirled, thinking something was wrong. He had never called for her. She rushed over to him.

"Thanks for being there for me," Cam said. "You've been—you've been a really good friend."

Hollowness opened in Karen's chest. She was overcome with a feeling she could not name. It was almost as if Cam were saying good-bye for good.

AFTER KAREN coordinated the surveillance duties, she returned to the SUV for a long day of keeping watch. With the extra bodies, they could cover more entry points. She stationed additional agents by the main entrance. They carried handheld metal detectors and would use them on anybody who tried to enter the school. School staff fully supported these precautions.

All Karen had to do was wait for the end of the day, which would come six hours from now. The agents did their jobs. They watched. They vetted. And nothing happened.

Around lunchtime, Karen received a phone call from Lee. She got out of the car, desperate to give her legs a good stretch. Long stints on surveillance duty served the younger set far better.

"We've got one," Lee said, sounding elated.

"Got one what? Where are you?"

"At the clinic with Paul. I'm reviewing medical records from the TPI, and we've got one." He spoke so quickly it was hard to understand.

"Noah Pickering," Lee continued. "He was a math student at the TPI. And surprise, surprise, one of the best. According to his medical records, Noah became irritable, moody, and withdrawn. Sound like anybody we know?"

"Yeah, Cam," Karen said.

"His record also shows a visit to the ER because of uncontrolled arm movements, jerking, according to his admission form. Clearly it's myoclonus. He hung himself in his bedroom closet a year before the Stewart twins had their tragic car accident."

"Autopsy?"

"Yes, but because cause of death was obvious they didn't do much. Specifically they didn't do any microscopic histology."

"What's that?"

"That's examining organ tissues under a microscope. They did note the liver seemed a little large, but unfortunately, again because of the obvious cause of death, they never explored it further."

Karen heard the hesitation in Lee's voice.

"You don't think it was suicide, do you, Lee?"

"No, I do not. Same as I don't think the brakes on the Stewarts' car just suddenly failed. These were murders, Karen, no doubt about it. Even without an autopsy on Noah Pickering, evidence of myoclonus is enough of a link. I wish I could have taken a peek at the poor kid's retina. I'm sure that red spot would have been there."

"But Cam doesn't have it—the red spot, I mean."

"He's younger than all of them," Lee said, postulating. "I keep returning to the same thought, that the length of exposure to some toxin dictates when symptoms appear and the level of severity."

"So Cam could have a red spot in his eyes at some later point?"

"It's highly unusual—unheard of, to be honest—but yes. Perhaps much later, along with myoclonic jerks, worsening organ enlargement, everything we've seen in Susie."

Karen gave this some thought.

"Whatever is happening to Cam," she said, "taking him out of the TPI hasn't solved the problem. Something is not right with him, Lee, and I'm not talking about his mood. His complexion is like ash. And this morning I noticed some weird bruising on his arms and he's itching them all the time, but there aren't any bites I could see."

"Yeah, Josh told me Susie has the same," Lee said. "Something, I don't know what, has metabolized in his system. Trust me on this, Karen, Cam's a very sick boy, we just can't fully see it yet. Everything we've seen in Susie is all headed his way."

THREE O'CLOCK could not come around soon enough. News reports of the Dirt Bike Shooter were incessant and frustrations continued to mount over the investigation's lack of progress. Karen wanted Cam out of school and home safe so she could finally relax. She had spent most of the day watching for threats and thinking of ways she and Lee could convince the president to increase the efforts on the TPI investigation.

Noah Pickering has changed everything, hasn't he?

At ten minutes to three, Karen and Lapham drove around to the front entrance to pick up Cam as soon as school let out. At three o'clock the school doors opened and a throng of students swarmed outside. They were smiling, laughing, with backpacks slung over shoulders, sunglasses in place to combat the afternoon glare. Normally, Cam exited with the first wave, but at five minutes past the hour there was no sign of him. He was not one to loiter when that final bell rang. When school was done, so was he. So where was he?

Ten minutes past the hour, still no Cam. Still not answering his cell phone.

"Get inside, get inside," she ordered Lapham.

Two minutes later.

The head of school, Ms. Barnes was her name, looked frazzled as she joined Karen and Lapham in the hallway in front of the main office. She was short, with dark hair, smoldering eyes, and a posture stiff and straight as a ruler. Other agents were inside, scouring the school. An announcement went out over the PA.

Six minutes later.

Still no word from Cam.

The agents on patrol returned, looking deeply troubled. According to the head of school, Cam's last class of the day was biology, so they had gone to that classroom to see if he was there. He was not, but his teacher was. The teacher said Cam had not attended class that afternoon. She had assumed he stayed home from school, given recent events.

Karen's world tilted. "Find him!" she snapped.

Within minutes the police were on the scene, helping with the search. Joint Special Operations Command had been notified. POTUS and FLOTUS had been alerted as well. Bishop was missing. A full search of the school was under way. Karen called Taylor, who said he had not seen Cam since the morning.

Twenty minutes later, the school was quiet.

No sign of Cam. Still not answering his phone, still not returning her texts.

Please God—please—let me find him.

He had a breakdown, Karen thought hopefully. *He's hiding out in a closet somewhere on the premises. He's scared. It was too soon to send him. Too soon!*

Thirty minutes later.

No Cam.

An agent radioed Karen. He had found something. Ms. Barnes led Karen and Lapham to a classroom on the lower level that would have been unremarkable were it not for one wide-open window. This side of the building had no entrances. Nobody had been watching the classroom, or seen what might have entered through that window.

"Do you ever leave these windows open?" Karen asked, hoping the answer was yes.

The head of school shook her head. "No, of course not."

"I want the classroom schedule. I need to know when it was last used."

Thirty-two minutes later.

"We aren't using this classroom at all," Ms. Barnes said.

Oh, God, no. He's gone, Karen thought. *Whoever tried to kill him—whoever killed the twins, and made Noah Pickering's death look like suicide—snuck into the school through the window of an empty classroom, hid out until the moment was right, and then took him. Gone—gone on my watch. I've lost Bishop. I've lost him.*

Agents and police were outside the window, scouring the grounds. A

separate team was trying to ascertain the location of every security camera in the area. Karen examined the window closely and saw something of
note.

"How would somebody open this window from the outside?"

Lapham studied the window closely, as did Ms. Barnes.

"They couldn't have," Lapham said. "It's built to open only from the
inside."

CHAPTER 43

For a brief period of time nobody could figure out what had happened. Had a kidnapper been hiding out inside the school? Did someone somehow sneak past all the security? All of these possibilities seemed hard to fathom. The security was too tight. Karen kept returning to the window that opened only from the inside. It was a critical clue, but she did not know how it factored into his disappearance. That is until a search of Cam's bedroom turned up the answer. On his bedroom dresser was a note addressed to his parents. Cam had not been abducted, as Karen first believed.

He'd run away.

> Mom and Dad,
> I'm so sorry to do this to you. But I needed space from every-
> thing and everyone. I couldn't stand the pressure and attention
> the shooting caused, not for one more second. If I stayed at the
> White House I was going to burst. I feel terrible doing this to
> you both. I know I'm going to cause all sorts of problems. But
> I don't feel safe anymore and this was the only thing I could
> think to do.
> I'm sorry. I'll be in touch.
>
> Love,
> Cam

There was no doubt about it—the note was in Cam's handwriting. It could not have been a forgery. Nobody could have snuck into the White

House and planted it in his room. The working theory was that Cam was not coerced into running away, but had done so of his own volition.

He was four hours gone.

Television monitors inside the White House Situation Room gave Karen a window into the world outside. It was not a pretty picture. Every network, reporters from all conceivable media outlets, descended on the White House to report on Cam's disappearance. Their portable lights glowed bright enough to hold back the twilight.

Creating an artificial barrier between the iron fence securing the grounds and the throngs of people who showed up to be at the epicenter of this national crisis stood a brigade of police, SWAT, and members of the National Guard. Guns were out in force to hold people back.

Every inch of the perimeter was professionally secured. Hidden from view were the best snipers the Secret Service employed. All active Secret Service agents in the D.C. area had been called into work. Meanwhile, the FBI, on top of hunting the Dirt Bike Shooter, was coordinating the search for Cam, mobilizing a truly massive interagency operation.

Karen took in the macro picture as a detached observer. Cam's disappearance was her fault, and the enormous response—the logistics, coordination, allocation of resources—was the fallout of her failure. There was no conceivable way she could ever take part in the actual search. Her job now was to provide information when requested. She would do so while coming to terms with her soul-shaking feelings of guilt, and fear for Cam.

Four chairs separated Karen from the president, yet she could feel the white-hot anger radiating off him like a scalding sun. Ellen Hilliard, looking shattered, was seated beside her husband, eyes hollow, hands clasped tightly in her lap, numb with grief.

Next to Karen, his gray suit a rumpled mess, sat the director of the Secret Service, Russell Ferguson. Ferguson had the air of a man facing the firing squad. Beads of perspiration sank into the deep creases of his furrowed brow. His eyes held no expression, his jaw set tight, a look of utter desperation on his face. The president's chief of staff, John O'Donnell, glared at Karen from his seat across the table.

"Go over it again," the president demanded.

Karen did. Starting with that morning, when she brought Cam to school against her better judgment, and ending with the open window in the classroom that never got used.

"And nobody saw anything?" The president spoke through clenched teeth, his voice almost a growl.

"No," Karen said softly, averting her gaze.

"We believe that is accurate. Our analysis there is complete," O'Donnell said.

"Show me," the president said.

O'Donnell used a computer connected to one of the wall-mounted monitors to bring up a satellite image of the school for all to see. A red circle marked the spot where it was believed Cam had slipped away undetected. Graphics of figures denoted the location of the Secret Service.

O'Donnell rose from his chair and went over to the screen. Using a laser pointer, he drew an imaginary line from the red circle to a football field a few hundred yards away.

"Given where Karen had her team positioned," O'Donnell said in a flat voice lacking any judgment, "if Cam went across the soccer field to Quebec Street, or headed straight to Thirty-seventh Street, he would not have been in their sight lines."

"So it wasn't Karen's fault," Ellen said, sounding almost relieved. "Cam must have known he could slip away without being seen."

"Why didn't we have agents guarding those points?" The president directed his attention to Ferguson, who in turn directed his to Karen.

"I added more agents to the detail given the resources that were available to me," Karen said, her voice shaky. "There were not as many as I would have liked, but we've had resource and scheduling issues for some time now."

Karen sucked down a weighty breath as her eyes met Ellen's.

"You added more bodies, but didn't expand the coverage area?" the president said, his voice rising in pitch.

"I increased the Secret Service presence as much as I could to guard against threats entering the building. That was what was on my mind, given that days ago someone had tried to kill Cam. How was I to know he was going to slip away on his own?" The force in her voice surprised her.

"It's your job to know, Karen," the president said with rising anger.

"I didn't think he should have gone to school in the first place."

The president's face turned red. "Protecting my son was your job, Karen. It was your only job and you failed me, you failed Ellen, and most importantly, you failed Cam."

"It's not Karen's fault, Geoffrey," Ellen said. "If anyone is to blame here, it's Russell. Not only did he ignore Karen's repeated requests for more resources, we have no idea the extent of corruption in his damn department."

"That's enough, Ellen," the president snapped. "You've made your point on that perfectly clear."

Russell Ferguson pulled at his shirt collar to release some trapped body heat.

The president said, "Talk to me about cameras."

"There are cameras near the elementary school close to Tilden Street," O'Donnell reported. "But there are a number of different routes Cam could have taken that have no surveillance activity whatsoever."

With a knock on the door, all conversation came to a stop.

"Enter," the president said sharply.

In stepped Dr. Gleason. Finding Cam was a singular mission and everyone at the White House was called in to participate, including his doctor.

"You wanted to see me, Mr. President?"

Gleason tugged on his white lab coat, unsure, it seemed, what to do with his hands.

The president emerged from his fog of anger. "Fred, good. Thank you for coming. The FBI was searching Cam's room, looking at his computer, trying to figure out where he may have gone, and they found something odd. I was hoping you could explain it to me."

Karen had heard about some sort of discovery in addition to Cam's note, but nobody had told her what had been found. It was doubtful she'd ever be told anything of consequence again as it pertained to the first family. What had to be obvious to all was that Dr. Gleason was suddenly uncomfortable in his own skin.

"What is it?" Gleason asked.

From a folder on the table, the president produced a publicity photo of Dr. Gleason, one that the PR flacks had commissioned for the White House Web site. He held a photo up for all to see, before handing it to

Gleason. Scrawled across the photograph, written in a black Sharpie with Cam's distinctive handwriting, were two phrases chillingly familiar to Karen:

I know what you are. I know what you do.

"What's this about, Fred?" the president asked. "Is this related to Cam's issue with Taylor? Help us understand."

"I'm—I'm as shocked by this as you are, Mr. President," Gleason said, stammering slightly.

Karen noticed that Gleason nodded his head yes, contradicting his denial of any knowledge about the photograph. His shoulders sagged as if weighted from whatever secret he was holding.

"Give us your best guess," Ellen said.

"May I speak freely?" Gleason asked. "I don't wish to reveal anything confidential regarding Cam's care, but this could be important."

"Patient privacy is the least of our concerns right now," the president said, looking at Ellen, who nodded in agreement.

Gleason cleared his throat. His actions seemed shifty to Karen. His body went still, but his feet were shuffling. He stopped blinking.

"As you're well aware, I'm the one who has been pushing for Cam to receive some psychological help for his issues. I believe the pressures of the White House and the resulting trauma from the attempt on his life have brought him to a critical point." Gleason kept putting his hand to his mouth—a sign, Karen recalled from her training, of deceit. "He needed someone to blame for his troubles, including troubles with his chess game, and I was the perfect outlet for his anger. I'm Taylor's dad, and, well, he already resents me for what I'm trying to do with his medical care. Obviously, I think his behavior here proves I was right. He's emotionally unstable, and I'm deeply concerned for his welfare."

Karen found him convincing. She remained tight-lipped about what she had seen in Cam's room—the printout with those two phrases written down the page, even what Cam had said to Lee—*Gleason's a liar*. Everything Dr. Gleason said could explain those things as well.

"Thank you, Fred, you can go now," President Hilliard said.

Gleason turned for the door, paused, and turned back around.

"Geoff, Ellen, I'm very sorry about what's happened." He shot Karen a look of contempt, and a shiver raced down her spine. *It's your fault,* his eyes were saying. *If only they'd gotten rid of you sooner, none of this would have happened.* His hard stare softened. "If there's anything I can do," he added.

"We'll let you know, Fred," the president said.

And with that, Gleason was gone.

Karen shrank under the weight of the president's hostile stare.

"Obviously, I can't have you working the White House detail anymore, Karen. As for your future with the Secret Service, Russell has made the difficult decision to put you on paid leave pending the conclusion of an internal investigation." Karen knew it was not Russell's decision at all, same as she knew the move was a formal precursor to her being fired. "If you have any information," President Hilliard continued, "I'm counting on you to do the right thing and share it with Russell, who will get it to the FBI. I'm final on this."

"Don't you think I should have a say?" Ellen interjected.

"No. This decision is effective immediately. Russell will handle the logistics," the president said, rising from his seat once more. "I thank you for your service. Now, if you'll excuse me, I have to go to the Oval Office to make a public address, an appeal really. Cam is one of the most well-known boys in the world. Someone is going to see him out there, and we're going to get him back."

The president exited the Situation Room with hurried steps and John O'Donnell followed.

Russell placed a hand on Karen's shoulder to comfort her. Worry stayed etched into his face. He knew he was next.

"I'm so sorry about this," he said. "It wasn't your fault."

"No, Russ," Karen said in a soft voice. "You're wrong. It was."

"I'll need to get your badge and guns," Russell said glumly.

Ellen approached. "Russell, will you give us a moment, please?" she said. "I'd like to speak with Karen alone, if I may."

With a nod, Russell Ferguson excused himself from the room.

"I'm so sorry about everything," Ellen said, her voice genuine and consoling. "It's—more than any of us can take."

"I should have done more to protect him."

"You couldn't have known," said Ellen. "Geoffrey is wrong to blame you."

"Someone has to be the fall guy—or gal," Karen answered glumly.

"You can still help Cam." Ellen sounded conspiratorial.

"How?"

"The girl. Susie Banks."

"I'm not following."

"From the beginning you told me to trust Lee, that he was one of the best doctors you knew. I took your advice to heart, didn't I? And you were right. I've come to trust him completely. Geoffrey does, too, in a way—though not to my degree, of course. Otherwise he'd have taken Lee's request seriously, and offered the girl protection."

"What are you asking me, Ellen?"

"Despite everything that's happened, I still trust you with my life and the lives of my family," Ellen said. "You saved Cam from Duffy. Cam did what he did on his own, for his own reasons, and I don't think there was any way you could have prevented it." Ellen looked away. "If anyone here is to blame, it's me," she said. "I let him go. I acted against your advice and you're the one who suffers the consequences."

"I would have done the same to me if I were in the president's position," Karen said.

Ellen nodded several times in quick succession. "You've always been so loyal to us. Even now. Which is why I want your help."

"My help?" Karen laughed at the absurdity. "Ellen, I've been suspended, and we both know that's just the first step before I'm officially let go."

"Yes, I realize. But you have a gun of your own, I suppose."

"I do. Several, in fact." Karen's eyebrows rose, along with her curiosity. *Where is this going?*

"Somebody tried to kill Cam, and that killer is still out there. If Lee's right, then the attempt on Cam's life must somehow be connected to his medical issues. It's reasonable to think that same person is going to go after Susie again. Assuming Cam comes back to us—"

"Cam will come back," Karen said, interrupting. "I'm sure of it."

"Assuming he does," Ellen continued, "we can't let anything happen to the girl."

"Josh is watching after her."

"He's not Secret Service."

"I haven't exactly been very good at my job."

"Your opinion. Not mine."

"It's your husband's, too."

"He's not asking you to help. I am."

"Asking me what, exactly?"

"Go to the camp and guard Susie. Guard her like you're protecting Cam. Don't let anything bad happen to her. I've heard that Lee has found another case from the TPI files. Enlarged organs, seizures too. And that boy's dead—a suicide, right?" Ellen's expression revealed her doubt. "If Lee's right, and Cam's symptoms worsen, Susie Banks might not just be the key to understanding what's going on with him—she could be the cure."

"Ellen, we don't know if there's a link or not, not for certain at least."

"What do you believe?" Ellen asked.

Karen thought about Lee. It was Lee who'd diagnosed Cam's splenic rupture before anyone else had a clue. He was the one who found five strangely sick kids with links to the TPI. She'd always trusted Lee. He was far from the perfect husband, but he was always an amazing physician.

"I'll pack my bags and head out tonight," Karen said.

CHAPTER 44

Karen listened to the news during her long drive to camp. Nonstop, every five minutes, came the "Breaking News" music, with Wolf Blitzer urgently announcing: "Security failure at the White House. The first family in crisis as Cam Hilliard is missing with the Dirt Bike Shooter still at large. Can the Secret Service be trusted to protect the president? What do we know about Karen Ray, the Secret Service agent in charge? Stay tuned."

The greatest failure in Secret Service history had occurred on November 22, 1963, the day John F. Kennedy was assassinated. Now Karen's name, her reputation, everything she believed she stood for, was intractably linked with what might be the second-worst moment in the agency's history. Instead of salvaging her father's legacy, Karen had trampled all over it.

I'm so sorry, Dad.

Tears welled in Karen's eyes, blurring the highway dividing lines.

Karen's suitcase was on the seat beside her, packed with enough clothes for a week, as well as a Glock 19, one of the weapons from her private arsenal—a sidearm the Navy SEALs favored. The gun was reliable and very accurate. Josh had her spare SIG. Combined with her father's guns in the basement safe, Karen felt she had ample weaponry at her disposal.

An hour from camp, Karen's phone rang.

"Hey, K-Ray, I heard. I'm sorry." It was Woody Lapham.

Karen's heart swelled and constricted at the same time. Already this was a voice from her past.

"Thanks for the call. You're the first."

"Ellen is still trying to get us all reassigned, but the president is holding firm—for now."

"No surprise there. Russell's gone. He knows it, too."

"No loss there," said Lapham, expressing long-held sentiments.

Karen smiled in the dark.

"What now?" Lapham asked.

It was nighttime and Karen was on a particularly lonely stretch of highway, grateful for the company—something to keep her mind sharp as the miles stretched on.

"Now? I'm out," she said, feeling the familiar crimp in her heart. "What's happening back in D.C.?" At Ellen's request, Karen had told no one of her new mission. It was obvious the first lady did not trust the Secret Service with anything, and that included keeping secrets.

"This isn't your typical teenage runaway, that's for sure," Lapham said. "The FBI is taking plaster footprints from around the school, trying to match them to Cam's shoes. They're looking at surveillance footage, tearing apart his room. Forensics is dissecting his computer and investigators are interviewing all of his friends. Basically, it's a giant mess."

"I can imagine."

"Then you can also imagine how many crazies are calling the tip line," Lapham said. "According to them, Cam is either at the Louvre taking selfies with *Mona Lisa,* or he's now driving for Uber."

To her surprise, Karen managed to laugh.

"I'm going to miss you, Woody," she said, still smiling. "You need anything from me, anything at all, just ask."

"Hey, you're only suspended, you're not going to the moon," he said.

Karen flashed on the job, what it meant to her, how it *was* her—how much she'd sacrificed to become this person she no longer was. The Service had taken Karen away from her family, and contributed significantly to her divorce from Lee. Karen was hardly the only agent to suffer those consequences.

"Woody, I'm just getting back to earth," she said. "It's you who's on the moon."

AS KAREN drove down the long dirt road to camp, her phone rang again. This time it was Josh.

"Hey, sweetheart," she said. "I'm almost there."

"Yeah, I know," said Josh. "My motion detector pinged me that someone was coming. Decided to call you first before I started shooting."

"Call first, shoot second. Good thinking, and thank you for your consideration," Karen said.

Up ahead the bright glow from the cabin's lights came into view. The air buzzed with the hum of countless critters. Karen parked her car on a grassy patch out front.

Josh gave Karen a big hello hug, and Valerie did the same. Karen took notice of Valerie's denim shirt and her faded dungarees, how the outfit went with her short hair. She seemed at home out here in the woods. Josh had on flannel and jeans, and his favorite boots. His face looked tired, but he was always at his best in the wild.

The cabin might have looked like a hospital ward, but it smelled nothing like one. The odors of pine and good cooking scented the air. As a whole, everything was clean and remarkably well maintained. It seemed Valerie and Josh were working well as a team.

"How's our patient?" Karen asked, eyeing Susie, who was propped up in her hospital bed. The poor thing looked utterly exhausted, with dark circles ringing her sunken eyes. Her long brown hair lay flat against her head. Her coloring nearly matched the white bedsheets.

"I'm doing okay," Susie said, her naturally quiet voice sounding fainter than usual.

She wore green cotton pajamas, which had to be far more comfortable than a starched hospital gown. The dialysis machine, resting atop a rolling metal cart pushed up to Susie's bedside, was on and churning away. Tubes hooked to her body took poisoned blood out and put clean blood back in.

To Karen's eyes, Susie seemed to be getting sicker. She observed a line of ugly bruises marking her arms. Bruises like the ones she had seen on Cam.

Karen noticed the open violin case on the floor by Susie's bedside.

"Josh tells me you've playing quite a bit," Karen said, looking for a distraction from those bruises.

"When my arms let me," said Susie, defeat ringing in her voice. Then she looked at Josh and Karen saw new life spark into her eyes.

"Have you had many attacks?" Karen asked.

"A few, I guess."

"She had one not long before you showed up here," Valerie said, taking no measures to mask the worry in her voice. "It was quite severe, which is why she looks so wiped out."

Valerie provided a frightening account of Susie's myoclonic jerks. They came on like a sudden thunderstorm, she said. One moment fine, the next—boom!—she was out of control, limbs flailing in all directions. Lee had called in a prescription for clonazepam, which Valerie had picked up at the hospital pharmacy in town, but the side effects were troubling. Fatigue. Blurred vision. Headaches. Muscle weakness. The jerking would come and go, but those side effects never went away.

"Imagine going through life afraid to even hold a glass of water," Valerie said. "She's getting used to these attacks in a way, I suppose. She doesn't exactly laugh when they happen, but with all she's going through, somehow, she still plays." Valerie brushed a loose strand of hair off Susie's face, pinning it behind her ear. "That's her resolve right there, shining brightly."

Karen touched Susie's arm. Her skin felt clammy. Valerie must have been aware, because she set a damp cloth to Susie's forehead.

Karen appraised Susie thoughtfully, again noticing the bruising similar to Cam's.

"What's causing those?" Karen pointed to a particularly nasty purple and black discolored area near Susie's bicep.

Valerie removed a printout from the portable blood analyzer sitting atop an antique dresser. She pointed to an array of numbers that meant nothing to Karen. "I'm not sure," Valerie said. "Her platelets are fairly low and her ProTime results are a bit high. That means her blood isn't clotting normally. I don't think it's alarming yet, but her liver and spleen are not functioning normally."

Karen thanked Valerie for the update, then took hold of Josh's arm. "Sweetheart, could we talk outside?"

"Sure thing."

Josh followed Karen out of the cabin and onto the wide front porch. The sounds of the night buzzed around them.

"Any news on Cam?"

"Nothing yet," Karen said, her eyes downcast. "And I'm sick with worry about it. But I'm also worried about your dad."

"Dad? Why?"

"He may be closer to the truth than anyone realizes. The Dirt Bike Shooter is still out there. Whoever is behind this managed to get to Stephen Duffy. Don't you think they'll be able to get to your father, too?"

Josh exhaled, low and loud. "Oh, damn. I didn't think of that."

"I'm here now," Karen said. "I'll keep everyone safe. Maybe you can go back to D.C. for a while and watch after your father."

Josh peered over Karen's shoulder to gaze through the window at Susie in her hospital bed.

"You have feelings for her, don't you?" asked Karen.

Josh shrugged in a way that reminded her of Cam.

"Believe me, you're not the first bodyguard to fall for their protectee."

"She's different—she's . . ."

"Cultured? Talented? Brilliant? Beautiful? The anti-Hannah?"

"Yeah, all those things," he said with a smile.

"I saw the way she looked at you. I'd say the feelings were mutual."

For a moment, Josh was quiet.

"Is she going to die?"

"Hopefully your dad can figure out what's wrong with her."

Josh peered again through the window at Susie resting in bed.

"I'll leave tonight," he said.

"It's late and it's a long drive. Your dad will be all right a few more hours without you. Just don't tell him you're coming to be his bodyguard." Karen had a crooked grin on her face. "He's got a lot of pride, and I'm not sure his ego can handle it."

Josh gave his mother a hug, then returned to the cabin. Karen stayed on the porch, enjoying the feeling of the chilly night air against her skin.

Through the window she watched Josh get a glass of water from the kitchen. He brought the glass over to Susie. Taking a seat on a tall metal stool, Josh put the straw to Susie's lips and held the glass for her while she drank.

It's the simple gestures, Karen thought, *that often mean the most.* In a way those little acts of kindness added up, and eventually coalesced into something far greater than the individual acts alone; they revealed a kind of deep commitment, not unlike the commitment it takes to dive in front of a speeding bullet meant for somebody else.

CHAPTER 45

TUESDAY, MAY 2

The TPI was closed for business, its doors bolted shut, and this made Lee happy. If he had not stumbled onto Noah Pickering, the fifth afflicted student, he doubted the FBI would have bothered to shut the place down. It was a small step, but an important one. It meant the president was taking his concerns seriously—even though he had not connected Susie's and Cam's symptoms, or those of the others, to any known disease, and even though Yoshi insisted he never gave the kids any experimental nootropics.

For the next several hours, Lee had to put his records search on hold, so he could concentrate on doing the job he was paid to do. He was back at the MDC, which was bustling with the usual late-afternoon rush. He worked diligently for several hours overseeing the residents before retreating to the staff lounge at the end of his shift. The TV was tuned to CNN, and, no surprise, the only story was Cam Hilliard's disappearance.

There was no break in that case either.

Karen seemed to be hanging in as best she could, or at least that was Lee's assessment from their phone conversation last night. He hurt for her, but there was little he could do to help her, or Susie for that matter, and frustrations were mounting.

After downing a cup of extra-muddy coffee, Lee touched base with Paul, who was still at the clinic after hours, sorting through medical records, hunting for another Noah Pickering.

"Any luck?" Lee asked. "Not that it would be luck to find another TPI kid with a bright future cut short."

"Nope, no luck at all," Paul said. "But thank you for another mountain of paperwork to go along with our other mountain of paperwork. We officially have a mountain range."

"You're a bitter man, Paul."

"No, I'm a loved husband and an adored father. I'm a bitter doctor. There's a difference."

"Noted."

"How about doing an old pal a favor and swing by Chip Kaplan's office while you're at the MDC," Paul said. "Tell him we'll take half of his last offer."

"I don't think that's how negotiations are supposed to work," Lee said with a laugh.

"I don't want to blow the deal," said Paul.

"And I'd like to avoid Chip at all costs if I could. Dr. Rajit gave him an earful about my abducting Susie Banks, and I got an earful from Chip about my continued role at the MDC."

"Fine. But next week, pitch him the sale and pitch him hard."

"Fear not, my good man," Lee said. "You help me figure out what the TPI is doing to these kids, and I'll help you get a job as the new White House doctor. Few patients, no insurance companies to deal with, and plenty of perks."

"Promise?"

"Just hang in there, buddy. We'll talk later."

Lee was headed back to the sixth floor to finish his charting, when his cell phone rang. He assumed it was Paul, but no, the number came up as the White House. Lee tensed. Was it about Cam?

He answered the call. "Dr. Lee Blackwood."

"Dr. Blackwood, please hold for the president of the United States," said an officious female voice Lee did not recognize.

A moment later, President Hilliard came on the line.

"Lee, it's Geoffrey—"

Geoffrey—I'm on a first-name basis with the president.

"We have an emergency and I need your help right away. Where are you?"

"I'm at work at the MDC. Is this about Cam? Is everything all right?"

"The MDC, you said? Good, that's where they brought him." The president pulled the phone away from his mouth. "Forget the car, Lee's already at the MDC," he said to someone else.

"Brought who to the MDC?" Lee asked.

"Yoshi," Hilliard said. "I've had the FBI watching his apartment."

"And?" Lee's voice rose with anticipation. "What's happened?"

"Our agents hadn't seen movement inside the home for some time. They got worried he might have snuck out. They broke in and found him unresponsive on the kitchen floor. There was a bag of mushrooms nearby."

"Oh no."

"He should be at the hospital now, Lee. If he knows something— anything—about Cam, he can't die. Promise me. Promise me, Lee, you won't let him die."

"I'll do everything I can, Mr. President," Lee said.

CHAPTER 46

Lee raced through the double doors to the emergency room, fully anticipating its atmosphere of everyday chaos and confusion. Doctors and nurses hurried about, but the intense commotion coming from bay 6 told him where his patient would be found. Two men dressed in dark suits with short haircuts—FBI, had to be—waved Lee over and pointed to that bay.

"He's in there," one of the agents said.

Lee rushed in, throwing back the curtain, and found himself looking down at Yoshi, lying flat on an emergency room bed surrounded by six nurses, gloved and gowned for isolation, scurrying about adjusting lines and monitor leads, drawing labs and calling for a stat portable chest x-ray and a head CT. Two ER doctors in scrubs barked orders.

Dressed in his trademark black, Yoshi lay unresponsive on a hospital gurney. A sickly bluish cyanosis signaled oxygen in his blood was dangerously diminished and presaged imminent death. Traces of blood dribbled from his nose, over his lower lip, and down his chin.

His long, white hair was helter-skelter and caked with blood, spittle, and vomit. Lee saw that he was bleeding from below, too, as one of the nurses inserted a rectal tube to help get some control over what appeared to be unstoppable choleric diarrhea.

"I can't get him to stop bleeding," another nurse said while she kept constant pressure on an intravenous access site.

The FBI had identified the type of mushrooms found on Yoshi's kitchen floor. Lee was hardly an expert on mushroom toxicity, but it was obvious this was no accidental ingestion. Yoshi, who had studied mycology, had to know what the *Amanita phalloides,* the death cap, would do to him.

Quick as that thought came, another followed. *What if it wasn't deliberate? What if someone forced Yoshi to eat them?*

These questions would have to wait. Right now, Lee was dealing with a dying man.

An FBI agent showed up, flashed a badge to the triage team. "This is a matter of national security," the agent announced. "Dr. Blackwood is taking over. Everyone please stay here to assist him."

The two ER docs showed no interest in defending their turf. As if someone had pinned a sheriff's star to his chest, Lee was officially put in charge.

"BP is sixty over palp," said a nurse, taking the measurement by palpating with her fingertips.

"Pulse one forty-eight by monitor. I can't even feel a carotid pulse."

"Call vascular surgery to see if they can help us with a central line," Lee said. "Right now, D-five normal saline at two hundred an hour. Wide open. What's his potassium? Let's get him intubated. Blood gases?"

The rhythm of the ER took practice to perfect, and Lee was surprised how easily, how naturally the orders came to him. Triaging Susie had apparently woken something inside him.

"We're just getting his labs back," a nurse in blue scrubs said. "Potassium is high at six point two. BUN is fifty. Creatinine two point nine. Both elevated. Sodium is low at one twenty-eight. Bicarb is low at eighteen. His blood gases show a pH of seven point two eight, pCO2 of thirty-six and a pO2 of sixty-four on room air."

Renal failure and metabolic acidosis, Lee concluded. *Not good.*

"What about liver function?" he asked.

Those labs indicated sudden, acute liver failure.

All markers pointed to hepatorenal syndrome, a rapid deterioration in kidney and liver function.

No, not good at all.

Yoshi's nonstop bleeding meant that his dying liver had run out of clotting factors. Nothing to do now except pull out all the stops and hope.

"Get him typed and crossed for transfusion," Lee said. "Let's try and stop that bleeding. Vitamin K ten milligrams and prothrombin complex concentrate five thousand units. Fresh frozen plasma at fifteen milliliters per kilogram."

The nurses ran about with schooled efficiency, preparing IVs and calculating infusion drip rates, stat calling labs and pharmacy, continuously monitoring leads, vitals, intake and output, and charting nonstop.

"Drop a large-bore nasogastric tube and start him on activated charcoal fifty grams every four. That should help to keep any poison that's still in his stomach from getting absorbed," Lee said. "Also get him on penicillin G, ten million units," he added. "See if it competes with the toxin."

"He's going to need dialysis," the ER doc said.

"Call in renal, gastroenterology, and hematology consults," Lee answered. "He's probably got cerebral edema from acute liver failure. He's going to need a CT scan once we get him stable—"

If . . .

"And a neuro consult," Lee continued. "Let's get him tubed. Can't wait for anesthesia. Get me a seven-oh endotracheal tube and a blade. Suction out his airway!"

Yoshi's organs were vanishing. He was bleeding out.

In the background he heard someone yell, "I can't get a blood pressure! He's flatline on the monitor!"

Lee called out, "Put the pads on him and start CPR. One milligram of epinephrine and two amps of bicarb."

Though it had been years since he had last intubated a patient, Lee's instincts and experience paid off, and he slid the endotracheal tube smoothly into Yoshi's trachea.

"Compressions at ten per minute. Give him forty units of vasopressin."

Lee took over giving compressions. His arms ached. Sweat dripped into his eyes. He kept pumping. His back started to hurt. He thought about Cam and the secrets Yoshi would take to the grave. He kept pumping. He thought about his promise to the president. He kept pumping.

"Still flatline," a nurse said after ten minutes. "No shockable rhythm."

Lee checked Yoshi's pupils. Fixed and dilated. No spontaneous respirations. No response to painful stimulations. No brain stem reflexes. No pulse. No blood pressure.

Dead.

CHAPTER 47

"Please hold for the president of the United States."

Lee was seated at a narrow desk in the ER, feeling his pulse hammer away in his fingertips. Yoshi's body was gone, shipped off to the MDC morgue. He was not the first person to have died despite Lee's best efforts, but it was the first time he'd let down the leader of the free world.

Lee's mind swirled with questions and possibilities while he waited for the president to come on the line. With Yoshi out of the picture was someone else's secret safe? Not surprisingly the first name to pop into Lee's mind was Gleason's. He did seem to know a lot about the ProNeural nootropics. Maybe he knew something else—something he worried Yoshi might reveal.

It was an interesting theory, but what to do with it?

Glancing at his phone, Lee noticed two voice mail messages in his inbox. He must have missed the calls while triaging Yoshi. He would have to check those messages later; the president had come on the line.

"Lee. What the hell happened in there?"

"Well, he died, sir. I tried to save him. There was nothing I could do. I'm very sorry."

The silence lasted so long Lee thought the call may have gone dead.

"Mr. President?"

Lee heard a shaky breath, followed by a loud sniff.

"Sir?"

"I just want—I want my son back. If Yoshi knew something—if—" *Is the president crying?*

"Mr. President, I understand. And again, I'm sorry." Lee did not know what else to say, but added, "I'll do anything I can to help."

President Hilliard sucked down a few more ragged breaths before regaining his composure.

"I'm sorry, Lee, I'm sorry. There's no room in the White House for a personal crisis, but I have one and there's not a damn thing I can do about it. Ellen blames me. Did you know that? She doesn't believe Cam suffered an emotional collapse. She thinks he was frightened, that he didn't trust anyone in the Secret Service to protect him, didn't know who might try to kill him next. She thought I should have done away with the whole damn lot of them, except for Karen. The one person I blame the most, she holds blameless. Now, we're barely speaking to each other. Oh hell, I shouldn't trouble you with this, I know."

But he did need to trouble Lee, or at least he needed to confide in someone. Having spent time inside the White House, Lee had come to have a better understanding of how truly isolating, how deeply lonely it was to be president. For the benefit of a nation, he had to hold his pain inside. Cracks in his façade meant cracks in the country. The little bit Hilliard did share had told Lee plenty. The family doc whom the president's physician held in such contempt was now one of the few people the president had come to trust.

Now, Lee thought. *Now is the time.*

The president had taken him into his confidence. Lee knew he'd never have this opportunity again.

"Mr. President, I have to ask you something, and it's difficult, but I have to ask."

A beat of silence, and then, "Go ahead."

"How well do you know Dr. Gleason? What I mean to say is, how much do you trust him?"

"Why are you asking me this?" The president's indignation was apparent.

"I'm trying to make the connection between the TPI and the symptoms I've seen, including those in Cam, not to mention everything else that's happened. Dr. Gleason is there in every link on the chain. From day one he's battled to keep me from examining Cam. Why? Maybe he knew the kids were taking something they shouldn't have been taking. Maybe he was the one giving it to them and Yoshi has been telling us the truth.

"The profit for a brain pill that could produce people like Cam and Susie would be enormous. Not to mention, he knew Stephen Duffy well. He could have been aware of the man's money troubles and promised to . . . well, you know . . . with Cam."

"Why, that's preposterous! Fred?!" There was a tremendous bite to Hilliard's voice.

For a moment, Lee shrank inside, but quickly regained his resolve. "Cam said something to me in private when I checked his eyes for the red spot on his retinas."

"And?"

"And he said, and I quote, 'Don't leave me. Dr. Gleason's a liar.'"

"He said that?"

"His words exactly, Mr. President. I wrote it off as teen anger, but now I regret it. I'm asking, for Cam's sake, for the sake of everyone involved—please, please look further into Fred Gleason. If nothing comes of it, well, then nobody knows anything and nobody got hurt. But if you find something—it might help us to find Cam."

Another excruciatingly long moment of silence ensued. Again Lee thought the president might have ended the call. He startled when the president spoke.

"Dr. Blackwood, thank you again for your service to me, to my family, and to our country," President Hilliard said. "I'll take your concerns under careful advisement."

This time, Lee had no doubt the president was gone. From behind, Lee felt a tap on his shoulder. He swiveled in his chair and his expression brightened when he saw Josh standing there, a big smile on his face.

Lee leapt up from his chair, opened his arms wide, and gave Josh a big hug.

"What are you doing here?" he asked as the two embraced.

"Mom's at camp. I figured you might need some company for a bit."

Lee was suspicious. "You're worried about me, aren't you?" he said.

"I think you should have a buddy around, is all."

Lee put an arm around his son. "I'm glad it's you," he said. "Would this buddy of mine like to go out and grab a slice of pizza and a beer? I've just had a really crappy couple of hours."

"You know I would."

Difficult as things had been of late, one lone bright spot for Lee was how this crisis had brought his family closer together. As he and Josh headed for the exit, Lee's phone buzzed with an incoming text message from Paul.

Come too office. Important.

The typo did not bother Lee, text messages were riddled with them, but "office" was a strange word choice. They always called it the clinic. Lee paused to send a reply.

Headed out with Josh, what's going on?

While waiting for Paul to answer, Lee remembered to check those voice mail messages, and sure enough the first call was from Paul.

"Hey, Lee—Paul here. I know it's getting late, but swing by the clinic if you can. I have an idea about what might be going on with Susie and Cam that I want to share with you ASAP. We've gone over it before, but I keep coming back to it because it's the only thing that makes sense to me."

Lee deleted the message. The next call, an hour after the first, was from Paul as well.

"Lee, where are you? I think I got something here. Call me."

Lee was intrigued. Paul sounded almost ecstatic. What could he have discovered? Instead of playing text tag, he returned Paul's call, but got no answer. A moment later, his phone buzzed again with another text message from Paul.

Come too the office. Need to speak with you.

Speak with me? Again the same typo, "too" instead of "to" as well as the odd word choice, thought Lee. Not really like Paul. Lee texted back.

Call me now. Let's chat.

Can't talk. On the phone. Just come quick.

Curious, thought Lee. Clearly, something was up.

"We're going to have to pass on the slice and suds," Lee informed Josh. "Gotta go to the clinic and meet up with Paul."

"I'm just the happy-go-lucky buddy," Josh said. "I go where you go."

TODAY WAS the day.

Mauser had been keeping a close watch on Lee. The busy hospital had provided excellent cover, but Mauser took additional precautions. He got rid of his bushy mustache and wore a baseball hat and thick reading glasses he had bought at CVS. Not much of a disguise, but he did not look like the hospital repairman anymore. It would have to do. He could have changed the plan, could have done it himself, but lately luck did not seem to be on his side.

He was also concerned about the guy who had left with Lee. The doc was a middle-aged lightweight, but this other fellow was muscled and probably knew how to handle himself. He guessed the man was Blackwood's son, who had military training. Everything was already in motion. Better to keep to the plan, Mauser decided. If things went south, nothing could be traced back to him or to Rainmaker.

Mauser got his fellow biker pal Willie Caine on the phone. "The texts worked like a charm," he said. "I think Blackwood's headed your way, but be ready, because he's not coming alone."

CHAPTER 48

Karen sat at the small wooden desk her father had bought at a local flea market years back. The rutted surface was papered with maps and notes, her modest contribution to the ongoing search for Cam Hilliard. In her gut, Karen knew how insignificant her efforts were—pointless, really—but she was not willing to abandon them in exchange for doing nothing at all.

She worked with her Glock secured inside her IWB holster, feeling the butt of the weapon pressed against her hip. Though she had traded suits for jeans, an office for a cabin, she would have felt naked without a weapon. Hours ago, Karen had oiled her father's AK-47 and leaned the rifle against a knotty pine bookshelf. The other gun they kept here, a bolt-action Remington, was locked in storage in the basement gun safe.

For Karen, it had been another day of frustration. With so many ways out of the city, finding Cam was like searching for a single needle in a row of haystacks. According to Woody Lapham, with whom Karen was still in contact, the FBI was investigating the possibility that Cam took an Uber out of the city. A taxi would have been a better choice. No digital trail for someone to follow. The Metrobus that stopped near the school could have taken him to plenty of places as well. The only sure bet was that the FBI and the Secret Service had their work cut out for them.

Karen's mind was active with ideas. She studied her maps and thought of avenues to explore. She shared her thoughts with Lapham, trusting he would present them as his own so they would not be ignored.

The twenty-four-hour news cycle did its part to perfection, broadcasting Cam's face on social media and every TV channel like a never-ending infomercial. The hunt for the Dirt Bike Shooter no longer kicked off the evening news. The search for Cam was now the lead story, and Karen's infamy seemed to be growing by the minute. If Lapham were to be believed, and why not believe him, landing an interview with Karen Ray was the major coup every reporter sought. But first they'd have to find her, and Karen's vanishing act had proved just as effective as Cam's.

She was so head-down on task that when the phone rang, Karen jumped. She glanced at the number displayed and felt uneasy eagerness take hold. It was Ellen's private cell phone. She answered the call, feeling the anticipation bubble inside her.

"Did you find him?"

"We're closing in," said Ellen.

"What does that mean?"

"We've received an e-mail from Cam."

"An e-mail? What did it say? Can you forward it to me?"

The lengthy pause opened a pit in Karen's stomach. For a moment she thought she had a real role to play.

"I'm sorry, but I can't," Ellen said. "Please understand."

"Yes, of course," Karen said, willing the defeat from her voice.

"But I am calling because I wanted you to know we think he's safe."

"Can you tell me anything more?" Karen could hardly contain her joy.

"He said he's fine." Ellen sounded strained, rife with exhaustion. "He's in a safe place, disguised, but didn't say where. He's got money for food. He's doing okay, but he's not ready to come home. He said, and I'm sorry to report what I already knew, that he couldn't trust the Secret Service to protect him. He feels safer and better now that he's gone. He's asked us for time and patience while he's sorting through some complicated emotions."

"Do we know where the e-mail came from? There must be a way to trace it, right?"

"Yes, there is," Ellen said. "The NSA thinks it came from a router at a coffee shop in Paterson, New Jersey. The FBI is concentrating search efforts there now. We're trying to keep it out of the news, hoping Cam will stay in one place and not think we're closing in on him. But you know how leaks can be. It's going to get out eventually, and I wanted you to hear the news from me before it breaks elsewhere."

"I appreciate that, Ellen. More than you can know."

"If Geoffrey had replaced the entire White House detail like I had asked, maybe Cam wouldn't have felt compelled to run away."

"I understand."

The guilt washed over Karen. *I should have known something was off with Duffy—I should have reassigned him. It's all my fault.*

"Not that I thought you were one of those who needed to go," Ellen said, as if reading Karen's mind. "You do know how much faith I have in you, how much I still have. But Geoffrey, the Secret Service, even the country it seems, needed a scapegoat. I'm just so sorry it had to be you."

"Don't worry about me," Karen said. "I'll be fine. My concern right now is for Cam and Susie."

"Promise me you'll do everything you can to keep Susie safe," Ellen said.

"Trust me when I tell you that I'll guard Susie with my life."

SUSIE DID not know why, but Karen made her feel sad. She did not know Karen well at all. She had no reason to pass judgment, but there was something, an air of melancholy, that followed her. It made Susie miss Josh, who had gone back to D.C., or at least that's what Karen had told her.

Not that Susie had a crush on Josh or anything. He was much older and she was inexperienced in dating because of her dedication to music. But he was sweet and nice to her—and, oh, who was she was trying to kid? Of course she had a crush on him. What girl wouldn't? But he was gone, and Susie was left with his mother.

Now sunset was fast approaching. Valerie had just returned from one of her long walks. The nurse had been taking lots of walks alone lately and Susie felt a sudden twinge of sadness. She was tired of being a prisoner—here at the cabin and in her own body. She was tired of the ugly bruises on her arms that appeared for no good reason, and the intense itching sensation that Valerie's creams could not soothe.

"I think I need some fresh air," Susie announced. "I want to go to the lake to watch the sunset."

Valerie's face registered surprise. "I'll go with you," she said.

"You just got back," said Susie.

"No reason I can't go out again. Let me just put the ziti in the oven."

Karen said, "I'll go too."

"You don't have to," Valerie said.

"I'm here to protect Susie, and I'm the only one with a gun."

Susie knew what Karen was really thinking: *I've already lost one kid, and I'm not about to lose another.*

Susie knew why Karen had replaced Josh as her guardian. Cam Hilliard had run away and the first lady wanted Karen, a seasoned and trained professional, to watch over her. Because she and Cam had similar health issues, the first lady evidently had taken a personal interest in Susie's well-being.

It was all so overwhelming.

Susie slipped on a light blue cotton dress, comfortable to wear around the cabin. It felt good to be in something other than pajamas for a change. The dress would not be warm enough in the evening chill, so she added a denim jacket to her ensemble. Valerie put the ziti in the oven, got her coat, and soon they were off.

The path to the lake was narrow and rocky in parts, with potentially treacherous roots lying in ambush under clusters of fallen leaves. They might have traveled a quarter mile, but to Susie, in her weakened condition, the journey felt more like a half marathon. Still, the effort was worth it just to see the reflecting sunlight glittering like starbursts across the rippling water; to watch pastel bands of pinks, reds, and yellows appear magically on the vast horizon as twilight neared; to hear the croaking of frogs and feel the gentle spring air tickle her flesh.

The trio sat at a red-painted picnic table near the water's edge, chatting as gentle waves lapped rhythmically against the rocky shoreline.

"Have they found Cam yet?" Valerie asked Karen.

"No," Karen said. "Hopefully soon. The FBI is good at what they do. Let's hope for Cam's sake they find him quickly."

Susie heard the sorrow in Karen's voice. It was obvious she wanted to be in on the action, back with her colleagues, doing the important work of finding Cam, not watching over some sick girl at a lake.

Susie wondered if Cam had her wan complexion. Was he developing bruises for no good reason? Itching constantly? Did his limbs go spastic without warning? Was he becoming forgetful? At times, Susie's sheet music was as foreign to her as Chinese. How could she forget something so ingrained in her memory, so rooted from years of diligent practice?

"He's just a scared kid," Susie said, trying to shake off the eerie feeling that she and Cam shared some terrible bond, a common fate. "He doesn't want to be hiding out. He wants to come home." She spoke with confidence, because she knew from experience. She was a scared kid herself.

Karen put an arm around Susie. Her touch felt surprisingly motherly and comforting.

"I hope you're right," Karen said.

"Everyone is going to be all right," Valerie said. "Including you."

Susie was hardly convinced. If the look in Valerie's eyes were to be believed, she would need either a cure or a casket.

CHAPTER 49

Traffic across town was mercifully light, thank goodness, allowing Lee to keep a heavy foot on the gas. Paul's voice messages had sounded downright giddy, while his texts were oddly detached. Strange.

It was seven thirty in the evening when Lee arrived at the clinic. Paul's Subaru was the only car parked in the lot. Lee put his key in the front lock and gave it a turn. To his surprise, the door did not open. He turned the key again, this time unlocking the door.

Lee said to Josh, "After hours we always keep this door locked, even if we're here."

Odd again, thought Lee, as he stepped into the dark foyer. Down the hall, well beyond the glass-enclosed reception area, light seeped from underneath Paul's office door. It was the only light on in the clinic.

"Paul, are you here?" Lee's voice sank into the gloom.

Josh came up close behind. "What's up, Dad?"

Lee flicked a switch, turning on the clinic lights. The sudden brightness temporarily blinded him.

"Something is wrong," Lee said in a whisper. "This—this isn't right."

"What's not right?" asked Josh, whispering as well.

Instead of answering, Lee ventured cautiously down the hall. Everything here was familiar, down to the antiseptic smells, but somehow it was different. Josh kept close on Lee's heels.

"Paul—are you here?" Lee called again.

No response.

Why isn't he answering?

All the doors in the hallway, including the one at Lee's back, were closed. *Is that normal?* He'd never paid particular attention, never noticed if the doors were shut after hours.

He turned the knob to Paul's office, opening the door a crack. He was about to open it all the way when Josh lowered his arm like a barricade.

Turning, Lee saw Josh had the gun Karen had given him in his hand. Josh motioned for Lee to back up a step. Smart move. If a threat awaited them inside, Josh was better trained and equipped to neutralize it.

Josh opened the door wider, edging around to his left as he sliced the space with his gun like cutting pieces of pie. He tried his best to see any threats before those threats saw him.

Is the office empty? Lee wondered.

It must have been all clear, because Josh went in. He glanced left, then right, and in a strangled voice, shouted: "Dad!"

Lee's heart sank. He burst into the room, where he saw Josh hugging the wall to the left of the open door, his gun aimed at a spot on the floor. Poking out from behind the desk, Lee saw Paul, facedown on the ground, arms splayed in front of him as though he were in freefall. The piles of papers his partner had complained about hours earlier were blotted with drops of red.

Dried blood matted Paul's dark hair. There was a huge wound in his right temple, a horrible jagged black hole ringed with blood. The carpeting beneath him was soiled dark. Blood sheeted down Paul's neck in thin streaks like exposed veins, some of it pooling in his ear canal. His neck was twisted in a grisly, unnatural angle. The pallor of his skin was the same bluish hue of Yoshi's, his body equally still.

A scream bubbled up in Lee's throat as he rushed to Paul's side. Dropping to his knees, Lee pressed his fingertips against his partner's cold flesh, feeling for a pulse and finding none. Images of Paul's wife and children flashed in Lee's mind as he took Paul's cold, lifeless hand in his own.

"Paul—Paul—please—oh God, Paul!"

A flash of movement drew Lee's attention to the doorway, where a man appeared as if out of nowhere. He held a gun in his right hand, pointing it at Lee. He was tall and thin, with a wispy dark mustache showing vividly against his ghostly pallor. A gray hooded sweatshirt shielded his eyes.

Josh was out of view, hidden behind the open door. The gunman fired three shots from six feet away. He should have hit something. A shoulder. Head. Neck. Something. Instead the bullets splintered only drywall. Turning with a quickness that belied his age, Lee leapt behind the desk to take shelter. The gunman aimed again, fired again, and missed again, as the desk shielded Lee from the bullets.

Before he could change positions, get settled, and squeeze the trigger once more, Josh kicked the door with his boot and sent it smashing into the killer's body with force. Snapping his arm out like a whip, Josh seized the gunman's wrist and gave a hard yank.

The man stumbled into the room and Josh, who kept hold of that wrist, went with him. The killer's free arm pinwheeled over his head in a wide arc as he fought for balance. His eyes, visible now, were wide and glossy with surprise.

The gunman slammed into Paul's desk, catching sight of Lee as he doubled over. Taking advantage, Lee jumped up and threw a punch, a solid jab that connected hard with the man's jaw. Pain exploded in Lee's knuckles.

The killer stumbled back. Josh grunted as he went with him, continuing his struggle to pry the gun loose. The two became entangled, momentum carrying them both to the floor. As he fell, the killer moved his gun in front of Josh's face.

Lee's body went rigid at the sound of the bang. Two other shots rang out. Had Josh been shot in the face? His shoulder? His neck? It had happened too fast for Lee to see. The entwined pair hit the floor with a thud.

Lee scrambled to his feet, leapt over the desk, and ripped the man off his son's body, screaming, "JOSH! JOSH!"

The killer went backward as Lee fell forward onto Josh. Even though the gunman was now behind him, the threat no longer registered. All he saw was blood on the front of Josh's shirt. Lee ripped the shirt open, popping several buttons as he flexed his arms back. He searched frantically for the entry wounds, seeing none.

Where has he been shot?

"Dad!"

Josh's voice lifted Lee from his drowning panic. The boil of his blood settled.

"Dad—Dad, I'm fine! I'm not hurt!"

Lee crumpled to the floor, chest heaving, gasping for air. Then he carefully regarded the gunman, specifically noting the three dark splotches marking the front of the man's gray sweatshirt. Josh stood and aimed his gun at the dead man—a gun Lee now knew had three fewer bullets in the magazine.

CHAPTER 50

"Who did the shooting?"

The person doing the asking was a tall, handsome black man with a smooth, shaved head and well-groomed goatee. He was Detective Neil Moore. Unlike the MPD officers roaming the clinic in police blues, Detective Moore wore dark slacks and a sharp-looking tweed blazer over a white shirt and red tie.

"I did, sir," Josh said, his deference to authority kicking in like a reflex. "It was self-defense. My father was a witness. This guy was going to shoot me."

Josh did not sound or act distraught. He never talked much about his experiences overseas in the military, but his calm and composed demeanor suggested this was not the first person to die by his hand. Lee thought about his own close brush with death, having a vague memory of Karen telling him how often people miss in close-quarters combat. He felt grateful she'd been proven right.

"Where's the weapon?" Moore asked.

"SIG Sauer. Bagged and tagged already," a nearby MPD police officer announced.

"It's my mother's gun," Josh said.

The detective responded with a nod. Lee studied the man's dark eyes, searching for any hint of aggression, seeing none.

Blood scented the air all the way to the waiting room, where Lee and Josh gave Detective Moore their statements. The clinic had become a beehive of activity, with cops everywhere and caution tape strewn about like a haphazard cobweb. Outside, strobes from a fleet of vehicles lit the sky like a display of fireworks. From down the hall, the sound of turning wheels drew Lee's attention to the medical examiner transporting a body zipped up in black plastic.

The detective reached out a hand, bringing the gurney to a stop.

"Who's that?" Moore asked in a rich baritone voice.

"The doc," said a young medical examiner in a white disposable body suit. Behind the ME stood an older gentleman dressed in a light blue jacket with the word CORONER emblazoned on the back. Lee's heart sank at the sight. His throat closed, his eyes watering with grief.

"He's not *the doc,*" Lee said, spitting out the words with ragged breath. "His name is Paul Tresell. And he was my partner and my friend."

Detective Moore gripped Lee's arm gently and with a nod, sent the coroner on his way.

"I'm truly sorry for your loss, Dr. Blackwood," the detective said, locking eyes with Lee. His sincerity was enough to hold back Lee's dark anger.

"Thank you," Lee said, a measure of calm returning. He took a seat next to Josh on one of the waiting room chairs.

Detective Moore pulled a chair over for himself, maneuvering it so he faced the father and son. He sat. "Do you keep narcotics here?" Moore asked Lee.

"Why are you asking?"

"The man your son shot is named Willie Caine. He's a doper, sometimes dealer, and let's just say he's earned a lot of frequent flyer miles with Police Air."

"You think he broke in here to get drugs?"

"Any other reason he'd kill your partner and ambush you?"

Lee was thinking there were plenty of reasons. He had no doubt Paul's murder was connected to the repairman. *But how?*

Lee locked eyes with Detective Moore. "Can I ask *you* something?" he said.

"Anything," answered Moore.

"Does Willie Caine have a tattoo of a skull wearing a pointed helmet on his body?"

The detective gave a shrug. "Why do you ask?"

Lee explained his encounter with the repairman at the MDC.

"Guess we can have a look," Moore said. "Willie won't mind."

Lee and Josh followed Detective Moore back into Paul's office, the smell of blood more pungent with each step. When they entered, Lee's breath caught. Paul was gone, but his echo remained in the form of a gruesome stain on the carpeting.

Lee's eyes turned down in reverence and memory. For Paul's sake, he vowed that sadness and anger would not cloud his mission. He would get answers. Paul would have justice.

The office was crowded with police and forensic specialists, all busily gathering evidence and processing the crime scene. On the floor, exactly where Lee had tossed him, lay Willie Caine. His gray and lifeless eyes stared vacantly at the ceiling, and his open mouth revealed a set of crooked, yellow teeth. A police photographer, encased inside a white plastic suit, took photographs with a digital camera.

Detective Moore knelt next to the body. With a gloved hand, he pushed up the sleeve of Willie's sweatshirt, exposing an array of tattoos decorating the forearm. One of them, framed by the tail of a winged dragon, was a skull head wearing a spiked helmet.

"That looks familiar to you?"

Lee nodded, then turned his head away.

"That tattoo could be gang-related," Moore said. "I'm not familiar with it. But there is a lot of narcotic activity in these gangs."

Lee believed this was about drugs—just not the kind sold on the streets.

"We have specialists who know a lot more about gangland than I do," Moore added. "I'll make sure to include this in my report."

"What about Josh?" Lee asked.

It was inconceivable to think that Josh could be in any trouble for saving his life.

"There's evidence to suggest you and Josh believed your lives were in imminent danger," Moore said, nodding toward Willie's sprawled-out body. "By law, you can use the amount of force which you reasonably believe is necessary to protect yourself."

"Meaning?" Lee asked.

"Meaning, don't use a gun when the other guy has a golf club."

"The other guy had a gun," Josh said.

"In D.C. you don't have a right to stand and kill, but there's no duty to retreat either," Moore explained. "We've got a healthy middle ground there. My sergeant and lieutenant will be down here soon enough. We'll have a sit-down. We'll talk it out."

"We'll have an attorney present," Lee said.

"It's your right," Moore said.

Lee did not know how it would play out, but he did not get the sense that Josh would leave in handcuffs.

Lee noticed one of the forensic specialists remove a cell phone from the back pocket of Willie's pants and slip it into an evidence bag. It was a Galaxy phone, the same kind Paul owned. Several thoughts came to Lee all at once. *What if Paul had called and left those voice mail messages before Willie ambushed him? What if Willie forced Paul to text Lee? Had Paul sent clues with the misspelling and the use of the word,"office"?* Aside from imagining Paul's visceral terror, another thought struck Lee. *What had Paul found out?*

"Detective Moore," Lee said. "I would like to look at my partner's computer before you take it away."

Moore shook his head. "It's evidence. I'm afraid that can't be allowed," he said.

"I understand," said Lee. "Would you mind if I made a phone call?"

"Be my guest."

Lee stepped into the hallway and returned moments later, handing his phone to Detective Moore.

"It's for you," Lee said.

Moore put the phone to his ear. "This is Detective Moore. Yes, yes of course . . . I'll hold." Moore appeared thunderstruck, his bravado retreating like the tide. He pulled the phone away and must have seen the number on the display come up as WHITE HOUSE because his eyes went wide. A few moments later those eyes grew even wider.

"Um, Mr. President? For real? Um—sir, yes, Mr. President, it's an honor. Yes—yes, of course. Of course, Mr. President . . . we'll have oversight, but yes, I'll make that happen. I understand, sir. Yes, sir. Thank you, Mr. President."

Moore handed Lee back his phone in a daze.

"The computer is all yours, Dr. Blackwood," he said.

CHAPTER 51

Lee sat at Paul's desk, trying to ignore the divot in the leather cushion—a reminder of where Paul once sat. He tried not to focus on the carpet's dark stain. Instead, he cleared his mind of grief and sorrow to focus on the task at hand. Paul had found something—maybe something critical, something that might have cost him his life.

Willie Caine's body had been taken away in a body bag and a lawyer friend of Lee's was on his way to the clinic. Josh was going to be interviewed, but it was increasingly doubtful he'd be charged. Josh would get Karen up to speed. She knew Paul well and would be devastated by the news. The police were on their way to Paul's house to notify Tracy, his wife, of her husband's murder. News that broke hearts was best delivered in person. Lee would speak with Tracy soon enough.

What did you figure out? Lee asked Paul, thinking again of those voice mail messages.

He assumed it was research related, so he opened Microsoft Word, checking the most recent files, and found nothing of interest. Next, he pulled up a Web browser and glanced through Paul's browser history, not because he had any strong feelings, but because he did not know where else to begin. To his surprise, Lee found a series of Web site visits, all of them specifically dealing with lipid storage diseases. He felt a little tingle at the base of his neck.

When this all began, he and Paul had discussed a metabolic disorder as a possible cause of Cam's symptoms, something genetic. But they had abandoned the theory when more young people turned up with similar symptoms and shared connections to the TPI.

Metabolic disorders, inborn errors of metabolism, were inherited at birth. The idea of a group of teens, all affiliated with the same organization, all having the same never-before-seen genetic disease, was inconceivable. The cause had to be environmental, a toxin, something the kids had ingested, something given to them, not a mutation inherited at birth.

Lee had put Occam's razor, a principle of scientific philosophy, into practice. The simplest explanation is usually the better one. An experimental nootropic was simple.

So why, then, was Paul looking up lipid storage diseases, a type of metabolic disorder and the least simple theory Lee could think of, hours before he called?

Because they could not come up with another answer, that's why.

Lee accessed Paul's e-mail. In the messages, he found recent correspondence with a geneticist named Dr. Ruth Kaufmann. Lee read through the e-mail chain and was surprised to read that Dr. Kaufmann did not at first dismiss the possibility of a genetic disorder.

Then again, Paul had started their correspondence by listing the symptoms with no mention of the ProNeural nootropics or the unusual clustering around the TPI. So in a way it was logical that Dr. Kaufmann had come up with a genetic cause, same as Lee and Paul had once discussed. But in Paul's next message, he gave new information, including the link between the patients and the TPI. This time, Dr. Kaufmann supported Lee's theory that an environmental factor made the most sense.

Lee was puzzled. What if they had focused only on the symptoms, as Dr. Kauffman had done in that first e-mail exchange? Could it be that Susie and Cam, the others too, all suffered from the same genetic disease—an illness that interfered with metabolism, causing progressive damage to multiple organs: brain, retina, liver, kidney—the whole body?

Paul was smart to reach out to somebody new, someone without bias. Dr. Kaufmann had given them a fresh perspective. In her e-mail to Paul, Dr. Kaufmann wrote:

> While I agree with you that a toxin makes the most sense,
> the red spots and other systems issues still make me think
> some genetic factor is at work. The only way to know for
> certain is to conduct comprehensive genetic testing. I think
> it's critical to rule out the possibility, as unlikely as it seems,
> that this condition is genetic in origin.

The idea of it baffled Lee. If the red spots in Susie's eyes had been there since birth, a precondition for them to be genetic disease markers, why didn't Cam have them as well? And what was the real likelihood of five TPI students, possibly more, all having the same incredibly unusual genetic disease? It seemed as probable as lightning striking one person five times.

Could it be Lee was missing something, some significant find that would tie everything together?

To get that answer, Lee knew what call he had to make next.

ON THE phone, Dr. Ruth Kaufmann had a husky voice with a rich and resonant sound. From her bio, Lee had learned that she was the director of the National Human Genome Center at Howard University, having earned her master of science degree in biology from Virginia Tech, and a Ph.D. in human genetics from the University of Maryland. According to her accompanying picture, she was a black woman in her late fifties with a round face, short hair, and a breezy smile. She was, from what Lee ascertained, internationally renowned for her expertise on genetic diseases. Paul had probably phoned her because of her reputation and proximity— Howard University was only a twenty-minute drive from the clinic.

Lee did not expect to hear from Dr. Kaufmann so soon after leaving her a voice mail with news of Paul's murder, but she phoned back minutes later. He took her call in his office, unable to bear another minute in the same room where his friend had died. He spent time giving Dr. Kaufmann an overview of the events leading up to Paul's murder, excluding names, focusing instead on the symptoms of the five known cases.

"The clustering is more than hard to explain, I agree," Dr. Kaufmann said, sounding baffled. "And I probably would have gone down the same rabbit hole you did."

"But you think it's still worth doing comprehensive genetic testing?"

"I do."

"A swab?" Lee asked.

"I don't think that will suffice," Dr. Kaufmann said. "For the kind of testing I have in mind we'd need a sample of blood, skin, or other tissue for a higher-quality analysis."

"One of the subjects, the one without the red spots in his eyes, is well—unavailable," Lee said, careful not to mention Cam by name.

"Then I'm afraid I can't be of much help."

Lee had no way to get tissue samples from Noah Pickering, or the Stewart twins. Those three were long dead and buried. He could easily get them from Susie, but to complete the picture he needed to test Cam. An idea came to him and his pulse jumped.

"What if I could get you tissue samples from a spleen?" he asked.

"That would work fine," Dr. Kaufmann said.

Three hours later, after the lawyer was gone, and the lieutenant and sergeant had finished questioning Josh; after the reporters were shooed away, no statements given; after Detective Moore gave them the green light to go home; after Lee spoke to Paul's wife, now widow, and made a promise to meet her at the medical examiner's office in the morning; after all that was done, Lee got in his car, Josh seated beside him, and drove off in the direction of the MDC.

MAUSER FIRED up his tracking app and followed Lee out of the parking lot. He was driving the white cargo van he used for his heating and cooling business (peel-away decals advertising his company removed). Hours ago, back at the MDC, Mauser had stuck a magnetic GPS locator to the undercarriage of Lee's car. He had followed Lee to the clinic and had been nearby when Willie Caine tried to do away with three people and came up two short. It was too bad for Willie, but Mauser had made the right call to use him as the sacrificial lamb. At least now he knew what he was up against.

Checking his rearview, Mauser spotted Drew Easley on his Harley, motoring right behind the cargo van. Easley, a fellow Blitzkrieg Biker, one of Mauser's top dealers, looked like a Viking with his long blond hair streaming in the breeze and a thick beard shielding much of his face. Unlike Willie Caine, Easley was someone Mauser could take to war. They had met up in Tenleytown and were together, drinking Starbucks coffees spiked with cinnamon whisky, watching police come and go from Lee's clinic. Now they were on the move, and Mauser thought he knew where they were headed.

His new plan was to trail Lee, because he and Rainmaker believed it would eventually lead them to Susie Banks. The situation was rapidly deteriorating, and things had to be dealt with in a permanent fashion. Prison was not an option. Willie's death would be a dead end, as in a junkie-desperate-for-a-fix kind of dead end, but if Rainmaker went down, Mauser had every reason to believe he'd take his henchman down with him.

It was time again for Mauser to get his hands dirty.

DR. BRIAN SENECA, the surgeon who had removed Cam's spleen, met Lee down at the path lab in the basement of the MDC. He was dressed sharply, in a tailored suit with stripes as bold as his scalpel cuts. The lab was closed at this hour, but Seneca was on friendly terms with a pathologist who had agreed to come in and procure a sample of the spleen for Dr. Kaufmann.

They spoke of Paul. Seneca knew him from the MDC, and was shocked and horrified by the news of his murder.

"What the hell are you involved with, Lee?" Seneca asked while they waited for the pathologist to prepare the tissue. "Fights in the hospital stairwell, poisoned girls, abductions, an assassination attempt, runaways from the White House, and now your partner's murder—it's, well, crazy."

"And I don't think I even know the half of it," Lee said bitterly. "There's a piece missing, something major, something I've overlooked, and I'm praying we'll find the answer in Cam's tissue."

The pathologist appeared ten minutes later with the tissue sample stored in a sealed clear plastic specimen bag. Lee put the sample inside the portable cooler the pathologist also supplied.

"What is it you're hoping to find in there?" Brian asked, pointing to the cooler.

"Something that proves my simple theories weren't the right ones," Lee said.

CHAPTER 52

Lee was dressed in his best suit and tie, and Dr. Kaufmann, warned ahead of time of their destination, had worn a lightweight tweed jacket with a blue blouse underneath and dark slacks. Her glasses, dangling from a gold chain lanyard, bounced against her chest as she took hurried steps to keep pace with Lee's much longer strides.

"I've driven by here so many times," Dr. Kaufmann said as they made their way to the South Portico entrance, "but never did I dream I'd be invited inside."

Lee's grim expression did not brighten. "Unfortunately, this dream is a bit more of a nightmare," he said.

Nightmare was an understatement. His head and heart were heavy with grief, having come from a harrowing experience at the medical examiner's office where Tracy officially identified Paul's body. Plans for the funeral were being hastily arranged. After the mania and activity died down, when the quiet returned and a profound sadness settled over everything like a fine dusting of malaise, Tracy and the kids would need Lee around. But for now, he could be here, guilt-free, doing the work he felt had to be done—getting justice for Paul.

Involving Dr. Kaufmann might be the right choice, but it still boggled Lee's mind. If a new genetic disease was affecting young people, why was it appearing now, and only at the TPI? What else could Yoshi and maybe Gleason have done to these teens?

He's a liar.

Cam's haunting words flashed again in Lee's mind.

What did he mean by that? Lee wondered. *And where on earth could Cam be?*

If the media reports were to be believed (and why not believe them), the search effort was still being concentrated on New Jersey, the location of Cam's e-mail message to his parents. Maybe the first family had new information to share.

With a uniformed guard standing by their side, Lee and Dr. Kaufmann traded a humid spring morning for the cool interior of a well-appointed conference room in the East Wing. Ellen Hilliard was there to greet them, and it was immediately clear to Lee how draining these past few days had been on her. Her face, normally radiant, had turned gaunt. She was dressed as if in mourning, wearing a black boat-neck outfit accented with a single gold chain. Her dark blond hair, often worn down, had been pulled back into a tight bun, revealing a neck far thinner than Lee had remembered. The spark in Ellen's electric blue eyes was extinguished.

Included among the small entourage awaiting Lee and Dr. Kaufmann's arrival was Dr. Gleason. Deep channels marked the corners of Gleason's eyes and his short brown hair seemed to have thinned out considerably. The stress seemed to be taking a toll on everyone—even the liars.

Lee had expected the president would be there, but Ellen said he had been called away suddenly for an emergency meeting and would return shortly.

Dr. Kaufmann seemed uncertain on her feet. Ellen noticed and took hold of her hand.

"It's all right," she said, her voice soothing. "I know this is a lot to handle, but please, try to think of this as just my home, and you are my guest."

"Thank you," Dr. Kaufmann said, her deep voice quavering ever so slightly. "I'm, well—well, a bit overwhelmed, as you can imagine."

"It's understandable," said Ellen. "I have some tea on the way. It'll help you relax."

As if on cue, a member of the service staff wheeled a cart into the room, with aromatic tea steeping inside a sterling silver pot. He poured four cups, adding milk and sugar as desired, while everyone took seats on the chairs positioned around the conference room table.

Once settled, Ellen expressed to Lee her deepest sympathies.

"We're all in shock," Lee said. "Utterly devastated. Tracy, Paul's wife, wanted me to thank you for the flowers you sent. She's deeply appreciative, and touched by your thoughtfulness."

"Anything we can do to help, please don't hesitate to ask. Do they still think the murder was drug related? That's what I heard on the news."

"We do keep some drugs in stock, samples to give out to our patients, so it's possible," Lee said. "It's the going theory, anyway. But it could also be connected to our investigation. Maybe Paul was onto something. It's why we're here, I guess—to find out." Sorrow swelled up in Lee, forcing him to will his eyes dry. He had to change the subject. "Is there any news on Cam?"

"No," Ellen said, looking crestfallen as her lips pulled tight. "But he did send another e-mail assuring us he's fine. He feels terrible for all the trouble he's causing."

"Someone tried to kill him and he felt betrayed by the people assigned to protect him," Lee said. "I can't imagine the kind of stress he's under."

"I can," Ellen said, her gaze shifting to the Secret Service agents standing sentry against a wall.

"I've been worried the media has been awful to you," Ellen said.

Lee got the reference. "They haven't made a connection between Karen and me," he said. "So I haven't been stalked, if that's your concern."

"Trust me, they will," Ellen said with vehemence. "How is Susie holding up?"

Lee provided a brief update on her condition.

"She's getting worse, isn't she?" Ellen asked.

"Yes," Lee said. "A tipping point could happen at any moment. If we have to move her to a hospital we will, but it won't make a difference. Until we figure out what's wrong with her, I'm afraid there's little anyone can do to help."

"What does it mean for Cam?"

"It means we need to find him fast and try to figure out if what's happening inside his body is the same thing happening to Susie. After we finish up here, I'm headed to camp. I'll biopsy Susie myself."

"Speaking of biopsies," Dr. Gleason chimed in, "I've done the two skin biopsies on the president and first lady you asked for." The venom in his voice was poorly disguised. Lee was his unshakable virus.

Yesterday, the three doctors, Lee, Ruth Kaufmann, and Fred Gleason, had come to an agreement to use a shave biopsy to procure the samples. Some bleeding was typically associated with the procedure, and the small bandage covering part of Ellen's right wrist might have hidden a stitch or two.

"The samples are in the refrigerator in the clinic," Gleason said. "I'll get them before you leave. We have a cooler you can use for transport."

Dr. Gleason leaned forward in his chair, his eyes boring into Dr. Kaufmann. "What exactly are you looking for in these biopsies of the president and first lady anyway?" he asked.

"A family history," Dr. Kaufmann answered calmly. "There could be mutation involved, something that might explain the unusual symptoms Lee has described."

"I've read your bio," Gleason continued. "You have an impressive background in the field of genetic diseases. In all your years doing research, you've never come across anything of this nature before, have you?"

Not really a question, Lee observed. *More like a prosecutor challenging a key witness.*

"No, I have not," said Dr. Kaufmann.

"And what's the likelihood these symtoms having a genetic cause?"

Suddenly, Lee got it. Just like his theory about the nootropics, any idea Lee suggested, simple or not, was instantly suspect in Gleason's mind.

"Respectfully, I don't like to speculate on such things, Dr. Gleason," Dr. Kaufmann replied. "I'm a woman of science, and these samples will help us make some determinations."

Inwardly, Lee was smiling. He'd liked Dr. Kaufmann before, but seeing her put Dr. Gleason in his place had elevated her status considerably.

Thinking of the long drive ahead, Lee was about to suggest they leave now to retrieve the biopsies, when the shuttered doors to the conference room flew open. In stormed a team of six men, all wearing FBI special agent Windbreaker jackets. Following them were several members of the Secret Service dressed in dark suits. The last to enter was President Hilliard.

Lee's heart leapt to his throat from the surprise. His shock morphed into confusion when the agents surrounded Gleason. With force, two agents seized Gleason by the elbows and hoisted him out of his chair. They spun him around, and as if by magic, had his wrists handcuffed behind his back.

The color drained from Gleason's face, his body shaking violently. "What's the meaning of this?" he shouted.

Instead of an answer, three FBI agents ushered Gleason out of the room in a hurried processional. Other agents joined them, along with most of the Secret Service.

President Hilliard hovered near the doorway, distraught.

Seized with anxiety, Ellen rushed to her husband's side. "Geoffrey—what—what's happening?" Her voice cracked with emotion. "Is everything all right? Is this about Cam?"

The president's aspect softened, but only a few degrees. "We'll talk," he said, nodding in Lee's direction, as if to say, *Not in mixed company.*

Lee took it upon himself to stand and approach. Dr. Kaufmann stayed rooted in her seat. The two Secret Service agents who had stayed behind tensed as Lee neared the president. With a wave, President Hilliard settled them down. Lee caught a flash of the bandage covering his president's right wrist, presumably concealing the location of his biopsy.

"Mr. President, is this in any way connected to my investigation into Cam and Susie? I need to know."

The president gripped Lee's arm forcibly, not hard, but with intent. "Right now all you need to know is that I appreciate the work you're doing. We'll focus on finding Cam, you figure out the rest."

"And Dr. Gleason?" Lee asked.

"Trust me when I say he's where he belongs."

CHAPTER 53

When Karen's phone rang, it was late afternoon. Her breath caught as she saw it was Woody Lapham returning her call. This was the call she'd been waiting for.

Hours earlier, Lee had phoned with more shocking news. The FBI had taken Gleason into custody. Lee had decided to delay his departure to camp until the evening. He wanted to stay local, see if Gleason's arrest had any connection to Susie and Cam.

Karen's calls to Ellen went unanswered. Much about Karen's new life troubled her, but being out of the loop was perhaps the most difficult adjustment of all. She no longer had access to the first family's schedule, had no idea where they were, or what they were doing at all times. It was like losing a limb.

She had made her call to Woody Lapham out of desperation. She could not stand not knowing any longer. It ate at her, made it impossible to think about anything else. Lapham had plenty of pals in the FBI, and she hoped he might be willing to share some privileged information with her. Goodness knew she'd done enough favors for him over the years.

"Are you sitting down?" Lapham said after the greetings and a brief catch-up conversation.

"I am," said Karen. She was perched on a queen bed in the tiny up-stairs bedroom. The room smelled of pine and mothballs. The heavy bedspread on which she sat could probably have shielded her from x-rays.

"I know why the FBI hauled Gleason away, and you're not going to believe it."

Her free hand gripped the edge of the bed with force. "Tell me."

"Guess who invested a huge chunk of his personal wealth in Pro-Neural?"

"What?" Karen's entire face screwed up.

"Yup. He was a major investor. For some reason the president had the FBI investigating Gleason and they found all sorts of incriminating evidence. Not sure why Yoshi didn't rat the guy out. Could have been saving the ammo for a plea bargain, but the CEO sang a different tune. Said it was Gleason who pushed Yoshi into supplying the TPI kids with Pro-Neural, and it was Gleason's scheme to fake the data to jack up sales and get more interest in the product. He was trying to make his hefty investment pay off."

Karen recalled the day she stole the ProNeural smart pills—how oddly Gleason had behaved, how he'd seemed to care a lot more about her snooping around his office computer than what she was doing in his office in the first place. Maybe he'd been corresponding about his scheme and had stepped away at an inopportune moment.

"Cam knew, didn't he?" Karen asked, even though she knew the answer.

"Someone had been sending Gleason anonymous messages warning him to stop or else kind of thing," said Lapham. "Why do you think it was Cam?"

"Because when the FBI searched his bedroom they found a picture of Gleason with the words *I know what you are, I know what you do* scrawled all over it. I'd found something similar days earlier—a piece of paper with those same phrases printed all the way down the page."

"Guess now you know what he meant by it," said Lapham.

"No doubt."

"It goes without saying this conversation never happened."

"You can trust me," she said.

Her lips might have been sealed, but her thoughts were spinning. The news did not change anything, not exactly. It was still possible Gleason was being cagey about Cam because he and Yoshi had done something besides peddle harmless pills. Like Lee had said, nothing added up.

Karen checked the time on her phone. Lee had left D.C. a few hours ago, and would be arriving at camp shortly.

She hoped he'd bring some answers with him.

IN MAUSER's opinion, following Lee was the easy part. The GPS locator did the lion's share of the work. Figuring out where Lee was headed was an entirely different matter. Lee had spent much of the day at the White House, which made sense because of Cam. The long wait had allowed Easley to gather supplies and stock up for whatever might be coming next.

It was time for next.

Mauser was dressed for battle, wearing black camo pants and a dark jacket. He was also well armed, with two AR-15 tactical rifles and plenty of ammo stashed in his van. He also had in his possession his beloved Mauser C96 pistol—a special gun he wanted to use for a very special kill.

Drew Easley rode shotgun. His long hair, pulled back into a tight ponytail, swayed across his broad shoulders while he diligently cleaned his Smith & Wesson .44 Magnum. He wore an outfit similar to Mauser's.

The landscape had been a desolate highway dotted with farmhouses, but now even those were few and far between. Mauser thought he had a good sense of things, a bit of clairvoyance—a gift from his mother, he supposed. She always knew when he was headed for some sort of trouble. His intuition had helped Mauser peg undercover cops, given him a sense which deals might go sour. He had ignored his gut once and it had cost him five years of hard time. He never ignored it again.

His gut was talking to him now, telling him in no uncertain terms they were going to hit the jackpot.

"You're sure this is worth it?" Easley asked, gazing at the darkness outside his window.

"You sure you want us to have supply to sell?" Mauser answered.

Easley snorted his displeasure. "You think Rainmaker would cut us off like that?"

"No doubt about it," said Mauser.

Easley mulled this over and offered a slight nod—his final approval. No going back now.

"You worried about the FBI?" Easley's voice was like a rumble of thunder.

"What? The shooting, you mean?"

"Yeah. That."

"They haven't produced a single useful lead, so no, I'm not worried at all," Mauser said. "If you ask me, Cam running away is the best thing that's happened to them. It distracts Joe Public from their incompetence."

Another nod from Easley. "What if Blackwood takes us to his girlfriend's house and not to the girl?" he asked.

"We're in the middle of nowhere, and he's with his kid. He's not going to a girlfriend's house."

"You know what I mean."

Easley was a man of few words, and Mauser knew exactly what he meant.

"If we get the chance, we'll take him at gunpoint and make him bring us to her."

"The girl is sick, right? She won't be alone. Someone's gotta be looking after her."

Mauser had thought the same. "Yeah, I'm sure other people will be there, wherever there is."

"What do we do about them?"

Mauser focused on the road. The van's headlights were like two knives slicing the void.

"I guess we'll do what we have to do," he said in a flat voice.

CHAPTER 54

Lee turned onto the dirt road to camp after 9:00 P.M. Scudding clouds made the moonlight come and go. Up ahead the cabin glowed like a jewel set against black velvet. His headlights illuminated a lone figure standing in the middle of the road, a rifle slung over her shoulder.

Lee slowed to a stop, rolled down his window, and waved to Karen.

"Do you greet all of your guests so heavily armed?" he asked with a wry grin.

Karen approached, leaning her body into Lee's open window. She smiled at Josh and blew him a kiss.

"You tripped the alarm," she said. "I thought you were going to call first."

Josh smacked his forehead in an admonishing way. "I forgot all about my own security system," he said. "How's it going, Ma? How's Susie?"

"We're all okay," Karen said. "Come in. You boys must be exhausted. We have meat loaf, if you're hungry."

Karen walked ahead while Lee parked his Honda on the grassy patch in front of the cabin. Hours of driving had been hard on his aching knees and tired joints. He was not looking forward to the return trip come morning, but he was anxious to get samples back to Dr. Kaufmann.

He had brought with him a small black medical bag marked with the presidential seal, which he had taken from Gleason's office. *I'm the White House doc now,* Lee thought mordantly. The medical bag contained all of the tools he would need to perform Susie's biopsy.

The procedure might have to wait until after dinner. The savory aroma of a fresh-cooked meal hit Lee as soon as he set foot inside the cabin. He paused a moment, marveling at the transformation of a rustic lodge into a functioning hospital.

Karen gave Josh a proper hug, and then, to Lee's surprise, turned and hugged him, tight and long, the way he remembered.

"I'm so sorry about Paul," she whispered in his ear. "I'm so sorry."

Lee thanked her as they broke apart.

"How is Tracy holding up?" Karen asked.

"Horrible, as you can imagine," said Lee, who was not faring much better. His guilt was oppressive. It was a constant companion that ate away at him like a disease.

Valerie approached and she and Lee greeted each other with a quick embrace. She seemed visibly stressed. The bags under Valerie's eyes had become pronounced, her short brown hair was no longer neatly brushed, and the tension inked into her pores had dulled her once-lustrous skin.

Lee wondered if camp life had taken a heavy toll, or if Susie's worsening health was the reason Valerie had aged a decade in days. He turned his attention to Susie, who was resting in bed, eyeing Josh with a sweet smile on her face.

"How are you holding up?" Lee asked, coming to Susie's bedside. It was good to see her again; good to know Karen and Valerie, Josh too, had done such an admirable job keeping her safe.

"Hey there, Maestro, long time no see," said Josh, joining Lee.

Susie's smile widened. "Hi Josh, Dr. Blackwood," she said in a quiet voice. "Nice to see you again."

Lee patted Susie's hand. "You too, kiddo."

"Been playing a lot?" asked Josh. "I miss your music. I think you've turned me into a classical junkie. I need my Bach fix."

"Worse things could happen," said Susie. "But no, I haven't been playing. I can't really play anymore because—well, you know."

Josh squeezed Susie's shoulder gently, which seemed to lift her spirits.

"Your attacks—I've heard they're getting worse, not better," Lee said. "Hopefully we can fix that for you."

Lee spoke with confidence, but Susie did not seem convinced. She had good reason to be skeptical, he thought. He checked her vitals, while Josh headed to the cabin where they'd be spending the night. Everything regarding Susie seemed normal, including the lab results from the blood and urine tests Valerie performed daily.

Everything was fine, and yet nothing was right.

"I'm getting worse, aren't I?" There was not a trace of doubt in Susie's voice.

"I guess I won't sugarcoat it. You're not getting better," Lee said. "I'm thinking of calling it Genius disease, because it only seems to affect the most brilliant people at the TPI. I'm counting on the biopsy to tell us a lot more, because my other theories have yet to pan out."

"I'm hoping the same," said Valerie.

"I'm hoping for a glass of water," Susie said.

Lee chuckled softly. "That I can do," he replied.

As he walked to the kitchen, a piercing sound erupted, rattling his eardrums. Spinning in a circle, Lee searched for the source. Karen came bounding down the stairs, grabbing the rifle leaning against a bookshelf without breaking stride. She snatched stacks of magazines and a box of ammo.

"What's that damn noise?" Lee asked, covering his ears.

"The perimeter alarm!" Karen shouted. "Did anybody follow you here?"

"No," Lee said.

Karen sidled over to a cylindrical device and soon the noise came to a merciful end. She cried out, "Everyone get upstairs. Now!"

She raced outside and Lee followed her.

"I thought I said get upstairs," she snapped at him.

Lee ignored her. A flashlight beam jouncing in the dark appeared from the direction Josh had gone.

"Josh, is that you?" Lee called out.

"Yeah, it's me," he announced.

"Get to the woods!" Karen yelled. "The perimeter alarm just went off."

Josh switched off his flashlight and vanished into nothingness. Moments later, he reappeared next to Karen and Lee. Karen removed a pistol from her holster and placed it in Josh's hand.

"Take this," she said.

MAUSER BROUGHT the van to a stop on the side of a dirt road. He and Drew Easley got out at the same time. The GPS tracker said Lee's car was parked close by. No need to announce their arrival with headlights and an engine. They followed the road for a time until lights appeared up ahead. Soon a two-story log cabin came into view, all lit up from the inside. Three people stood out front in the wash of the cabin's glow, bathed partly in moonlight. Two of them were armed.

Dropping to a crouch, Mauser raised his rifle and took aim. He motioned for Easley to do the same. Clearly, they'd come to the right place. As luck would have it, Lee had led them to a remote location with what seemed like nobody around for miles.

KAREN'S HEART beat so hard she thought it might snap a rib. Adrenaline flooded her as if a dam had let go.

Focus. Let your training take over, she urged herself. *It could be a deer. Perhaps bear. Could be nothing. Probably nothing.*

But instinct told her it was something. It was too coincidental for Lee to show up and moments later have the alarm get tripped. She took the flashlight from Josh and put the beam to the undercarriage of Lee's car. She asked herself: how would *she* track someone here? Long, straight roads in the middle of nowhere made it difficult to follow someone discreetly. You'd have to keep your distance. She searched with the flashlight. Nothing. She was about to give up, but backtracked, focusing the beam on an object sticking out just enough to be out of place. It was black, square, and small. She plucked off a piece of metal and felt its weight in her hand. She shined her light on it. Recognition kicked in. She'd been trained in surveillance techniques. She knew the tricks of the trade.

A scream rose in her throat.

"Get down!" she yelled.

Lee and Josh dropped to the ground on her command.

A moment later, bright flashes cannoned from the gloom as metallic pings signaled bullets hitting their parked cars. The ground near Karen's head erupted with a geyser of dirt and loose rocks. She ducked reflexively as a bullet whizzed close enough for her to hear it pass. Everyone scrambled to get behind those cars.

Readying her weapon, Karen got on one knee and aimed at the next flash she saw. She fired. The recoil pushed the butt of her AK-47 sharply into her shoulder. The blast swallowed her hearing and left an unpleasant ringing in her head. She fired again. And again.

Bullets answered her bullets, streaking in the dark, coming at them from all directions, it seemed. Josh returned fire with his handgun—her Glock. She heard the distinct sound of shattering glass behind her.

The cabin! They were shooting at the cabin!

Karen yelled one word that got Josh moving fast.

"Susie!"

Lee grabbed Josh's arm with force. "No! You've got the gun. Stay here. I'll get Susie."

MAUSER SAW the guy—his guy, Lee Blackwood—crawling up the cabin stairs like Spiderman on the move. He had a good shot, took aim, but a sudden burst of gunfire from behind those parked cars forced him to take cover in the woods. Easley must have had the same idea about Lee, but gunfire kept him pinned to his position. The shooting continued back and forth. One volley dispensed, another volley returned. Conserving ammo became a concern. In addition to his fully loaded C96 pistol, Mauser had four AR-15 magazines stuffed in his pockets, each carrying twenty rounds. Four became three when he needed to reload. It was time to get strategic.

"Easley, keep laying it down," Mauser said. "I'm going to the cabin."

Bullets spit from Easley's gun barrel with a *rat-tat-tat*. Being a man of few words, it was Easley's way of saying yes.

FROM HIS knees, Lee pulled open the cabin door a crack, then slid inside on his belly. He went straight to Susie's bed, but saw she wasn't there. He called her name in a whispered voice.

From upstairs came Valerie's faint reply. "Lee, we're here."

His thoughts were gummed with terror. The steady report of gunfire barked in the background. He bounded up the stairs without caution, a sudden burst of bravado spurring him on. The doors to the two upstairs bedrooms and the bathroom at the end of a narrow hallway were closed.

"Valerie? Susie?"

"Here."

Again it was Valerie's muffled voice Lee heard.

Opening a door to his right, Lee poked his head into the bedroom where he and Karen slept when they were married. The room was empty. Crouching, Lee lifted the dust cover and peered underneath the bed. Two sets of terrified eyes peered back. He coaxed Susie out first, before helping Valerie to her feet. Both women were pale, breathing shakily.

"Come on," he said, speaking briskly. "We'll go out the back. Val, did you call nine-one-one?"

Valerie shook her head. "I didn't have my phone on me when we ran upstairs."

Lee had a phone on him, but would not waste precious time calling now. He'd wait until they got somewhere safe.

"Come with me," he said.

The trio raced down the stairs in a line, holding hands as they descended. Lee took the lead, with Susie behind him and Valerie in the rear. They sprinted through the cabin, keeping their hands clasped tightly together. They went out the back door, a chain on the move, scampering along the narrow, twisting path to the lake.

Moonlight guided their way as the steady bark of gunshots echoed in the night.

CHAPTER 55

Mauser adjusted his strategy. He would go after Lee and the girl, which meant getting to the cabin. Easley cloaked his approach with a steady barrage of gunfire. Bullets went flying and the stench of gunpowder soured the crisp night air. Easley would have ammo issues at some point soon, so Mauser scrambled with purpose through a dense copse of brush, then hurdled a fallen tree with ease, before pushing through a thicket of prickly pines.

Emerging from the woods on his belly, Mauser crawled across the dirt road like a soldier going under razor wire. Two targets were off to his right, but he could not get off a good shot without stepping into open space. He'd let Easley handle them for now. After taking care of business, he could think about a sneak attack from behind.

Mauser slithered to the cabin on his stomach. The building concealed him from those two shooters. He peered into a first-floor window, surprised to see a hospital bed in the center of a large room, along with an assortment of modern lab equipment. Craning his neck to get a better look, he saw something that put a smile on his face. Somebody had left the cabin's rear door wide open.

It was like a compass needle showing him where to go.

KAREN CROUCHED beside Josh, using Lee's bullet-riddled Honda for cover. She focused on the task at hand—eliminate the threat in front of them. To do so, she blocked out all distractions, meaning Lee, Susie, and

Valerie. It took great effort and tremendous concentration not to let her brain become overwhelmed.

Popping up from behind the car, Karen sent a fresh burst of AK-47 gunfire at the last flash she saw. Teeth clenched, her jaw set tight, Karen felt her muscles relax after absorbing the intense recoil. A reply flash came a second later, followed by the whizzing sound of more bullets. Bangs and bullets, but only one flash now, Karen observed.

A thought pulsed in the back of her mind. There had been two shooters. Had she or Josh gotten off a lucky shot? It was doubtful, meaning the second gunman could be anywhere—dead, injured, even readying a surprise attack.

Karen knew what to do. They had to change positions. Their opponents gained advantage every second she and Josh remained in one spot. Sitting ducks were seldom the lucky ones. The best option was to move laterally toward the threat to change their position relative to the shooter.

They could seek shelter in the woods, she thought. Make the shooter waste ammo attacking them through cover. Either way, this engagement had to end quickly. The longer it went on, the more likely it was she and Josh would end up injured or dead.

She scanned the trees to their right, guessing they were twenty yards away, far enough from the cabin to be cloaked in darkness.

Moonlight illuminated Josh's face. He appeared calm, practiced at this, it seemed, as though he had slipped into a familiar second skin. It also seemed he had the same idea. Using hand signals, Josh pointed first to his face—*Look at me*—and next to the trees she'd been eyeing. *That's where I'm going,* he was telling her. Fingers counted up one . . . two . . . three . . .

When the count hit three, Josh sprang up and ran for those trees.

Karen stood the moment Josh broke into his sprint. She fired a fusillade at the shooter, her focus splintering between her target and her son. She sank back down when the return fire came.

Seconds later, a burst of gunfire erupted from the trees. Josh was providing cover. Hunched over, Karen zigzagged toward the tree line, careful to avoid ditches and loose rocks. Bullets slapped at the ground near her feet seconds before she took shelter among the pines. She worried her labored breathing might give her away.

Josh pointed to a tall tree with low branches. "Are you a good shot, Mom?" he asked in a whisper.

"I am," Karen whispered back.

"Good. Because I know what we've got to do."

LEE GRIPPED Susie's hand tightly as they made their way down the path to the lake. She squeezed back hard enough to make his knuckles ache, but the chain remained unbroken. An exposed root hidden in the dark caught Lee's foot and when he stumbled, all stumbled, but nobody let go. The frantic dash continued at a reckless pace, all three panting like galloping horses. Tree branches clawed at Lee from the dark, leaving painful scratches across his face and arms.

To his back, a rumble of gunshots rolled off into the distance. It took effort not to lose focus. Josh was back there, so was Karen, and despite his tremendous faith in their abilities, fear consumed him.

Without warning, Lee's right knee, the more bothersome of the two, buckled beneath him. Stumbling again, Lee managed to grab a tree branch and keep from falling. His overstressed lungs took in sips of air. Branches canopying overhead blocked most of the moonlight, but occasional glimpses lit the path like lanterns on a runway. They were getting closer to the lake. Good. There were cabins along the shoreline where they could take refuge. He could make a phone call from there, try to summon help.

The shooting stopped and Lee felt panic rise up in him. Had Josh been shot? Karen? His thoughts shifted when he heard a chilling sound not far behind them. It was the crack of a fallen branch breaking underfoot. His chest tightened with a fresh band of terror.

Someone else was on the path.

Cloud cover cast everything in an impenetrable darkness. Another rolling boom sounded, this one much closer. Whoever was back there seemed to be gaining ground, shooting blindly in the dark, or maybe not blindly at all. The trees offered some cover and Lee was wondering if they should take shelter there, when he felt a sudden, very strong tug on his arm. The force of the pull sent him backwards. Reflexively he pushed off the ground to get the chain moving in the right direction. They had to hurry.

He could hear footsteps.

As Lee leaned his body forward, another strong tug pulled him back again with such force he let go of Susie's hand. He heard Susie make a muffled, anguished sound. Valerie cried out as well, but hers seemed to be a cry of panic. Moonlight returned, revealing Susie, down on the ground, her arms twitching incredibly fast. They moved up, down, and sideways in variable patterns. Lee bent to pick her up, but the twitching made it impossible to take hold of her. He tried again, managing this time to hoist her off the ground, but she skittered like a live fish in his arms and soon slipped from his grasp.

Back on the ground, Susie grunted and moaned. It was like nothing he had ever seen. She had not lost consciousness, another indicator this was a seizure unlike any other.

"I can't stop it—I can't stop!" she cried out frantically.

Valerie sank to her knees and made shushing sounds, hoping to keep Susie quiet, but her arms jolted and jerked as though she were continuously awakening from a nightmare. Lee bent down to try and pick her up again when a lone figure, broad in the shoulders, materialized on the path behind them.

He stepped into a wide swath of sudden moonlight. Even without his mustache, Lee would have recognized the repairman anywhere. The pistol in his hand was more like a miniaturized machine gun, an old-looking weapon.

He aimed the gun at Lee, but hesitated as his gaze turned to Susie still twitching on the ground. He seemed baffled by her, maybe even intrigued, and for the briefest of moments, he was distracted.

Lee saw murder in the man's eyes and his mind went blank as his fear fell away. A single notion drove him: *act or die.* Springing forward like he was back on the high school football team, Lee stretched his arms out wide, his body leaning, fully airborne, almost horizontal to the ground. The repairman swiveled, aimed his pistol at Lee's streaking frame, and fired.

JOSH POINTED to the nearby tree with low branches.

"I'm going to draw him out," he said.

Karen's ears may have been ringing, but she had heard him.

"No," she said sternly. *I'm still the parent here.* "Whatever we do, we do it together."

"Whatever *you* do, Mom, don't miss," he said.

Before she could get in another word, Josh was gone, on the move, headed for that tree.

Gunshots rang out, following the sound of Josh's fast-falling footsteps. Without breaking stride, Josh swung himself up onto a sturdy tree branch. The gunman targeted the same tree, bark splintering where his bullets struck.

Karen lost sight of Josh in the branches as he ascended. The rustling leaves became her son's heartbeat. She understood now. Josh was drawing the gunman's attention away from Karen and onto himself. He was bait. Chum in the water. Karen held a breath. *What's next?* she wondered. *Whatever you do . . . don't miss. What could he be thinking?*

Flashes exploded from the dark, still targeting that tree.

Raising her rifle, Karen aimed at the last flash of light she saw . . . and she waited. Something told her she would know when to shoot. From the corner of her eye, Karen watched the tree where Josh was hiding. The branch he was on had to be at least ten feet off of the ground. It swayed from her son's weight. More shots came from across the road. A moment later, Josh tumbled from the tree, landing with a thud in a tangled heap on the rocky ground, unmoving. Karen's thoughts went black.

He's been shot—he's dead—Josh!

She tried to scream, but no words came out. A noise from across the road drew her attention: not gunshots, but footsteps. She watched Josh, hawklike, praying he would move. Shock and panic eclipsed every thought, but still she had the wherewithal to realize something of possible importance. Josh had landed in the middle of a fairly deep culvert. Her father had dug the ditch years ago to keep rain runoff from flooding the road. From her vantage point, Karen could see Josh lying down there, still as the dead, but the shooter could not. He was drawing him out!

A second later, the gunman emerged from the shadows, seeking his target. Karen sighted him right away—dark clothes, long flowing hair, a thick beard. The instant his head caught the moonlight, she fired. Blood, like black raindrops, sprayed out from a bullet hole placed in the center of his forehead. The shooter's knees buckled as he fell forward.

With no brain function telling him to brace for impact, he landed face-first on the dirt road, arms at his sides.

Off to her right Karen heard another sound—it was Josh whistling for her attention. Her heart leapt when she saw him push to his knees. She rushed to him, her hand covering her mouth, overcome with exquisite relief. She dove into the culvert and wrapped her arms around her son.

Mischief glinted in Josh's eyes. "Nice shooting, Ma."

MAUSER HAD his rifle slung over his shoulder and his namesake C96 pistol in his hand. He had wanted the Mauser gun to do the killing, but Lee gave him no chance to aim, so he fired blindly. He might have hit pay dirt, or maybe not. The big man did not seem to slow. He fired again, but a second later it was Mauser on the ground with Lee on top of him. Blood dripped into Mauser's face and mouth. Oh yeah, he had hit something all right. A blow to the side of Mauser's head seemed to come from out of nowhere. He felt a tooth loosen, his jaw suddenly on fire.

Mauser aimed to take another shot, but Lee had smartly pinned his hand to the ground. He bucked and kicked to get free; the strength of Lee's grip surprised him. With his free hand, Mauser clutched Lee's throat and squeezed. Lee rolled onto his back, wheezing and gasping for air. Mauser rolled with him. On top now, Mauser squeezed harder, digging his fingers into the sides of Lee's neck. He tried to reposition his gun, but Lee pushed back with surprising counterforce.

Mauser felt the pulse beating in Lee's veins start to weaken. Soon all his strength would be gone. He increased the pressure, choking the life from Lee. He would have kept going, but several weak blows struck the back of his head. It was the woman, whoever she was, attacking him from the side. Mauser let go his grip on Lee's throat to uncork a vicious, rising left hook that caught the woman square in the jaw. She fell backward and might have struck her head on a rock or root, because her body went limp when she hit the ground.

Using his left hand again, Mauser punched Lee in the side of his head—once, twice, three times, hard blows, all of them. Lee finally let go of Mauser's wrist to clutch his injured throat, gasping for air. Mauser scrambled to his feet and aimed his gun at Lee. The twitching girl had gone still, but she was moaning, moving slowly. The other woman was breathing, but still unconscious.

This was the end for all three.

Take the bull out first, Mauser decided, before getting the cow and calf.

LEE HAD been too weak to shield his head from the blows, his arms too heavy to move. The pain from the gunshot wound to his shoulder pulsed angrily. His throat felt on fire. A bitter taste filled his mouth. Blood thrummed in his ears, his chest. Death now. The repairman took aim with his strange-looking gun. No choice but to die—and then Susie and Valerie—all three would soon be gone.

An odd feeling washed over him. Was it peace? It was an unfamiliar calmness, whatever it was. His clinical mind understood he was in shock. Hormones flooded his bloodstream. Cortisol and adrenaline pumped from the adrenal glands spiked his heart rate and quickened his pulse. An infusion of glucose should have given Lee the energy to run, to evade, but to where? The repairman was practically hovering over him. There was no place to go. By the sound of it, Karen and Josh were engaged in a battle of their own. Nobody was coming to the rescue.

Lee's instincts took over, and his body went perfectly still. It was what all animals did when faced with death, when there was no place to run, no means of fighting back. They froze and hoped the threat would simply go away. But the repairman was not going anywhere.

The face of his son—of Paul—of Karen—those came to him. *It won't hurt,* Lee promised himself. He was just so sorry he had failed everyone.

"Why?" Lee managed to squeak out the word. "Why?"

The repairman steadied his aim at the same instant a tall shadowy figure loomed up behind him. The shadow's arm came forward with speed as if throwing a ball. There was a horrible cracking sound, bone breaking, and the repairman crumpled to the ground clutching his head, howling like a wounded animal. In an instant, Lee became unfrozen and he pounced for the gun the repairman had dropped. Incredibly, the repairman had managed to scramble to his feet, and was coming at Lee with rage in his eyes, blood streaming down his face. Spinning on his back, Lee picked up the gun, pulled the trigger, and fired three shots at close range, all of them into the repairman's chest. This time, when the repairman went down, he stayed down.

Lee stood shakily, ignoring the intense pain in his shoulder and the steady ache in his throat. His eyes searched all directions for the shadowy figure who had saved them all, but he was gone.

He searched again.

"Please. Come out. Please." Lee's voice was barely a rasp. "We won't hurt you."

Rustling in the trees drew Lee's attention. There was movement in the brush nearby. Lee dropped the gun to the ground. "We won't hurt you," he said again as a figure emerged from the shadows and stepped into the moonlight.

Lee's eyes went wide. His mouth fell open.

It was Cam.

CHAPTER 56

Thank goodness they had built a hospital in the woods.

Valerie had suffered a terrible blow to the head. She was badly disoriented, unsure where she even was. She looked normal enough when Lee examined her, and moved normally too, but she was definitely in a daze, and probably concussed. They would have to get her to a more robust facility soon, possibly for a CAT scan, but nobody was going anywhere just yet.

Josh's hands and knees were badly scraped from his fall, the right ankle sprained and swollen, but overall he was in fairly good shape. He was more than a little relieved Susie was safe.

"I got the idea to play possum when Dad thought I got shot," Josh had said in describing his ordeal.

Lee was in need of treatment himself. In addition to his many cuts and contusions, he'd been shot in the shoulder by the repairman. The bullet, luckily, went clean through, but according to Josh, had the shooter used his AR-15 instead of the Mauser handgun (an odd choice of weaponry, Josh observed), he speculated the outcome might have been far worse. The AR fired bullets with twice the muzzle energy in foot-pounds as the antique Mauser gun, and it would have shattered Lee's bones and shredded his flesh.

Karen applied a field dressing, following Lee's instructions on how to properly clean and dress the wound.

"I know how to do this, Lee," Karen said, her tone playfully snarky. "I'm trained to provide emergency medicine to the president, after all."

"You're trained to do a lot of things," he said.

He was thinking about the dead guy out front. They had searched him and the van, found more guns, ammo, even rope, but nothing of real value—no IDs, no hint of who they were, or who might have hired them.

Nobody had called the police, but that was life in rural Virginia for you. The last thing Lee or Karen wanted was Marine One landing out front, joined by an armada of federal agents and thousands of reporters. The dead guys weren't going anywhere, and Karen thought it was best to get in touch with the first lady and the president before taking any action.

Lee got Ellen on the phone, and she said something rather surprising.

"I'm glad you're all safe. Don't bother calling the president. I'll tell him myself. I'll be there in a few hours."

She sounded calm, oddly detached, and nothing about their conversation sat well with Lee. Karen did not know what to make of it either, but they followed her instructions anyway, figuring answers would come soon enough.

Karen was giddy with excitement. Lee could tell her adrenaline rush was still going strong. They were alive, and Cam was safe. He was with them. But what was he doing at camp?

Cam had refused to answer any of their questions. He sat quietly at the kitchen table, obviously nervous, staring at his clasped hands, remaining tight-lipped.

"Please, Cam," Karen pleaded. "Tell me what you're doing here. How did you even get here?"

Susie came over to the kitchen table and took a seat next to Cam. She was weak, moving slowly. Her face and clothes were dirty.

"Please, Cam, talk to us," she said, looking him in the eyes. "Whatever you're doing here, whatever secret you have, you can let it go now. You're safe with us."

The way Cam looked at Susie made Lee think the boy might speak.

"I think you and I have a lot more in common than the TPI," Susie said. "I never talked to you there, but I wish I had. I was always too nervous to say anything."

"Why?" Cam asked.

Susie laughed as if it were obvious. "Because you're the president's son."

"I get what you mean," Cam said. "But I'm no different than you."

Susie nodded like she got it—she understood him.

"Do you like it? Having your talent, I mean, being so good at what you do?"

"You're good at what you do," Cam said. "Do you like it?"

Susie gave this some thought. "Sometimes yes," she said. "Sometimes no. I don't like the pressure."

"Believe me, it's a lot less pressure than living in the White House."

She laughed sweetly. "Do you have what I have?" she asked. "Dr. Blackwood called it Genius disease."

Cam shrugged. "I don't think so. I don't have that red spot in my eye, I know that."

Lee decided it was time to interject. Susie had worked her magic. Cam's barriers were coming down.

"Cam, please, talk to us. Who brought you here?"

"She did," Cam said, pointing at Valerie, who was resting and recovering in Susie's hospital bed. Valerie screwed up her face, searching for a memory.

"Me?" Valerie sounded confused.

"I don't understand," Lee said.

"Call my mother back," said Cam. "She'll tell you everything."

THEY DID call back, but Ellen said an explanation could wait until she arrived. Josh left to drive Valerie to the hospital. He would tell the admissions nurse Valerie had a slip and fall, possible head injury. Susie was taking a nap upstairs. Her myoclonus attack had left her completely drained.

Cam maintained his silence. Ellen showed up hours later in a black SUV driven by Woody Lapham. She burst into the cabin and clutched Cam in a tight embrace. They broke apart and Ellen dabbed at her eyes, where tears had formed.

Karen went over to Lapham. "Where's her entourage?" she asked. The first lady would never travel all the way out here with only one Secret Service detail.

"The president knows where we are," Lapham said. "He wants this quiet. We all want this quiet. Cam goes home tonight. The story is going to be that he called us and arranged for a pickup. Secret Service went and got him. We're not saying where he went, or what he did while he was gone. He's back home and that's all that matters. He's safe. End of story."

"What about the bodies? I have two dead guys on my property."

The cabin suddenly lit up as bright lights streamed in through the front windows. Karen flinched, thinking attack, but Lapham showed no concern. Glancing outside, Karen saw a small fleet of black SUVs and sedans driving down the road to camp.

"We're going to clean it all up," Lapham said. "These are people we can trust."

Karen nodded. To her knowledge, the FBI did not employ cleaners, but the CIA did.

"Talk to us, Ellen," Lee said, joining her and Cam at the kitchen table. "We're in the dark here."

Karen came over, bringing four glasses of water with her.

"I was afraid for Cam's life, Lee. Truly afraid. Honestly, it's as simple as that."

"I suspect there's a bit more to it," said Lee.

Ellen said, "I thought whoever was after Susie was coming after Cam, too, and somehow they'd infiltrated the Secret Service. I tried to get Geoffrey to fire everybody, start fresh, clean house so I could feel safe, but no, it couldn't happen, not on my timetable, so—I guess—I guess I snapped. That's the only explanation I can give you. I wanted Cam somewhere where he'd be safe until we figured everything out, until we vetted every damn agent we employed."

"So you brought him here?" Karen sounded incredulous.

"Why not here? Should I have brought him to Camp David, where there'd be more government types I couldn't trust watching over him? No, there was only one person working for me I trusted completely, who I trusted all along. You, Karen. It was you."

A realization seemed to come to Karen's face. "You told me to come here to watch over Susie because you knew you were going to bring Cam here, didn't you? That's why you pushed for him to go to school that day."

"Cam would be taken care of," said Ellen. "He'd have the best Secret Service agent, along with a trained nurse, someone Lee trusted, to monitor his health. All bases covered."

"So you got in touch with Valerie," said Lee.

"I'm paying her salary, I knew how to contact her. When I told Valerie what had happened to Cam and what I wanted done to protect him she agreed to help. She fed him, cared for him, checked his vitals, all that, and all under the condition she not tell a soul—not even you, Karen."

"All those walks Valerie started to take make a lot more sense now," said Karen.

"I thought she looked extra stressed," Lee added. "Poor thing, she was shouldering a terrible burden. What made you think she'd go along with this?"

Ellen eyed Lee slyly. "I'm the first lady of the United States. Let's just say I can be . . . persuasive."

"How did you pull it off?" asked Karen. "We were watching the school. We were on heightened alert."

"Cam knew the blind spots. He went online and figured out the places where there weren't any surveillance cameras. We put together a disguise he brought to school in his backpack—a wig I bought him, dark glasses, and some baggy clothes—and then he took a bus to a place where I had a cab waiting. The cab drove him out of D.C., where Valerie picked him up. She got him settled in one of the cabins. And that's where he's been ever since."

Of course Valerie could get through that perimeter alarm, thought Karen.

"Good thing, too," Cam said. "When I heard the gunshots, I went through the woods to get to your cabin, thinking you might have to help me."

"Turned out to be the other way around," said Lee. "What about New Jersey?"

"What about hacking a router at some coffee shop and sending out an e-mail so people thought it came from there," said Cam. "Yeah, I fooled the NSA." He said it with pride.

"I had to get word to Geoffrey that Cam was all right," Ellen added. "But I couldn't give away his location for obvious reasons."

Karen shook her head in dismay. "Ellen, you've caused . . . a nightmare. The search effort alone, my damn job. Think of what you've done!"

"When you're absolutely convinced the alternative is to bury your son, you can overlook quite a lot," Ellen said with attitude. "So forgive me for not giving a damn about the consequences."

"Black Bear," Lee murmured softly.

"And now?" asked Karen.

"Now, I think Cam's former doctor needs to give us some real answers."

"Gleason?" Lee was baffled by her statement.

"You do know he's been arrested on fraud charges, don't you?" Ellen said.

Lee sent Karen a confused look, while Ellen appeared contrite.

"Oh, my bad," said Ellen. "I know Woody told you, Karen, so I figured——"

"I keep my secrets when asked," Karen answered quickly. "I'm loyal like that."

"We all keep secrets," Ellen said. "Especially Dr. Gleason."

"Wait——wait a second here," Lee said, clearly unnerved. "What fraud did Gleason commit?"

Karen explained Gleason's role——his substantial investment in Pro-Neural and the scheme to use bogus test data to increase sales and product interest.

"No wonder Gleason tried to keep me at arm's length. He knew I'd eventually figure out Cam was taking nootropics and worried it could jeopardize his scheme."

"The printout, the photograph. 'I know what you are——I know what you do,'" Karen said to Cam. "You knew all along, didn't you?"

"Remember when I told you about doxxing?" Cam said.

Karen gave a nod. "Yeah. You said it was harvesting information about individuals from the Internet."

"Right. Well, I did some serious harvesting on Dr. Gleason, including hacking into his work computer," Cam said. "I was angry because he kept trying to send me to a shrink, you know? I just wanted to mess with him, instead I found out he was scamming all of us. So, I started sending him anonymous messages to get him to stop."

"Why didn't you tell someone right away?" asked Lee.

"He was worried what the scandal might do to his father," Ellen said, placing her hand over Cam's. "Fred and Geoffrey were close friends. He feared guilt by association, didn't want to tarnish his father's reputation, not to mention what it would do to his friend Taylor. They may be rivals, but Taylor's also Cam's closest friend.

"Gleason must have somehow figured out Cam was onto him. We're still trying to sort it out. There were e-mails in the draft folder of Duffy's Gmail account—someone, we don't know who, offering to take care of all of Duffy's financial troubles in exchange for Cam's life. The NSA is trying to track down the source."

Karen knew the technique well. The Secret Service had dealt with plenty of nutcases who used the draft folder and a shared e-mail password to collude without broadcasting their plans over the Internet.

"My God," Karen said, her color draining. "Gleason knew about Duffy's financial troubles and he had motive to kill Cam to protect himself."

"That's our working theory," said Lapham, joining the conversation.

"Either Duffy or Gleason hired the Dirt Bike Shooter, but my guess is Duffy," Lapham said. "Hopefully, now we'll be able to track that guy down."

Lee looked out of sorts. "That means Gleason didn't hire the repairman to kill Susie," he said. "His only target was Cam."

"We think so," Lapham said.

"How did we find out about Gleason in the first place?" Karen asked.

"Because of Lee," Ellen said.

"Me?" Lee touched a finger to his chest.

"After Yoshi died, you said something to Geoffrey that convinced him to check into Gleason—exhaustively."

Karen's head was buzzing. "If Gleason was only after Cam, that means we still don't know what's the matter with Susie and the link between all of the TPI kids, Cam included," she said.

Just then came a sound of breaking glass, loud enough to cause everyone to jump. Ellen gasped. Lee rose from his chair in a flash. Karen gripped the edge of the table with force, terror in her eyes. Cam's expression was a blank, his body oddly still—but his arms were twitching violently in all directions, just like Susie's, and on the floor at his feet lay the shattered remnants of the water glass he'd been holding.

CHAPTER 57

Cam had been home for three days and the media could not get enough of him. Every major news outlet again had him as the lead story Where had he gone? What had he been doing? Why did he run away? The president and first lady had formed a united front. They insisted this was a personal, family matter, and no details would be shared with the press or public. Period. No exceptions.

Lee was amazed at how well the secret had held. Ellen's involvement somehow had been kept under wraps, and the team the president ordered to camp for the cleanup job had done remarkable work. There were no news reports anywhere of two dead guys from the same biker gang as Willie Caine. They disappeared. Vanished. Wiped clean from the face of the earth. Lee wondered if he'd ever learn their true identities. One would always be the repairman, and the other his lackey.

The FBI charged Dr. Frederick Gleason with conspiracy to commit murder for the failed assassination attempt of Cam Hilliard. As everyone expected, Gleason's lawyers had their bail request denied. However, the case against him remained circumstantial, though Lee felt confident investigators would soon find more evidence linking him to the sensational crime. The media continued their feeding frenzy, with everyone speculating about the location and identity of the elusive Dirt Bike Shooter.

Since his return from camp, Lee had spent as much time with Tracy and the kids as possible. He closed his clinic, referred all patients to the MDC, and attended Paul's memorial service. With his arm in a sling— an injury he explained as a strained shoulder from a fall—he gave a moving eulogy that praised Paul's commitment to family medicine, to his community, his friends, and above all else, to his family. There might not have been a dry eye in the room, but Lee could hardly tell because his own vision was blurred with tears.

As far as he knew, there were no connections that tied Cam's and Susie's sickness back to Yoshi, nothing to Gleason either. The nootropics seemed to be a dead end.

The big concern now was for Susie and Cam. No doubt about it anymore. Those two were linked symptomatically. Before he was officially welcomed home, Cam was rushed to the MDC for evaluation. Only he was not given a typical checkup. He had been brought there under a false name (again), with Lee put in charge of his care and testing.

CT scans were used to measure the size of Cam's organs. Sure enough, the liver was enlarged: 12.5 centimeters. His prostate was abnormally sized as well. Lee no longer needed an EEG to prove Cam had been suffering from seizures all along.

It was obvious now why Taylor began beating Cam at chess. Just as Susie had experienced, Cam's seizures, his illness in general, made it difficult if not impossible to concentrate for extended periods of time. Regardless of the physiology, Cam would forget key chess moves and strategies the way Susie would sometimes forget how to read sheet music.

The most startling find, though, was the last test Lee performed.

After giving Cam eye drops, Lee used the ophthalmoscope to look into his eyes.

"Focus on the light," he said.

And there it was, soon as the macula came into focus: the cherry-red spot. Lee blinked, thinking *his* eyes must be playing tricks on him, but no, it was there all right, bright and cherry red.

"It's unheard of," Lee said to the president and first lady during a debriefing session held in one of MDC's conference rooms. "Cam is very sick, and honestly I can't tell you why. The red spot in his eye—it should have been there since birth. If this was a genetic disease, it should have been there when I checked him the last time."

"I don't understand how the red spot would suddenly show up." Ellen's puzzled expression mimicked Lee's.

"I don't know either," he said. "All I can tell you is that whatever this disease is, it's new to medicine, something nobody has ever seen before."

"What made you think to check again?" Ellen asked, massaging her fingers nervously.

"Nothing about this case has ever been logical. So I guess I thought to do an illogical thing."

The one test Lee had not performed on Cam was the one Dr. Kaufmann was coming to the White House tomorrow to discuss.

The results of her genetic testing were now complete.

THEY MET in Ellen's office, at Dr. Kaufmann's request. She had specifically asked to hold this initial meeting with the first lady alone, and not with the president. It was an odd request, extremely odd, thought Lee. But Ellen had agreed, and now they were in her spacious East Wing office, anxiously awaiting news. Sunlight streamed in through the tall bank of windows overlooking the emerald green South Lawn, but the glorious morning and resplendent views did little to counter the somber mood inside.

Seated at the round conference table were Lee, Karen (whose rehire had been kept quiet), Ellen, and Dr. Kaufmann. Everyone wore grave expressions. Lee understood why Ellen had wanted him and Karen to attend. They were deeply involved, and she needed the support. But an important meeting about Cam without the president there? Nobody knew what to make of it, including Ellen, but all agreed to the conditions and trusted that Dr. Kaufmann had good reason for her unusual request.

"I'll get right to it," Dr. Kaufmann said, slipping on her glasses to read from a report stapled inside a yellow folder. "The results of my testing, and I have copies to share with you all, do show a gene mutation in Susie and Cam that could explain their symptoms."

Tears sprouted in Ellen's eyes. Lee's shoulder throbbed angrily. He had misread all of the signs—he went down the rabbit hole, as Dr. Kauffman had said. But genetic diseases weren't clustered! He felt baffled, lost in these uncharted waters.

"This particular type of genetic mutation, though it's a variant I've never seen before, is known to cause lysosomal storage diseases," Dr. Kaufmann continued.

"What are those?" asked Ellen, her voice shaky.

"It's a group of approximately fifty rare inherited metabolic disorders that result from defects in lysosomal function. Lysosomes are organelles in almost every cell. They hold various enzymes, but their main function is to break down things, digest food, or dispose of cells when they die. Problems with lysosomal function result in a variety of cell deficiencies that could explain Cam and Susie's highly unusual symptoms, including why Cam had developed the red spot in his eyes so late in life."

Lee knew one did not cure genetic diseases; one lived with them, adapted to them.

"It's near impossible for me to map the specific deficiencies to a specific symptom, but suffice to say, if the system itself is in disarray then the entire metabolic process can be thrown off-kilter. I'm sorry, this is not the news I'm sure you were hoping to receive."

Ellen had gone into shock, as would any parent receiving such a devastating outcome, but she also seemed perplexed. Lee thought he knew why.

"Dr. Kaufmann, thank you. I have a million questions to ask, but the most important question of all is why isn't my husband here? He should know all of this. I followed your advice and didn't even tell him we were meeting. You said this was related to me, that we needed to talk in private first, and you were insistent. Now, I demand to know why."

Dr. Kaufmann cleared her throat and eyed Lee with unsettled look. "Ellen, I can deliver this news to you in private, if you'd like."

Ellen turned fierce, panic eclipsing her face. "No! Tell me now!" Her breathing turned shallow, and Lee worried she might faint. "Tell me now," she said in a softer voice.

"I don't know—I don't know how to say this," Dr. Kaufmann stammered, "so I guess I'll just come right out and say it. According to the results of the biopsy and all of my genetic testing, you are Cam's mother, but the president is not Cam's biological father."

CHAPTER 58

The Greater Washington Fertility Center, located on M Street NW, was a little over a mile from the White House, but D.C. traffic turned it into a twenty-minute trip. Woody Lapham did the driving, while Karen rode shotgun. Lee sat in the back with the first lady. Three other agents followed in a separate vehicle. Lee's arm, still in a sling, throbbed steadily. The tension of the moment seemed to have elevated his pain.

Ellen phoned the president while en route, informing him that the meeting with Dr. Kaufmann, on his schedule for tomorrow—the meeting he knew about—was being postponed. Further testing had to be done, she said. The president did not seem to press for details, maybe because he expected the process could be a long one. Ellen ended the call with four words: "I love you, too."

The cars pulled up to the front entrance of a six-story beige brick building with panes of tinted rectangular glass to give the structure a modern aesthetic. Dozens of medical-related businesses were housed in the complex, but the office they wanted was situated on the fourth floor, in suite 410. Ellen instructed Karen and Lapham to have the other agents wait for them in the car.

She was first to enter the wide, marbled foyer. Since she was without a disguise, several people stopped to stare. At the elevators, Karen asked a group to wait for the next one so they could ride alone, and refused to let anybody get on with them when the elevator stopped on the second floor.

The fertility center had a spacious reception area with a waiting room straight out of a Pottery Barn catalog. The anxious process of attempting to conceive a family through IVF was made a little less so through the homey décor. The company slogan, etched into the glass behind the curved reception station, read: *Delivering Miracles Every Day.*

Karen flashed her badge at the receptionist seated behind the desk. "Dr. Hal Hewitt," Karen said coolly. "Where is he?"

The receptionist, noticing Ellen Hilliard, blanched. "He's—he's in his office. I'll—I'll tell him you're here," she said, stuttering.

"No, you'll buzz us in right now," Ellen responded sharply, "and you won't say a word."

Karen pointed to Woody Lapham, who understood his order was to enforce the first lady's wishes.

"Nobody is to come in," Karen said to him.

The door to the clinic area buzzed and Ellen ripped it open, quaking with fury. She stormed down the hall in long, purposeful strides, passing offices, exam rooms, and open lab areas, seeming to know exactly where she was headed. Employees and patients gawked, but said nothing as they passed.

Lee and Karen followed closely behind, exchanging nervous glances. Less than an hour ago, Lee had no idea this was where Cam was conceived. Ellen came to a shuttered mahogany door with Hewitt's name written on a brass plate. She threw open the door without knocking.

Hal Hewitt, seated behind a glass-topped desk, jumped out of his chair when Ellen barged in. One of his sunspotted hands went to his chest. His heart had to be beating fast, though Lee was not sure he'd perform CPR if called upon.

"My goodness, Ellen, you nearly scared me to death."

Hewitt stood. Everything about him was rumpled and out of sorts— from his wispy hair to his wrinkled yellow shirt and mismatched green tie. He seemed hapless and haphazard, but Lee knew better. He was cunning and perhaps responsible for everything, including Paul's murder.

"What have you done?" Ellen said, striding over to his desk. His office was spacious. Nice furniture. Good views outside. Again, the sort of place anxious would-be parents might feel a little more relaxed.

Reflexively, Hewitt backed up a step, bumping into the wall behind him. "Ellen—I . . . I don't know what you're talking about."

"I had a geneticist test my family. Geoffrey is not Cam's father! Now, I demand an answer."

Hewitt's mouth moved, but for a time no words came out. "That's . . . wrong. It's got to be wrong—the test—it's flawed. That's impossible."

Ellen was not buying it. "What did you do?" she asked, moving behind Hewitt's desk, closing in on him.

"I did nothing. I swear."

"No, that's a lie," said Lee. "Dr. Kaufmann is an expert in her field. She wouldn't make this claim unless she was absolutely certain. The report is irrefutable. You owe us an explanation."

"It's a mistake, I'm telling you," Hewitt insisted.

"There is no mistake. Now you tell me, dammit. Who is my son's father?" Ellen said through clenched teeth. Her face turned crimson. "Who?"

Hewitt held her gaze.

"I am," he said.

Ellen got a faraway look in her eyes like she could not quite process what she had heard. A second later, she snapped back into herself.

"That's not true," she said. "You take it back." Her face was now flushed with ripe anger. She took several steps toward Hewitt. Karen stepped forward, pushing back her blazer to reveal her service weapon, while simultaneously placing her hand on Ellen's shoulder. She must not have liked her proximity to Hewitt.

The next moment happened so fast Lee barely saw it happen at all. Ellen pushed Karen back with force at the same instant Hewitt lunged at Karen's waist. One second Ellen was confronting Hewitt with an accusatory finger, and the next Hewitt was pointing Karen's gun at the first lady's head.

Ellen staggered backwards with a fearful look.

"I can't let any of you tell," Hewitt said in a voice as shaky as the hand holding the gun. "I'm sorry—I'm so sorry. My work is too important. Too important. I'm still experimenting, still working. I'll change the world for the better."

"You can't explain three murders," Lee said. "This is the first lady of the United States!"

"I'll—I'll figure something out."

But Lee could see it in Hewitt's face, in his eyes: he had no plan. Still, he took an off-balance firing stance.

Karen became a blur of motion. She launched herself into the air at the same instant Hewitt fired. The bullet struck Karen in the chest and she curled in a ball as she fell to the floor. Lee rushed at Karen, seeing Hewitt aim the gun at her. But before he could do anything, Karen, with stunning quickness, pulled a second gun from her ankle holster and fired four times at Hewitt.

Each bullet found a home. Two sank into Hewitt's fleshy stomach. Another vanished into his arm. But the last bullet shot struck him in the head, and put a stop to his cold, beating heart.

CHAPTER 59

Karen arrived at Ellen's office in the East Wing of the White House at the scheduled time of half past seven in the morning. She was dressed sharply in a blue suit. In a few hours she'd be facing the cameras, part of a team of people who would be giving a press conference to discuss the shocking events that had taken place inside Hal Hewitt's office at the Greater Washington Fertility Center.

Day and night, reporters continued to scavenge for information, attempting to piece together some kind of story using what few facts they had, spreading disinformation with the speed of a mouse click.

Karen winced in pain as she took a seat in the empty chair placed in front of Ellen's cherrywood desk. The bullet Hewitt fired had bruised her ribs badly, but otherwise she'd escaped serious injury. A few inches lower and the projectile would have bypassed her bulletproof vest and could easily have severed her spinal cord. Karen was well aware of her good fortune. Her gaze settled on a manila envelope on the desk in front of her.

"Is that what I think it is?" she asked.

"Bump in salary, promotion to senior management, everything we discussed," replied Ellen. "I told Russell that I wanted to give you the news personally."

A lump sprang into Karen's throat, making it difficult to swallow. Finally, after so many setbacks, she'd get a chance to put into practice many of the reform ideas she and her father had spent years championing.

"Ellen . . . I'm——" Karen paused. Not one to normally be at a loss for words, she was suddenly unsure exactly what to say. "I'm sorry" hardly seemed adequate. What Hal had done to her, to Geoffrey, to so many others, was unconscionable.

"You don't have to say anything, Karen. You of all people understand how hard I fought to have Cam, and I'll never, ever stop fighting for him, no matter what that monster did to our family."

Ellen picked a piece of paper off her desk and flipped it over. "I found Hal's e-mail to me," she said. "He sent it ten years ago, but I had it in my archives. He wrote to tell me that he was now on the board of the TPI and he could get Cam in right away, no waiting list. I didn't need much convincing."

Karen sighed with disgust. "Guessing he sent similar letters to the parents of the other children," she said.

"Yes, he did," said Ellen, anger rising in her voice. "From what the FBI could piece together, Hal Hewitt got close to Yoshi and worked his way onto the board so he could steer all his offspring to the institute from the shadows, then he carefully observed their progression.

"Five families took him up on his offer. Those that couldn't afford tuition were told they could get scholarships, when in reality it was Hewitt secretly paying their bill. Three families declined his offer entirely. One of those families had relocated to Ohio. They're all dead. Home invasion. No arrests ever made. The other two have children younger than Cam. They haven't presented with symptoms yet."

"Have they been notified?" Karen could hardly imagine how difficult that news would be to receive.

"It's in process," said Ellen. "Should we go over the press statement? I wanted to get your reaction before I present it to Geoffrey and his senior staff and cabinet members. Some of this might not make it to the final press statement, but the public is clamoring for answers and we have to give them something. I'm not sure how much I'm comfortable sharing, or what to even say. Either way, I'll need you with me to answer any questions pertaining to the assault."

"Sounds good."

The only thing the public knew for certain was that Dr. Hal Hewitt had illegally fathered Cam Hilliard, along with other children, and that the first lady had confronted him after learning the devastating news.

The story leaked to the press was that Karen shot Hewitt, who had brandished a weapon of his own. Everyone agreed that America did not need to know that Hewitt had threatened the first lady with a gun seized from the Secret Service.

As for figuring out Hewitt's various crimes, he had left behind a substantial digital trail, which had allowed the FBI and other investigative agencies to piece together his methods and motives. It took three minutes for Ellen to dispense with background information, including the development of Cam's strange symptoms, Lee's involvement, links to other TPI students, concerns over the ProNeural nootropics, and Gleason and Yoshi's fraud scheme.

Ellen began reading the press statement:

> In every case, the murders and assaults, including the attempt on my son's life, were the result of one man's horrifically misguided deeds. Dr. Hal Hewitt's sick and twisted vision for the future began with the struggles of his son, Liam Hewitt.
>
> Liam was a gifted artist who had fallen victim to drug abuse. From analysis of Dr. Hewitt's digital archives, we now know that he confronted his son about his drug problem. Liam insisted that drugs were essential to his creative process and would not stop taking them. Dr. Hewitt became obsessed with saving Liam and set off on his destructive path to discover if it was possible to unlock a person's creative potential without any reliance on drugs of any kind.

Ellen paused and took a drink of water.

"It sounds great so far," Karen said, encouraging.

> Dr. Hewitt's work as a fertility specialist made him uniquely qualified to shape the formation of human life. He spent years perfecting his protocol and developed a rudimentary form of gene editing in sperm that predated today's modern CRISPR-Cas systems for targeted genome editing.

Using his technique, Dr. Hewitt could snip out a piece of any organism's DNA cheaply, quickly, and precisely—like a film editor altering frames of a movie. We can only speculate that Dr. Hewitt did not share his breakthrough research with the broader scientific community because he wanted to further his selfish and misguided ambitions without interference.

Dr. Hewitt believed he had correctly identified the genes that control our neuroplasticity, which is how the brain learns and retains information. In one of the papers the FBI recovered during this ongoing investigation, Dr. Hewitt referred to his procedure as, and I quote, "putting the brain's ability to form new neural connections on steroids."

What Dr. Hewitt strived for was a genetically modified child capable of quickly mastering skills requiring tremendous creativity. Music. Art. Chess. Mathematics. Any endeavor combining creative thought and cognitive ability.

In his prodigious writings, Dr. Hewitt expressed a desire to maximize people's potential, to help usher in a new golden age. He imagined a planet full of artists and brilliant abstract thinkers who could solve humanity's greatest challenges, and believed wrongly that the sacrifices of a few would be worth such a result.

Dr. Hewitt used his sperm without the knowledge or consent of any of the parents who had entrusted him with their fertility treatment, as a way of presumably reducing the variables of his horrific experiment. From the data analyzed so far, it appears Dr. Hewitt's procedure did augment to some capacity the brain's natural neuroplasticity and enabled a type of genius that far surpassed what was obtainable without genetic enhancement.

To put his theory into practice, Dr. Hewitt required a vehicle to expose each child to different skills to master. It was his hope an innate interest would take root, and because of the genetic enhancement, Dr. Hewitt theorized these children would develop tremendous skills quickly. He believed rapid skill acquisition would subsequently foster an interest in obtaining true mastery. For this reason, the TPI became an essential component of Dr. Hewitt's plan.

It is our strong belief that Dr. Hewitt was well aware of the risks involved and he intentionally limited his manipulations to a handful of test subjects so that he could monitor them most carefully. He made a vow, which he had put into writing, to see each child through to adulthood before he went public with his discovery.

However, when these children reached a certain age of maturity, they experienced symptoms of a systemic genetic disease unlike anything known to medicine. The symptoms that presented in these young people—organ enlargement, seizures, among others—were unequivocally the result of Dr. Hewitt's nightmarish eugenics procedure.

We believe Dr. Hewitt became worried that doctors would eventually discover the genetic anomaly and trace it back to him. However an autopsy, if performed, would show evidence of a new type of genetic disease, but would not offer any links back to his fertility clinic. It is the opinion of the FBI, and other investigative authorities, that Dr. Hewitt commissioned the murder of all affected young people, and in some cases their families as well, to hide his many crimes and protect his research.

It is the strong belief of the FBI that the people responsible for the attempted murder of my son were part of this elaborate scheme and that Dr. Fredrick Gleason, Cam's personal physician, played no part in the attempt on my son's life.

Ellen put the paper down.

"Is that all?"

"No, there are a few paragraphs about what this has done to my family, to the others. I just can't read it right now."

Karen reached across the desk and briefly took hold of Ellen's hand. "Are you sure you can go through with this?"

"I have to," said Ellen.

"How did he get to Duffy?" The question had been bothering Karen for some time.

"Mark Mueller—he was the man Lee killed at the farm, nickname Mauser—was a drug dealer who sold narcotics to an employee at the NSA. That employee went looking through various computers at the people closest to Cam, to learn their secrets."

"And found Duffy's."

"Right. That employee has since been arrested and has been cooperating, as I understand it."

"What about Mauser and his crew?"

"The FBI is still piecing that together," said Ellen. "They believe Mauser was Liam Hewitt's drug dealer. Hewitt may have hired Mauser as some sort of nanny to keep his son supplied, monitor his intake, keep him safe, and in exchange for their protection services, Hewitt fed them Oxy-Contin to sell, which he siphoned from his clinic's pharmacy by replacing real narcotics with counterfeit pills he bought online. He even had a code name; called himself Rainmaker. When the children started having medical issues, Hewitt threatened to cut off Mauser's supply unless they cooperated."

"Cooperated by killing those kids."

"I guess in Hewitt's mind his son Liam wasn't like the others. Liam could still live as an addict, but the other kids were going to die, no matter what anyone did to try and save them."

"And now?"

"And now . . ." Ellen's eyes grew misty. "Now they're still going to die, Karen, and I can't stop it. I can't save my son. Lee can't. Nobody can."

EPILOGUE

THREE MONTHS LATER . . .

The World Junior Chess Championships took place inside the prestigious Marshall Chess Club in New York City. The four-story redbrick building on a leafy street in Manhattan housed the second-oldest chess club in the United States. In this building thirteen-year-old Bobby Fischer had defeated Donald Byrne in "The Game of the Century." Adorning the walls in the high-ceilinged tournament hall were framed photographs of famous matches and players who had come and gone over the course of the club's storied hundred-year history. Included among the thirty or so spectators who occupied folding chairs set up along the hall's perimeter were Lee, Karen, Josh, Susie Banks, Valerie Cowart, the president, and the first lady.

Cam sat with the U.S. team, a tense look on his face. Everyone was sweating, and not just because the air-conditioners struggled to cool the room on a brutally hot August day. Taylor Gleason, who had taken Cam's place on the U.S. team, was presently engaged in a tense match against a sixteen-year-old boy from Belarus, who was known as an aggressive player.

It was incredibly difficult and emotional for Cam to withdraw from the tournament. The decision he made showed not only tremendous maturity, but also acceptance of his disease, his limitations.

To stay involved, Cam turned to coaching. He and Taylor worked together for hours on end, forging strategies, practicing complex moves. With Cam's guidance, Taylor's game had improved remarkably, but nobody could have predicted this level of success.

Taylor was playing for more than just the tournament win. He was playing for redemption. His disgraced father had had the murder charges dropped, but was still facing prison time for his ProNeural scheme. As much as Cam had showed his maturity by backing out of the tournament, Taylor had demonstrated inspiring grit and resilience.

Much of the game Taylor spent shoring up his weaknesses. He repulsed many of the speculative attacks with defensive moves, but according to the president's running commentary, that was not enough. His opponent simply regrouped and tried again, creating space on the board while waiting for Taylor to make a mistake. To win, Taylor had to counterattack, pursue vigorously, and create counterthreats of his own. Cam had drilled Taylor on this tactic. The president insisted it was time to put that strategy into action.

"This is just like boxing," the president told Lee. "Everyone has a plan until he gets punched in the mouth."

Taylor was looking increasingly anxious, and it was understandable. A victory or draw here would give him enough points to claim the tournament title. His opponent moved his knight to f6, trying to control the center of the board. But Taylor countered, moving his rook to e3, supporting his pawn on e4. Cam gave a subtle thumbs-up sign, clearly approving.

Lee did not understand the strategy, but a projector displayed the game onto a large screen so at least he could follow the action.

Susie sat next to Josh, her hands clasped tightly in his in nervous anticipation. She was still adapting to her new reality as well, playing themes on her violin instead of full pieces as she battled her depleted concentration and memory loss. Her myoclonus could be controlled somewhat with medication, but she still needed to be on dialysis. Her organs were still growing larger. Josh had been her rock, a steady presence in her life despite her declining health.

"You don't get to pick only the good parts of the people you love," Josh had said to Lee. "You get the whole package, and I'm fine with that."

Susie was everything that Hannah was not. She was affectionate and adoring. What she could not be was healthy. Without a cure, she would die, and so would Cam. Valerie had been looking after Susie these days, and the two had grown close. In many ways, Valerie was as much a surrogate mother as she was Susie's caregiver.

Over the course of the match Susie and Cam locked eyes frequently, speaking some unspoken language. In the months since the terrible truth came out, the two had grown extremely close, which made sense given they were half siblings who shared a tragic bond.

The game continued. Taylor took his opponent's pawn with his pawn to d6, but his opponent countered, moving his rook to c6 in what turned into an exchange of material.

"Taylor needs to cramp this guy's style, force him to defend the pawn in the center of the board, not exchange material."

The president sounded exasperated. Lee nodded his agreement but was incapable of visualizing the game to Hilliard's extent. Karen looked on in rapt attention. Normally she'd be on duty, but it was Woody Lapham leading the team keeping the president and first family safe during the tournament. For the first time in Lee's memory, Karen did not seem to be missing the action. She was happy to be a spectator. Hell, she was happy to be alive.

Physically Lee was relatively fine, his shoulder throbbing only intermittently, but it was the emotional strain that had contributed most significantly to his suffering. He blamed himself not only for Paul's death, but for Yoshi's as well.

Yoshi, like Paul, was an innocent in all of this. He took his own life because Lee had shamed him, exposed him as a fraud. While Yoshi's methods were clearly misguided, his intentions all along were ultimately good.

But it was Paul that kept Lee up at night. The guilt he felt pulsed more painfully than his bullet wound. Lying awake in the darkness, Lee kept seeing his friend's face, hearing his voice, aching for a different outcome.

He would never stop blaming himself for Paul's death, so he did what he felt he had to do. He sold his practice to the MDC. He did not do it for the money or to honor Paul's wishes. He sold it because he could no longer practice without him. He and Paul were in a marriage of sorts, and the business simply felt empty with him gone.

It was heartbreaking to let the business go, to sell off a final link to his father, to give up on family medicine, but it paled compared to the suffering of Paul's family. But in a way it was also freeing. It gave Lee time to concentrate on his new life's mission: saving Susie and Cam.

At the moment there was no cure for what they had. Twice during the tournament, Cam's myoclonus had struck without warning, sending his arms into spasm. Lee would have to live with lingering guilt, but Cam and Susie had to live with something far worse: a progressive, genetic disease.

But there was hope.

The process Hewitt had used to engineer the gene augmentation could potentially be reversed into a new therapy. CRISPR technology had advanced greatly since Hewitt had pioneered a rudimentary technique from the shadows. Advancements now offered the possibility of precisely directed gene therapy that not only might cure Susie and Cam, and the other two surviving children Hewitt had fathered, but could someday treat a host of terrible diseases. As with all science, though, its potential for abuse would never disappear. New Hewitts might always emerge.

The president would fund the research and development using his personal wealth, as well as future money he would make on the speaking circuit, opening a new battlefront in the ongoing war against genetic disease.

President Hilliard had appointed Lee as program director, and his first act in his new role was to hire Dr. Ruth Kaufmann to lead the research teams. The future of gene therapy had yet to be defined, but Lee had tremendous faith in Dr. Kaufmann's leadership and her abilities. Their efforts by no means guaranteed a cure, but they did offer hope, and that was the next best thing.

Taylor moved his knight to g8, and about half the room gasped, while Cam leapt from his seat like there'd been a buzzer-beater basket. The other half of the room, Lee included, had no clue what had happened.

"I think he just forced the game into a draw," the president said, pumping his fist in victory. A draw was worth half a point for each player, but Taylor's total points would give him the tournament title. Even though their roles had been reversed, Cam concentrated on the game as if he were the one playing in the finals, and in a way he was. Without Cam as the catalyst, without his tutelage, Taylor would never have made it this far.

Lee's phone buzzed. He glanced at the screen. The two-word message filled him with joy.

I accept.

Now it was Lee who pumped his fist in a quiet show of victory. Lee was committed to reopening the TPI to honor Yoshi's memory and mission. With the help of involved parents, Lee had raised several hundred thousand dollars toward that goal. Fundraising would be an ongoing effort, and for that, they needed a new director. Ellen had used her contacts to find the perfect person. Her name was Nozomi Arakida, a Japanese woman who had studied at the TPI under Yoshi and who had gone on to found a similar school in St. Louis. It was Nozomi who had texted Lee, accepting his offer to take over the Washington school, extending her brand's reach in the process. In a strange way, Hewitt's dream of ushering forth a new golden age of culture and learning had taken a small step toward becoming a reality.

The game continued. Taylor forced his opponent to trade off queens. Lee saw now what others saw earlier as the inevitable outcome. Black did not have enough material to get to checkmate. The game ended in a draw. In a way, it was a fitting conclusion. There was no clear victor, but it was a clear victory nonetheless.

Thunderous applause shook the room. Taylor stood shakily and waved to the crowd. His smile was broad and beaming, eyes elated. Cam and Taylor shared an embrace. They broke apart, and while holding hands, raised their arms overhead in shared triumph. Everyone knew they had won as a team.

The rest of the U.S. team soon swallowed Taylor and Cam in a large group hug. Cam slipped away from the huddled masses as Susie rushed the floor. Nobody in the Secret Service moved as she neared him. They knew how important she was to Cam and Cam to her. They hugged tightly. Then Cam raced over to his parents. He threw his arms around his mother and held her as she gave him a kiss on the forehead. Tears filled her eyes. Cam broke away and approached the president.

The president wiped his tear-lined eyes, opened his arms, and pulled Cam into a tight embrace. He pulled his lips tight, straining against raw emotion. "I'm so proud of you, son," he said. "I'm so proud."

Son.

It did not matter what Hewitt had done to this family. Cam was Geoffrey's son regardless, his pride and joy. His boy. The first family gathered in a huddle, bodies leaning forward, foreheads pressed tightly together in an unbroken circle.

Lee watched, his heart swelling with joy.

Josh put an arm around Lee. "Pretty awesome, Dad," he said.

Karen came over and stood beside them.

"Yeah, pretty awesome," Lee said in a quiet voice.

Valerie and Susie had joined the first family in their victory celebration. All were talking excitedly.

"I got something else that's pretty awesome," Josh said. He handed a piece of paper to Lee, who read it before handing it to Karen.

"You've applied for the Secret Service?"

Karen's voice rose sharply. She put a hand to her chest, looking as excited as Cam post-victory.

"Hey, I need a job, right?" Josh said. "Can't think of a better place to work or a better person to work for." Josh winked at his mom.

"I'll put in a good word for you," Karen said, laughing as she stifled a cry.

Lee, Josh, and Karen huddled together, touching foreheads just like the first family had done. Eventually, the two families converged, forming a larger group huddle, with Susie and Valerie joining as well.

Strange as it was, a peaceful feeling washed over Lee. He knew everyone would soon go separate ways. Josh and Susie's relationship would either blossom or wither, while Josh and Karen would become closer working together for the Secret Service. Susie would continue to play music, follow her dreams. Valerie would take a nursing job at the MDC and still care for Susie and Cam as needed. Ellen and Geoffrey would spend their last year in the White House working to raise money for the genetic research initiative. Lee would go to work for the president and first lady, committed to finding a cure for the survivors. Everyone would be involved in something new, but they would have an unbreakable connection for years to come.

In that way, they had all become family.

ACKNOWLEDGMENTS

This novel began with a simple premise: write a story about the president's family. In many ways, this book is an homage to my father, whose book, *The First Patient*, which had received (along with stellar sales) glowing praise from President Bill Clinton. It became apparent quite early in the writing process that I sorely lacked knowledge in numerous areas of expertise. To that end, I'd like to thank my uncle and trusted medical advisor, Dr. David Grass, without whom my character's medical deeds, as well as the trials of running a family practice, could not have been told with any degree of verisimilitude. David was also my sounding board for plot and story arc, and it's safe to say he played a vital role in making sure the novel never flatlined.

My brother and fellow thriller scribe, Matthew Palmer, also graciously shared with me his insider knowledge of the White House and various facets of how the government machine operates. I owe additional thanks to another writer friend, Lisa Gardner, who opened my eyes to how I could open the book. My brilliantly talented and dedicated mother read every page of the manuscript and offered her candid feedback, which I appreciate to no end. In that same regard, my thanks also go to super agents Meg Ruley and Rebecca Scherer, as well as to Clair Lamb, who helped improve the novel immeasurably with their careful reading and thoughtful critique. Special gratitude goes to Jennifer Enderlin, my father's devoted editor, who has taken me under her wing and allowed me the opportunity to carry on my dad's legacy while sharing with me her incredible gifts for story and character.

My deep appreciation also extends to Ben Beauchemin of Wicked Weaponry, and U.S. Secret Service, Office of Government & Public Affairs, who assisted with tactical details portrayed in the book; and to Dr. Ethan Prince, who provided invaluable medical consultations. My thanks, too, to the generous individuals who purchased character names in support of the Multiple Myeloma Research Foundation and the Greater Nashua Food Bank: Karen Ray, Valerie Cowart, Woody Lapham, and Dr. Marilyn Piekarski. A special note of appreciation I extend to the sales and marketing team at St. Martins for doing all they do to put these books into the hands of eager readers.

It goes without saying that my father, Michael Palmer, is a huge presence in every word I write and that we all miss and love him. I'm grateful for the opportunity to carry on his legacy, and I hope this novel does him proud.

Last, but hardly least, my deepest thanks goes to my wife, Jessie, and my two children, Benjamin and Sophie, for your love and support, and the joy and meaning you bring to every day.